THE MISTLETOE SELLER

It's Christmas Eve. Flurries of snow fall on the cobbled streets of Whitechapel and an abandoned baby, swaddled in a blanket, is found on a doorstep in Angel Alley...

Named after the street on which she was abandoned, Angel Winter is taken into a loving home. But fate deals a cruel blow and she's thrown out to fend for herself. Angel scratches a living selling mistletoe in Covent Garden market. Although struggling, she will never sell her only treasure, the gold and ruby ring that was hidden in her swaddling when she was abandoned. It could hold the key to the secrets of her past...

THE MISTLETOE SELLER

THE MISTLETOE SELLER

by

Dilly Court

Magna Large Print Books
Long Preston, North Yorkshire,
BD23 4ND, England.

British Library Cataloguing in Publication Data.

A catalogue record of this book is
available from the British Library

ISBN   978-0-7505-4591-4

First published in Great Britain by HarperCollins*Publishers* 2017

Copyright © Dilly Court 2017

Cover illustration © Gordon Crabb by arrangement with
Gordon Crabb Illustration

Dilly Court asserts the moral right to be identified as the author of
this work

Published in Large Print 2018 by arrangement with
HarperCollins Publishers Ltd.

Magna Large Print is an imprint of Library Magna Books Ltd.

Printed and bound in Great Britain by
T.J. (International) Ltd., Cornwall, PL28 8RW

In loving memory of Harry House

2013–2016

Taken too soon but never forgotten

Chapter One

St Mary Matfelon Church, Whitechapel, London – Christmas Eve 1859

'I found her in Angel Alley, Vicar.' The verger cradled the infant in his arms, protecting her from the falling snow. 'She was all alone and no one else in sight.'

'Bring her into the warmth, Fowler, before she freezes to death.' The Reverend John Hardisty stood aside, ushering the verger into the candlelit church. The bells were ringing out to summon worshippers to midnight mass, and the first of the faithful were already starting to arrive.

'What will we do with her, Vicar?' Jim Fowler gazed down into the blue eyes that regarded him with an unblinking stare. 'She must be cold and no doubt she'll be hungry soon. Where will we find someone to care for her at this time of night, and at Christmas, too?'

'Take her to the vestry. My wife will know what to do.'

A married man himself, with nine little Fowlers to raise, Jim carried the infant to the vestry and as he pushed the door open he was greeted by the sound of female chatter, which stopped abruptly when the assembled ladies spotted the baby.

'Good gracious, Jim, what have you got there?' Letitia Hardisty surged towards him, peering at

11

the baby with undisguised distaste. 'Not another foundling, surely?'

'Oh, Letty, that's not a very Christian attitude.' Cordelia Wilding, a plump woman wearing a fur-trimmed velvet bonnet and matching cape pushed past her to snatch the infant from the verger's arms. 'What a beautiful child. Just look at those soft golden curls and big blue eyes. She's a little angel.'

The third woman, Margaret Edwards, the deacon's wife, plainly dressed in serviceable grey linsey-woolsey with an equally plain bonnet, leaned over to take a closer look at the baby. 'A Christmas angel, to be sure. I believe she's smiling, Cordelia.'

'It's probably wind.' Letitia stood back, frowning thoughtfully. 'If you'll stop cooing over her, ladies, you'll realise that we have a problem on our hands.'

Margaret touched the infant's cheek with the tip of her finger. 'Where did you find her, Fowler? Was there a note of any kind?'

Jim puffed out his chest, pleased to be able to tell the deacon's wife something she did not know. Margaret Edwards was notoriously opinionated and very conscious of her husband's standing in the community. 'I took it to be of the female gender, ma'am. Judging by the lace dress, which must have cost a pretty penny, in my humble opinion.' He glanced round the small group and he realised that they were unimpressed. He cleared his throat. 'Ahem... I was taking a short cut through Angel Alley and I heard a sound. She weren't crying, but sort of cooing, as if to call out to me.'

'Very interesting,' Letitia said sharply. 'But was she on a doorstep? If so, the mother might have intended the householder to take her in. Or was she in some sort of shelter? It's been snowing for several hours.'

Cowed by her supercilious stare and the caustic tone of her voice, he bowed his head. 'She was left in a portmanteau, ma'am.'

'A portmanteau?' Margaret tapped her teeth with her fingernail, a habit that never failed to annoy Letitia.

'I think we all know what a portmanteau is, Margaret.' Letitia moved closer to the verger, fixing him a stern look. 'Did you bring it with you? It might help us to identify the child. This is obviously a matter for the police.'

He shook his head. 'It were sodden with snow, ma'am. I was too concerned about the little one to think of anything but getting her to safety.'

'You stupid man. There might have been a clue as to who she is, if indeed it is a girl.' Letitia cocked her head, listening. 'The bells have stopped. It's time for the service to begin. We can't stay here talking all night.'

'What will we do with the infant, Letty?' Cordelia clasped her hands to her bosom, her grey eyes filling with tears. 'Someone must take her in. I would, but I'm afraid Mr Wilding would object. We have visitors staying with us, important business contacts, you understand.'

'I can't have her,' Margaret said firmly. 'I must support the deacon during this busy time of the year. He has his duties to perform, as has the vicar.'

'And for that reason I cannot have her either,' Letitia added, nodding. 'Besides which, the child needs a wet nurse.' She turned to Jim. 'You have a large family, Fowler. Surely one more would make little difference, and I seem to remember that your youngest is only a few months old.'

Jim took a step backwards, holding up his hands. 'My Florrie has enough to do, ma'am. We can barely feed and clothe the young 'uns as it is. Maybe the Foundling Hospital would take her in, or else it will be the workhouse.'

'Send for a constable,' Letitia said hurriedly. 'The police station in Leman Street is the best place for the child. They're used to handling such matters, and you, Fowler, must go to Angel Alley right away and fetch the case in which you found the baby. It might prove to be vital evidence for the police to find and apprehend the mother who committed the crime of abandonment.'

'Oh, no, Letty,' Cordelia said tearfully. 'The poor creature needs sympathy. Where is your compassion? It is Christmas Eve, after all. Remember the babe that was born in the stable.'

'The stable in Bethlehem is not Angel Alley in Whitechapel, Cordelia.' Letitia shooed the verger out of the room. 'You had best stay with the child, Cordelia, since she seems to be taken with you. Come, Margaret, the service has started.' She left the vestry with the deacon's wife following in her wake.

Cordelia sank down on one of the upright wooden chairs – comfort was not the main purpose of the vestry furniture. She unfolded the woollen shawl, which was new and of the best

14

quality. The flannel nightdress was trimmed with lace and the yoke embroidered with tiny pink rosebuds. Someone, perhaps the expectant mother, had put time and effort into making the garment. Cordelia was not the most imaginative of people, but it seemed unlikely that someone who had taken such trouble over a simple nightgown would desert a much-wanted infant. The baby had not uttered a sound, and that in itself was unnerving and seemed unnatural. Cordelia had long ago given up hope of having a child of her own, and although part of her longed to take the little one home and give her the love and attention she deserved, a small voice in her head warned her against such folly. Her husband, Joseph Willard Wilding, was a successful businessman who had bought a failing brewery and turned its fortune around. They entertained regularly and she was expected to be the perfect hostess. A child would not fit in with their way of life.

'You are a beautiful little girl. If you were mine I would christen you Angel, because that's what you are.'

The baby gurgled and a tiny hand grasped Cordelia's finger with surprising strength. She felt a tug at her heartstrings and an ache in her empty womb.

How long Cordelia sat there she did not know, but she felt a bond growing with the child and the sweet, milky, baby smell filled her with unacknowledged longing. Then, just as Angel was becoming restive and beginning to whimper, the door burst open and Jim entered, carrying a large portmanteau. He was followed by a police

15

constable. The last words of 'Come All Ye Faithful' echoed around the vestry as the policeman closed the door.

'This is the infant, Constable Miller,' Jim said importantly. 'The one I found in Angel Alley, lying in this here case as if she was a piece of left luggage. I don't know what the world is coming to.'

Constable Miller took the portmanteau from him and proceeded to examine it in the light of a candle sconce. 'There doesn't seem to be a note of any kind, Mr Fowler.' He raised his head, giving Cordelia a questioning look. 'Was there a note pinned to the baby's shawl, ma'am? The child's name, maybe?'

Cordelia shook her head. 'Nothing, Constable. The baby is well cared for and clean, and her garments are of good quality.'

Constable Miller ran his hands around the lining of the case. 'Aha. As I thought. There is generally something personal to the mother left with found-lings.' He held up a gold ring set with two heart-shaped rubies. 'This might be valuable,' he said thoughtfully, 'but I'm not an expert in jewellery. Anyway, it might help us to find the mother, or it's possible she will have second thoughts and return to the place where she abandoned her baby. Women do strange things in such cases.'

'What will happen to the child now?' Cordelia asked anxiously. 'You won't lock her in a cell overnight, will you?'

A wry smile creased Constable Miller's face into even deeper lines. 'I doubt if the other occupants of the lock-up would appreciate a nipper howling its head off, ma'am. I'll have to report back to the station, but I expect she'll end up in the workhouse if the Foundling Hospital can't take her.'

Jim backed towards the door. 'I've got to go, Constable. The service has ended and I'll be needed to tidy up ready for the Christmas Day services.' He let himself into the body of the church, closing the door behind him.

'Busy for all of us,' Constable Miller said drily. 'No doubt we'll be scooping the drunks off the streets and arresting the pros–' He broke off, his face flushing brick red. 'I'm sorry, ma'am. I mean we'll be keeping the streets as free from crime as possible in this part of the East End.' He reached out to take the baby, but Cordelia tightened her hold on the tiny body.

'I don't like to think of Angel in such a place, Constable. Or in the workhouse, if it comes to that.'

'She has a name, ma'am?'

Cordelia blushed rosily. 'I've been calling her Angel because she was found in Angel Alley and because it's Christmas, and she looks like an angel.'

'I don't suppose you'd like to take care of her for a couple of days, would you, ma'am? It would make my life easier and you obviously have some feelings for the little mite. Which,' he added hastily, 'I can understand, being the father of five. I'd take her myself, but for the fact that my wife is sick in bed and the nippers are having to look after themselves.'

'I wish I could, Constable,' Cordelia said with genuine regret, 'but my husband wouldn't agree,

17

and anyway, she needs a wet nurse.'

'Give her to me then, ma'am. I'm sure the sergeant at the station will know of some woman who'd like to earn a few pence for her labours.'

Cordelia hesitated. 'I suppose that means some slattern who might be disease ridden and most certainly of low morals.'

'That I can't say, ma'am.' Constable Miller kept his tone moderate but he was tired and coming to the end of his shift. His only wish was to take the tiresome infant to the station and see it safely settled before he went home to his family, left in the care of his eldest daughter, a child of ten. Whether or not they were asleep in bed was something he would discover when he opened the door of their two-up, two-down terraced house. No doubt they would have searched the cupboards for their presents, such as they were, but all he could afford on a constable's pay were wooden toys made from offcuts by the carpenter who lived at number six, and rag dolls that his wife had spent many evenings sewing by the light of a single candle.

Cordelia rose to her feet, still clutching Angel, who was growing restive and her whimpering was rapidly growing in volume. 'I must come with you, Constable. I have to make certain that this child is placed in safe hands.' Cordelia turned her head as the door opened to admit Letitia, the vicar and Joseph Wilding, and judging by the expressions on their faces she realised that her decision was going to attract strong opposition. She explained hastily, but Joseph barely allowed her to finish speaking.

18

'It's ridiculous, Cordelia. The child has been deserted by her mother and goodness knows where it came from. The thing might be riddled with disease and you have a delicate constitution. Come away and leave the matter to the authorities.'

'Yes, my dear,' Letitia said smoothly. 'Your caring attitude is admirable, but misplaced. There are institutions that care for this type of child.'

'And what type is that?' Cordelia demanded angrily. 'Angel is an innocent, just like the Child whose birth we are supposed to be celebrating at Christmas.'

Shocked, Letitia stared at her wide-eyed. 'That is blasphemous, Cordelia.' She turned to her husband. 'Pretend you didn't hear that, John. Cordelia is obviously beside herself, and it's very late. Time we were all tucked up in our beds so that we can be ready for tomorrow – or rather, later on today. Go home, Cordelia, and leave the matter in the hands of the police.'

Cordelia held the child closer as she rose to her feet. Rebellion was not in her nature and she would normally have complied with her husband's wishes, but this was different. 'No,' she said firmly.

'No?' Letitia and Joseph spoke in unison.

'It's all right, ma'am,' Constable Miller said hastily. 'I will make certain that the child is well cared for.'

Cordelia shot a sideways look at her husband. 'I am not abandoning this infant. I intend to accompany Constable Miller to the police station, and I will stay with Angel until I am satisfied that appropriate arrangements have been made for her care.'

'Cordelia, I forbid you–' Joseph broke off mid-sentence. The stubborn set of his wife's normally soft jawline and the martial gleam in her large grey eyes both startled and confused him. Used as he was to commanding his army of workers at the brewery and generally getting his own way by simple force of his domineering nature, he was suddenly at a loss.

'I am going with her,' Cordelia said simply. 'It's Christmas Day and my little winter angel needs the comfort of loving arms. I will never know the joy of holding my own child, so please allow me this one small thing, Joseph.'

John Hardisty cleared his throat, touched to the core by the simple request of a childless woman. 'I will accompany you, my dear Mrs Wilding. If Joseph feels he must tend to your guests then please allow me to be of assistance.'

'That won't be necessary, Vicar.' Joseph moved to his wife's side. 'I'm sure my friends will understand. I don't agree with what you're doing, Cordelia, but I am prepared to humour you – just this once.'

She met his gaze with a steady look. For the first time in the twenty-five years of their marriage she knew that she was in control, and it was a good feeling. She said nothing as she followed the constable out of the church, wrapping her cape around the baby to protect her from the heavily falling snow.

'Get into the carriage, Cordelia,' Joseph said sternly. 'Might I offer you a lift, Constable?'

'I'm supposed to be walking my beat, sir.' Constable Miller squinted up into the swirling mass of feathery snow. 'But I suppose under the circumstances it would be appropriate.'

The desk sergeant dipped his pen into the inkwell. 'Name, please?'

'Cordelia Wilding.'

'No, ma'am, the infant's name, if it has one.'

'Angel,' Cordelia said firmly.

'Angel?' He looked up, frowning. 'Surname?'

'Really, Officer, is this necessary?' Joseph leaned over the desk. 'My wife knows nothing of this child. She's simply caring for the infant until someone comes to take her away.'

A shaft of fear stabbed Cordelia with such ferocity that she could scarcely breathe. 'Angel Winter. It's the name I've given the poor little creature who's been cruelly abandoned by her mother. She needs someone who can take care of her bodily needs, and a home where she will be loved.'

'Don't we all, ma'am?' Sergeant Wilkes said drily.

'I suggested the Foundling Hospital, Sergeant,' Constable Miller took his notebook from his pocket. 'The infant was found at approximately eleven forty-five in Angel Alley by a Mr James Fowler, the verger at St Mary's church, and taken into the vestry where this good lady has been taking care of the said babe.'

The sergeant glanced at the clock. 'It's nearly half-past one in the morning, and it's Christmas Day. I doubt if anyone would be happy to be awakened at this time.'

As if acting on cue, Angel began to cry and this

21

time no amount of rocking or soothing words made any difference.

'She's hungry,' Cordelia said apologetically. 'A wet nurse must be found immediately.'

'Lumpy Lil is in the cells, Constable Miller. Go and fetch her, if you please. She's up for soliciting again.' Sergeant Wilkes shot an apologetic glance in Cordelia's direction. It was bad enough having a nipper howling its head off fit to bust, without the added complication of there being a lady present. He thought longingly of home and a warm fireside, a pipe of baccy and a glass of porter to finish off a long day. 'Begging your pardon, ma'am.'

'Lumpy Lil,' Cordelia repeated faintly. The image this conjured up made her shudder, but Angel's cries were becoming more urgent, and she supposed that one mother's milk was as good as another's, even if the woman was of questionable morals.

Joseph moved closer to her, lowering his voice. 'Come away now, Cordelia. You've done your best for the infant. Let the police deal with her.'

She turned on him in a fury. 'You make Angel sound like a criminal. I won't abandon her, and I intend to remain here until I'm satisfied that a good home has been found for her.'

'This is ridiculous, my dear,' Joseph said through clenched teeth. 'You cannot stay here all night, and possibly all day too. I won't allow it.'

Cordelia turned away in time to see Constable Miller escorting a large, raw-boned woman along the corridor that presumably led from the cells. Lumpy Lil lived up to her name – her torn blouse was open to the waist, exposing large breasts, purple veined and threatening to burst free from the confines of tightly laced stays.

'Good grief!' Joseph stared at her in horror. 'Surely not this creature.'

'Where's the little brat then?' Lil's words were slurred. It was obvious that she had been drinking and was still under the influence, but Angel was screaming by this time, and much as Cordelia hated the thought of this unwashed, drunken woman laying hands on her pure little angel, she could see that there was little alternative. She cleared her throat, meeting Lil's aggressive glare with an attempt at a smile.

'I know it's a lot to ask, but would you be kind enough to give sustenance to this poor little child, Miss Lumpy?'

'It's Miss Heavitree to you, lady.' Lil tossed back her shaggy mane of mouse-brown hair. 'You never told me the queen was visiting Leman Street nick, Constable Miller.'

'Less of your cheek, Lil. You know what's required of you.'

'Give us the kid, missis.' Lil held her arms out, exposing tattoos that ran from her bony wrists to her elbows. 'I'll be glad to get some relief from me sore titties. My babe only lived three days, and then the cops brought me in for trying to make a living.' She spat on the floor at Constable Miller's feet, narrowly missing his boots. 'I provides a valuable service, they knows that.'

'Less of your lip, Lumpy.' Constable Miller poked her in the back. 'If you're willing to take care of the nipper you can use the inspector's office. He's at home with his family, where we all should be, and I'm going off duty, so don't give me any trouble.'

'All right, I'll see to the little thing. What's her name?'

'I call her Angel.'

'There's no accounting for taste. I dare say she'll be as much of a brat as the rest of 'em when she's old enough to answer back.' Lil flung the baby over her shoulder with careless abandon. 'Lead on, Constable. You can stay and watch if it gives you pleasure.' She winked at him, but Constable Miller merely shrugged and gave her a push in the direction of the office.

'It would be nothing new to me, Lil. I've got five of my own, but I'll be outside the door, so don't try to escape.'

'I'll keep an eye on her,' Cordelia volunteered as Constable Miller ushered Lumpy Lil and the baby into the inspector's office.

'You don't want to mix with the likes of her, ma'am,' he said in an undertone. 'She's not your sort at all.'

'She most certainly is not.' Joseph laid his hand on his wife's shoulder. 'You've done your duty by the infant, Cordelia. It's time to go home.'

Cordelia Frances Wilding had been brought up to be a dutiful daughter and a biddable wife, but at that moment something inside her snapped. The need to protect the infant was stronger than any other emotion she had felt in her whole life, and nothing anyone said or did would make a scrap of difference.

'Go home, Joseph,' she said firmly. 'I intend to

remain here until I am satisfied that Angel will be looked after properly.'

'You are telling me to leave you here? In a police station with common prostitutes and villains of every kind?'

'Yes, I am. I won't move from this spot until I know what arrangements have been made.' She looked him in the eye. 'Or else I'll bring her home and hire Miss Heavitree as her wet nurse.'

'This is ridiculous. Have you lost your senses, Cordelia?' Joseph paled visibly. 'What about my status in the business world – have you considered that?'

She turned her back on him. 'I'm not listening.'

Joseph stared at her in horror. This angry person was not the docile wife who had run his household and acted as hostess to his business acquaintances for more than twenty-five years. He barely recognised the mutinous woman who was openly defying him, and worse still he felt a wave of sympathy emanating from the desk sergeant. There seemed to be little he could do other than admit defeat and save face by appearing to support his wife.

'Very well, my dear. I can see that this means a lot to you, so I'll do as you ask, but only if you promise not to do anything rash.'

'I'll do what I think best, Joseph.'

Defeated for the first time in his married life, Joseph turned to Sergeant Wilkes. 'I have to go now, but I'll send the carriage back to wait for my wife.'

'Yes, sir. I understand.'

Joseph lowered his voice. 'I would be prepared

25

to make a generous donation to any charity of your choosing if a suitable home can be found for the infant. My wife will not leave until she is assured of this.'

'I can't promise, sir, but I'll see what I can do.'

Joseph turned his head to see his wife looking directly at him and his heart sank. 'You heard what I said, Cordelia?'

'Yes, I did, and I'll stay here until I'm satisfied that Angel will be loved and cared for, but don't be surprised if I bring her home with me, Joseph. I will not be swayed on this matter. It's Christmas Day – a time for children and families – I can't abandon her, and I won't.'

Chapter Two

Spital Square, Spitalfields – 1871

Angel put down her sampler and stared out of the window. The square was bustling with life and the sun was shining. She longed to go outside but she was forbidden to leave the house unless accompanied by Lil Heavitree, her nursemaid, although at eleven years of age she thought it ridiculous for a big girl like herself to be waited upon hand and foot by an old woman. Lil must be forty, if she was a day, and her large ungainly figure seemed to broaden with every passing year. Clumsy and prone to using bad language when she forgot herself, Lil was looked down upon by the other servants and Angel was constantly flying to her defence, particularly when her guardian's personal maid, Miss Nixon, used her wiles to get poor Lil into trouble. Quite often, when Lil's innate clumsiness had caused her to smash a valuable figurine or one of Mrs Wilding's best Crown Derby dinner plates, Angel had taken the blame. Aunt Cordelia might grumble, but she would forgive Angel, whereas Lil would probably lose her job. There were times when Angel heard the under-servants calling Lil names, referring to her as Lumpy Lil and taunting her about her former life. Angel was not sure what Lil's crimes had been, but they haunted the poor woman even after nearly twelve years of devoted service.

Angel leaned forward, attracted by the cries of a young woman selling strawberries. Aunt Cordelia loved the sweet succulent fruit and the season when they were at their best was far too short. Angel leaped to her feet with a show of lace-trimmed pantalettes and a swirl of her silk taffeta tartan skirts, and she ran from the room, grabbing her reticule on the way out. The coins clanked together merrily as she raced down three flights of stairs, flying past the startled housemaid as she crossed the entrance hall and let herself out into the street, just in time to catch the strawberry seller before she moved on to Norton Folgate.

With a punnet clutched in her hand Angel went to find Aunt Cordelia, but her way to the drawing room was barred by Miss Nixon.

'Where do you think you're going, miss?'

Her enthusiasm dashed by Miss Nixon's tight-lipped expression and sharp tone, Angel wafted

27

the strawberries under the maid's nose. 'I bought these with my own money as a present for my aunt.'

'Have you no sense, child?' Miss Nixon's voice was laced with acid. 'The master is dead. Do you think that a few berries will mend a broken heart?'

Angel stared at her blankly. She heard the words but they made no sense. 'He can't be,' she whispered. 'I saw him yesterday and he greeted me with such a kind smile.'

'That may be so but he was taken suddenly. An apoplectic fit, so the doctor said. Anyway, it's none of your business. Go to your room and don't bother Mrs Wilding. She's prostrate with grief.'

Slowly, Angel ascended the stairs. The smell of the warm berries was suddenly nauseating, much as she loved the fruit, and she abandoned the punnet on one of the carved mahogany tables that were placed strategically on each landing. The old nursery on the third floor was now a schoolroom, but Angel's governess had retired recently, leaving a gap in her life once filled with lessons on history, grammar and mathematics. Aunt Cordelia had insisted that Angel should receive an education fit for a young lady, although Uncle Joseph often stated within Angel's hearing that filling girls' heads with knowledge was a waste of time – and now he was dead. It was hard to believe that a large, ruddy-faced man, seemingly in the prime of life, should have been struck down so cruelly. Angel entered the schoolroom to find Lil waiting for her.

'You've been told, have you?'

'Miss Nixon said my uncle is dead. Is it true, Lil?'

'Dead as a doornail, love. Felled like an ox, he was. Just got up from the breakfast table, so Florrie says, and collapsed at her feet, and her still holding the coffeepot. It's a wonder she never spilled it all over him. Not that he'd have felt a thing. He were a goner for sure, and the missis screamed and fell down in a dead faint. Such a to-do.'

'How awful,' Angel said sadly. 'It must have come as a terrible shock. I ought to comfort her. Do you think I should go to her now, Lil?'

'Not at this minute, my lovely. The doctor's been and given her a strong dose of laudanum, and the undertaker will be here any minute. Just stay up here until the missis sends for you.'

'I bought her some strawberries.' Angel walked over to the window and peered out. 'It's such a lovely day.'

'It don't matter whether it's raining or sunny – when your time is up, that's it. The master has gone to his Maker, and I don't doubt that worry was partly to blame.'

'Worry?' Angel was quick to hear the change in Lil's tone. 'Why was he worried?'

'Well, whatever it was he's out of it now.' Lil smoothed her starched white apron with her work-worn hands. 'I can't dawdle about here all day. There's work to do. I just came to make sure you was all right.' Lil gave her a searching look. 'You ain't going to pipe your eye, are you?'

'No, I feel sad, but somehow I can't cry for Uncle Joseph. I know he never wanted me to

29

come and live here.'

Lil twisted her lips into a crooked smile. 'That was true at the outset, but he came round in the end. The missis can be very persuasive when she puts her mind to it. Now I really must get my carcass downstairs and offer to help or I'll never hear the last of it.' She waddled to the door, but she hesitated and turned to give Angel an encouraging smile before leaving.

Left to her own devices there was little that Angel could do other than wait for her aunt to send for her, but the call did not come. Luncheon was normally brought to the schoolroom at midday, unless Angel was invited to take the meal with her aunt, but she waited until she heard the clock in the hall strike one, and then she took matters into her own hands and went downstairs to the basement kitchen.

Cook and the young housemaid, Gilly, stared at her as if she were a ghost.

'You should be upstairs in the nursery, miss,' Cook said severely.

'It's not the nursery now,' Angel countered. 'It's the schoolroom, and I'm hungry. Where's Lil?'

'She went to the pharmacy to purchase some laudanum for madam – doctor's orders. She's to be kept quiet in a darkened room, and she don't want to be bothered with the likes of you.'

Angel was taken aback by Cook's response. She had never been a cheery soul, but now her tone was belligerent and downright disrespectful. Angel had known from an early age that she was not related to the Wildings by blood, and that she had been adopted by Aunt Cordelia when she was just a baby, but the servants had always treated her with due deference, until now.

'I would like my food sent to the schoolroom, Cook. When Lil returns, please send her to me.' Angel shot a withering look at Gilly, who was giggling helplessly. 'I'm glad you think it's funny. This is supposed to be a house of mourning.'

Gilly's jaw dropped and she backed into the scullery. 'Sorry, miss.'

'On second thoughts, I'll help myself,' Angel said, ignoring Cook's tight-lipped expression as she cut several slices from a freshly baked loaf of bread. 'Is there any ham or meat left from dinner last evening?'

Reluctantly Cook opened the larder door and took out a plate of cold beef. She placed it on the table. 'Is there anything else, miss?'

'You wouldn't treat me so rudely if my uncle were still alive.' Angel added some meat to her plate and a pat of butter. 'My aunt will hear of this.'

'You've got a nasty surprise coming to you, miss. You won't be so high and mighty when the bailiffs arrive.'

Angel hesitated in the doorway. 'I don't know what you mean.'

'You'll find out soon enough.' Cook turned her back on Angel and returned to the range where she had been stirring a bubbling pan of soup.

Angel took the plate to her room, but as she nibbled a slice of bread and butter her appetite deserted her and she left the remainder of the food untouched. She wanted to go to her aunt and comfort her, but Lil's words of warning made

31

her hesitate, and just when she had made up her mind to ignore them anyway, Lil burst into the room. She trailed her woollen shawl behind her and her straw bonnet was askew, allowing wisps of hair to cling damply to her forehead.

'I've just run all the way from the pharmacy, Angel. The undertaker's arrived, love. Mrs Wilding is prostrate with grief and there's no one but you from above stairs to tell him what's required.'

Angel leaped to her feet. Something to do at last. 'I'll speak to him.'

'Are you sure?' Lil followed Angel out of the room, clumping down the stairs in her wake. 'I'll come with you so that he doesn't take advantage of your tender years.'

'I'll deal with it, Lil. Don't worry about me.' Angel hurried to the ground floor where she found the undertaker. He clutched his top hat in his hands, but as he turned to greet her his conciliatory smile faded.

'I'm sorry, miss, but I really need to see your mother. Will you tell her that Jeremiah Chancellor is here to await her convenience?'

'Mrs Wilding is my aunt and she is resting at the moment, sir. She must not be disturbed but she will let you have her instructions as soon as possible.'

'If you would be kind enough to tell her that I called, I'll come again tomorrow.'

'Just you wait a minute,' Lil said brusquely. 'You ain't going and leaving the dead body here, are you? The master is stretched out on the dining-room table. It took me and Cook to heave him off the floor and he's no lightweight.'

'I have a coffin in the hearse, which is at your disposal,' Mr Chancellor said stiffly. 'But it's customary for the loved ones to rest at home until the funeral.'

'There is the morning parlour,' Angel said hastily. 'I'm sure that would be suitable, but you aren't going to leave him here for long, are you?'

He looked over the top of Angel's head, addressing himself to Lil. 'There's the question of the necessary arrangements to be made, and there are certain financial matters to discuss. I can only do that with the lady of the house or someone in authority.'

'My aunt will see you when she is rested, but I'm sure she will agree to any suggestions you might care to make.' Angel raised her voice, just a little, but even to her ears she sounded youthful and uncertain.

Mr Chancellor turned to Lil. 'I can't take instructions from a mere child. Tell your mistress that I'll be pleased to call on her when she is feeling better.'

Angel could see that Lil was simmering with indignation and was flexing her hands as if at any moment she might seize Mr Chancellor by the collar and eject him from the house. Angel was well aware that Lil had once floored a would-be intruder with an upper cut that would not have disgraced Tom Cribb. It had been the talk of the servants' hall for months after the event.

'I can speak for my aunt, sir,' Angel said firmly. 'Please go ahead with the necessary arrangements, and if you would be kind enough to call tomorrow morning I am sure Mrs Wilding will be able to see you in person. You must understand that she is too upset to see anyone at the moment.'

Jeremiah Chancellor screwed up his face, as if calculating the risks of taking instructions from a minor, but after a quick glance at his surroundings and the obvious trappings of wealth, he managed a sickly smile. 'Of course, miss. I'm sorry if I caused offence, but you must realise that in my line of business I have to be careful.'

'I understand, sir.' Angel inclined her head graciously, although secretly she would have been pleased to let Lil loose on him. She had a satisfying vision of the pompous gentleman flying down the front steps aided by a shove from Lil, but she managed to control a sudden desire to giggle. 'Please see Mr Chancellor out, Lil.'

Angel waited until the door closed on him before making her way slowly up the stairs, but as she reached the first floor she could hear her aunt's sobs through the closed bedroom door. If ever anyone was in need of loving care, it was Aunt Cordelia and, ignoring Lil's advice, Angel entered the room. The curtains were closed and the four-poster bed loomed large in the shadows. Angel tiptoed over to stand at her aunt's bedside.

'Aunt Cordelia, it's me, Angel.' When there was no response, Angel lay down on the coverlet and cuddled up to her aunt. 'Don't cry. I'll take care of you just as you took care of me when I was little.' She rested her cheek against her aunt's back, placing a protective arm around the slim body, racked with sobs. Angel's tears, which had been so long in coming, fell unchecked.

Angel was considered to be too young to attend the funeral, despite her protests that she wanted to be there if only to support her aunt, but Cordelia was adamant. She had recovered enough from the shock of her husband's sudden death to agree to Mr Chancellor's arrangements for the interment. The day after Mr Chancellor's visit Angel had accompanied her aunt to Jay's Mourning Warehouse in Regent Street, where Cordelia was fitted out with her widow's weeds. Angel was in the awkward stage where she was neither child nor adult, but she wanted to show her respect for her adoptive uncle and she chose a plain grey tussore gown, which she wore with black armbands, similar to those purchased for the servants.

At home the curtains were closed and black crepe ribbon tied to the door knocker indicated that the occupants were in deep mourning. The house in Spital Square had never been filled with music and laughter, but now it was a sad place and the only sounds that echoed throughout the building were the servants' footsteps on the back stairs and the closing of a door or window.

Two days after the interment, Angel was on her way to her uncle's study in search of something to read from his small collection of books, when the door flew open and a man hurried out, almost colliding with her.

'I'm so sorry, my dear. I didn't know you were there.'

Angel recognised the tall, thin gentleman whose balding head was compensated for by grey mutton-chop whiskers, a curly moustache and a goatee beard, which was a similar shade of ginger to his bushy eyebrows. Geoffrey Galloway was her aunt's solicitor and when Angel was younger he used to bring her a poke of peppermint creams or a stick of barley sugar. He still treated her as if she were a charming five-year-old. Sometimes growing up was very hard, especially when people failed to see that she was on her way to adulthood.

'I was going to borrow a book, sir.' Angel kept her tone neutral and she met his amused gaze with a stony stare.

'Admirable, young lady. Admirable.' He smiled vaguely and crossed the hall to where Gilly waited, holding his hat and cane. 'Good day.'

A warm draught laced with the smell of horse dung and fumes from the gasworks wafted in from the street, and Gilly closed the door after him. She shot a sideways glance at Angel, her mean little face contorted with spite. 'You won't be looking down your nose at us servants for much longer, so Cook says.'

Angel paused in the doorway. 'What do you mean by that?'

'Just you wait and see. Cook knows a thing or two.' Gilly scurried off in the direction of the back stairs, leaving Angel staring after her.

'Darling, is that you?' Cordelia's voice from the depths of the study brought Angel back to reality and she hurried into the room.

'Are you all right, Aunt Cordelia? What did Mr Galloway want?'

Slumped in her late husband's leather chair, Cordelia made an effort to smile, but her heart-shaped face was deathly pale and her eyes red-rimmed. 'We're ruined, Angel. There's no easy way to put this, but your uncle's business venture failed miserably. The brewery has had to close and we've lost everything.'

Angel sank down on the chair recently vacated by Mr Galloway – the seat was still warm. 'I don't understand. How could that happen?'

'I don't pretend to understand business matters, dear. All I know is what Geoffrey just told me. Apparently Joseph played the tables to try to recoup his losses when the business was failing and his last gamble didn't pay off. Everything has gone, and he mortgaged the house without my knowledge. I'm virtually penniless.' She buried her head in her hands and her shoulders heaved. 'We'll be living on the streets.'

'No, that can't be true,' Angel said stoutly, but then Gilly's spiteful words came back to her. How the servants could have found out was a puzzle, but then they always seemed to know things before she did. 'There must be something we could sell to raise money. Perhaps we could find a smaller house to rent.'

'You don't know what you're talking about, Angel. Everything has to go – the furniture, my jewellery, the silver – all the things I treasure. The household bills haven't been paid for months and if I can't raise the money the bailiffs will come in and take everything. I can't bear the disgrace.'

'Isn't there anyone who could help us?' Angel asked in desperation. 'Do you know anyone who could lend you some money to keep us going for a while?'

Cordelia raised her head, gazing at Angel with

tears sparkling on the tips of her dark lashes. 'There is one person who has offered to help, but I don't think I can bring myself to accept his offer.'

'Who is it, Aunt? What does he want in return for a loan?'

'Geoffrey asked me to marry him,' Cordelia said dully. 'I've known him for years. He's been Joseph's solicitor for as long as I can remember, and he used to dine here quite often, but I can't marry a man I don't love, even for the sake of keeping a roof over our heads.'

'He seems like a nice man,' Angel said slowly. 'But if you don't like him...'

'I do like him, darling. I've always liked him, but I loved Joseph.' Cordelia mopped her eyes with her sodden hanky. 'I know he was domineering and sometimes impatient, but ours was a love match and I miss him terribly. Anyway, I'm in mourning, and I will be for a year or maybe two.'

'You mustn't give it a second thought.' Angel leaned over the desk to grasp her aunt's hand. 'We'll manage without him, Aunt Cordelia. I'll find work and we'll look for somewhere else to live. You won't have to marry a man you don't love. I'll look after you now.'

'My darling, you're just a child. I wouldn't think of placing such responsibility on your young shoulders. But you're right, we will survive somehow, and the first thing I will do is take my jewellery to the pawnbroker. I won't allow the bailiffs to take it.'

'There is my ring, too,' Angel said slowly. The

thought of parting with the one thing that might have belonged to her mother was agonising, but she could not allow her aunt to make all the sacrifices.

'No, Angel. That is yours and you must keep it always.' Cordelia frowned, staring down at the jewels on her left hand. 'I will part with everything other than my wedding ring. Joseph placed that on my finger when I was just twenty, and it will remain there until the day I die.'

Angel knew that at any moment her aunt would burst into tears and that would only make matters worse. She jumped to her feet. 'There must be other things we can sell, Aunt Cordelia.'

'The bailiffs will be here this afternoon. We must act quickly if we're to salvage anything, and even then I dare say it's against the law, but at this moment I don't care.'

'You must stay here,' Angel said firmly. 'I'll go to the pawnshop with Lil. It would be a brave man who tried to get the better of her.'

'Perhaps you're right, my darling. I'm afraid I would give in too easily.' Cordelia rose from the chair, patting the leather arm rests as if saying farewell to an old friend. 'I have the onerous duty of informing the servants that they will have to find employment elsewhere, but first I'll fetch my jewellery box. I have a fine gold chain, which you must keep. Thread it through your mama's ring and hang it around your neck.'

Angel swallowed hard. 'Thank you, Aunt Cordelia. I'll treasure it always.'

Angel and Lil returned from their trip to the

pawnbroker's in White's Row to find the bailiffs already at work. The dining-room table was being hefted onto a cart, together with the chairs, and the sideboard stood on the pavement waiting to be treated with equal lack of care. Angel would have run forward to snatch the portrait of her aunt as a young bride from the hands of a burly carter, but Lil restrained her.

'Just go indoors, love,' she said in a low voice that sounded more like a growl. 'You can't stop 'em, and they might start asking questions.'

Angel realised that her weighty reticule might cause comment and she tucked it under her arm as she marched up the steps to the front door. It was wide open and Gilly was ineffectually flapping her apron at a porter who was carrying a tea chest filled with Cordelia's Crown Derby dinner service.

'Robbers,' Gilly cried hoarsely. 'That belongs to the mistress.'

'Not no more, my duck.' The man winked at her and continued on his way. A second cart had drawn up outside and a second bailiff pushed past Angel as he entered the house.

Gilly screamed, 'They'll have the clothes off our backs next, miss.'

'No, they won't. You'll be quite safe below stairs. We have to leave them to do their work.' Angel pointed the distraught maid in the direction of the baize door. 'Stay in the kitchen with Cook.'

'I can't, miss. Cook done a bunk and Miss Nixon went last night. I dunno how to cook dinner, and that's a fact.'

Lil grabbed Gilly by the arm. 'Do as Miss Angel

40

says, you halfwit. There's nothing to be done up here.'

'What shall I do, Lil? I ain't got no money, and me dad will skin me alive if I goes home.'

'Just wait in the kitchen,' Lil said with a surprising show of patience. 'I'll be down in a minute and we'll decide what's to be done.' She gave Gilly a shove and the girl stumbled off in the direction of the back stairs.

Angel sidestepped two porters. 'You'd best go after her, Lil. Goodness knows what she'll do left on her own in the kitchen. She'll probably burn the house down.'

'She's daft enough,' Lil said grimly. 'Leave her to me.' She strode off with a determined set to her jaw.

Angel was about to go in search of her aunt when she heard someone call her name. Her heart sank as she recognised the voice and she turned slowly to see the Reverend John Hardisty and his wife standing in the doorway.

'Angel, my dear child, what a sorry state of affairs, to be sure.'

'Poor Cordelia, she must be distraught,' Letitia said with a smile that did not reach her eyes.

'Yes, ma'am,' Angel answered meekly, but she was not fooled by Mrs Hardisty's words of sympathy. She suspected that Letitia harboured some kind of grudge against her aunt, although it was hard to imagine Aunt Cordelia merited such ill feeling. Whatever the cause – and Letitia Hardisty always managed to appear conciliatory and pleasant – Angel had often felt an undercurrent and on this particular day it was more obvious

41

than ever.

'Is there anything we can do?' John Hardisty spoke with genuine concern.

'I don't think so, sir,' Angel said hastily. 'I think my aunt is resting. This has all come as a terrible shock.'

'Is it true that you are losing everything?' He looked round, shaking his head. 'If so, where will you go?'

'I dare say Cordelia has relatives who will take her in. Although I wouldn't relish such a change after being mistress of my own house for so many years.' Letitia pursed her lips and there was a malicious gleam in her dark eyes. 'Poor thing,' she added, clutching her husband's arm. 'We should leave, John. I fear we are intruding.'

He cleared his throat noisily as if about to embark on a sermon. 'If there is any way I can be of assistance, Angel, please ask your aunt to contact me.'

Letitia dragged him towards the door, which was propped open to allow the bailiff's men easy access. 'A penniless widow is a pitiable object in the eyes of society. My condolences to your aunt, you poor child.'

The words that tumbled from Letitia's lips should have given Angel comfort, but the reverse was true. She had attended church every Sunday for as long as she could remember, and there had been interminable tea parties either at the vicarage or here at home, when the ladies of the parish gathered together to discuss their charitable actions and exchange gossip. Even as a child it had been obvious to Angel that women like

Margaret Edwards, the deacon's wife, and the good ladies who tried to alleviate the suffering of the poor, were all in awe of Letitia Hardisty, if not actually afraid of her and her sharp tongue.

Resisting the temptation to rush after the vicar and his wife and slam the door, shutting them out of her life for ever, Angel took a deep breath. Whatever befell her and her aunt in the future, the one good thing to come out of this terrible state of affairs was that Aunt Cordelia would be free to start her life again, away from the tittle-tattle and covert glances of those who were supposed to be her friends. Even so, the future looked bleak and for the first time in her life Angel was scared.

Chapter Three

Two days later, Angel stood in the middle of the entrance hall, glancing round at the walls. Ghostly patches on the wallpaper marked the places where paintings and gilt-framed mirrors had hung until the bailiff's men took them away. The slightest sound echoed through the empty rooms like thunder, and the home she had known all her life was being ripped apart. Strange men had robbed them of everything that was much loved and familiar, and the house itself was to be sold by auction. Where they would go and what they would do was something that Angel had hardly dared to imagine, but now she was facing reality.

Childhood was over and she must grow up fast. It was a terrifying prospect.

The bailiffs had left them with very little other than their personal belongings. Lil had stuffed those haphazardly into three large valises, and the pots and pans from the kitchen were piled into wicker baskets and a tea chest. Lil had packed these herself and had insisted that Gilly must guard them with her life, if necessary. Angel had heard the child sobbing and had gone down to the kitchen to investigate. She found her clutching the chest like a shipwrecked mariner clinging to a floating spar.

'What are you doing?' Angel demanded.

'She told me not to let no one near this or she'd tan me hide. I know that Lumpy Lil would do it, too.'

'You silly girl, she only meant for you to stop the bailiff's men from taking everything. I doubt if they'd set much store by old saucepans and chipped china. Get up, for heaven's sake.'

Gilly staggered to her feet. 'I got cramp in me legs thanks to her.'

'You won't let Miss Heavitree hear you talking like that if you've got any sense, and don't call her Lumpy Lil or she'll have your guts for garters.'

'Where did you hear that vulgar expression, Angel?' Cordelia's shocked tones made Angel spin round to see her aunt standing at the foot of the stairs.

'I'm sorry, Aunt Cordelia. I didn't know you were there.'

'We mustn't allow our standards to drop simply because we're in a difficult situation,' Cordelia said primly. 'I want you to come upstairs, Angel. Mr Galloway is here and he has something to tell you.'

'What is it?' Angel asked anxiously.

'I'll allow him to tell you, darling. Come along, don't keep him waiting.'

Dragging her feet, Angel followed her aunt up the steep staircase. Geoffrey Galloway was waiting for them in the study, which, denuded of its books and furniture, seemed like a different place. The only item left by the bailiff's men was a chair with a threadbare seat and a castor missing off one leg. Cordelia perched on it, balancing with difficulty. 'I haven't told Angel anything, Geoffrey. I think it would be best coming from you.'

He stood with his back to the fireplace, feet wide apart, hands clasped. 'You must be aware of the seriousness of the situation in which your aunt finds herself, Angel.'

'Yes, sir.'

'I've been thinking it over very carefully, you understand, and your aunt agrees with what I am about to say.'

Angel knew instantly that his solution was not going to benefit her. She shot a wary glance in her aunt's direction, but Cordelia was studying the bare floorboards as if they were something new and interesting.

'My sister, Mrs Adams, is also recently widowed,' Galloway announced in a sonorous tone. 'Rebecca owns a small house in Maddox Street and she is in need of a genteel lady to be her companion. I think it would suit your aunt admirably.'

Angel turned to her aunt. 'Is this what you want, Aunt Cordelia?'

'My darling, what choice do I have?' Cordelia met Angel's gaze with a tremulous smile. 'It's very kind of Mr Galloway to go to so much trouble on our account, and I have met Mrs Adams on a couple of occasions. She seems a very agreeable lady.'

'Am I to go with you, Aunt?'

'No, Angel,' Galloway said firmly. 'My sister is childless and she loves to travel. It would not be appropriate for you to live with your aunt, but of course you may visit her sometimes.'

'What is to become of me, Mr Galloway?' Angel met his stern gaze squarely, without flinching.

'You are fortunate to have been brought up like a young lady. Mrs Wilding has been more than generous in making sure you have had a good education, and you know how to behave in polite society.'

'What Mr Galloway is trying to tell you, my love, is that he's found a suitable place for you with a good family, where I hope you will be as happy as you have been here, with me.' Cordelia held out her hand. 'I hate the thought of being parted from you, Angel, but I hope and pray that this is just a temporary arrangement.'

Angel refused to be placated. 'Am I to be a servant like Lil?'

'No, definitely not.' Cordelia's lips trembled. 'I wouldn't allow such a thing.' She cast a beseeching look at Galloway. 'Tell her, please. You know more about the Grimes family than I do.'

'Phileas Grimes is a client of mine, known to

46

me for many years. He is a wealthy man who's made his fortune from buying tracts of land in the East End for building. He has a daughter about your age, and he is often away from home.'

'So we are both to live with strangers,' Angel said slowly. 'Aunt Cordelia is going to stay with your sister, and I am going to...' she paused. 'Where exactly is this house? Is it in London?'

'Ah, there you have spotted the best part of the plan.' Galloway beamed at her, puffing out his chest. 'Mr Grimes owns a lovely old house in the Essex countryside. You will have plenty of freedom and you will share lessons in art and music with his daughter. It will be an idyllic existence away from the dirt and disease of the East End.'

Angel threw herself down on her knees beside her aunt, clutching both her hands in a desperate grip. 'Don't let him separate us, Aunt Cordelia. You are more important to me than anyone who might claim to be my real mama. Please tell him that you will not be parted from me.'

Cordelia's eyes filled with tears and she raised Angel's hands to her lips. 'If only I could, darling. I would do anything to keep us together, but you must see that it's just not possible at the moment. I'm penniless, my love. The money from my jewellery has been spent on food and necessities and now everything has gone and I can't support myself, let alone you, but Geoffrey has promised that Lil can go with you, and Mrs Adams has a place for Gilly in her household. We will all be taken care of, but I hope in the future we will be together again. This isn't for ever, darling girl.'

Dazed and struggling to come to terms with the

sudden change in events, Angel rose slowly to her feet. 'And if I refuse? What happens then?'

Galloway's lips tightened to a thin line beneath his quivering moustache. 'You will comply with your aunt's wishes if you know what's good for you. You're an orphan, Angel Winter. That isn't even your real name, so how do you propose to manage if your aunt cannot look after you, as she has done for the last eleven years? Have you any idea how fortunate you are, little girl?'

Angel shook her head. 'You are not a nice man, Mr Galloway. I hope my aunt never marries you, because you have a cruel nature. A kind man wouldn't separate us, and you are not a kind man, even though you pretend to be.'

'That's enough, Angel. You must apologise for being so rude to Mr Galloway.' Cordelia stood up, swaying on her feet and Galloway leaped forward to support her.

'You see the real nature of the child now, Cordelia,' he said angrily. 'You do not know her pedigree and I think it's becoming obvious that she came from the gutter. You've harboured romantic fantasies as to her birth, but she's a child of the slums and needs a firm hand.'

Cordelia uttered a muffled cry and fainted in his arms.

'You hateful man,' Angel cried passionately. 'You planned all this.'

'Don't be ridiculous, child. Fetch your maid. I need her to accompany Mrs Wilding to my sister's house. You will come with me.'

'I won't leave Aunt Cordelia.'

'We'll see about that.' Galloway swept the unconscious Cordelia off her feet and carried her from the room. He came to a halt at the sight of Lil, who had a valise in each hand and a bundle of clothes tucked under one arm. 'My carriage is outside. I need you to accompany your mistress to Maddox Street.'

Lil dropped the cases on the highly polished floorboards. 'I ain't going nowhere without Angel.'

'It's Miss Winter to you,' Galloway snapped. 'Do as you're told. I'll look after the young lady.' He glanced at Gilly, who was cowering in a corner clutching a basket filled with kitchenware. 'You, too. Get in the carriage.'

'I ain't moving until I knows what's happening to Angel,' Lil said angrily. 'What's up with the mistress, anyway? What have you done to her?'

Galloway chose to ignore her and he left the house, staggering beneath the voluminous folds of black crepe that enveloped Cordelia like a shroud.

Angel grasped Lil's hand. 'Look after Aunt Cordelia. He's promised that you can come to me in the country. I don't know where I'll be but he gave his word you would be with me.'

'And you believed him?' Lil curled her lip. 'I don't trust that man, but for your sake I'll see that the mistress is settled comfortably and then I'll come and find you. It don't matter where you are, you can trust me, Angel.'

'I know I can. I wouldn't go with him if he hadn't promised that we'd be together.'

Lil beckoned to Gilly. 'Come along, nipper. Let's get this over and done with.' She followed Galloway out of the house.

Seized by a feeling of panic, Angel ran after her

but Cordelia was already in the carriage and Lil climbed in beside her, followed by Gilly.

'Wave goodbye to your aunt, my dear,' Galloway said loudly. He seized Angel's arm and pumped it up and down so that from the carriage window it must have looked as though she was waving. 'Smile,' he said through clenched teeth as the coachman flicked the whip and the horses moved off.

Angel tried to break free but Galloway tightened his grip on her arm. 'No you don't.' He gave Angel a shove that sent her stumbling backwards. 'My sister doesn't want to be troubled by a brat like you.'

'Aunt Cordelia.' The words were ripped from Angel's throat in a hoarse cry of anguish. The only mother she had ever known had been taken from her in the cruellest way, and even Lil had deserted her. She faced Galloway with tears streaming down her cheeks. 'I hate you. You pretend to be kind but you're a monster.'

She did not see the blow aimed at her head until too late and she crumpled to the ground, stunned and barely conscious. Then, before she had a chance to gather her wits, she was hoisted over Galloway's shoulder like a sack of coal. In a haze of pain she heard him hail a cab and the next thing she knew she was in the vehicle and Galloway climbed in to sit beside her. Overcome by a feeling of nausea and a throbbing headache, she slumped against the leather squabs, taking deep breaths of the fetid air. The stench of the river and the manufactories on its banks was overpowering.

'Where are you taking me?' she demanded angrily.

'The workhouse in Bear Yard, if you must know.'

Angel stared at him in disbelief. Surely the bump on her head must have addled her brains. 'The workhouse?'

'That's what I said. You're a pauper now. You are the devil's spawn and you're going back where you belong. It's a new building, opened only last year. You'll be quite comfortable there.'

'But you promised Aunt Cordelia that I would be taken care of. You said I was to be a companion to a girl my own age somewhere in Essex.'

'I lied,' he said complacently. 'It comes naturally to a lawyer – you'll learn not to believe everything you're told. This is a valuable lesson in life.'

'You can't do this to me.'

'There's no such word as can't. That's what my old nanny used to tell me and she was right. You will do as I say or I'll inform the workhouse master that you are a simpleton and must be tied to your bed for your own protection. You won't get the better of me, Angel Winter, so don't try.'

Despite Angel's protests she was admitted to the workhouse and forced to undergo the humiliation of being stripped of all her fine clothes, scrubbed down with lye soap and her hair rinsed with vinegar. It trickled into her eyes and made her yelp with pain, but a quick slap from the older inmate charged with this task made Angel catch her breath, and she bit her lip, determined not to cry. Finally, after being given a coarse huckaback towel, she dried herself as best she could and with

51

the greatest reluctance dressed herself in a shift and a shapeless, faded blue-and-white striped dress. A calico pinafore and a white mobcap completed the outfit and a pair of boots that had seen better days pinched her toes. When she tried to protest and ask for her own shoes, she received a clout on the ear that sent her sprawling onto the flagstone floor. In all her life she had never received anything more brutal than a smack on the wrist, and that was for a misdemeanour so small that she could not remember what she had done to deserve the punishment. Now in the space of a couple of hours she had been knocked to the ground, humiliated and imprisoned amongst total strangers. The comfortable life she had led in Spital Square seemed like heaven and now she was in hell. There was only one thing left that linked her to her past, and, when the woman turned away to hang up the towel, Angel took the ring and chain from inside her cheek where she had concealed it before the undignified assault on her body. She just had time to slip the chain around her neck and tuck the ring beneath her shift, before the older woman rounded on her. She yanked Angel to her feet.

'Come with me.'

'Where are you taking me?'

'Don't speak unless you're spoken to or you'll get another wallop.'

Angel had no alternative but to follow the hunched figure from the communal washroom into a long dark corridor that led, eventually, to a flight of stairs. An unpleasant odour of damp and dirty laundry wafted up from the basement in clouds of steam. The large room, little more than a dank cellar, ran the length of the building, and the heat from the coppers was stifling. The red-faced women worked silently, washing the bedding, rinsing it and feeding it through giant mangles, which they operated by hand. Huge baskets were piled high with sheets and blankets and taken to the drying room. The deafening sound of hobnail boots clattering on the stone floor combined with the bubbling noise from the coppers and the rhythmic grinding of the mangles. Added to all this was the constant chorus of coughing from diseased lungs. It was a horrific place, but this was where Angel was destined to spend the rest of the day, and, as far as she knew, the rest of her life.

Angel had missed the midday meal by a whisker and she had eaten very little at breakfast. As she worked on throughout the afternoon all she could think about was the bowl of thick, creamy porridge, sprinkled with golden sugar and slathered with thick cream that she had left barely touched. The boiled egg had fared little better, and she had only nibbled the buttered toast. Her stomach growled and by suppertime she was faint with hunger, dazed with exhaustion and could barely drag one foot after another as the inmates were marched to the dining hall. A hunk of dry bread accompanied a bowl of thin gruel, and this was eaten in silence with the matron watching every move.

That night, trying to sleep on a hard wooden bed with just a thin flock-filled mattress, one blanket and no pillow, Angel made up her mind to escape. The other girls in her dormitory ranged in age from seven to fifteen: the younger ones cried themselves to sleep and the older girls talked in hushed voices for a while. Sobs, snores and coughing filled the night air, and a strong smell of carbolic emanated from the floorboards, which were scrubbed each morning until they were bleached white. This, Angel had learned from Lizzie, the older girl who shared her bed, was the job of those who were too young to pick oakum or work in the laundry, and too old for the schoolroom.

Despite her aching limbs and physical exhaustion, Angel's mind was surprisingly clear as she plotted her escape. The first thing she would need was her own clothes. She had seen them folded and placed on a shelf in the area next to the washroom. They were to be sold off to pay for her uniform, so Lizzie had said, and Angel had no reason to doubt her. Lizzie had been born in the workhouse and had never seen her brothers, who had been admitted with their mother. The unfortunate woman had died some years earlier, but what had happened to her father Lizzie could not say. The thirteen-year-old lived in hope that one day someone would come and take her from here. She smiled as she slept and Angel could only imagine what dreams her new friend must be enjoying. At least Lizzie could escape from the reality of her incarceration for a few hours each night. But it was not so for Angel; she kept her eyes open, waiting until all was quiet. She had no idea how she was going to make a break for freedom, but she was determined to try. Anything and anywhere would be better than this dire place.

At last it seemed that everyone slept. Angel raised herself carefully from the narrow bed so as not to wake Lizzie, and crept out of the dormitory, barefoot and still in her calico nightgown. At the sound of footsteps, she dodged into a cupboard and peered through a crack in the door as the light from an oil lamp bobbed up and down, and the sound of footsteps drew nearer. She held her breath until the woman was out of earshot. She had not bargained for the night watch, but this put her on the alert and made her even more determined to get away. The long corridor ran parallel to the dormitories and moonlight streamed in through the tall windows, its benevolent rays illuminating the way to the staircase.

She made it to the ground floor without mishap, although she had to hide from the night patrol several times. The reception area was deserted and silent and the doorkeeper had, for some reason best known to himself, deserted his post. To Angel's intense relief she found her garments still neatly stacked on the shelf. Her fingers shook as she took off the nightgown and put on her own clothes. Her red flannel petticoat caressed her bare legs like a whisper after the coarse material of the workhouse uniform. She slipped the green silk bodice and overskirt over her head, fastening it with difficulty. Every second counted and she was about to put on her stockings when she heard approaching footsteps. She pushed her bare feet into her boots and tiptoed across the room to open the outer door. The bolts drew back with little more than a click and the door opened with just a sigh of well-oiled hinges. The night air enveloped her in a warm hug as she stepped out into Bear Yard. She picked up her skirts and ran. Where she was going she had no idea, her only aim was to get as far away from the workhouse as her legs would carry her.

But as she emerged into Vere Street she realised that night time in this notorious area of London was not a friendly place. The workhouse might be sleeping silently, but it was not so outside its walls. Gaudily dressed women bared their charms in doorways, while others hung out of upstairs windows, calling out to the men who staggered along the pavements, some with bottles clutched in their hands and all of them the worse for drink. Skeletally thin dogs rummaged in the gutters for scraps of food and feral cats howled and fought over the carcasses of vermin, while big black rats slunk from alley to alley, on the lookout for any-thing they might attack and gobble up. Gangs of ragged boys hung about beneath the gas lamps, smoking pipes and watching out for the unwary. Angel hid in a doorway as a youth plucked a wallet from a passing stranger's pocket, but his victim rounded on him and a fight ensued. Every-one seemed to join in and there was much shout-ing and flailing of arms and legs. Angel took the opportunity to make a break for it and ran, dodg-ing down alleys and avoiding the grabbing hands of men who lurched out of doorways, offering her money and promising her a good time. She had no idea what they were talking about, but she did not stop to find out.

The narrow courts and alleys were unlit, but in the distance she could see a pool of light. Emerging from the darkness was like entering heaven – she could hear voices and the scent of fruit and flowers filled the air. Her feet barely seemed to touch the cobbled streets as she ran towards this oasis in the darkness of the wicked city. She came to a halt in a square where wagons were being unloaded by porters, who balanced baskets filled with produce on their heads. They added one on top of the other until their burdens reached improbable heights, but somehow they managed to deliver the fruit and vegetables to the stall owners without dropping a single apple. Angel watched, fascinated and excited by the bustling activity. She might have been invisible, for all the notice anyone took of her, and that was oddly comforting after the terrifying moments in Clare Market. Suddenly overcome by exhaustion, she made her way between the carts and barrows to the far side of the square and comparative safety beneath the portico of St Paul's Church. She huddled in a corner and fell asleep.

She awakened to bright sunshine and a cacophony of noise. Cart wheels rumbled over the cobblestones and the clip-clop of heavy horses' hoofs echoed off the surrounding buildings. The shouts of the traders bargaining for fruit and vegetables vied with the cries of the flower girls and the raucous laughter and chatter of the porters.

'What are you doing here? This ain't no place for the likes of you.'

Angel shielded her eyes from the sunlight and

found herself looking up at an older girl with a freckled face and a mop of carroty curls escaping from a straw bonnet. 'Who are you?'

'I asked first. You ain't one of us, so what d'you think you're doing taking my pitch?'

Angel scrambled to her feet. 'I don't know what you're talking about. What place is this?'

'Are you a bit of a simpleton? This here is Covent Garden Market. Where have you been all your life?'

Angel eyed her warily. 'What's your name?'

'Hoity-toity, ain't yer? And you wearing duds what must have cost a pretty penny. Come on then, tell us who you are and what you're doing here.'

'To tell you the truth I'm lost. My name is Angel Winter and I ran away from the workhouse last night.'

'You was in the workhouse?'

'Only for a few hours. I told you, I ran away. I wasn't going to stay in a place like that. Mr Galloway left me there, but he was supposed to take me to a family in Essex. I have to get to Maddox Street and tell my aunt what he did. She thinks he's a nice man, but he isn't. He's bad and he's cruel, and I worry about Aunt Cordelia.' Angel's voice broke on a sob and she turned her head away. She didn't want this strange creature to see her cry.

'Seems to me you've had a run of bad luck, nipper.' The girl laid her hand on Angel's shoulder. 'I'm Dolly Chapman and I sell flowers, when I can get hold of 'em.'

Angel looked up. 'What do you mean?'

'Flowers cost money, stupid. I have to sell buttonholes and such to earn enough to keep body and soul together. I ain't got no money to pay them hawkers what they ask.'

Dolly's snub-nosed face seemed to fade away and Angel closed her eyes.

'Here, don't pass out on me, nipper.' Dolly gave her a shake. 'You don't look too good. Are you hungry?'

'I think so. My tummy hurts.'

'You're a baby,' Dolly said scornfully. 'Sit there and I'll see what I can do. I'm a bit peckish meself, as it happens.' She sashayed off in the direction of a coffee stall and returned minutes later carrying a steaming mug and two bread rolls. She handed one to Angel. 'Get that down yer and you can share my coffee.'

'I'm not allowed coffee,' Angel said before she could stop herself.

'Hark at you, miss. I dunno where you come from, but it weren't from round here. You'll put up with coffee or you'll have to go and find a horse trough and drink the water them big brutes have slobbered in.'

Angel swallowed a mouthful of buttered roll. 'I'm sorry. I'd be grateful for a sip of your coffee, please, Dolly.'

Dolly handed her the mug. 'I dunno how a young lady like you ended up in the workhouse, but it'll make a good tale to tell the others of a night when we're warming ourselves round the watchman's brazier.'

'Are there more of you?'

'Lord love you, my duck. You might have dropped out of the sky like a real angel, for all I knows. Eat your grub and I'll show you how to snatch some blooms, but you'll have to look out for yourself. Them as come from east of Clare Market are the ones to watch – spiteful little cats, all of 'em. They'd do their own mothers down to pay for a tot of blue ruin.'

'Blue ruin?'

'Gin, my duck. Don't you know nothing?'

Angel took a sip of coffee. It was hot and sweet with an overlying hint of bitterness, but it warmed her stomach. 'I'm a quick learner,' she said hastily. 'Thank you very much for the bread, and the coffee.'

'Come on then. Stir your stumps, Angel. We've got work to do. You'll need some brass to pay for a night's lodging, otherwise you'll be sleeping here again. It ain't easy to survive on the streets.' Dolly led the way across the cobblestones to the floral hall where the perfume of garden flowers mingled with that of more exotic blooms, and the explosion of colour made Angel gasp with delight. Despite her recent traumatic experiences she was transported to a world where peace and beauty abounded – but not for long. Dolly grabbed her by the arm and dragged her outside to where the blooms were being unpacked. A sea of heads and flailing arms, flying skirts and cat-like howls accompanied the frenzied actions of the women and girls who were snatching the fallen blossoms from the dusty ground. Dolly dived in head first.

Angel could only stand and stare, but in a heart-beat it was all over and the crowd dispersed, each of the women clutching handfuls of flower heads and sprigs of greenery. Dolly faced up to an older woman who attempted to snatch a rosebud from her grasp. Their colourful language made Angel recoil in a mixture of horror and admiration. She had heard costermongers and draymen swearing at each other, but the expletives used by these two would have made a sailor blush.

Dolly surged towards her. 'Don't tangle with Smutty Sue. She's a nasty bitch and she once bit a porter's finger off when he tried to stop a fight.'

Angel shot a wary glance in Smutty Sue's direction and she was convinced. The woman had long pointed teeth that looked like fangs, and straggly grey hair that barely hid the scars on her cheek and neck. Smutty Sue hawked and spat, sending a pool of tobacco juice onto the cobblestones.

'She scares me,' Angel whispered.

'Rightly so.' Dolly jerked her head in the direction of a group of younger girls who were now seated cross-legged outside the floral hall. 'They're all right, so long as you don't pinch their flowers or their men. C'mon, Angel. I'll show you how to make buttonholes.'

Angel shook her head. 'Thank you, but I really ought to go and find my aunt. Do you know where Maddox Street is?'

'It's up West somewhere. Not my territory, duck. Go if you want to, but from what you told me I doubt if the old girl will be able to help. She's either sweet on your Mr Galloway, or she's scared of him, and if he holds the purse strings she'll do what he wants.'

'I don't think so,' Angel said, frowning. 'She

61

really loved Uncle Joseph and I'm sure she only did what Mr Galloway said because she was scared. He pretended to be nice and kind, but he was putting it on.'

'Men are all the same. They're like puppeteers and women are the ones dancing on strings. But not me. I seen many women beaten and driven to an early grave by their fellers and no man is going to do that to me.'

'I hadn't thought about it like that. I suppose Aunt Cordelia did do exactly what Uncle Joseph said. It's just the way things are.'

'Not here it ain't.' Dolly winked and tapped the side of her nose with her forefinger. 'We suit ourselves.'

'I suppose I'd better go and find a few flowers then,' Angel said reluctantly. 'Smutty Sue won't mind, will she?'

'Sue don't run our lives. Anyway, she's got what she wanted. You go and see what you can rescue.'

Angel made her way back to the floral hall, keeping an eye out for anyone who might take exception to her. Lumpy Lil would give Smutty Sue a run for her money, but the memory of Lil brought tears to Angel's eyes. She must not cry or the flower girls would laugh at her. She took a deep breath, turning her attention to finding anything that the others had missed. A waft of sweet scent reminded her of her aunt's linen press, where crisp Egyptian cotton sheets were strewn with sprigs of lavender, and she stopped at the stall where the plant was on sale.

'What's a young lady like you doing in a place like this?' The stallholder eyed her curiously.

'Why do you ask, sir?'

He threw back his head and laughed. 'Well, well, so you are indeed a well-bred girl and not of the normal sort who fight and scrap and swear like troopers. I thought perhaps you'd stolen those fine duds, but it seems I was wrong.'

'I'm looking for broken flowers, sir. I hope to sell them to pay for my lodgings.'

'Where are your parents, or have you run away from home?'

'No, sir. I'm an orphan.'

'Do you have a name, Miss Orphan?' His eyes crinkled at the corners when he smiled, and his grin was infectious.

Despite her fear that he might realise that she was a runaway and call a constable, Angel found herself returning his smile. 'My name is Angel, sir.'

'An Angel – aptly named, I'm sure.' He plucked a few sprigs of lavender from a container and handed them to her. 'Take these. You'll find the sweet-smelling flowers go best. Pinks, carnations and stocks are popular.' He leaned forward, his expression suddenly serious. 'But take care. Some of those girls are bad 'uns. Don't be led astray.'

Angel bobbed a curtsey. 'I won't, sir. Thank you.'

'Be gone with you, and if you come and find me tomorrow I'll see that you have something to sell.' He proffered his hand. 'Jack Wicks.'

She shook his hand. 'Angel Winter. Much obliged to you, sir.'

The girls were chatting and giggling as their

nimble fingers turned the discarded blooms into pretty nosegays and buttonholes. Dolly made room for Angel.

'Well, I'm blowed,' she said, whistling through her teeth. 'How did you get hold of all that lavender?'

'A kind man gave it to me.'

Angel's words were received with hoots of laughter.

'What did you do to earn that, nipper?' One of the older girls chortled with laughter and nudged her neighbour. 'Did he put his hand up your skirt, love?'

'No, of course not,' Angel said, horrified by the suggestion. 'He's a nice man.'

'There's no such thing. They're all out for what they can get.'

'That ain't true, Nelly.' One of the smaller girls spoke up. 'My pa was ever so nice. He wouldn't hurt a fly.' She began to snivel. 'He were drownded when his lighter got mowed down in the dark by a steamer.'

'Pay no attention to her,' Dolly said hastily. 'Nelly's had a bad time, haven't you, Nell?'

That seemed to open the floodgates and before Nelly had a chance to tell her story they were all swapping experiences they had had at home and on the streets. Angel was shocked and alarmed by what she heard, but Dolly seemed to understand and she gave her a hug. 'You just have to learn to be careful, my duck. Jack Wicks is all right, so you don't have to be afraid of him, but be wary because they ain't all like him.' Dolly picked up a stem of pinks, discarding those blossoms that were crushed. 'Now, watch what I do to make these into a buttonhole, and copy me. Then I'll take you out on the streets and see how you do.'

'Why are you helping me?' Angel asked, bewildered by Dolly's kindness.

'I had a younger sister once.' Dolly's nimble fingers twisted the pinks into shape, adding a sprig of baby's breath. 'She was fair-haired like you and she had big blue eyes. Grace was always smiling, even though she was mortal sick. She were only ten when she went down with the fever that took Ma and me three brothers, all within days of each other. Dunno why I was spared, but here I am, and here you are, so let's make the best of things and get on with our business.'

'I know what you say is true,' Angel said slowly, 'but I must see my aunt again, and Lumpy Lil. I'm very grateful to you for helping me, Dolly, but I have to find them or die in the attempt.'

Chapter Four

Angel kept close to Dolly all day and she soon realised that she was in the hands of an expert when it came to persuading a reluctant public to part with its money. Dolly combined bare-faced cheek with friendly banter, which worked better with men than with women. By the end of the afternoon Angel had earned threepence, but that was not enough to pay for a night in the doss-house used by many of the flower girls.

'Don't worry, my duck,' Dolly said cheerfully. 'I'll help you out this once, but tomorrow you've got to stand on your own two feet. We'll get to the market early and see what we can scrape off the floor, but you must make your own buttonholes and nosegays and you'll have to find your own pitch.'

'You mean I'll have to go out on my own?'

'You can do it, Angel. I wouldn't suggest it if I didn't think you could use them big blue eyes to your advantage. Choose the older gents; they'll be more likely to feel generous to a poor little orphan. The younger coves are a bit chancy. They might have other ideas, if you get my meaning.'

'I think I do, but what about the girls? How do I know if I'm trespassing on someone's pitch?'

'You'll have to use your loaf, and take my tip and talk a bit more like the rest of us. You talk like a toff and you dress like one too. We ought to get you some duds from a dolly shop, but that costs money. Anyway, we'll worry about that tomorrow. The main thing now is to get something to eat and pay for a night's snooze in Mother Jolly's palace.'

'A real palace?'

Dolly sighed. 'It's a joke, Angel. You've got a lot to learn, my duck.' She examined the contents of her pockets. 'Sixpence – not a bad day. It costs fourpence a night at Mother Jolly's, sixpence if we shares a bed. So if you add your threepence to my sixpence that comes to...' Dolly started adding up on her fingers.

'Ninepence,' Angel said eagerly. 'That leaves threepence for our supper.'

'You're a quick one, ain't yer? You did that in your head.' Dolly gazed at her with genuine admiration. 'I wish I had more learning.'

'You seem to do very well without it.' Angel handed her three pennies. 'What will we get for that?'

'A pint of pea soup costs a ha'penny and a ha'penny for a mug of cocoa. That leaves us tuppence for breakfast. We can get by on that, but you'll need to earn more tomorrow, nipper.'

'I'll try, Dolly. I'll try really hard.'

Mother Jolly's lodging house in Monmouth Street was a four-storey building divided into a male section, on the top two floors, and a women's section on the ground and first floors. Mother Jolly lived in the basement and put in an appearance only to take money or to throw an unruly tenant out onto the street. The women who paid fourpence for the privilege of sleeping in a wooden cot with a lumpy straw-filled mattress and a single blanket, regardless of the temperature outside, were mostly workers from Covent Garden market, but the male occupants were poor Irish migrant workers, and Angel's first night was disturbed by the clumping of boots on the bare stair treads and even louder altercations. She huddled up against Dolly's back and tried not to think of her old room in Spital Square and her comfortable feather bed. Perhaps this was all a bad dream, and when she awakened in the morning she would find herself at home with Lil grumbling as she drew back the curtains, and the aroma of the hot chocolate tempting her to sit up and drink from a bone-china cup.

But next morning Angel was awakened by Dolly giving her a shake, and the smell of unwashed bodies filled her nostrils. She tumbled out of bed.

'What time is it?'

'Time to get to work before the others wake up,' Dolly whispered.

Angel had slept in her shift and she retrieved her clothes from the end of the bed. 'I think I've got measles or something, Dolly. I'm itching all over.'

Dolly gave her a cursory look. 'You ain't sick, my duck. The bed bugs have been having a feast on you.' Dolly pulled her ragged dress over her head and slipped her bare feet into her boots.

'Bed bugs – that's disgusting.' Horrified, Angel stared at the red marks on her pale skin. 'I'm not sleeping here again.'

'You'll get used to it,' Dolly said casually. 'Come on. We've got enough money for a cup of coffee and a bread roll.' Dolly tiptoed from the room and Angel hurried after her. She could not wait to get away from the bug-infested dosshouse, and the thought of another night in such a place made her even more determined to find her aunt.

Dolly tried to dissuade her, but Angel would not be deterred. She made as many buttonholes as she could before the flower girls descended on the market like a flock of noisy seagulls, and kindly Jack Wicks loaned her a wicker basket.

'You can return it to me in the morning,' he said, adding a few sprigs of lavender for good measure. 'Just steer clear of the other flower sellers. They won't tolerate anyone they think is trying to steal their pitch.'

'I'll remember that,' Angel said, nodding. 'Can you direct me to Maddox Street, sir? My aunt is staying there and I need to find her.'

'A well brought-up girl like you shouldn't have to hawk buttonholes to all and sundry. I'd like to have a few words with that lady.'

'Oh, no, sir. It's not Aunt Cordelia's fault. She thinks I'm safe in the country with a respectable family.'

Jack Wicks stared at her, frowning. 'I don't know your story, girl, but if I had a daughter I wouldn't want her to roam the streets and mix with the likes of those flower girls.' He took a pencil from behind his ear and drew a sketch map on a scrap of paper. 'You can read, I suppose.'

'Yes, sir. Thank you, Mr Wicks. I'm much obliged to you.'

He shook his head. 'I'd take you there myself if I didn't have to look after my stall. Good luck, Angel. I hope you find your aunt.'

It was mid-morning by the time Angel reached Maddox Street. She had sold a couple of button-holes, but most people were too busy going about their daily routine to be interested in purchasing such fripperies. She told herself it did not matter – she was going to find Aunt Cordelia and Lumpy Lil, and they would be reunited. Aunt Cordelia would realise that Mr Galloway was not to be trusted, and they would live happily ever after, just like in the storybooks. The only trouble was that she had no idea which house belonged to

Mrs Adams, and the passers-by seemed reluctant to stop and answer her questions. Eventually, after waylaying an errand boy, she discovered that Mrs Adams owned a house in the middle of an elegant terrace.

Angel struggled to control her excitement as she knocked on the door. Aunt Cordelia was so close she could almost smell the gardenia-scented perfume she always wore. But it was a prim housemaid who opened the door.

'No hawkers or traders.'

Angel put her foot over the threshold just in time to prevent the girl slamming the door in her face. 'I'm not selling anything. I've come to see Mrs Wilding. I'm her niece, Angel Winter.'

The girl did not look convinced. 'You might be the Angel Gabriel for all I know, but your aunt isn't here.'

'She must be,' Angel insisted. 'Mr Galloway brought her here the day before yesterday. He said she was to stay with Mrs Adams.'

'Mrs Adams has gone to the country for the rest of the summer. She don't like the heat of London.'

'That can't be true. Mr Galloway said–'

'Get off the doorstep, girl, or I'll call a constable. I told you, Mrs Adams and her guest have gone to the country.'

'Did Miss Heavitree go too?'

'If you mean that frightful creature who came with her – she was sent separate with the baggage and that stupid halfwit girl. They'll be sacked for certain and left to find their own way back to London.'

70

Angel fought back tears of disappointment and frustration. 'Where have they gone? Please tell me. I must find my aunt.'

'I wouldn't be allowed to say, even if I knew. Now go away and leave us in peace.'

'Is there anyone in your household who might know my aunt's whereabouts?'

'There's only me and the cleaning women here. The house is being shut up until the autumn, so come back then.'

'Just a minute.' Angel took the scrap of paper from her basket. Mr Wicks had written directions on the back of a receipt with his name printed in bold black letters and the number of his stall in Covent Garden. 'Will you take this and give it to my aunt or Miss Heavitree when they return to London? It's very important.'

The girl snatched it from Angel's hand. 'Anything, if you'll just go away and leave me in peace. Now will you leave or do I call a copper?'

Angel sank down on the front step as the door closed. Her last hope had gone and she was alone in the great city, except for Dolly. How long she sat there she did not know, but eventually she rose to her feet and started retracing her steps, and after taking one apparently wrong turning after another, she found herself in Regent's Circus, and was about to ask a gentleman the way to Covent Garden when the lady with him spotted the sprigs of lavender. With a cry of delight she plucked one from the basket.

'Lavender, my favourite flower. It smells so sweet.'

The gentleman smiled down at her. 'Just like

you, my darling.' He took a handful of small change from his pocket and dropped it into Angel's basket. 'I'll take all the lavender.'

Angel gathered the sprigs into a bunch and handed them to him, hardly able to believe her luck. He presented them to his lady and she blushed and thanked him so prettily that Angel thought he was going to kiss her there and then, but he tucked her hand in the crook of his arm and they walked away, arm in arm. Angel gathered up the coins – sevenpence ha'penny in all – slipped the money into her reticule and picked up a nosegay.

'Flowers, lovely flowers. Buy a buttonhole for your lady, sir?'

By late afternoon Angel had sold every single flower in her basket and was the richer by eleven-pence ha'penny. Compared to a meagre three-pence the day before, it seemed like a small fortune. She made her way back to Covent Garden with a smile on her face for the first time since she had been wrested from her home. She found Dolly chatting to one of the other flower girls. They stopped talking when Angel approached them.

'Did you find your aunt?' Dolly asked.

Angel's smile faded. 'No, they'd gone away and the maid didn't know where.'

'I'm sorry.' Dolly gave her a hug. 'I suppose that means I'm stuck with you for a bit longer.' She eyed the empty basket. 'How much did you make today?'

'Elevenpence ha'penny,' Angel said proudly.

'Crikey, you done well.' Dolly turned to her

friend. 'How much did you take, Ivy?'

'Sixpence, and I thought that was good. Maybe the nipper has something we ain't got.'

'Big blue eyes and a la-di-dah manner of speaking,' Dolly said, chuckling. 'Never mind, Angel. You can pay me back by buying me a ham roll and a cup of tea for supper.'

Angel smiled and nodded, but inwardly she was crying for her aunt and her old life, which was fading into nothing but a happy memory. The realisation that this was how she was going to scratch a living from now on hit her like a thunderbolt, and there seemed to be no escape.

Gradually, day by day, Angel became accustomed to life in Covent Garden market. She learned the tricks of the trade from the other girls and soon became as adept at turning broken blooms into buttonholes and nosegays as the very best of them. But it was far from an easy way to earn a living and she was out on the streets in all weathers. Summer turned into autumn, when the chill turned the leaves on the London plane trees to shades of copper, bronze and gold, and icy winds rattled the windows of Mother Jolly's doss-house. Angel's fingers and toes were numbed with cold as she stood on street corners. She managed to save a few pennies to purchase a rather moth-eaten woollen shawl from a dolly shop in Shorts Gardens, but the soles of her boots were worn into holes and leaked when it rained. It would take months to earn enough to buy a second-hand pair, and winter was on its way. Angel knew that she was not suffering alone – it was the same for all the flower girls – but that was little comfort. As the nights grew frosty and the evenings drew in, Dolly developed a cough that dampened even her normally buoyant spirits.

Summer flowers had long since vanished from the stalls, and hothouse blooms were hard to come by and costly. The girls were forced to find alternatives to hawk round the streets. Some of them chose watercress, oranges or even matches, and, in desperation, others took to the streets at night selling themselves.

Angel visited Maddox Street several times in the months following that first visit, but the house was always shuttered and empty. On the last occasion she slid a note under the door, giving her address as Mother Jolly's, in the hope that one day her aunt would return to London. She had heard nothing since and times were hard. Gardenias and carnations made wonderful buttonholes, but they cost more than she could afford and she had taken to selling watercress. Even then, there were plenty of much younger children engaged in the trade, and their pinched faces, stick-thin limbs and bare feet, blue with cold, touched the kind hearts of many a housewife, whereas Angel found herself largely ignored.

She no longer had Jack Wicks to help her out with bunches of lavender as he had closed his stall until the spring, but on his last day he had given Angel his address in Hackney. With Dolly too sick to work, Angel scraped the money together to pay Mother Jolly, but selling watercress at four bunches for a penny brought in barely enough to keep them from starvation. Dolly insisted that she was getting stronger every day, but she was weak and simply walking to the washroom exhausted her. Angel knew that she must do something drastic or neither of them would survive the winter. She had an open invitation to visit the Wicks family, and she was in dire need of help. Perhaps Jack could find her work in his market garden. Winter was closing in and Angel was growing more desperate with each passing day.

It was a long walk to Pratts Lane and it took Angel all morning to reach the red-brick cottage surrounded by market gardens. Her breath curled around her head and her cheeks tingled from the cold, but the air on the edge of the city was remarkably fresh and free from the worst of the smoke and stench from overflowing drains. She stopped to gaze out at the vast expanse of marshes that stretched as far as she could see, with the canal at Hackney Cut threaded through them like a silver ribbon. She knocked on the door and waited, hardly daring to breathe. Mr Wicks might have forgotten her or, even worse, he might regret having asked her to visit his home. The temptation to retrace her steps and hurry back to Seven Dials was almost irresistible, and she was about to turn on her heel when the door opened.

'Good Lord. If it isn't Angel Winter. You'd better come in out of the cold.' Jack Wicks ushered her into the narrow hallway, and the warmth of the cottage and the smell of baking bread was almost too much for Angel. She leaned against the wall, struggling with a sick feeling in the pit of her stomach and Jack's voice seemed to fade

75

into the distance.

The next thing she knew she was seated in a chair by the range and someone was chafing her cold hands.

'Are you feeling better, dear?'

Angel's vision cleared as she met the woman's concerned gaze. 'I'm sorry. I felt a bit faint.'

'Jack says you must have walked all the way from Seven Dials. Is that right, Angel?'

'Yes, ma'am. I shouldn't have come.'

Jack's face loomed into view. 'I invited you here on many an occasion back in the summer, so let's not hear any more of that talk.' He handed Angel a steaming mug of tea. 'Here, love, take a sip of this. I dare say you haven't had a bite to eat since breakfast. Is that right?'

Angel did not want to admit that she had eaten nothing at all and very little had passed her lips the previous day, but she managed a nod as she sipped the hot, sweet tea.

'I thought so.' Jack exchanged meaningful glances with his wife. 'Well, we can soon remedy that. Sally bakes the best bread you'll ever have the luck to taste.'

Sally Wicks straightened up, wiping her floury hands on her apron. 'We were about to eat, my dear, so I hope you'll join us. But sit awhile first. You look done in.' She turned away to stir the contents of a large black saucepan.

'Thank you, but I don't want to impose,' Angel said anxiously. 'I came to ask your advice, Mr Wicks. Things have been a bit tight lately.'

Jack pulled up a chair and sat down beside her. 'I can understand that very well. Winter is always

76

hard for those who depend on the market for their living. That's where we're fortunate in having our own market garden. I dunno how we'd survive the cold months if we didn't have a store of vegetables and the sale of the dried lavender to rely on.'

'I wouldn't have bothered you, but Dolly is sick, and selling watercress doesn't pay well. I wondered if you could give me some work. I'll do anything.'

'There, there, don't fret, love. We'll talk about it after you've got some good vittles inside you,' Sally said, waving the wooden spoon in the air and sending drips of hot soup onto the floor, which were immediately lapped up by a small terrier who had been asleep in the corner and suddenly awakened.

Angel handed the mug to Jack. 'Thank you for the tea. I feel better already.' She leaned over to stroke the dog, and it leaped onto her lap, licking her face and wagging his stumpy tail.

'Well, then,' Jack said, laughing. 'Stumpy doesn't always take to strangers, but he obviously likes you, Angel. You must have a way with dogs.'

'I've never had a pet,' Angel said, laughing at the animal's enthusiastic greeting. She stroked Stumpy's head and he settled down on her lap. Warmth was beginning to seep into her bones and the sweet tea was also having its effect. 'I'd like to have a dog like him. He'd keep me warm at night.'

'And he's a first-class ratter.' Jack rose to his feet. 'We get plagued by vermin, particularly in the winter. Stumpy deals with them for us.'

Stumpy looked up, wagging his tail and panting.

'He looks as if he's laughing.' Angel gave the

terrier a hug. 'You are a funny little fellow.'

Jack moved his chair to the table. 'Come and sit down, Angel. Sally's vegetable broth will set you up for the rest of the day.' He turned to his wife. 'Where's Danny? Are we waiting for him?'

Sally shook her head. 'No, love, he's gone looking for holly and mistletoe. I doubt if he'll be back before dark.'

Angel made a move to rise and Stumpy clambered unwillingly to the floor. Behaving like a sulky child, he made his feelings very clear as he threw himself down on the scrap of blanket that served as his bed. Angel took her place at the table and Sally passed her a bowl of soup.

'Help yourself to bread, my dear. It's still warm from the oven.'

'Thank you.' Angel took a slice and buttered it sparingly. The fragrant aroma of the broth made her stomach rumble with anticipation, but, mindful of the manners drilled into her in the old days, she waited for her hosts to take their seats before she tasted the soup.

'You could make a little money before Christmas if you sold mistletoe, Angel,' Jack said thoughtfully. 'Holly is always popular.'

Angel gulped down a mouthful of hot soup. 'I'd try anything, Mr Wicks, but where would I get a supply? I haven't seen any in the market.'

'Mistletoe grows on all manner of trees. It's particularly prolific in orchards and easy to pick from fruit trees. Danny will have gone a long way to find enough to fill his cart. Those who are in the know guard their sources as if they was gold dust. It's a short season so they have to make the most of it.'

'Maybe Danny could help her there, Jack.' Sally took a slice of bread and broke it into small pieces. 'A young girl selling mistletoe might be very appealing.'

'We'll ask him when he comes home.' Jack turned to Angel with a beaming smile. 'You'll stay to meet our son, won't you?'

'I'd like to, but it gets dark very early, so I should start out soon. Thank you, all the same. Maybe I'll just stick to watercress. After all, mistletoe isn't wanted after Christmas.'

'There's plenty more soup in the pot,' Sally said, smiling. 'Help yourself to more bread, too.'

'Thank you. This is so good, Mrs Wicks. I haven't tasted food like this since I left home.' Angel's voice broke on a sob and she looked away. The memory of Aunt Cordelia and Lumpy Lil still brought her to tears. She tried to put all thought of her former life behind her, but it was not always possible.

'Jack told me something of your past, dear. You're a brave girl.'

Angel stared down at her plate. Their kindness was overwhelming, and if she allowed herself to cry she was afraid she might not be able to stop.

Sally patted her on the shoulder. 'It looks like snow, maybe you ought to stay here for the night. We can put you up with no trouble, and you do look quite done in.'

'That makes good sense, Sally,' Jack said, frowning. 'I saw the signs earlier this morning. Let's hope Danny gets home before it starts.' He turned to Angel. 'You won't make it back to

Seven Dials before the weather breaks. Stay here tonight and I'll see you safely home in the morning.'

Angel was about to refuse but Sally forestalled her. 'Yes, you must. You can sleep in the parlour. I'll light a fire in there as soon as I've cleared the table, and it will be nice and warm.'

'What about Dolly?' Angel said anxiously. 'Who will take care of her if I'm not there to make sure she has something to eat and drink?'

'I'm sure she'll survive for one night without you, dear.' Sally rose from her seat. 'You wouldn't be any use to her if you got lost in a snowstorm, would you?'

'I suppose not.'

'Good girl.' Jack also stood up. 'If you've finished your meal you can come outside and help put the tender plants under cover. I've built a lean-to shed so that the lavender can be protected from the worst of the winter weather. It's our main source of income, so I can't afford to lose a single plant.'

Angel could see that it was useless to argue, and the thought of being part of a family again, even for one night, was too tempting to refuse. She would have slept on the floor if necessary and the only thing that worried her was Dolly, but she had been a little better that morning, so perhaps she could manage on her own for a few more hours. Maybe one of the other girls would share their food with Dolly. Judy could be kind, if she was not in one of her sulks, and Maisie always seemed to have enough money to spend on feathers for her bonnet and ribbons for her hair.

80

Dolly said that Maisie was not a good girl and would come to a sticky end, but Angel had not questioned her further. Although she had a vague idea how Maisie made her money, she preferred to remain in ignorance.

Outside the sky was the colour of slate and although it was early afternoon, darkness was creeping up on the marshes so that it was hard to tell the difference between land and the corpulent bank of cloud. Angel worked hard, helping Jack heft the large clay pots into the shelter of the lean-to, and they finished just as the first feathery flakes began to fall. At that moment the grating sound of a handcart's wheels on the gravel path preceded Danny Wicks' arrival. He stomped round the side of the house, stopping in surprise when he spotted Angel.

'Who's this, Pa?'

'Where are your manners, son?' Jack placed a protective arm around Angel's shoulders. 'This young lady is Angel Winter, one of the flower girls from Covent Garden. Angel, this rough fellow is my son, Daniel.'

'How do you do?' Angel said politely.

Danny glared at her. 'She don't sound like one of them girls, Pa.'

'Never mind that. Put the cart away and come inside. Your ma has been fretting about you since noon.'

'I'm fifteen, not five,' Danny muttered as he pushed the laden cart under the sloping roof of the lean-to. 'I'm doing a man's job, aren't I?'

Jack shrugged and opened the back door. 'Go inside and get warm, Angel. I want a few words

81

with my son.'

Angel was only too glad to return to the kitchen and was greeted by the aroma of hot cocoa. Sally handed her a mug. 'Here, love. You'll need this. You look frozen.'

'Thank you.' Angel wrapped her numbed fingers around the tin mug. 'Your son has come home, Mrs Wicks. He's got a big load of holly and mistletoe.'

'Danny's a good boy. He wanted to go to sea, but Jack managed to convince him that working the garden was a better life. I'm not too sure myself.'

Angel said nothing. She tucked herself away in a corner of the room, pulling up a three-legged stool to sit beside Stumpy. The dog nuzzled her hand and butted her with his head until she relented and made a fuss of him, but he lost interest when Danny walked into the house and he ran to him, jumping up and down and barking excitedly.

Danny picked the small dog up in his arms. 'You silly fellow,' he said fondly. 'I'd have taken you with me, but I didn't want to lose you down a rabbit hole like last time.'

Sally rushed forward to give her son a hug. 'Come and sit by the fire, love. It's freezing out there. Are you hungry?'

'Don't fuss, Ma.' Danny shot a sideways glance at Angel. 'What's she doing here?'

'Don't be rude, Danny. Angel came all the way from St Giles to seek advice from your father, and I asked her to stay the night. It's not fit for man nor beast out there in the snow.'

Danny put Stumpy back on the floor and the

dog raced over to Angel and jumped onto her lap. 'Just so long as you haven't given her my room. I don't want a kid meddling with my things.' Danny accepted a mug of cocoa from his mother, giving Angel a withering look as he left the room.

Sally shook her head. 'Don't take any notice of him, Angel. Danny doesn't mean half of what he says. He's a good, kind boy really.'

'I'm sure he is,' Angel said doubtfully. 'I don't mean to be a nuisance, Mrs Wicks.'

'You are more than welcome here, Angel. Don't let Danny upset you. He's probably tired, and hungry too.' Sally made a move towards the door. 'Come into the front parlour and see the bed I made up for you on the sofa. I've loaned you a nightgown, too. It will be much too big, but it will keep you warm, and tomorrow Danny will see you safely back to your lodging house. I'll pack up some food for you to take to your poorly friend, so you mustn't worry about a thing.'

Later, at the supper table, Jack persuaded Danny to part with some of his mistletoe so that Angel could have something to sell when she returned to St Giles. Danny agreed reluctantly and was even less enthusiastic about the prospect of seeing Angel safely home.

'She got here on her own, didn't she?' he demanded crossly.

'Danny, my son, you might think you're a man, but you've got a lot to learn,' his father said sternly. 'You might take a leaf out of Angel's book. She's suffered more in her short life than you'll ever know, so I want you to do this one thing for her. Is that understood?'

Chapter Five

Few words passed between Angel and Danny during the long walk back to Mother Jolly's establishment. He carried a sack filled with mistletoe and Stumpy trotted along at his heels, but Danny paid little attention to Angel, even when she slipped on a particularly icy patch and fell to her knees. She scrambled to her feet and continued without saying a word, but her hands stung and she had torn her skirt.

'Why don't you like me?' she demanded when they came to a halt on Mother Jolly's doorstep.

Danny dropped the sack at Angel's feet. 'Who says I don't like you?'

'You've made it very obvious.'

'I don't like people taking advantage of my dad's good nature. He's always helping some lame dog or another and then they disappear and he never gets a word of thanks.'

'I'm not like that,' Angel protested. 'I'll pay you for the mistletoe when I've earned some money, and I'll write a letter to your parents, thanking them for their hospitality.'

'That's what I find odd,' Danny said warily. 'You talk and act like a young lady, so why are you in this place? I don't believe that story you told Pa. If your aunt loves you so much, why did she abandon you?'

Angel snatched up the sack, which for all its

bulk weighed next to nothing. 'It's got nothing to do with you. You are a rude boy, just like your ma said. You should be ashamed of yourself. I'm younger than you, but I think I'm a lot more grown up than you are, Danny Wicks.'

She faced him angrily and he glared back at her. Then, to her surprise he threw back his head and laughed. 'You're a funny little thing. But I never meant to hurt your feelings.'

'Then you should watch your tongue,' Angel said crossly. 'I didn't ask you to bring me home.'

'No, you didn't.' He held out his hand, smiling ruefully. 'I've said I'm sorry, Angel. My dad would kill me if he knew I'd been mean to you, and I didn't mean half of it. Cross my heart and hope to die.'

'I won't tell him, if that's what's worrying you.' Angel tossed her head. 'And I won't bother you again.' She let herself into the house and slammed the door behind her.

Forgetting everything other than Dolly's welfare, Angel raced up the stairs to the dormitory. 'Dolly, are you all right?' She came to a halt at the sight of the empty bed, neatly made up, and her heart sank. Her worst fears were realised. 'Oh, no...' An empty bed meant one of two things: the occupant had recovered and gone to work, or she was heading for a pauper's funeral. Abandoning her sack of mistletoe, Angel ran downstairs and hammered on the basement door.

'Who is it and what d'you want?' Mother Jolly wrenched the door open. She took the clay pipe from between her broken teeth and breathed smoke in Angel's face. 'Oh, it's you. I thought you'd run off. You're lucky I didn't give your bed to someone else.'

'Where's Dolly?'

'How would I know? She owes me for last night, and so do you. If I haven't got the money by midday you'll have to find another dosshouse.'

'I will pay,' Angel said urgently. 'I've got mistletoe to sell. I'll have plenty of money but maybe not until later on. Has Dolly gone to the market? She's not...?' Angel could not bring herself to speak the word.

'Dead?' Mother Jolly cackled with laughter. 'She was well enough to get dressed and go out in the snow. Although who knows what's happened to her since seven o'clock this morning. She might be frozen solid on the foreshore or floating down the Thames towards the sea.'

Angel turned her back on her landlady and took the stairs two at a time.

She found Dolly, barefoot and shivering, in Covent Garden market. She was slumped against the wall in the floral hall, surrounded by a collection of bruised and broken carnations and chrysanthemum petals.

'What are you doing here?' Angel was relieved to find her, but Dolly's pallor was alarming. Her flame-red hair seemed to have sucked every last scrap of colour from her face and there were bruise-like shadows under her green eyes. 'You're not well, Dolly.'

'I got no money to pay Mother Jolly. You never came back last night and I thought I might earn a penny or two here.'

Angel took off her shawl and wrapped it around Dolly's thin shoulders. 'You'll catch your death of cold, sitting here on the bare stone. Can you get up?'

'I can't walk another step. Me feet are so numb I don't think I can stand.'

Angel sat down beside her and took off her boots. 'Put these on. They leak but they're better than nothing.'

Dolly's eyes widened in horror. 'I can't take your boots. How will you manage?'

'I've got some money,' Angel said, crossing her fingers behind her back. 'I'll get another pair at the dolly shop, so don't worry about me. We've got to get you back to the warmth.'

Dolly was too weak to offer much resistance, and eventually Angel managed to get her to her feet. They made their way slowly back to Mother Jolly's, Dolly dragging her feet and Angel trying hard to ignore the pain of being barefoot in the snow. She helped Dolly into bed but it was only a few degrees warmer in the dormitory than outside, and Mother Jolly's worn blankets offered little protection from the cold. Having made sure that Dolly was comfortable, Angel put on her boots and went out to find a coffee stall. She returned minutes later with a hot drink and a ham roll, but Dolly complained feebly that her throat was too sore to allow her to eat. She sipped the coffee and collapsed back onto the lumpy mattress.

'It's no good, she'll turn me out on the street, Angel. I'm done for.'

'Don't say that. I've got plenty of mistletoe and

I'm going out to sell it right away. I'll earn enough to pay Mother Jolly for both of us. Keep warm and try to sleep. I'll be back later, I promise and I'll bring you some nice hot cocoa. You like that.' She picked up the sack and slung it over her shoulder.

Trade was slow. The threat of more snow to come seemed to have kept many people indoors, and those who were out on the street were intent on getting to their destinations as quickly as possible. Even so, by the end of the afternoon, Angel had earned enough to pay Mother Jolly with some left over, which would pay for a pint of pea soup, a bread roll and, more importantly, a pennyworth of laudanum to ease Dolly's aches and pains. Better still, there was enough mistletoe in the sack for another day's trading. That night Angel crawled into bed beside Dolly with a feeling of achievement. Gradually their shared warmth lulled her to sleep, despite Maisie's loud snoring and the scrabbling of vermin behind the skirting boards.

Next day the snow that had fallen during the night lay thick on the ground, although its pristine whiteness was rapidly degrading into slush as people walked to their places of employment. Angel made her way eastwards along the Strand towards Fleet Street, pausing occasionally to linger outside shop windows and peer longingly at the festive food. The sight of crusty pork pies, snowy iced cakes, mince pies and Christmas puddings, stuffed with dried fruit, made her mouth water. Costermongers' barrows were decorated with sprigs of berried holly and piled high with rosy red applies, dimpled oranges, bunches of black and green grapes and heaps of crinkled walnuts. It seemed like another life when such food had been plentiful, and the scent of chestnuts roasting on a brazier at the roadside made her stomach growl with hunger. She quickened her pace, heading towards the City where she hoped to sell the remainder of the mistletoe before noon, and that would enable her to go round the street markets in the hope of finding a fresh supply at a reasonable price. Up West she could make more on each sprig than she could in the East End, and every farthing counted. She stood on the steps of St Paul's barefoot and shivering, having had to discard her boots when the uppers finally parted from the soles. Her feet and legs were blue with cold, but oddly enough she felt no pain from the blisters that she had incurred during the long walk to and from Hackney. If she could just earn enough pennies she could buy herself a good stout second-hand pair of boots, and some woollen stockings would be a bonus. She cried her wares, hoping to attract the sympathy of City gentlemen who might take pity on a ragged girl in the season of peace and goodwill.

By mid-afternoon the light was fading and her purse was satisfyingly heavy. She had one last bunch of mistletoe to sell as she started on the walk back to her lodgings, but on Ludgate Hill she came across a group of ragged boys who taunted her and threw pebbles at her. She quickened her pace, but they followed and when she broke into a run, they caught her up and she was surrounded.

'Give us yer money, nipper.' The biggest boy grabbed her by the neck and another boy snatched the purse from her hand.

Laughing, they raced off, leaving Angel shaken and angry, but unhurt. All her work had been for nothing, and now she could not pay for their lodgings and she and Dolly would go hungry. She glanced down at her left hand and realised that she was still clutching the last bunch of mistletoe. One of the boys stopped to look back and for a moment she was afraid that he was going to return. The single bunch of mistletoe meant the difference between sleeping in the dosshouse and being cast out into the night. To someone in Dolly's condition it would be a death sentence, and Angel was not prepared to allow that to happen. She dodged into Naked Boy Court, but discovered to her dismay that the narrow alley was a dead end with no way of escape. She flattened herself against an iron-studded door, hoping that her tormentors would not see her. The sound of their raucous voices taunting her grew closer with each passing second, and she held her breath, praying that the youths would not find her. The cold iron hinges pressed into her back and she was trembling with fear, but just as she thought all was lost the door swung open.

She found herself gazing into the snow-covered courtyard of a large house with mullioned windows and a portico over the front entrance. A tall gentleman wearing a broad-brimmed hat and black overcoat was about to place a bowl of scraps on the ground for two greyhounds. The dogs, clad in blue woollen coats, were better dressed for the snowy weather than Angel herself, and she found herself envying the animals. She knew it was wrong to spy on the gentleman and his pets, but the gentleness of his tone as he spoke to the dogs brought tears to her eyes. Overcome by a feeling of loneliness, she choked back a sob and the dogs sprang to attention, alerting their master to her presence.

Angel wanted to run but somehow her tired limbs would not obey the command of her equally exhausted brain. Lack of food and the intense cold had turned her temporarily to stone and she could not move a muscle. The gentleman straightened up and walked towards her, flanked by his faithful hounds. Angel could only stand and stare. He was handsome in a forbidding way, with dark eyes beneath heavy brows and a full moustache that reached to his chin. Over his arm he carried a red woollen blanket and in his hand he clutched a hunting whip with a long white thong. He advanced on Angel like the god of wrath and she knew she was in trouble, but she could hear the boys shouting insults, daring her to come out and face them, and she had nowhere else to go.

'Well, what have we here?' The gentleman clicked his fingers and the dogs came to a halt at his side. 'Who are you, girl?'

'Would you like some mistletoe, sir?' She held the bunch up for his inspection. 'It's only a penny a bunch.'

He stared at her with a puzzled frown. 'What the devil would I want with mistletoe? It's pagan nonsense.'

Angel glanced nervously over her shoulder as two of the boys skidded to a halt outside the great oak door.

'I see.' The gentleman raised the whip and brought it down with an expert flick of his wrist. The crack of the leather thong echoed off the walls like a pistol shot. 'Brave fellows, aren't you? Chasing a little girl for sport. Get out of here or the next time I'll lop your ears off.' He raised the whip again and the boys fled. He slammed the door and bolted it.

Angel experienced a moment of sheer panic. The man with the whip was even more frightening than the street Arabs. 'I – I should go, sir.'

He turned to give her a searching look. 'Who are you, child? You look like a ragamuffin but your manner of speech is that of a young lady.'

Angel backed towards the door. 'I'm a flower girl, sir. I was selling mistletoe to pay for a night's lodging for me and my friend, Dolly, and those boys stole my purse.' She bit back tears of fear and exhaustion, and one of the greyhounds licked her hand, its liquid brown eyes brimming with empathy, as if it too knew of hardship and cruelty.

'It seems that Juno has taken to you, girl. What's your name?'

Her teeth were chattering so much that she could hardly speak. 'Angel Winter, sir.'

A hint of a smile flickered across his face. 'An angel has landed in our midst, dogs. What shall we do with her?' His expression changed. 'You must go home, Angel Winter. Where do you live?'

'M-Mother J-Jolly's dosshouse, sir. If you will give me sixpence for the mistletoe I can pay for one night's lodging for me and Dolly. She's very sick, sir. I fear she might die.'

'What the hell is a child such as yourself doing in a place like that?' He wrapped the red blanket around her shoulders. 'You'd better come indoors while I decide what to do with you.'

The thick woollen cloth was still warm from contact with his body and it smelled of bay rum and cigars, bringing back memories of Uncle Joseph and her old home.

'Thank you, sir, but I really must return to Monmouth Street.'

'Monmouth Street? We'll see about that. Come, dogs.' He strode across the snow-covered courtyard and thrust the door open. 'Don't dawdle, child. Follow me.' He stepped inside. 'Baines, where are you? Come here, man.'

Juno nudged Angel's hand with her velvety head and the two dogs followed their master into the house. Angel hesitated, but large flakes of snow were spiralling to the ground, and the warmth of the blanket was too comforting to surrender lightly. Her options were limited and surely someone who was kind to animals could not be all bad? She plucked up the courage to go inside.

The entrance hall was dark and cool, with a flagstone floor, oak wainscoting and a beamed ceiling. The gloomy atmosphere was far from welcoming, and Angel was nervous. She came to a halt.

'Who are you, sir?'

'What is that to do with you, child?' He laid the whip on the carved top of an oak chest and took off his hat. His hair was dark and straight and it came to his shoulders, giving him the look of a tragic poet, but his military bearing and weathered features were those of a man used to command.

'What's up, Colonel?' A man who appeared suddenly from the depths of the house came towards them wiping his large bony hands on a hessian apron covered with chicken feathers. 'I was just plucking a nice fat capon when you called, sir.'

'Take this child to the kitchen, Baines. Give her something to eat while I decide what to do with her.'

Baines glared at Angel beneath shaggy sandy eyebrows. 'Who have we here, then, sir?'

'Her name, it seems, is Angel Winter and she was set upon by a band of youths who stole her purse.'

'I'd send her home, sir. Not wanting to tell you what to do, as it were, but nippers this age are nothing but lies and trouble.'

'I'm not a liar,' Angel protested. 'I wanted to go, but he wouldn't let me.'

'Watch your tongue, nipper. That is Colonel Sir Adolphus Grantley you're speaking of, and if he says you're to stay here a while, then that's what you'll do. Come with me, and none of your lip.'

'Take Thor and Juno with you, Baines. I'll be in my study.' Sir Adolphus walked away, leaving Angel with the disapproving Baines and the greyhounds for company.

Baines ambled off with a decided limp and the dogs followed him, leaving Angel little alternative other than to follow him too. The long passages were poorly lit and smelled damp and musty, but

Angel was past worrying about such details. All she could think of was Dolly and the desperate need of a shilling to pay Mother Jolly for two nights' lodgings. She was too cold and exhausted to worry about her empty belly, but when she walked into a kitchen the aroma of something savoury bubbling away on the range made her stomach rumble. Juno and Thor went to lie together on a pile of blankets in the inglenook, and Baines motioned Angel to take a seat at the pine table in the centre of the room. She sank down on the nearest chair. Outside the window feathery snowflakes clung briefly to the diamond-shaped panes and then melted and trickled down the glass like tears.

'I have to go soon,' Angel said firmly. 'It's very kind of Sir Adolphus to invite me in, but the boys will have gone now, and I need to get back to the lodging house. My friend Dolly's life depends on me bringing home the money to pay Mother Jolly. You must understand that, Mr Baines.'

'Sergeant Baines to you, girl.' Baines filled a bowl with soup thickened with lentils and floury dumplings. 'Here, get that down you. I seen healthier-looking corpses than you.'

Angel did not argue. She spooned the herb-flavoured potage into her mouth, burning her tongue in the process, but it tasted good and she felt the warmth of it seeping through her veins, bringing life back to her chilled body.

Baines resumed his position by the back door, sitting on a stool as he finished plucking the chicken. 'There's more in the pot, if you're still hungry,' he said grinning. 'You polished that off quicker than old Thor, and he's a fast eater.'

'It was very tasty. Thank you.'

He wiped his nose on the back of his hand. 'How has a well-spoken little miss like you landed up in such a fix?'

'It's a long story,' Angel said wearily. 'I'm very grateful for the food and the chance to get warm, but please let me go, Sergeant Baines.' She fingered the ring hanging round her neck on Aunt Cordelia's gold chain. Until now she had resisted the temptation to pawn it, knowing that she would never be able to redeem the only thing that connected her to her mother, but Dolly's life hung in the balance, and there was no choice.

'Why the hurry? The master won't let you go unless he thinks you'll be safe. He's like that.'

'I have to get to the pawnshop before it closes. If I can't pay Mother Jolly we'll be thrown out on the street, and I'm in desperate need of a pair of boots.'

Baines tossed the last of the feathers out onto the snow and closed the door. 'Come with me, nipper. You'll have to tell that to the Colonel. He's a good man.'

Sir Adolphus was standing with his back to the fire in the book-lined study. 'I thought I told you to keep her in the kitchen, Baines.'

'She needs to get to a pawnshop, Colonel. I'd be inclined to ask her where she got a valuable ring from. The police might be interested in this young lady.'

'Leave us, Baines. Bring me coffee and some hot milk for our fallen angel.'

Baines shuffled from the room with a grunt, closing the door behind him.

'I didn't steal it,' Angel said angrily. She hooked her finger round the chain and showed him the ruby ring. 'This is mine. It was left with me when I was abandoned as a baby. Aunt Cordelia gave me the chain, and I wouldn't part with it unless I was desperate, which I am. Please let me go, sir. I fear for my friend's life if she doesn't get some food inside her and some medicine.'

He sat down in a leather wing-back chair by the fire. 'Are you expecting me to believe such a cock-and-bull tale?'

'I swear it's the truth.' Angel tucked the ring back inside her torn blouse. 'It's all I have of my mother's, Colonel. I've never stolen anything in my life.'

He was silent for a moment, staring at her with an unreadable expression. 'For some reason I believe you, girl.' He held out his hand. 'Let me see the ring, if you please.'

Reluctantly Angel unhooked the chain and laid the ring on his palm. He examined it, holding it up to the firelight with a critical eye. 'I'm no expert, but I'd say these are fine stones – worth quite a lot of money, I should imagine. Fetch me the magnifying glass off my desk. I'd like to take a closer look.'

Angel did as he asked and he studied the ring, turning it round in his fingers until Angel could have screamed with frustration.

He looked up. 'Did you know there are initials engraved on the inner edge of the ring?'

'No, sir.'

'And you don't know who your parents were?'

'No, sir. I was found in Angel Court, White-chapel on Christmas Eve twelve years ago. I was just a few weeks old. They named me Angel Winter.'

'An apt name, indeed. I was going to send you back to the lodging house with enough money to keep you and your sick friend for a week or two, but I've changed my mind. You obviously came from a good family, Angel Winter. I'm intrigued, and that doesn't happen very often.'

'What are the markings, sir?' Angel asked eagerly. Any link with her real mother would be wonderful.

'J E M,' he said, peering through the magnifying glass. 'Does that mean anything to you?'

'No, sir. I know nothing of my true identity.'

'A mystery, indeed. However, I can't allow you to pawn the only thing that connects you to your real mother, and a pawnbroker would give you just a fraction of its worth.'

'But, sir, I've already—'

He held up his hand. 'You've told me several times of your desperate need to pay this blood-sucking woman her dues.' Sir Adolphus leaned back in his chair, eyeing Angel with a speculative gaze. 'What am I going to do with you, Angel Winter?'

'Nothing, sir. Please let me go. I don't want to cause you any bother, and the soup was delicious. I feel better already.'

'Just look at you, child. Those rags won't protect you from the cold and you certainly can't go bare-foot in this weather.' He was silent for a moment, as if considering what course of action to take. 'Are you literate, Angel?'

'Yes, sir. Aunt Cordelia was very particular about my education. I had a governess until I was eleven.'

'And where is this aunt of yours now?'

'I don't know, sir. Mr Galloway, her solicitor, arranged for her to stay with his sister, a Mrs Adams who lives in Maddox Street. I went there because I wanted to tell Aunt Cordelia that Mr Galloway had gone back on his word, but she had left for the country with Mrs Adams, and the maid wouldn't tell me where. I've been back several times since then, but there was no one at home, not even a servant.'

'And where is this man Galloway now?'

Angel shuddered. 'I don't know, sir. He left me in the Bear Street workhouse, but I escaped and ran away. He's a bad man.'

'I see. Perhaps I ought to pay a visit to this Mr Galloway.'

'I couldn't ask you to do that, sir.'

'You are not asking me, Angel. I dislike cheats and liars, and you have been badly done by.' He leaned over to tug at a bell pull. 'We will visit this Mother Jolly, and rescue your young friend. After that I think I might have a solution that would benefit us all.' He looked up as the door opened to admit Barnes.

'Take Angel to Miss Susannah's room. I think she might find some more suitable clothing there, and something to put on her feet.' He fixed Angel with a piercing stare. 'My niece stays here sometimes, although she lives in my country house.

99

Find yourself something to wear and be quick about it. We'll go to your lodging house directly.'

Angel was too stunned and surprised to argue. She followed Baines, who led her across the entrance hall and up the wide staircase to the upper floor. The light was fading fast despite the reflection of the snow outside, and the dark wood panelling and yellowed ceilings added to the sombre atmosphere. Susannah's room was at the far end of the landing. Baines opened the door and stood aside. 'There you are, miss. I dunno if you'll find anything to suit, but take what you want. Miss Susannah won't be needing any of the things you'll find in the clothes press.'

'Why not?' Angel demanded anxiously. 'Is she dead?'

'Not that I know of. She doesn't come here often these days and I doubt if any of the duds you'll find would fit her now. Can you find your own way back to the master's study?'

'I think so.'

'If not I'll send the dogs to find you.' Baines grinned and saluted as he closed the door, leaving Angel alone in the room that was dominated by a large four-poster bed. Heavy mahogany furniture slumbered in the shadows like sleeping giants and, to Angel's imaginative mind, there was a lingering feeling of sadness in the still air. Dust lay like fuzzy blankets on all the surfaces and a faint waft of lavender seemed to float past her like a spirit of a long-departed lady of the house. Angel suppressed a shiver and concentrated on the task in hand.

The clothes press was packed with garments

ranging in size from those that were suitable for a five-year-old to others that were on the large side for Angel, but were infinitely better than the rags she was wearing. She found a plain grey merino dress with a slightly yellow white collar and cuffs, a cotton shift and some woollen stockings. In a cupboard she discovered a selection of shoes, again in all sizes, and several pairs of boots that were hardly worn. Miss Susannah must have led a very sheltered existence and had never had to walk far. Angel discarded her rags and dressed herself in the new garments. The smell of camphor clung to them, but at least it had prevented the moths from feasting on the expensive cloth. She pulled on the stockings, revelling in their warmth, and slipped her feet into the boots, which fitted as if they had been made for her. Despite her hurry, she scraped a layer of dust off the cheval mirror and examined her reflection with a satisfied smile. A feeling of optimism surged through her as she tidied everything away and went downstairs to find Sir Adolphus. Why he had decided to help her was a mystery, but even if he changed his mind, as adults often did, she was warmly dressed, even if the cherry-red velvet cape she had selected made her feel like Little Red Riding Hood.

'Good grief!' Sir Adolphus stared at Angel, his dark eyes twinkling. 'What a transformation from crushed rose petal to young lady.'

'I'm glad you find my appearance amusing, sir.'

He rose to his feet. 'I'm not laughing at you, silly girl. My instincts were correct, it seems. Underneath those rags there lurked a presentable young person. I think Susannah might warm to you, Angel Winter. You might very well be the answer to my prayers.'

'I don't understand, sir.'

'No, of course you don't, but you will.' Once again he tugged at the bell pull and Baines appeared so quickly that Angel suspected he had been loitering outside the door.

'What can I do for you, Colonel?'

'Find me a cab, Baines. We're going out.'

Chapter Six

Dolly was put to bed in the four-poster with a stone hot-water bottle wrapped in a towel at her feet, and another placed at her side. Baines had lit the fire and left a brass scuttle filled with enough coal to keep the room warm all night. The damp feeling and musty smell were already, fading into a distant memory, and the shadows seemed less dense and frightening.

A doctor was sent for and after examining Dolly he drew Sir Adolphus aside. Angel strained her ears to hear what he was saying.

'The child is severely malnourished, but I don't think she is consumptive. A few days in bed, and an invalid diet should work wonders. I've seen it before in some of the less fortunate children. They're born tough in order to survive the rigours of life on the streets.' The doctor shot a glance in Angel's direction and she hastily averted her eyes.

'What about the other child?' Sir Adolphus did not bother to lower his voice. 'She has also led a harsh existence.'

'But not for long, I think.' The doctor nodded his head. 'She has obviously been well cared for as an infant and it shows in her general physique. They are an interesting example of two very different social classes.'

'Thank you, Doctor. Come downstairs and share a glass of buttered rum punch with me before you go out into the night.' Sir Adolphus glanced over his shoulder as he ushered the doctor from the room. 'I'm sure you heard all that, Angel. Baines will see to your needs. I'll see you in the morning.'

Dolly raised her head from the pillows as the door closed. 'Am I dreaming, Angel? This don't seem real.'

'Don't ask me how it came about,' Angel said, smiling. 'I feel it too. One minute I was in fear of my life and freezing to death, and now look at me. Look at both of us, with a bed several times the size of the one we've had to share, and a fire blazing up the chimney just for our benefit. It's like it used to be when I lived with my aunt and uncle, but I'm afraid that at any moment I might wake up and find myself back on the streets.'

Dolly's thin frame was racked with a bout of coughing and she fell back onto the feather pillows. Angel moved to the bedside and pulled the coverlet up over Dolly's shoulders. 'Try to sleep. You'll feel better in the morning, and I'll be here at your side if you need anything.'

'Ta, Angel.' Dolly closed her eyes and curled up

with the hot-water bottle clutched in her arms. 'I never had so much fuss made of me afore in me whole life.'

Next morning, leaving Dolly still sound asleep, Angel made her way downstairs to the kitchen. Baines looked up from stoking the fire. 'You're bright and early.'

'I'm used to going to the market. You have to be quick or the others will have snatched the best blooms and there'll be nothing but broken stems and leaves trodden underfoot.'

'The master said you're to have breakfast with him in the dining room.'

'Can I do anything to help, Mr Baines? It seems we're putting you to a lot of trouble.'

He straightened up, staring at her in surprise. 'Well now, you are a proper young lady, ain't you? You ain't no street urchin.'

'I was brought up to be polite, if that's what you mean.' Angel eyed him curiously. 'This is all very strange. Do you know what the colonel has in mind for me and Dolly, Mr Baines?'

'It's just Baines, miss. As to the master, we've been on many a campaign together, but I don't presume to question his actions. Anyway, he likes to have breakfast early and he don't like to be kept waiting. The dining room is on the left of the entrance hall. D'you need me to show you the way?'

'I'll be all right on my own, thank you, Baines.'

The atmosphere in the old house seemed friendlier somehow as Angel made her way through the maze of passages, or maybe she was just getting used to the drabness of the wooden panelling and the low ceilings. One thing was certain: the house lacked a woman's touch, and although she had never been in a barracks, this was exactly how she imagined it might be.

Angel entered the dining room to find Sir Adolphus already in his chair at the head of a table that would have seated twenty, with room to spare. The furniture was heavily carved and a mahogany buffet was groaning beneath the weight of salvers filled with devilled kidneys, buttered eggs and a silver breakfast dish containing sausages and bacon.

'Help yourself, Angel,' Sir Adolphus said casually. 'I believe a good breakfast is the only way to start the day.'

Angel's mouth was watering. She had not seen food like this since she left the house in Spital Square, and she was very hungry. She took a little of everything, apart from the kidneys, which she had never liked, and went to sit at the table.

'I'm very grateful to you for taking us in,' she said in between mouthfuls, 'but I don't understand why you're being so kind to strangers.'

He sat back in his chair. 'I don't like injustice, Angel Winter. I could tell, despite your rags, that you weren't a common street girl, and I'm curious. The tale you told me is a mystery that intrigues me somewhat, and I intend to visit your Mr Galloway.'

Alarmed, Angel paused with the fork halfway to her mouth. 'Why, sir? He not a good man. He promised Aunt Cordelia that he would look after me, but he broke his word.'

'Exactly. That's why I intend to meet the gentleman. It occurred to me last night that I must first seek your aunt's permission if I am to take you to Grantley Park.'

'Grantley Park, sir?'

'We'll talk about that later, after I've had words with Galloway.'

Angel spent the morning attending to Dolly's needs. Baines kept the scuttle filled with coal and Angel dusted and swept the bedroom, opening the casement windows just enough to allow the air to circulate. Outside the snow was still falling and she was glad that she and Dolly were somewhere warm and safe. The dogs now recognised her as a friend and they followed her upstairs. Thor took up residence in front of the fire while Juno settled for the bed, and curled up beside Dolly, and soon all three were sound asleep, leaving Angel free to take a closer look at her surroundings.

She opened a cupboard and came across a shelf packed with children's books. The pages were dog-eared and someone, maybe the mysterious Miss Susannah, had obviously been a keen reader. On a higher shelf sat a wooden doll with a painted face and jet-black hair, its jointed arms outstretched as if begging a small girl to take it to her heart. Next to the doll was a wooden Noah's ark with chipped paintwork and, on closer examination, Angel realised that most of the animals were missing. She found a giraffe and an elephant tossed carelessly in a box containing wooden building blocks, and a monkey head-down in an empty inkwell. She put everything back in its place before moving on to the dressing table. The drawers were filled with lace-trimmed handkerchiefs, kid gloves, odd stockings and lengths of satin ribbon. A jewellery box contained glass beads and jewelled hair combs, knotted silver chains and odd buttons. Angel was getting a clearer picture of Miss Susannah in her head, and she decided that she must be a very spoiled and over-indulged young lady.

At midday Dolly managed to take mouthfuls of chicken broth, and she nibbled some bread and butter. Having eaten reasonably well, she went back to sleep, and Angel took the tray downstairs accompanied by Thor, although Juno chose to remain on the bed, guarding her new friend. Angel left the dishes in the kitchen, Baines having refused her offer to wash up, and she was on her way upstairs when Thor left her and raced to the front door. A gust of icy air preceded Sir Adolphus as he strode into the house. He looked up and saw Angel, who was about to ascend the stairs.

'Come into my study. I need to speak to you.' He discarded his hat and greatcoat and walked off in the direction of his study.

Angel hurried after him. 'Did you see Mr Galloway, sir?'

'I managed to track him down eventually.' Sir Adolphus went to stand by the fire, holding his hands to the heat. 'A despicable person. I disliked him on sight.'

'Did he say anything about Aunt Cordelia, sir? Is she well?'

Sir Adolphus turned slowly to face her, his expression grim. 'I'm sorry to be the bearer of bad news, but it appears that your aunt went out walking in the rain and caught a chill. She succumbed to lung fever several weeks ago.'

Angel sank down on a chair. 'She's dead?'

'I'm afraid so, but if it's any comfort, she believed to the last that you were living with a family in Essex and that you were happy and well cared for.'

Too stunned for tears, Angel stared at him, unable to put her feelings into words.

'I'm no good at this sort of thing, child. But there is someone here who might be able to offer you comfort. Apparently she's been camped outside Galloway's office, refusing to move on until he told her where you were. The wretched fellow was glad to be rid of her.'

Angel's breath hitched in her throat. 'Lumpy Lil?'

'An apt description. I've never seen a woman who so resembled a badly stuffed sofa in all my life. I sent her round to the kitchen to help Baines, although heaven knows what he'll think of her. He has no liking for the female of the species since his wife left him for another man. You may go downstairs and see your friend, Angel, but keep her away from me at all costs.'

Angel rose to her feet. Her head was spinning and she was too shocked to think clearly, but one thing was foremost in her mind. 'What will happen now, sir?'

'Nothing has changed as far as I'm concerned. You have no legal guardian and I have a use for a girl like you. As soon as your friend is well enough to travel I'm taking all three of you to Grantley Park. You will be looked after, never fear.'

'Why, sir? Why would you take us in?'

'I have my reasons. Now go and find your friend. Make sure she isn't upsetting Baines. He'll only take so much from a woman.'

Dazed by the sudden turn of events, Angel left the study and went downstairs to the kitchen where she found Lil and Baines in the middle of a fierce argument.

'Lil,' Angel cried. 'Lil, I can't believe you're here.'

'She's here, all right,' Baines said grimly. 'It ain't my lucky day, that's for certain.'

'Darling girl.' Lil held out her arms and Angel ran to her, cuddling into the familiar curves of Lil's ample body.

'Oh, Lil. I thought I'd never see you again.' The tears that Angel had been holding back flowed freely down her cheeks and she rested her head against Lil's shoulder. 'Is it true that Aunt Cordelia died?'

Baines cleared his throat. 'I'll make a brew. Once you women start piping your eyes there's no stopping you.'

'Can we go anywhere quiet, away from that ignorant man?' Lil demanded angrily. 'He's rude and coarse and I don't want nothing to do with the likes of him.'

'Come upstairs to my room,' Angel said hurriedly. 'There's so much I want to ask you about poor Aunt Cordelia.' She took Lil by the hand and led her from the kitchen before she had a chance to continue her verbal battle with Baines.

'I don't think much of this place,' Lil muttered as she followed Angel upstairs to the first floor. 'It needs a good spring clean and I'd have all those carpets out on the line and beat the dust from them. Haven't these men ever heard of soap, and water and elbow grease?' She stared at Dolly's sleeping figure. 'Who is that? And who said that hound could get on the bed? It's not right. You'll get fleas and such.'

'It's all right, Lil,' Angel said hastily. 'Juno is a good dog and very clean, and she's keeping Dolly warm.'

Arms akimbo, Lil pursed her lips. 'I'm going to sit by the fire and you can tell me exactly what's been going on.'

Lil's mobile features registered every emotion from shock and horror to indignation and anger as Angel relived the events that had brought her to Sir Adolphus Grantley's house.

'What I don't understand,' Lil said frowning, 'is why a toff like him would take in two children, and why would he show such an interest in your past?'

'I don't know. Maybe he's just a kind man who likes to help people.'

'Hmm.' Lil's eyebrows knotted together in a frown. 'In my experience men don't do anything for nothing. There's something in it for him.'

'I don't know what you mean, Lil.'

'Of course you don't, my little innocent. I'm here to protect you now. I nursed you as if you was my own babe, and heaven help anyone who tries to lay a finger on you.'

'Sir Adolphus is a good man, Lil. He was a colonel in the army and Baines was his sergeant. They're brave soldiers.'

'That lot are often the worst.' Lil raised herself

from the chair with a groan. 'This weather affects my rheumatics something shocking.' She hobbled across the room. 'Where does this door lead?'

'It's a small room, like Aunt Cordelia's dressing room.' Angel's eyes filled with tears and her throat constricted. 'You haven't told me what happened to her, Lil.'

Lil opened the door and peered inside. 'This will do. I'll sleep in here so that I'm close to you girls. I'll need a bed and some linen.' She paused, slanting a worried look in Angel's direction. 'Your aunt didn't suffer, love. It was pneumonia, the doctor said, and she went very quick. She weren't in pain, but the last thing she said was, "Find Angel, Lil. Make sure my baby girl is well and happy."' She cleared her throat noisily. 'I'll go downstairs now, and tell that windbag Baines what I need to make meself comfortable.'

Baines and Lil were never going to get along – that was clear from the start – and during the next few days Angel found herself acting as peacemaker. Sir Adolphus was rarely at home to witness the spats that occurred between his sergeant and Angel's former nursemaid, but two days before Christmas he sent Baines to find Angel with instructions to send her to his study.

She hurried downstairs wondering what could be so urgent. Baines had been uncommunicative, but that could have been due to the fact that both Lil and Juno were growling at him like angry guard dogs.

'You sent for me, sir?' Angel stood with her hands clasped tightly behind her back.

111

Sir Adolphus was seated behind his desk. He stopped writing and put his pen down on the silver inkstand. 'We'll be leaving for Grantley Park tomorrow. I take it that your young friend is well enough to travel, and she's welcome to come with us, but she'll have to earn her keep. My housekeeper will find work for her and your aunt's servant too, if she chooses to accompany us.'

'I can't speak for the others, sir.'

'Then you must talk it over with them, Angel. I'm not a charity, but I feel somewhat responsible for the flower girl, and your servant has a mind of her own. Galloway would vouch for that, I'm certain. He did his best to poison my mind against Miss Heavitree, but I'm a man who likes to use his own judgement.'

'Might we know where we're going, sir?'

'Grantley Park has been in my family for two hundred years. It's a Tudor house in its own grounds, on the edge of Low Leyton marsh. There, does that satisfy your curiosity?'

'A little,' Angel said doubtfully. 'Is it far from London, sir?'

'About seven miles, which is far enough to be away from the stench and corruption of the city.'

She did not know whether to question him further, but he had picked up his pen and it was clear that she had lost his attention. She realised that she had been dismissed and went to find Dolly, who was now out of bed and dressed in garments they had discovered in the clothes press. Lil had had to make some alterations in order to make them fit, but Dolly was thrilled with her acquisitions and even more delighted when they found a pair of boots that were too small for Angel but fitted Dolly to perfection.

She was in the middle of a twirl when Angel burst into the bedroom.

'See how fine I look,' Dolly said delightedly. 'I ain't never had nothing so grand in me whole life. I shall be a young lady like you, Angel.'

'I think Sir Adolphus has other plans, Dolly. He said you would have to earn your keep when we go to his country house.'

'I suppose it's only to be expected,' Dolly said philosophically. 'I was just dreaming. I suppose I'd better take these clothes off then.'

'No, certainly not. They were left to the moths so obviously they weren't wanted. It's a crime to leave them to rot. You look splendid, Dolly. I won't let them turn you into a slavey. If it isn't nice where we're going, we'll leave and set off on our own. We've earned our living before, and we can do it again. Now all I have to do is convince Lil that it is for the best.'

Starting out early on Christmas Eve, Angel, Dolly and Lil travelled in Sir Adolphus' barouche, with Thor and Juno. Baines sat on the box next to the coachman and Sir Adolphus rode his chestnut stallion, Caesar. It had stopped snowing but the going was slow and difficult. At times it seemed that they would have to turn back, but Sir Adolphus was determined to reach Grantley Park. The bricks that Baines had heated on the kitchen range and placed on the floor to keep their feet warm had cooled, and despite their layers of clothing and woollen blankets the cold was insidious,

113

creeping into their bones and chilling them to the marrow.

Angel peered out of the window at the vast white expanse of the marshes, with tufts of bleached grasses poking through the snow and steel-grey pools of frozen water reflecting the leaden sky. Dolly had fallen asleep with Juno resting against her, and Thor settled down at Angel's feet, sharing her warmth. Lil sat with her arms folded and her head nodding, but each time she felt herself overcome by the desire to sleep she jerked herself back to consciousness.

Eventually, when the light was fading, they arrived at their destination. There had been moments during the journey when Angel thought the carriage was going to overturn, and others when they were stuck in a particularly deep snowdrift, and Baines had had to dig them out. But they had arrived safely and Baines leaped down to open the door. Sir Adolphus dismounted, handing the reins to a groom, who came slipping and sliding from the stable block.

The dogs jumped out first and danced across snow to be reunited with the master. Angel climbed to the ground more slowly. It was a relief to stretch her legs and feel firm ground beneath her feet after the rocking motion of the carriage. She paused, staring at the sprawling red-brick Tudor mansion, which was much larger than she had imagined. Even in the half-light she could see that the house and grounds were extensive, but she did not have time to dwell on the grandeur of her new surroundings as the front door opened, shedding a beam of light on the pristine whiteness of the snow. A manservant hurried out, followed by a maid and a girl with long dark ringlets who threw herself into Sir Adolphus' arms with a shriek of delight.

'Uncle Dolph, you've come home at last.'

'Go indoors, Susannah. It's freezing out here.' Sir Adolphus gave her one of his rare smiles as he disengaged himself from her embrace.

'Who are these people?' Susannah demanded, staring over his shoulder. 'Who have you brought with you, Uncle?'

'All in good time, Susannah.' Sir Adolphus strode into the house. 'Come inside, everyone. Leave the servants to bring the baggage.'

Angel clutched Dolly's hand and led her into the entrance hall. The warmth of the house was almost overpowering after the chill in the carriage, and the first thing Angel saw was a huge Christmas tree decorated with glass balls and tinsel. Swags of holly and ivy had been looped around the banisters, and the scent of the applewood logs burning in the huge stone fireplace mingled with the aroma of pine, with a friendly hint of beeswax and lavender furniture polish. She had only just stepped inside Grantley Park and somehow it felt like coming home. Angel was struggling to come to terms with the unfamiliar feeling when the maid stepped forward to take their outer garments, and a woman wearing a chatelaine hung with a weighty bunch of keys hurried to greet her master. She was dressed in black bombazine and her dark hair was scraped back so that it appeared to have been painted on her head, reminding Angel forcibly of the doll she had found in the toy cupboard.

'Good afternoon, Sir Adolphus. Welcome home, sir.'

'Thank you, Mrs Kerslake. We're very glad to have arrived without mishap. The weather is truly atrocious.' Sir Adolphus laid his hand on Angel's shoulder. 'This young lady is my ward, Angel Winter, and she is going to be part of the family from now on. I leave it to you to make a room ready for her.'

'Of course, sir, but what about the others?' Mrs Kerslake eyed Lil and Dolly with suspicion.

'Miss Heavitree is my maid,' Angel said quickly. 'And Dolly is willing to work, but she's been poorly and she needs to rest.'

Mrs Kerslake's lips folded into a pencil-thin line. 'I see.' She shot an enquiring look at her master. 'Is this so, sir?'

'I should think there must be space for a small person in the servants' quarters. The child is stronger than she looks, and I'm sure that Cook can always do with an extra pair of hands in the kitchen.' Sir Adolphus handed his greatcoat and top hat to the maid who was hovering by his side. 'Is my sister in the drawing room?'

Susannah grasped his arm. 'Of course she is, Uncle. Where else would Mama be on Christmas Eve? Hector and Toby arrived home from school yesterday and we've been in uproar since then. They've been teasing poor Humpty until they made him cry.'

'Have they,' Sir Adolphus said grimly. 'We'll see about that.' He turned and beckoned to Angel. 'Come and meet your new family. Don't worry

116

about your little friend. Miss Heavitree will look after her.'

'That I will,' Lil muttered. 'We'll be fine, Angel.'

'I'll see you later,' Angel whispered, eyeing Mrs Kerslake warily. She was not sure whether the stern-looking woman was friend or foe, but she was not going to question her authority, and she followed Susannah and her uncle to the drawing room with the dogs trotting along at her heels.

Angel hesitated in the doorway, taking in the scene. Illuminated by dozens of expensive wax candles, and warmed by a log fire roaring up the chimney, the room was large and furnished for comfort rather than the latest fashion. Another Christmas tree, slightly smaller than the one in the entrance hall, stood in the corner of the room, ablaze with tiny candles. Presents were piled beneath it and garlands of holly and ivy were draped from the ornately carved stone fireplace. Bowls of oranges studded with cloves scented the air and vases of jewel-bright chrysanthemums brought colour to dark corners.

An elegantly dressed woman was seated on the sofa, sandwiched between a boy of eight or nine and an older boy, whom Angel thought must be her own age or a little older. A youth stood with his back to the fire and it was his voice that had been the loudest, but he was silenced by the arrival of his uncle.

'Eloise, my dear. Don't get up.' Sir Adolphus crossed the floor to embrace his sister. 'I see your errant sons have returned from Rugby in time for Christmas.' He slapped the tall, dark-haired youth on the shoulder. 'So you've made it through your last term, Hector. Congratulations, my boy.'

'Thank you, sir. It was a close-run thing at times, but I'm ready for Sandhurst now. I can't wait to commence training.'

'I wish you would reconsider, Hector.' Eloise sighed heavily. 'Your father died on the North-West Frontier, and now you want to follow in his footsteps and join the army.'

'Your dear departed, as I recall, was run over by a brewer's dray,' Sir Adolphus said, winking at his nephew.

'He was on his way to the barracks,' Eloise protested, mopping her eyes with a cotton lawn hanky.

'Don't cry, Mama.' The youngest boy gave his mother a hug. 'Would you like a peppermint? I have some in my pocket.'

His elder brother reached out and cuffed him round the head. 'Ignore him, Mama. If it's been in his pocket it will be covered in fluff. Humpty is a grubby little beast.'

'That's enough, Toby.' Eloise wrapped her arms around Humphrey, who was trying hard not to cry. 'Leave him alone, both of you. He's just a baby.'

'The boy is eight years old, Eloise,' Sir Adolphus said sharply. 'Don't turn him into a milksop.'

Susannah rolled her eyes. 'I told you they were being beastly to poor Humpty, Uncle Dolph. Hector and Toby are bullies.'

Angel stood back, watching and listening to the family banter with a feeling of detachment. She had fallen in love with Grantley Park the moment she stepped inside the house, but she felt like an intruder. Sir Adolphus seemed to remember her presence and he drew her forward. 'Angel, I'd like you to meet my sister, Mrs Devane, and my nephews, Hector, Toby and Humphrey. You've already met Susannah, and I hope she will look after you and make you feel like one of the family.'

Angel bobbed a curtsey, not knowing quite how to respond. Mrs Devane was staring at her with a shocked expression that might, in any other circumstances, have been comical.

'Adolphus, I think you should explain yourself.'

'Angel Winter is my ward, and as such is now part of the family.' Sir Adolphus regarded his sister with a steady gaze. 'I'll explain further when we are on our own. Suffice it to say that Angel is one of us, and I expect her to be treated as such.'

Angel fingered her mother's ring, taking comfort from the familiar object covered by the bodice of her woollen frock, which paled into insignificance when compared to the gown Susannah was wearing. Angel had seen well-dressed young ladies promenading in the Strand, and the creation in shimmering shot taffeta that changed colour from pink to purple with every movement of Susannah's lithe young body, was undoubtedly the height of fashion. Her glossy curls, the colour of a raven's wings, were tied with matching ribbons and her large brown eyes sparkled with health and vitality. Angel was suddenly conscious of her own pallor and her skinny body. She was as flat chested as young Humphrey, whereas Susannah was developing the curves of adolescence and would soon blossom into a beautiful young woman. Angel felt like a sparrow confronting a peacock, and when she caught Hector's quizzical glance she could see that he had formed the same opinion. His dark eyes twinkled with amusement as they met her defiant look, and his generous lips curved in a grin. He was undoubtedly the most handsome young man she had ever seen, and he had the height and bearing of an athlete.

'Welcome to Grantley madhouse, Angel,' Hector said, chuckling. 'You are the first and probably the last angel I'll ever meet.'

'Are you really an angel?' Humphrey asked innocently. 'Where are your wings?'

'They're locked up in Mrs Kerslake's office,' Toby said, struggling to keep a straight face. 'She's only allowed them when she goes to heaven for a visit.'

'Stop it, boys.' Eloise rose from the sofa with a swish of starched petticoats and a waft of tuberose and orris-root perfume. 'Uncle Dolph has brought Angel to live with us, so I expect you to treat her kindly.' She turned to Susannah. 'That goes for you, too, miss. Having a girl close to your own age can only be beneficial.'

Angel met Susannah's cold stare with a sinking feeling in her heart. She had seen that expression many times in the eyes of the flower girls, usually before they pulled her hair or threatened her with bodily harm. Life at Grantley Park might appear to be one of luxury and fun, but she had felt the undercurrents and she knew it was not going to be easy.

Chapter Seven

Grantley Park, Summer 1878

Angel hitched the trug over her arm as she let herself into the walled garden. The sun blazed down from a clear azure sky and the air was filled with the droning of bees, birdsong and the heady fragrance of flowers. The scent of lavender never failed to take her back to Covent Garden market and the stall owned by Jack Wicks. Despite the ease and luxury of living in Grantley Park, she had never forgotten the kindness that Jack had shown her, and although she had often wondered how the Wicks family were getting along on the other side of the marsh, there had never seemed a right time to pay them a visit. Danny Wicks had made it clear that he considered her to be a nuisance, but that was years ago and it was more lack of opportunity that had kept her tied to Grantley. Life here was never dull, especially when the boys were at home.

Angel took a pair of scissors from the pocket of her hessian apron and snipped sprigs of lavender to add to the trug, which was already filled with pink moss roses and sprays of baby's breath. It was another world within the red-brick walls of the kitchen garden, peaceful and well ordered, and an escape in times when family squabbles and strife became too much to bear. Angel wan-

121

dered along the gravel paths between the neatly tended beds of vegetables and the flowers grown to adorn the house. Arranging them was one of her favourite tasks, whatever the season. In midwinter she gathered branches groaning with red berries and bulrushes from the edges of the lake, but in the months when there was next to nothing worth picking, and the berries had been consumed by the hungry wildlife, she had to rely on flowers grown the previous summer, which had been hung to dry in the flower room. As always, she could not wait for the spring, when snowdrops covered the ground on either side of the carriage sweep, followed by sunshine-yellow clumps of primroses peeping out from beneath the hedgerows and the final glory of scented bluebells that carpeted the woods.

She bent down to cut a small bunch of clove-scented pinks to put in a cut-glass vase for Aunt Eloise, as she had been instructed to call Mrs Devane soon after her arrival at Grantley. Their relationship was fragile and often quite difficult, but Angel had learned to hold her tongue when Eloise chose to needle her into an argument, although sometimes she was driven beyond the limit and retaliated in kind. The result of these spats often lasted for days, until eventually Angel was forced to apologise, if only for the sake of the whole household, who suffered miserably when Mrs Devane was in one of her black moods. Oddly enough, the only person who could deal with her during one of these bouts was Lil. She was a little older now, and a few pounds heavier, and her hair was an odd shade of pepper and salt, but she had lost none of her fighting spirit and she knew exactly how to handle Eloise Devane.

The trug was filled to the brim and Angel was about to leave the peace and tranquillity of the walled garden when she heard Susannah calling her name. There was a note of urgency in her voice that made Angel hurry, when normally she would have made Susannah wait until she was ready to deal with whatever the young lady wanted. They were friends, most of the time, but Susannah was still the spoiled darling, adored by her mother and indulged by her uncle. Her brothers teased her, but Susannah had them exactly where she wanted them, and with a flutter of her ridiculously long eyelashes or a persuasive smile that showed off her dimples, she could usually wrap them round her little finger. But there was one exception and that was Hector.

Angel's hand trembled as her fingers closed on the sun-warmed metal latch. Hector, for all his bluff and bravado, had been her favourite from the moment she first saw him. He was too hand-some for his own good and she knew that all the young ladies in the neighbourhood were madly in love with him. He was, after all, heir to Grantley Park and he was a dashing captain in the Royal Artillery.

'Angel. Where are you? Come here at once – I need you.' Susannah's voice rang out loud and clear, echoing off the walls of the kitchen garden.

Angel opened the gate and emerged into the cool green shade of an ancient oak tree. Humphrey had once climbed it as a dare and had reached the top, startling the nesting birds. In his hasty descent he had missed his footing and come crashing through the branches to land badly. Toby, who had egged him on mercilessly, had run to the house for help, leaving Angel to minister to the dazed nine-year-old. Humphrey had broken his arm and suffered a mild concussion. Although she had had nothing to do with the dare, Angel had been implicated simply by her presence. Toby's allowance had been stopped for the whole of the following school term, and Angel had been confined to the schoolroom for two weeks and given a pile of mending, which Aunt Eloise inspected every day. If her stitches were too big or her darning not considered neat enough, Angel had to unpick the work and start again.

She walked to meet Susannah, who came hurrying across the smooth grassy sward, holding her blue-and-white dimity morning gown above her ankles in what her mother would have considered the most unladylike manner. 'What are you doing, Angel? Why are you wasting time picking flowers? You're needed in the house.'

'What's the matter, Sukey?'

'Don't call me that,' Susannah said crossly. 'It makes me sound like a housemaid.'

Angel fell into step beside her. 'And, of course, you're a young lady now. This is all about you, isn't it?'

'I don't know what you mean.' Susannah quickened her pace. 'Blanche will be here in less than an hour and Mama is lying down with one of her headaches. I need you to help me get ready and you must sit with us in the drawing room.'

'So you need a chaperone,' Angel said, laughing. 'I take it that Blanche won't be on her own, or you wouldn't need me.'

'I suppose Rupert might be with her, and it wouldn't be proper for me to entertain them on my own.'

'You could have asked Lil.' Angel linked her hand through Susannah's arm. 'I'm just teasing. Of course I'll be there for you. Rupert is very dashing, even if he isn't very bright.'

'If you say anything to embarrass him I'll never speak to you again, Angel Winter.'

'I promise to be the perfect chaperone. I'll sit quietly and I won't say a word that will put Rupert Westwood's nose out of joint.'

Susannah gave her a withering look. 'Your vulgarisms betray your time on the streets, Angel. Haven't you learned anything during your time here with us?'

'I am one of you,' Angel said softly. 'Sir Adolphus adopted me legally. We are cousins, Sukey.'

'On paper, maybe.' Susannah came to a halt outside the front entrance. 'You don't know who your mother was.'

'Thank you for reminding me. I might have forgotten that I'm not like you.' Angel thrust the door open and stepped over the threshold. The house, as always, seemed to wrap itself around her with a gentle welcoming hug.

'I didn't mean it,' Susannah said urgently. 'I'm sorry, Angel. It's just that I don't know what I'll do if Blanche doesn't invite me to their ball. I'm nineteen, and what chance do I have of meeting eligible young men if I never go anywhere other than church, and the occasional stay in the dreary London house in the most unfashionable part of town?'

'Then we have to be extremely nice to Blanche and hope that she obliges with an invitation to her coming-out ball.'

Susannah headed for the staircase. 'It's not as if it's a proper coming-out ball. I mean, she isn't being presented at Court, even though Sir Eugene is a Member of Parliament.'

'I know that, Sukey, and Rupert is in the same regiment as Hector, and he might get posted to India or South Africa, and then what would you do?'

'I think I'd die of a broken heart.'

'Come on, Sukey, it's not as bad as that,' Angel said wearily. 'Let's go upstairs and choose an afternoon gown. I'll do your hair.'

Susannah stopped halfway up with wide stair-case. 'I should have asked Cook to make some little fancy cakes. You will have time to do the flowers, won't you? Just in the drawing room, and in the hall, too.'

'Stop worrying. I'll ask Lil to do the cakes – she has an amazingly light hand when it comes to such things – and I'll see to the flowers as soon as you're settled.' Angel gave her a gentle shove. 'Up you go, Sukey. I'll make you so beautiful that Captain Westwood will fall at your feet.'

'Maybe Hector will be home in time for the ball.'

Angel had no answer to this and she followed Susannah upstairs to the large bedroom overlooking the parterre garden at the rear of the house. Having gone through every afternoon gown that

Susannah possessed, they opted for the cream shantung trimmed with blonde lace. Angel had to tug hard as she tightened Susannah's stays in an attempt to whittle her waist down to nineteen inches, but after a great deal of effort on her part and groans of protest from Susannah, they managed to fit her into the gown.

'I shan't be able to eat anything, not even the smallest fairy cake,' Susannah said breathlessly. 'If anyone says anything to upset me I'll probably swoon.'

'Make sure you faint into Rupert's arms then.' Angel moved to the rosewood dressing table and picked up the silver-backed hairbrush. 'Sit down and stop grumbling. As Lil always says – pride feels no pain.'

'She doesn't wear a corset, or if she does it's very loose. That woman always looks like a sack of potatoes.'

'I wouldn't let her hear you say that,' Angel said, laughing. 'Lil is a wonderful friend but she hasn't got a sense of humour.'

Susannah lowered herself stiffly onto the stool, staring at her reflection in the mirror. 'I think I have a spot coming, right on the tip of my nose. It will be huge by the time they arrive.'

'Nonsense. It's just your imagination, Sukey. You look perfectly fine.' Angel brushed Susannah's thick hair until it shone, and then pinned it up in a deceptively simply style, allowing a few tendrils to curl around Susannah's forehead. 'There, you're done. If that doesn't knock Captain Westwood for six, nothing will.'

Susannah regarded her reflection critically, and

for a moment Angel thought that she was going to complain, but her pouting lips curved into a delighted smile. 'Thank you, Angel. If you end up a spinster you could become a coiffeuse or a lady's maid. Anyway, that's by the bye – you'd best see to the flowers, and remind them in the kitchen that we have important guests coming for afternoon tea.'

'And what will you be doing while I'm running round after you, Your Highness?'

'Don't be sour, Angel. Just because I have a gentleman admirer and you don't. Maybe one day Hector will notice you, but beware of that because he'd never marry you. He has his sights set on becoming a major-general at the very least, and he's on the lookout for a rich wife with a good pedigree.' She turned her head to give Angel a pitying smile. 'I'm sorry, but there it is. You don't know who your parents were.'

'Don't be sorry, Susannah. I have no intention of marrying anyone. I intend to become a woman of means. I'm not sure how I'll go about it, but I wouldn't want to risk ending up like my poor mama, whoever she was.' Angel left the room before Susannah had a chance to ramble on in her tactless way and make matters worse. Of course, she had only spoken the truth and Angel was well aware of the disadvantage of her birth. She would probably never know the identity of her parents, and no gentleman would want to marry a foundling. She went to the kitchen to pass on Susannah's message, but Lil had already made a batch of small cakes and was in the process of icing them. Considering the size of her hands and sausage-like fingers, she could execute surprisingly delicate work and her sugar-paste flowers always earned praise, even from Eloise, who was notoriously fussy.

'I should be doing this for your benefit, not her ladyship's,' Lil said grudgingly. 'That young madam has it all her own way.'

Cook looked up from the pastry she was rolling out. 'You shouldn't speak of the family in that way, Lil. It ain't respectful.'

'I respect those who earn it,' Lil retorted, sniffing. 'Miss Susannah is a spoiled minx and Angel is worth ten of her.'

Angel could see that this was going to turn into a heated argument and she held up her hand. 'Whatever you think of the family, just remember that we're beholden to Sir Adolphus and Mrs Devane for taking us in, Lil. In any case, Miss Susannah thinks very highly of your cakes, and she is always praising Mrs Jones's cooking skills.'

'So there, Lumpy Lil,' Cook said, pointing the rolling pin at her. 'Maybe you should think before you speak.'

'It's Miss Heavitree to you, Eudora Jones.' Lil added a sugar-paste flower to the last tiny cake and stood back, admiring her work. 'I could have been a confectioner if I'd had the advantage of training.'

'Indeed you could,' Angel said smiling. 'Do you know where Dolly is? I might need her help with the flowers as I'm running out of time.'

'What a palaver.' Lil shook her head. 'You'd think the Queen was coming to tea.'

Angel made her escape from the kitchen. Cook

and Lil were constantly at loggerheads but she suspected that they quite enjoyed their spats, and Dolly wisely kept out of the way when the two of them were working in the kitchen. Lil had no particular duties at Grantley. She helped out where she was needed, and Angel knew that Aunt Eloise would have sacked her years ago if it had not been for Sir Adolphus. He had a soft spot for Lil and had said on more than one occasion that, had she been a man, he would gladly have had her in his regiment. But Lil had one particular gift that earned her permanent position in the household: she had a way with animals and a knowledge of herbal remedies that could ease the suffering of a lame horse or cure a sick dog. She spent much of her time in the stables, and Caesar was her particular favourite. He was too old to be taken on active service and Sir Adolphus had reluctantly had to leave him behind when he returned to duty in South Africa. The horse had been off his feed after his master's departure, and Lil was the only one who could tempt him to eat. She slept in his stall for several nights while he was on the brink of collapse, grooming him and talking to him with such tenderness that it brought tears to Angel's eyes. Lil might not be beautiful, and outwardly she was belligerent and short-tempered, but she had a big heart, as Angel knew only too well. It was Lil who had been her surrogate mother since that snowy Christmas morning when Uncle Joseph had paid her fine and had her released from police custody. Lil was her friend and confidante, and the one person on whom she knew she could rely.

Angel found Dolly in the laundry room, helping Meg fold the freshly ironed sheets. Meg Potter was a girl from the village who had started as a scullery maid and risen to the position of chambermaid under the aegis of Mrs Kerslake. But times had changed, as had the fortunes of Grantley. Mrs Kerslake had retired to live in Hampshire with her brother, and Miss Langdon, Mrs Devane's personal maid, had found employment elsewhere. Meg now did the work of chambermaid and lady's maid. In a similar fashion, Dolly had been a scullery maid at the beginning, but she was quick and willing and had been promoted to parlour maid. Angel was certain that her friend could do even better and, for the last year or so, had been encouraging her to hone her skills so that she might rise to the dizzy heights of lady's maid. In their free moments they studied the fashion plates in the *Young Ladies' Journal*, the *Ladies' Companion* and the *Queen*, and Dolly practised her hairdressing skills on Angel, with varying degrees of success. Susannah laughed at their efforts but she was quick enough to enlist Dolly's help when it came to mending the lace on her petticoat or darning her expensive silk stockings. Sir Adolphus gave Susannah a generous dress allowance, but it was soon spent and then she was forced to make economies. Angel had no such luxury and she had to rely on Mrs Devane's charity and Susannah's cast-offs, but even so, she was much better dressed than she had ever been since leaving Spital Square. She did not waste time fretting about what might have been or envying Susannah her good fortune. Her brief time in the workhouse and selling flowers on the streets had ever shown her a way of life that was hard and brutal and, even though she knew she would never be considered part of the family, she was grateful to Sir Adolphus for giving her a second chance.

With Dolly's help Angel completed the flower arrangements in good time for the Westwoods' arrival, and Susannah waited until her guests arrived before making a grand entrance. She wafted down the staircase, a vision in cream silk and lace, with a tea rose pinned to her gown.

'Blanche, how lovely to see you again.' Susannah kissed her friend on the cheek, but her gaze was focussed on the young army officer who stood behind his sister. 'And, Rupert too. How kind of you to spare some of your hard-earned leave to visit us at Grantley.'

Rupert Westwood was pleasant-looking rather than handsome and about average in height, but his generous mouth and humorous grey eyes made him instantly likeable. He bowed over her hand. 'It's always a pleasure to see you, Susannah.'

'Thank you for inviting us,' Blanche said sweetly. 'We had such a pleasant carriage drive that it seems a shame to come indoors.'

Susannah's smile faded but she made a quick recovery. 'Yes, of course. I thought we might take tea on the lawn.' She sent a mute appeal for help to Angel. 'But first you must come to the drawing room for a glass of lemonade. Angel, my dear, would you be kind enough to check that the table has been set in the shade?' She uttered a trill of laughter. 'You can't always rely on servants to use what little common sense they have.'

'Absolutely true,' Blanche said, tucking her small hand through the crook of Susannah's arm. 'And I would love a glass of cool lemonade. It's so very hot outside.'

'Might I be of assistance?' Rupert turned to Angel, who was about to slip away to arrange for a table and chairs to be set up outside.

'That won't be necessary,' Susannah said sharply. 'You must join us in the drawing room, Rupert. I want to hear all about your experiences in the Cape.'

'It wasn't a holiday, Susannah.' His smile faded and his eyes darkened. 'There are some things it's better not to talk about.'

Susannah merely shrugged and moved on, turning her attention to Blanche, but Angel could not simply walk away and leave Rupert with his painful memories. 'It's almost impossible for us to put ourselves in your position,' she said softly.

'I wouldn't have it any other way.' He proffered his arm. 'Shall we join my sister and Susannah?'

She shook her head. 'I'll come in a moment, but I have to make sure that everything is set up in the garden.'

'You aren't a servant.'

'No, Captain Westwood, but I'm more than happy to help where necessary.' Angel hurried to the kitchen, leaving him standing in the entrance hall. There were more important things to be done, and he was familiar with the layout of the house. He could find his own way to the drawing room.

A tea table and four chairs were brought from the house and set out in the shade of a tall elm tree, and Dolly rushed around laying a cloth and bringing napkins and cutlery. A silver spirit kettle was brought from the dining room and the best silver tea set. Angel knew that Susannah was desperate to make a good impression on Rupert, as this was only his second visit to the house. She did her best to make the table setting look perfect, before joining them in the drawing room.

Susannah looked up enquiringly. 'Is everything all right, Angel?'

'Perfect,' Angel said, smiling.

'Then we'll go outside and enjoy the sunshine.' Susannah rose gracefully from the sofa, extending her hand to Rupert, who hurried to her side like a well-trained lapdog.

'I hope there's plenty of shade.' Blanche followed them into the garden. 'My skin is so fair that I burn easily, and freckles are so unbecoming.' She shot a sideways glance at Dolly, who was standing to attention by the table.

Angel knew that Dolly was sensitive about the sprinkling of freckles on her nose and cheeks, but she had grown into her looks and was really very pretty, although she was still convinced that she was as plain as a pikestaff.

'Cucumber sandwiches,' Angel whispered. 'We'll have those now, I think, Dolly.' Angel watched her friend hurry back to the house and she could tell by the set of Dolly's shoulders that she had heard Blanche's tactless remark. She could have shaken the silly young woman, but she managed to keep a smile on her face as she took a seat at the table.

She covered her annoyance by making the tea, leaving it to Susannah to fill the cups and pass them round to her guests like the perfect hostess.

Angel remained silent and Rupert said little, although to be fair to him he would have had difficulty getting a word in edgeways when Susannah and Blanche got on to the subject of fashion, and ball gowns in particular. Blanche was describing a garment she had seen in a magazine with expressive movements of her arms when Dolly attempted to place a plate on the table, and she caught Dolly's hand, sending a shower of dainty cucumber sandwiches into the air. They came down in a buttery rain, most of them landing in Blanche's lap. She leaped to her feet with a shriek.

'You stupid, clumsy idiot.'

Dolly clapped her hands to her mouth, her eyes wide with horror. 'I – I'm so sorry, miss.'

'It was an accident,' Rupert said calmly. 'And it was your fault, Blanche. If you hadn't been swinging your arms like a windmill this would never have happened.'

'Shut up, Rupert. It's not funny, and it was that stupid girl's fault.' Blanche stared down at the grease stains on her pink silk skirt. 'My gown is ruined.'

Susannah had apparently been frozen to the spot, but the colour rushed to her cheeks and she pointed a shaking finger at Dolly. 'You're dismissed. Pack your bags and leave immediately.'

It was Angel's turn to rise to her feet. 'You can't do that, Susannah. It wasn't Dolly's fault.'

Rupert tugged at his sister's arm. 'Sit down and stop making a spectacle of yourself, Blanche. I'm

135

sure the stains will come out in the wash. You can't allow this poor girl to lose her job because of a mishap.'

Blanche sank down on her chair and burst into tears. 'I don't care about her.'

'Well, I do.' Rupert turned to Susannah. 'I apologise for my sister's outburst. You mustn't allow her hysterics to influence your decision. It was an accident.'

Angel placed her arm around Dolly's shoulders. 'Don't cry, dear. I'm sure that it was said in the heat of the moment.' She fixed Susannah with a hard stare. 'Please tell her that you didn't mean it.'

Susannah's lips quivered and she nodded. 'I suppose so, but I am truly sorry about your lovely gown, Blanche.'

Blanche fumbled in her reticule and brought out a hanky. 'I think I'd like to go home now.' She mopped her eyes and blew her nose.

'Don't be ridiculous, Blanche,' Rupert said angrily.

'I want to go home. I'll go on my own if you wish to stay here, but I need to change my clothes.'

'I'm sorry, Susannah.' Rupert sighed and shook his head. 'Blanche is being extremely childish over a mere trifle.'

'It's lucky it wasn't trifle. That would have made a real mess.' The words left her lips before Angel could stop herself. She glanced anxiously at Blanche, who was staring at her open-mouthed, but Rupert threw back his head and laughed.

'That's exactly it, Angel. You've put the whole silly fuss into perspective.' He turned to Blanche, the laughter fading from his eyes. 'Come on, Blanche. Stay for tea and then I'll take you home. Dammit, I'll buy you a new frock if that one is ruined.'

'Watch your language, Rupert,' Blanche said crossly. 'You're amongst ladies now, not your common soldiers.' She pouted mutinously, but sat down anyway.

'If Blanche can forgive Dolly then surely you must, Susannah?' Angel held on to Dolly, sensing that she was about to run away.

Susannah threw up her hands. 'Oh, all right. You can stay, girl, but be more careful when you bring a fresh plate of sandwiches, and you have Captain Westwood to thank for your reprieve.' She smiled at Rupert and fluttered her eyelashes. 'You are a fair man, Rupert.'

Dolly bobbed a curtsey. 'Thank you, sir. Thank you, Miss Susannah.' She backed away, turned and raced across the grass, her fiery curls escaping from beneath her mobcap.

'The girl has no finesse,' Susannah said dismissively. 'We keep her on because Uncle Adolphus insisted on it, otherwise she would have been sent packing long ago.' She sent a challenging look in Angel's direction.

'You were talking about the ball at Westwood before the accident,' Angel said, refusing to take up Susannah's subtle challenge. 'When is it to be?'

Rupert pulled up a chair and sat down beside her. 'That was skilfully done,' he whispered. 'You've deflected the conversation nicely. You're a born tactician, Angel.'

137

Angel sat back and smiled. Susannah and Blanche had launched into an animated discussion about the coming ball and Dolly's mishap seemed to have been forgotten.

The rest of the visit passed off reasonably well. Lil's dainty cakes were praised and a message was sent to the kitchen complimenting the cook, and Dolly managed to get through the afternoon without any further accidents.

When it was time for the Westwoods to leave, Blanche and Susannah were again the best of friends and as Dolly handed Rupert his hat and cane, he leaned over to whisper something in her ear. Dolly's cheeks reddened and she smiled shyly. 'Thank you, sir.'

Angel waited until the Westwoods' carriage had driven off before challenging Dolly. 'What did he say to make you blush?'

'He said he hoped I wasn't too upset and it weren't my fault. He's such a lovely gentleman and so handsome, too.'

Angel stared at her in dismay. 'Don't get any ideas, Dolly. He's a gentleman through and through, but he's not for you.'

Dolly tossed her head. 'I don't see why it's so impossible. I'm just as good as he is, and a sight better than his sister, if you ask me. Why shouldn't a girl like me raise herself in the world? He likes me, Angel. He treated me like a lady.' Dolly flounced off in the direction of the servants' quarters.

Angel watched her with a sinking heart. She could see endless problems arising in the future.

Chapter Eight

Rupert Westwood rode over from Westwood Hall every day. Sometimes he was accompanied by Blanche, but she preferred a genteel carriage ride, whereas her brother liked to exercise his horse and keep them both in trim. It was understood that he had only short leave, but the details were never discussed in front of Angel, and Susannah was either unaware of this or had chosen to put it out of her mind. She was convinced that Rupert had fallen in love with her and nothing Angel could say would bring her out of her state of euphoria. All she could talk about was the coming ball at Westwood Hall and the fact that Rupert had already claimed her for the first dance. She fully expected him to propose and had already decided where she would like to go for their honeymoon.

Angel liked Captain Westwood well enough, but she was suspicious as to the motives for his frequent visits. At first she had accepted Susannah's assumption that the gallant captain came to see her and her alone, but a chance encounter one hot afternoon in early August had shattered that illusion. Angel had been in the walled garden picking lavender and allowing it to dry for use in the long winter months, when she heard voices. Recognising Dolly's light tones, she opened the gate and then closed it again. She leaned against the wall,

shocked by the sight of Dolly and Rupert Westwood in a tender embrace. They were standing in
the shade of the oak tree, out of sight of the main
house but clearly visible from the walled garden.

Dolly had tried to deny it when Angel challenged her later that day, but it was obvious that
she was lying and in the end she had to admit
that she had fallen in love with Captain Westwood, and that he returned the feeling. Angel
had tried to convince her that it could only end
badly, but Dolly had become sullen and mulish
and refused to listen to reason. Angel could only
hope that the infatuation would pass, that Rupert
would consider the difficulties that such a relationship would create for both of them, and
would realise that Susannah was being used in a
heartless fashion. Having failed to convince
Dolly, Angel decided that she would have to face
Rupert. The ball was only two days away and
Susannah was blissfully unaware of the dual life
that Rupert was leading.

He arrived, as usual, soon after luncheon but
Angel was waiting for him outside the stables. He
dismounted, flinging the reins to a groom, who
hurried out to take the horse.

'Angel, this is a pleasant surprise? You aren't
dressed for riding, so am I to assume that you
came to meet me?'

She did not return his friendly smile. 'Yes, I
did.'

'Is anything wrong?' He took off his hat and
tucked it under his arm. 'Is Susannah unwell?'

Angel glanced over her shoulder. 'We can't talk
here. Will you walk with me?'

'Of course. I'd be delighted to have your company for a while. I hope you don't feel that I've been neglecting you.'

'No, why should I? You come to see Susannah, don't you?' Angel started walking towards the parterre garden and he fell into step beside her.

'I do, but I am always pleased to see you too.'

Angel came to a halt, just out of sight of Susannah's bedroom window. A tall magnolia leaned against the wall of the house, its huge creamy blossoms shedding saucer-like petals onto the gravel path. 'I saw you kissing Dolly. She's in love with you, Rupert, and you're not being fair to her or Susannah.'

He recoiled as if she had slapped his face, and he dropped his gaze. 'I know, Angel. I can't deny it and it's been tormenting me.'

'Then do something about it, or you'll break both their hearts.'

'What can I do? I was genuinely attracted to Susannah. Who wouldn't be? She's beautiful and intelligent and she comes from a family who can trace their lineage back to William the Conqueror, but Dolly is an original. She's sweet and uncomplicated and she makes me laugh.'

'She came from a poor family and was forced to live on the streets until I brought her here, but I agree with you in every other way, and I love Dolly as if she were my sister, which is why I can't allow you to use her for your entertainment. You'll go away and forget about her.'

He bowed his head. 'That won't happen.'

'What do you mean by that?'

'I intend to take her with me. She knows that

141

and she's willing to face the rigours of life in camp.' He looked up, his grey eyes pleading for her approval.

'So you intend her to live as a camp follower. You don't want to marry her but you'll make her your mistress, an object of scorn for all your fellow officers and friends to snigger at behind her back.' Angel could barely contain her fury. 'And when you're tired of her or you decide to marry a woman from your own class, you'll abandon Dolly to the next man who will take her on.'

'No, that won't happen,' he said earnestly. 'I promise you that I'll love her and take care of her.'

'You might think I'm naïve, Rupert, but I was brought up by a respectable couple and I know the ways of society. One day you'll succumb to pressure from your family to marry and produce an heir to Westwood, and that woman won't be your mistress. You might set Dolly up in rented rooms somewhere out of the way, but she would be an outcast. Better leave her now, while she has a chance to make something of her life.'

'I really do love her, Angel.'

'Then prove it. Tell her the truth and finish it here and now. She'll be devastated, but she's young and she'll get over you eventually.'

'Are you going to tell Susannah about this?'

She thought for a moment and then shook her head. 'No, I'll say nothing if you settle matters with Dolly. You must be completely honest with her, and I just hope she'll understand.'

'My father wants me to marry Susannah,' Rupert said sadly. 'I admire her greatly, but the thought of marrying without love is abhorrent.'

'That's something only you can decide. Susannah is a good person and I'm very fond of her. She'd make you a dutiful wife and everyone would approve of the match, but it's your choice.' Angel met his tortured gaze with an attempt at a smile. 'I know you'll do the right thing, Rupert.' She walked away, bracing herself for a stormy session with Dolly later in the day.

But everything went on as before. Dolly was dreamy-eyed and barely conscious of her surroundings and Susannah spent the afternoon in Rupert's company with no outward sign of distress. It was obvious that he had either ignored Angel's warning or had given himself time to think about how he would go about telling Dolly that their brief affair was over. Either way, it led to a sleepless night for Angel and a nerve-racking day prior to the ball.

Rupert did not pay his usual visit, but neither Susannah nor Dolly seemed to be upset or worried by his absence. Susannah was too busy sorting out which fan she would take to the ball and whether to wear a tiara or silk flowers in her hair, and Dolly went about singing at the top of her voice, until Lil told her to shut up and Cook threatened to throw a bucket of water over her. Angel happened to be in the kitchen at the time, discussing the menu for dinner due to Eloise's continuing bout of migraine, which had kept her in a darkened room for yet another day. It should have been Susannah who took over when her mother was incapacitated, but Susannah had no interest in the running of the house and, as

143

always, it was Angel who took up the reins.

She left the servants discussing the ball, with preparations for dinner a secondary concern, and she was about to go upstairs to check on Eloise when a loud hallooing outside preceded the rumble of carriage wheels. Angel ran to open the door and her heart thudded uncomfortably against her stays at the sight of Hector, handsome as ever in his uniform as he dismounted from his horse. Thor and Juno appeared as if from nowhere, moving as swiftly as their ageing bones would allow, and they greeted him enthusiastically. Toby leaned out of the carriage window, shouting and waving to Angel with Humphrey looking over his shoulder. They practically fell out of the vehicle as it drew to a halt and Humphrey rushed over to hug her. At fifteen he had grown tall, having lost his youthful chubbiness, but he still possessed the boundless enthusiasm for life that had led him into scrapes at school. Toby, on the other hand, had matured into a good-looking young man, who was in his third year at Oxford, studying law, which always made Susannah laugh. She had teased him when he announced his choice of career, calling him the poacher who had turned gamekeeper, referring to the fact that he too had always been in trouble at Rugby, and was constantly being gated for playing pranks that all too often backfired.

Humphrey released Angel but Toby took his place, giving her a hug that lifted her off her feet. Hector smiled and walked on.

'He always was a cold fish,' Toby said crossly. 'Can't you do better than that, Hector? Or are you too grand now?'

Hector paused in the doorway. 'Angel knows that I'm pleased to see her. Grantley wouldn't be the same without her.'

'I suppose that will have to do.' Toby slipped his arm around Angel's waist and they entered the house together. 'It's good to be home. Where's Mama? I thought the noise would have brought her running.'

'I'm afraid she's rather unwell today,' Angel said hastily. 'It's one of her migraine attacks, but I hope she'll be well enough to join us for dinner.'

Humphrey looked up as Eloise appeared on the landing, looking wraithlike in her voluminous white wrap. 'Mama, Angel says you're feeling poorly. You should be in bed.' He bounded up the stairs to throw his arms around his mother, dwarfing her in the process.

'Humpty, you've grown a foot at least since last term.' Eloise smiled up at him, a hint of colour tinging her cheeks. 'How lovely to see you. I wasn't expecting any of you for a week or so. I thought you would be having a wonderful time in London.'

'We'd run rather low on funds, Mama,' Toby said ruefully. 'And we missed you, of course.'

Hector crossed the floor to stand at the foot of the stairs with the dogs at his heels. 'I collected them from Naked Boy Court, Mama. I was on my way home and I knew you would want to see your boys.'

'And it's a lovely surprise, darling.' Eloise beckoned to Angel. 'Will you help me dress? I gave Meg the day off to visit her sick mother, but now I wish I hadn't been so generous.'

'Of course.' Angel was tempted to put Dolly forward, but she knew that Aunt Eloise liked things to be done a certain way and, even though Meg had no formal training as a lady's maid, she was used to Mrs Devane's foibles.

Hector stood aside to allow Angel to pass and she could feel the heat of his body and the familiar smell of saddle soap, leather and fresh air that clung to his uniform. He gave her an encouraging smile. 'What would we do without you, Angel?'

It was the sort of praise he might have given to a trusted servant, but even so it brought a blush to Angel's cheeks and she acknowledged him with a hint of a smile as she hurried upstairs.

'I'll see you in the drawing room in half an hour,' Eloise said firmly. 'And get those dogs out of here, Hector. The stables is where they belong. It's bad enough having them in the house when Adolphus is at home.' She turned on her heel and headed for her bedroom, leaving a waft of rose and violet perfume in her wake.

Angel was used to Aunt Eloise's little ways and her megrims. She had grown fond of her adoptive aunt, and was accustomed to her moods. Getting her dressed took a while, but eventually Eloise was ready to go downstairs and Angel followed her at a discreet distance. She had learned to keep the delicate balance of being neither servant nor a member of the family. Life was easier when Sir Adolphus was in residence, but Hector said that his uncle's return home was far from imminent. When questioned further, Hector told them that the unrest in the Zulu kingdom was likely to escalate into outright war,

146

and he would be returning to duty very soon. Angel was devastated by the news, but she had to hide her emotions or risk being teased mercilessly by Toby. She suspected that Humphrey, who had suffered so much ridicule as a young child, would be more sympathetic, but one thing was certain, and that was the displeasure she would endure from Aunt Eloise if she thought that her adored Hector might throw himself away on a foundling. He had always taken Angel's side during arguments when they were younger, but he had never given her cause to believe that he regarded her with anything other than brotherly affection. The secret she kept close to her heart, like the ring that her mother had left with her, was not to be shared lightly.

Angel sat slightly apart from the family group, as always, distancing herself but ready to join in when anyone remembered her presence. Susannah joined them and was mildly pleased to see her brothers, but she quickly turned the conversation to herself and the forthcoming ball at Westwood Hall.

'It's going to be a splendid occasion,' she said eagerly. 'You must come, Hector. Wearing your uniform, of course, because it makes you look quite dashing. You remember Blanche, don't you?'

Hector shrugged. 'She seemed nice enough.'

'Nice?' Susannah exchanged wry glances with her mother. 'Blanche is lovely and very sweet, most of the time. She's an heiress too. You could do much worse, Hector.'

'Thank you, Sukey, I'll choose my own bride, if you don't mind.'

'Don't call me Sukey. I've only just managed to stop Angel using that silly, childish name.'

Toby winked at Angel and Humphrey slapped his hand on his knee. 'Good for you, Angel. Keep Susie in her place, that's what I say.'

Susannah tossed her head. 'You're still a brat, Humpty Dumpty.'

Humphrey opened his mouth to retaliate but his mother held her hand to her forehead with a pained expression. 'Stop it, both of you. I've only just recovered from a sick headache and you're bringing it back.'

'Sorry, Mama.' Susannah poked her tongue out at Humphrey, but he shot a wary look at his mother and subsided.

'Sorry, Mama,' he said humbly.

'Anyway,' Susannah continued triumphantly, 'getting back to the important things in life, you must come to the ball, Hector. You could come too, Toby, if you promise to behave yourself.'

Toby stood up and stretched, stifling a yawn. 'Can't think of anything more boring. I'd rather be out hunting rabbits for the pot or fishing, thank you.'

Angel was sitting quietly by the window, listening to the exchange so reminiscent of her early days at Grantley, but she realised that Hector was studying her face with a thoughtful expression in his dark eyes.

'Are you going to the ball, Angel?'

'Yes, as a matter of fact I am.'

He nodded. 'Then it seems it's my duty to accompany you both.'

'Really, Hector?' Susannah stared at him in

surprise. 'Do you mean it?'

'I've just said so, haven't I?'

'So you *are* interested in Blanche. I knew you would be when I mentioned the fact that she's the catch of the county.'

A smile curved his lips and his eyes twinkled with golden lights. 'I thought that was your claim to fame, Susannah.'

Angel stood up quickly. She could see this turning into a squabble and she did not want Hector to change his mind. 'Well, I think it's very gallant of you to escort us, Hector. I wasn't really looking forward to the ball, but I am now.'

'Well, you would, wouldn't you?' Susannah said spitefully.

'And why is that?' Hector demanded.

Eloise rose majestically to her feet. 'Don't spoil the boys' homecoming, Susannah. You're supposed to be a young lady, and young ladies don't squabble with their brothers. I'm going to rest before luncheon. Angel, I want you to go to the kitchen and tell Cook that we have three extra mouths to feed.'

'Four, if you count Humpty Dumpty, who can eat for two,' Toby said, chuckling.

'I'll do that right away.' Angel hurried from the room. She was used to Susannah's lapses, when resentment bubbled to the surface. There had been jealousy on her part from the moment Sir Adolphus had brought Angel to Grantley, and she could understand that. Until she arrived Susannah had been the spoiled only daughter, and suddenly she was expected to share everything with a complete stranger. Angel was used to making allow-

149

ances for her, and she knew that beneath the prickly surface Susannah was a kind-hearted girl. Perhaps growing up with three brothers had made her compete for their mother's affection, but whatever the reason for Susannah's behaviour, her moods never lasted long. She would repent and apologise and give Angel a trinket from her jewellery box, or a lace handkerchief and they would be friends again.

Angel went slowly to the kitchen. She had intended to wear her muslin gown to the ball, which was pretty enough, but nothing like Susannah's elegant creation, made especially for such a grand occasion. Hector's decision had thrown Angel's plans into turmoil, and the fact that she did not possess anything more suitable to wear was suddenly a problem. She would go to the ball looking like Cinderella before the fairy godmother had done her magic. But she suspected that Hector would have eyes for no one but Blanche, and she had to admit that Blanche was strikingly pretty, as well as being very rich and well connected. Angel sighed and went to the kitchen to pass on the news that three healthy appetites would be joining them for luncheon. Cook had better order in more food, or Toby and Humpty would go hungry.

'What's up with you, miss?' Lil demanded when Angel walked into the kitchen. 'Don't say "nothing", because I won't believe you.'

'You do look a bit down in the mouth,' Cook added, eyeing Angel curiously.

'I'm perfectly all right, thank you, but you might not be when I tell you that the boys are home, for how long I don't know. There'll be three extra for luncheon.'

Cook threw up her hands. 'I knew the peace and quiet wasn't going to last. They'll eat us out of house and home.'

Lil rolled up her sleeves. 'I'll peel some more potatoes, Eudora.' She gave Angel a searching look. 'I suppose Mr Hector is home too?'

'Yes, he's on leave for a while. Anyway, we won't be in for dinner tomorrow. He's accompanying us to the ball, so you'll only have Toby and Humphrey to feed.'

'So that's it.' Lil drew Angel aside when Cook bustled into the larder. 'He's upset you, has he? I'll skin him alive, even if he is a grown man.'

'No, Lil. You've got it all wrong.'

'Then what is it? I know you, Angel. There's something bothering you.'

'It's silly really. I shouldn't be so vain, but I've just realised that my gown will look old-fashioned and dowdy compared to the other young ladies.'

'And Miss Susannah will be done up to the nines and my little angel will look like a common-or-garden sparrow,' Lil said angrily. 'I'm not having that. We've got the rest of today and all night if necessary. We'll see what we can do. Dolly – where are you, girl? You're needed here. I've got other things to do.'

Dolly popped her head round the door. 'I'm busy, Lil. Can't it wait?'

'Do you want Angel to go to the ball looking like a drab? Captain Hector has come home.'

Angel met Cook's curious gaze with an attempt at a smile. 'It's not just the fact that Hector is

151

escorting us to the ball – it's just that–'

'You don't need to explain,' Dolly said hastily. 'We all understand, don't we, Cook?'

Eudora nodded and a slow smile spread across her plump face. 'I think we do, Dolly. I'm quite nifty with my needle.'

'You don't have to go to all this trouble.' Angel looked from one eager face to the other. 'I can always stitch a few ribbons on my gown, or something.'

'Nonsense.' Lil curled her lip. 'You've had that muslin frock for two years at least, and all the other young ladies will be dressed in the latest fashions. I ain't having my baby girl go to the ball looking like a poor relation.'

'But that's what I am,' Angel said, laughing. 'Who's going to look at me?'

'Captain Hector, for one.' Dolly winked at Lil. 'I'm sure we can make you presentable.'

'We have an hour or two between clearing up after luncheon and the preparation of dinner,' Lil said firmly. 'Anyone who wants to help can meet me in the sewing room at three o'clock. You'll be there, Angel, no matter what her ladyship upstairs says. Do you understand me?'

'Yes, Lil,' Angel said meekly. There was no gainsaying Lumpy Lil when she had set her mind on something.

Luncheon was a lively meal with Toby and Humphrey chattering non-stop about their experiences at university and at Rugby School. Humphrey announced proudly that he had beaten the bullies, having turned himself into the form clown by keeping his classmates amused with anecdotes and comic impressions of the schoolmasters.

'I think I might go on the stage, Mama,' he said, having succeeded in making his family laugh.

'Don't say such things, Humphrey.' Eloise stared at him in horror. 'Your education is costing my brother a small fortune, and he will expect you to achieve something better than becoming an entertainer.'

'He's joking again, Mama.' Toby flicked a pellet of bread roll at his brother, but a look from Eloise prevented Humphrey from retaliating.

'A spell in the army would do you both good,' Hector observed casually. 'Don't worry, Mama. Humphrey has a warped sense of humour.'

'At least I have one,' Humphrey countered. 'You are always so serious, Hector. Do you ever allow yourself to relax and have a good laugh?'

'I wonder if Rupert will visit us this afternoon,' Susannah said, seemingly oblivious to the argument between her brothers. 'You must know him, Hector. He's in the same regiment as you.'

'But a different battalion, Sukey.'

She shrugged and tossed her dark curls. 'I don't know the difference – it's just the army, as far as I'm concerned.'

'Sacrilege, Sukey,' Toby said, chuckling. 'You've ruined Hector's day, if not his whole leave.'

Angel glanced anxiously at Hector. 'South Africa and Natal Province are so far from here that it's hard for us to imagine what it must be like.'

He responded with a smile. 'That's true and I wouldn't expect anyone here to understand,

153

neither would I want you to. War in any shape or form is abominable, and I'm afraid it's inevitable.'

'That's rich coming from a man whose profession it is to fight and kill,' Toby said seriously.

'You might think differently if the enemy was on our doorstep. Anyway, this is hardly the topic for discussion at a family meal.' Hector acknowledged his mother with a nod. 'It's good to be home, Mama, even if it's only for a short time.'

'Oh, Hector, don't say that. I was hoping you would have a few weeks in which to rest and regain your strength. You look very thin, my dear boy.'

'I'm sure a week of home cooking will put that to rights, Mama.' Hector leaned back in his seat. 'That was an excellent meal. The best I've had for weeks.' He looked up as Dolly began to clear their plates and gave her a dazzling smile. 'Please pass the message on to Cook and thank her for me.'

Dolly bobbed a curtsey. 'Yes, sir.'

'I think I'll go and lie down for a while,' Eloise said, rising from the table with a weary sigh. 'All this excitement is too much for me.'

Hector stood up to pull back his mother's chair. 'You mustn't overexert yourself, Mama.'

'No, dear. You're quite right.'

'I'll see you to your room, Mama.' Susannah leaped to her feet. 'Might I have a look through your jewel case? I have to decide what to wear with my ball gown.'

'Don't you ever think of anything but yourself, Sukey?' Toby demanded crossly. 'You used to be more fun.'

'She used to pull my hair,' Humphrey said darkly. 'At least she doesn't do that now.'

'Brothers are horrid.' Susannah followed her mother out of the room, pausing to turn her head and pull a face at Toby. 'And don't call me Sukey.'

Angel was about to help Dolly clear the table when Hector laid his hand on her arm. 'You shouldn't do that. You're not a servant.'

'It's only a few plates, Hector. I wasn't intending to do anything more strenuous.'

Toby was already at the door. 'Who's coming for a ride? What about you, Hector? That nag of yours must need exercising.'

'Yes, that's what I had in mind.' Hector released Angel. 'Would you like to come too? It's a lovely afternoon.'

'What about me?' Humphrey asked plaintively. 'Don't I count?'

'Of course you do, Humpty old boy. Let's all go.' Toby rushed from the room, leaving the door to swing shut of its own accord.

'Well?' Hector faced Angel with a quizzical look. 'Do you dare to accompany us?'

Angel glanced at the mantel clock. There was an hour before she was supposed to join Lil in the sewing room, but an invitation to ride out with Hector was an honour for which she would have walked barefoot over broken glass. 'Yes, I dare, and you might be surprised to find that I'm quite a good horsewoman now, Hector.'

'We'll wait while you change into your riding habit and meet you at the stables in fifteen minutes. Can you manage that? Or are you like Susannah and take hours to get ready?'

155

Angel headed for the doorway. 'I'll be with you in ten minutes. Eleven at the most.'

They rode out of the grounds at a sedate trot, breaking into a canter as they approached Epping Forest, and slowing to a walk beneath the cool green canopy of trees until they emerged once more into the sunlight and the gleaming expanse of the Hollow Pond. Toby and Humphrey urged their horses to a gallop on Leyton Flats, but Hector rode more slowly, taking in the scenery with an appreciative smile.

'I'll miss all this, Angel. Memories of home keep me going when I'm away.'

'When will you have to leave us?' Angel asked, although she already knew the answer. It was clear from the bleak expression on his face.

Chapter Nine

It was only when Angel handed the reins to the groom that she remembered her promise to Lil. She raced from the stables, the skirts of her riding habit flying out behind her like wings, and her blonde curls escaping from the confines of a snood. She reached the sewing room to find Lil, Meg and Dolly hard at work. Dolly looked up and smiled but Lil's face was set in grim lines. Angel knew she was in trouble.

'I'm sorry,' she began breathlessly. 'I lost track of time and it was such a lovely day for a ride.'

'We're spending our time doing things for you and you couldn't be bothered to turn up for a fitting,' Lil said crossly. 'Lucky for you Dolly's about your size.'

'Oh, don't get on to her, Lil.' Dolly snipped a thread and smoothed out the material. 'I wouldn't turn down an invitation to go out riding with the captain, if it was me he asked, and if I could ride a horse, which I can't.'

Angel gazed at the shimmering satin gown in a shade of brilliant turquoise, embellished with tiny crystal beads and seed pearls. 'Where did this come from? It's not mine.'

Meg looked up from the hem she was stitching. 'It's one of Madam's. It's been packed away in a trunk for a couple of years, and I doubt if she'll even remember it. We've altered it so I don't think she would recognise it anyway.'

'Since you've decided to join us, you'd better try it on.' Lil rose from the wooden stool and held the gown up, giving it a shake.

'It's beautiful.' Angel dashed her hand across her eyes, overcome by emotion. 'I've never seen anything so lovely. It shimmers like the sunlight on the Hollow Pond.'

'Never mind that, you silly girl. Take off your riding habit and let's see if the frock fits. If it doesn't we've wasted a whole afternoon.' Lil frowned, but there was a note of pride in her voice. 'I'm not having you go to a ball looking like a dollymop. You'll outshine Miss Susannah or my name ain't Lilian Heavitree.'

On the evening of the ball Eloise was still not

157

feeling well enough to chaperone Susannah and Angel, but as Hector was accompanying them she had not raised any objections. He was waiting for them at the foot of the stairs, looking dashing as ever in his dress uniform. Susannah trailed her gloved hand on the balustrade as she descended slowly, leaving a cloud of heady perfume in her wake. Her gown, in crimson silk, was trimmed lavishly with black lace, with the overskirt drawn back into an elaborate bustle, and a long train. Angel had to watch her step or she might have trodden on it with disastrous consequences.

'You look like an empress, Sukey,' Hector said gallantly, but his smile faded and his eyes widened when he saw Angel. 'Great heavens, who would have thought that the little duckling my uncle brought here one Christmas would have turned into a beautiful swan?'

'Don't be ridiculous, Hector.' Susannah came to a halt, fixing him with a stony stare. 'It's amazing what one of Mama's old frocks, cut down by the inexpert hands of the kitchen maids, can do for a girl from the streets.'

Hector's winged eyebrows snapped together in an ominous frown. 'That was mean even by your standards, Susannah. I want you to apologise to Angel. She looks lovely and whoever altered the gown has worked wonders. No one would know that it hadn't been made by the same hand that created your theatrical garment.'

'Are you saying I'm overdressed?' Susannah demanded angrily.

'I'm surprised that Mama approved of something as elaborate and colourful, especially for an

158

unmarried girl.'

'I don't see why I should apologise for looking stylish,' Susannah said, pouting.

'Don't spoil the evening, Sukey. You're beautiful and you know it. I'm sure Westwood will fall at your feet when he sees you.'

The tension between brother and sister was broken by the appearance of Toby, who rushed downstairs, struggling with his bow tie. 'I've changed my mind, Hector, I'm coming to the ball, but I'm in need of assistance. I've been struggling with this wretched thing for half an hour or more.'

Susannah stamped her foot. 'Really, Toby, you're impossible.'

'Come here, you buffoon.' Hector placed his hat and gloves on a side table while he fixed his brother's tie. 'You've lost a collar stud. You really are a disaster, old man.'

'I have a spare.' Toby felt in his waistcoat pocket and took out a stud. 'I'm always losing the damned things so I carry a couple of extras with me at all times.'

Hector tried and failed. 'You'll have to take your tie off and start again.'

'Let me have a go.' Angel took off her gloves. 'I remember helping Uncle Joseph with his collar studs. There's a knack in it, especially when replacing one. Let's see if I can remember how to do it.' Within seconds she had it in place. 'There you are, Toby. I hadn't forgotten.'

Susannah tapped Toby on the arm with her fan. 'Come along, we'll be late and the ball will have begun. Why do you always have to spoil things?'

'Never mind, Sukey,' Hector said pleasantly.

159

'You always did like to make a grand entrance. Your audience will be waiting for you.'

She rounded on him, her eyes narrowed. 'If you call me Sukey once more I'll forget that I'm a lady and I'll scratch your eyes out.'

'I always knew she had talons,' Toby said, chuckling. He seized Susannah by the hand and dragged her towards the door. 'I pity poor Westwood if you get your claws into him, you wildcat.'

Hector proffered his arm to Angel. 'Might I have the pleasure of the first dance, Miss Winter?'

The twinkle in his eyes was impossible to resist. 'I'll have to check my card, Captain Devane, but I think it might be arranged.' Angel smiled up at him. Despite Susannah's tantrum it was going to be a wonderful evening.

Flaming torches set at intervals along the carriage sweep led the way to the imposing entrance of Westwood Hall. Built in the Palladian style, it was a large country house set squarely in open parkland. A liveried footman hurried to open the carriage door, and Hector and Toby stepped down to help the girls alight. Susannah laid her hand on Hector's arm, clearly intending to make a grand entrance, leaving Angel to follow with Toby. The spacious hall was lit by dozens of candles, and the scent of warm beeswax mingled with the perfume of white lilies, roses and jasmine. Angel realised that her attempts at flower arranging paled into insignificance when compared with the spectacular displays spilling over from silver urns and cutglass vases, placed on every available surface. Music floated through from the ballroom and they were greeted by Sir Eugene Westwood with Rupert and Blanche at his side.

Susannah did not bother to hide her annoyance when Hector claimed Angel for the first dance, but Angel was in heaven. Her feet hardly seemed to touch the ground as the orchestra played a Viennese waltz and Hector held her in his arms, whirling her round until she was dizzy with delight. She danced the quadrille with Toby, and Rupert claimed her for a lively polka, leaving Susannah to take the floor with Sir Eugene.

When Angel returned to their table she was dismayed to find Blanche seated beside Hector. She was talking animatedly and Hector was listening with what appeared to be rapt attention. A worm of jealousy crawled into Angel's heart and suddenly Blanche took on the aura of a vile temptress – a siren who was luring Hector with her lovely voice. Angel took a deep breath and forced her cold lips into a smile. She was being ridiculous, and she knew it. Hector was his own man and Blanche was both beautiful and an heiress. It was a match made in heaven and she, Angel Winter, the foundling child, was not even in the running.

'Thank you, Miss Winter,' Rupert said with a courtly bow. 'May I get you some refreshment? A glass of fruit punch, perhaps?'

Angel sank on a chair beside Blanche. 'That would be lovely. It was a very lively polka.'

'It was indeed.' He glanced over his shoulder as his father came towards them with Susannah on his arm. 'Miss Devane, might I bring you a glass of fruit punch?'

Angel could see that Susannah was still simmering with resentment, but she gave Rupert a sweet smile and accepted his offer. Sir Eugene handed her into a chair opposite Angel.

'Thank you, Miss Devane. I regret I must leave you now and do my duty as a host, but I hope you might have another dance free after supper.'

'I'll be sure to save one for you, Sir Eugene.' Susannah's smile faded as he walked away and she leaned across the table, fixing Angel with a warning look. 'Keep away from Rupert,' she hissed. 'He's not for you.'

The words 'It's not me you need to worry about' hovered on Angel's lips but remained unspoken. She could not betray Dolly's secret, nor could she bring herself to dash Susannah's hopes, even though she was being particularly trying this evening. Angel could understand this latest show of animus, even if it was aimed at the wrong person. Rupert Westwood's heart was already lost, but to someone that Susannah would have thought the most unlikely recipient. The truth would hurt even more deeply than if Susannah's suspicions had been correct. For a man from such an illustrious family to form a liaison with a servant would bring disgrace upon his good name and ultimate ruin for Dolly. Angel reached out to lay her hand on Susannah's. 'You need not worry about me. I think he's very handsome and charming, but that's all, and he was being chivalrous by asking me to dance.'

Susannah shrugged and looked away. 'Of course I knew that.'

Hector turned his head. 'Are you two arguing again?'

'Mind your own business, Hector,' Susannah said with a bright smile. 'We were just discussing dance partners.' She fixed her gaze on Blanche. 'Did my brother tread on your toes?'

'That's not fair.' Blanche blushed prettily. 'Hector is the perfect partner in every way.'

'I was joking, you silly goose,' Susannah said airily. 'Of course Hector is good at anything he chooses to do. We all agree on that, don't we, Angel?'

'Susannah has such a wicked sense of humour,' Angel said hastily.

'You'll get used to my sister in time, Blanche.' Hector rose to his feet as the orchestra struck up a mazurka. 'Are you willing to risk having your toes trodden on, Angel?'

She had thought he was going to ask Blanche to dance, but he was smiling and holding out his hand, and it would have been impossible to refuse. She could feel Blanche's eyes boring into her back as she walked onto the crowded floor, but as the music started all the other couples seemed to melt into nothingness. Angel had only practised the mazurka once or twice, but when Hector took her hand she found it easy to follow the steps, and she began to relax and enjoy herself. It was an elegant dance and Hector was seemingly an expert. She wondered how many ladies he had partnered in the past, and how many hearts he had broken, but that seemed un-important – he was hers for as long as the orchestra kept playing.

It was over all too soon and they rejoined their party. It was Blanche's turn to give Angel a look that would have curdled milk, which was some consolation. After all, if a lady like Blanche Westwood could be jealous of a foundling, there might yet be hope for her.

Angel accepted a cup of fruit punch from Rupert and drank it down thirstily. This might be her first and last ball and she was determined to enjoy every minute. But disappointment almost overcame her when Hector escorted Blanche into the supper room. Long tables were set with white damask cloths where crystal glassware sparkled in the candlelight, and silver epergnes were filled with fruits and flowers. Toby pulled up a chair for Angel and she sat down next to Rupert with Susannah on his right. Hector and Blanche were on the opposite side of the table.

Toby slumped onto the chair beside Angel. 'Dashed boring affairs, but at least the food looks good and I'm starving.' He glanced at Angel's empty plate as he helped himself from a salver of cold ham and tongue. 'What's the matter? Lost your appetite?'

Angel was not hungry and her stays were laced so tightly that she doubted if she could manage to eat anything more substantial than an ice cream or a spoonful or two of one of the enormous wobbling and shimmering fruit jellies. 'I'm not very hungry, Toby.'

He summoned a footman with an imperious wave of his hand. 'A strawberry ice cream for the lady.'

'That wasn't necessary,' Angel said, glancing

anxiously at Hector, but his attention was fixed on Blanche, who was talking animatedly.

'Now that would be a match made in heaven,' Toby said, grinning. 'The Westwood fortune might save Grantley from bankruptcy.'

Angel stared at him in horror. 'What do you mean by that?'

He speared a slice of tongue on his fork. 'Didn't you know? I thought everyone was aware of our shaky finances. Uncle Dolph is hopeless with money, and Mama was left penniless when our father died.'

'I'm sorry,' Angel murmured, acknowledging the footman with a hint of a smile as he placed a glass dish filled with strawberry ice cream on the table in front of her.

'Papa was a gambler,' Toby said casually. 'Lost everything and walked out in front of a brewer's dray, leaving Mama to cope on her own. I don't know where we would have been if Uncle Dolph hadn't taken us in.'

'That's terrible. I didn't realise that he committed suicide.'

'No reason why you would. It's not the sort of thing to brag about, but it means that Hector, Humpty and I have to earn our living, or marry heiresses, or rich widows.' He attacked his food with relish, leaving Angel to eat her ice cream in silence, but every time she glanced at Hector she had visions of him walking down the aisle in the village church with Blanche on his arm, and her appetite deserted her. Susannah was doing her best to charm Rupert, and Angel realised with a pang of guilt that the reason for Susannah's determination to marry well was one of survival and not avarice. The news that Grantley was in financial difficulties brought back memories of her comfortable childhood with Aunt Cordelia and Uncle Joseph, which had ended so abruptly. If the family lost Grantley she could see the past repeating itself: finding herself homeless again, and living on the streets of London was a distinct possibility.

'What are you thinking about?' Toby demanded. 'You were miles away.'

She came back to earth with a start. 'Yes, I'm sorry. I was thinking about what you just told me. How terrible for Aunt Eloise to be living with the threat of losing everything yet again. No wonder she suffers from megrims.'

'I dare say we'll manage,' Toby said casually. 'When I pass my law examinations I'll be in a position to help Mama. I rather fancy myself as a country solicitor, doing as little work as possible and spending my spare time hunting and fishing.' He glanced at her empty plate. 'How was the ice cream? I'm not sure if I fancy that or a plateful of jelly. On the other hand the tipsy cake looks good.'

'You'd better marry a wealthy woman, Toby. With your love of good food she had better have a large fortune so that she can keep you in style.'

He chuckled and reached for a slice of tipsy cake.

The rest of the evening passed pleasantly, but as far as Angel was concerned the magic was lost. All she could think of was the threat to Grantley and the life she had come to enjoy and the people she had come to love. The thought of losing everything for a second time was almost too much to bear, but the only person who noticed a change in her mood was Hector. She had, at his request, saved the last waltz for him. If she had not been so pre-occupied with the news that Toby had so casually imparted, she might have wondered why he chose to honour her, and not the beautiful Blanche, with the last dance, but until they were whirling around the floor the thought had not occurred to her.

'What's the matter, Angel?' Hector tightened his clasp on her hand. 'You've lost some of the glow you had earlier. Are you tired?'

'Not at all. I'm perfectly all right, thank you.'

'There's something wrong, I can tell.'

It was neither the time nor the place to tell him what she knew and she shook her head. 'Perhaps I am a bit tired. It's been an exciting evening.'

'I'm glad you've enjoyed yourself.'

Angel had promised herself she would not ask the question, but she could not stop herself. 'What I don't understand is why you're dancing with me and not Blanche?'

If he was startled he hid it well. 'Perhaps I prefer dancing with my adopted cousin.'

'Or maybe someone had claimed her first and you missed your opportunity?'

'What does it matter? I haven't trodden on your toes, as far as I know.'

'She's rich and beautiful. Blanche Westwood is the catch of the county, according to Susannah.'

'I see where this is leading. Toby told about our precarious financial position, didn't he?'

'How did you guess?'

'My brother is a man of few words, which is odd for someone training to be a lawyer, but I could see by the look on your face that he was revealing something that shocked you. You would not make a good poker player, Angel.'

'I was really sorry to hear it. Your poor mama must be so worried.'

'My uncle and I have managed to keep the worst of it from Mama. She's had enough to put up with and she's delicate. I think losing Grantley would be too much for her to bear.'

'So what will you do?'

'Nothing at the moment. We're paying the interest on the mortgage that Uncle Dolph took out on Grantley, and we'll find a solution somehow. You mustn't worry, and please don't repeat any of this to Susannah. She doesn't know, and it would serve no purpose to upset her unnecessarily. Luckily she has her heart set on marrying a wealthy man, although I think Sir Eugene might be a bit old for her.'

Angel turned her head and caught sight of Susannah locked in Sir Eugene's arms. There was something about the way that he was holding himself, and the angle of his head as he looked into Susannah's eyes that made her wonder if the gentleman was looking for a young wife. Rupert was dancing with a pretty blonde girl who was flirting outrageously and he seemed to be enjoying himself. Angel had never experienced such happiness as she was feeling now, but the lives and loves of those around her were as tangled and intricate as a spider's web, and she knew that her own personal bubble might burst at any moment.

She met Hector's gaze and smiled. 'It's been a wonderful evening, Hector. I wish it would never end.'

But all too soon the guests began to depart and the orchestra stopped playing. It was time to return home to Grantley, but in the confines of the carriage Angel felt closer to Hector than she had during the ball. It had been a magical evening and over far too soon.

Next day a feeling of anticlimax hung over the household at Grantley. Despite having arrived home in the early hours of the morning, Hector had left for London before breakfast, leaving a message to say that he'd be back in time for dinner. Angel read the note, wondering why he had not made any mention of it the previous evening.

She found Susannah and her mother already at breakfast in the dining room. Humphrey was nowhere to be seen, and Toby had not yet put in an appearance, which was hardly surprising as he had drunk far too much and had fallen asleep in the carriage on the journey home, snoring loudly until Susannah prodded him in the ribs.

Angel took her place at table, toying with a plate of buttered eggs and grilled bacon, while Susannah nibbled a slice of toast.

'I take it from your sulky expression, Susannah, that the ball was not an unqualified success.' Eloise touched the silver coffeepot with the tips of her fingers and pulled a face. 'I refuse to drink cold coffee.' She picked up the hand bell and rang it. 'Where is that girl?'

Almost immediately, as if she had been waiting

169

outside, Dolly hurried into the room. 'You rang, madam?'

'More coffee, please. And will you go upstairs and tell Master Humphrey that breakfast won't be kept for him?' She turned to Susannah with a weary smile. 'I suppose Toby drank too much, as usual, and won't rise until noon at the very earliest.'

Dolly bobbed a curtsey. 'If you please, ma'am. Master Humphrey was up very early and left for town with Captain Devane.'

'Thank you, Dolly. That will be all. Just bring fresh coffee and some more toast.'

'Yes'm.' Dolly hurried from the room, closing the door behind her.

'Well, then,' Susannah said, frowning. 'What do you make of that, Mama? Why would Hector and Humpty Dumpty go to town without saying a word?'

'I had a letter from our solicitor yesterday.' Eloise sighed and shook her head. 'That man only contacts me when there is bad news.'

'What could be wrong, Mama?' Susannah asked anxiously.

Eloise held her hand to her head. 'I don't know. Perhaps Hector can sort it out. Things always happen when Dolph is away, and I have no grasp of business matters.'

'Hector will know what to do.' Angel could see that Susannah was not going to let the matter rest, and Aunt Eloise seemed to be on the brink of admitting that they were in serious financial difficulties. It was not difficult to imagine what effect such information would have on Susannah, who was still visibly upset about her lack of success in charming Rupert Westwood.

'You monopolised Hector all evening,' Susannah said angrily. 'Blanche only had one dance with him and you must have had three or four. You'll ruin everything if you continue to flirt with my brother.'

'I did not flirt with him.' Angel's good intentions evaporated like morning mist. 'Hector was being kind and considerate because he realised I didn't know many of the guests.'

'If what Susannah says is true, you should have reminded my son of his duty to the other young ladies at the ball,' Eloise said severely. 'Hector has a kind heart and you've always played on that, Angel. You might not realise it, but you do.'

A rap on the door preceded Dolly, who entered carrying the coffeepot and a jug of hot milk. 'Will there be anything else, ma'am?'

'That's all for now. You may clear the table when we're finished. My son will have to forgo his breakfast if he can't be punctual for meals.'

'Yes'm.' Dolly curtseyed and backed out of the room.

'I sometimes detect a hint of insolence in that girl's attitude,' Eloise said crossly. 'You brought her here, Angel, therefore you must speak to her severely. Warn her that if she doesn't mend her ways she will find herself out of work, and I would not recommend her to anyone else if she cannot properly respect her betters.'

Angel rose hastily to her feet. 'I'm sure she doesn't mean to be rude, Aunt Eloise. I'll speak to her right away.'

'Thank you, and please see to the flower arrangements. The water needs changing. The smell of it is bringing on my migraine.' Eloise filled her cup with coffee. 'I'm going to rest for a while when I've finished my meal, and I don't want to be disturbed.'

'I thought I might ride over to Westwood Hall this afternoon,' Susannah said cautiously. 'I'd like to thank Sir Eugene and the family for their hospitality in person.' She glanced at Angel, who was about to leave the room. 'Will you ride with me?'

'Not today. I have things to attend to here. Perhaps one of the grooms could accompany you.' Even as she spoke Angel could hear the sound of a horse's hoofs on the gravel and she went to look out of the window. 'You won't have to bother, Sukey. Rupert Westwood has saved you the trouble.'

Susannah's cheeks flamed with colour and she leaped to her feet. 'Oh, Lord. I must go to my room and put my hair up. Keep him occupied until I come down, Angel.'

Angel had just seen Dolly rush out to greet their visitor and she held her breath, hoping that Susannah did not change her mind and catch the couple in a fond embrace. Angel could only hope that vanity had won the day and Susannah had gone upstairs to make herself beautiful.

Eloise rose more slowly to her feet. 'Send him to the drawing room, Angel,' she said firmly. 'I will keep the young man entertained until Susannah is ready to receive him.'

Glad of the reprieve, Angel hurried outside to greet Rupert, who was standing at the bottom of the steps with Dolly. They moved apart and Dolly backed away nervously.

'Good morning, Captain Westwood,' Angel said pleasantly. 'Won't you come inside?' She sent a warning look to Dolly.

'Good morning, Miss Winter.' Rupert doffed his top hat. 'You look remarkably fresh for someone who danced the night away.' He handed the reins to a groom, who had come running from the direction of the stables.

'It was a lovely ball,' Angel said, smiling. 'And Westwood Hall is a beautiful house.' She turned to Dolly. 'I'm sure you have work to do.'

Dolly hesitated. 'Could you let us have a few moments together?'

'Are you mad?' Angel said angrily. 'What would have happened if anyone other than myself had been looking out of the window?'

'Don't scold her, Miss Winter.' Rupert moved swiftly to Dolly's side. 'I'm truly grateful to you for keeping our secret.'

'Just how long do you think you can keep something like this quiet?' Angel looked from one to the other. 'It's Dolly who will suffer, Captain Westwood. You already know that, so why are you pursuing her?'

'We're in love,' Dolly protested. 'You know we are, Angel. I thought you were on our side.'

'I am, of course, which is why you must end this now.' Angel turned to Rupert. 'You're not being fair to anyone.' She could see from the horrified expression on his face that someone had overheard her words, and she turned to find Eloise standing behind her.

173

Chapter Ten

'Leave us, Chapman.' Eloise glowered at Dolly, who fled into the house. 'What were you saying, Angel? I think an explanation is due.'

Rupert stepped forward. 'Forgive me, Mrs Devane. It was my fault. Angel was trying to protect you from a difficult situation.'

'Come inside, both of you.' Eloise turned on her heel and led the way to the drawing room where she sank down on one of the damask-covered sofas. 'Now tell me exactly what is going on.'

Angel glanced nervously at Rupert but once again he took the lead. 'I have to be honest with you, ma'am.'

Eloise raised a pale hand. 'Please spare me the histrionics, Captain Westwood. It seems to me that you've taken advantage of one of my servants and you've been toying with my daughter's affections. Now tell me that I'm wrong.'

'It's not like that,' Angel said hastily.

'I wasn't speaking to you.' Eloise turned her back on Angel. 'Well, Captain Westwood. I'm waiting.'

'I love Dolly, ma'am. I'm not apologising for a feeling that is both deep and genuine. I admit that I presumed on my acquaintance with Susannah in order to visit Grantley, and for that I do apologise most sincerely, but you must see that I was placed in a difficult position.'

'All I can see is that you have been using my daughter and abusing my hospitality. I thought better of you, sir. We'll see what your father has to say about this.'

'Why shouldn't he care for Dolly?' Angel could keep silent no longer. 'She's a splendid girl and she loves him truly. Why can't they marry and be happy?'

'Marriage?' Eloise raised a delicate eyebrow. 'Are you telling me that you wish to marry a girl who was plucked from the city streets?'

'Yes,' Rupert said simply. 'I don't care about any of that, Mrs Devane. I love Dolly and I intend to make her my wife.'

Angel stared at him in amazement. She had not believed him at first when he told her his intentions towards Dolly were entirely honourable, but the look in his eyes and the passion in his voice left her in no doubt as to his sincerity.

'And what will Sir Eugene say to that?' Eloise voiced Angel's unspoken thoughts.

'He'll have to get used to the idea, ma'am, but when he sees how happy we are and what a good army wife Dolly will make, I think he'll come round.'

'I hope so, for your sake, but you realise that I cannot continue to employ the girl now?'

Angel could keep silent no longer. 'Dolly has done nothing wrong.'

'Kindly keep your nose out of my business. You brought the creature to my house and she has deceived us all. I won't tolerate that sort of behaviour from a servant.' Eloise reached for the bell pull and tugged on it. She shot an angry glance at

175

Rupert. 'You've deceived my daughter, sir.'

'No, ma'am. I can't allow that,' Rupert said urgently. 'I really like Susannah. She's a beautiful young woman, but the life of a soldier's wife is not one I would wish on her. She deserves better.' He looked over his shoulder as the door opened and Susannah breezed in, followed by Dolly. A dull flush stained his cheeks and he sent a pleading look to Eloise, but she chose to ignore him.

'Susannah, I wish I could have spared you this, but Captain Westwood has just told me something very interesting.' She fixed Dolly with a stony stare. 'You can pack your bag, Chapman. You're dismissed and don't expect to receive a character from me.'

Dolly's mouth opened in a silent cry of distress and Angel rushed to her side, placing a protective arm around her shoulders.

'What on earth is going on?' Susannah demanded, laughing. 'You look as if you're part of a Greek tragedy, and what has Chapman done to deserve the sack, Mama?'

Eloise folded her hands neatly in her lap and her eyes glinted with malice. 'I think Captain Westwood can answer that better than I.'

Dolly bowed her head and wept.

'How can you be so cruel, Aunt Eloise?' Angel said angrily. 'This isn't Dolly's fault.'

'Susannah, I owe you an apology,' Rupert said tentatively. 'I never meant to mislead you as to my intentions, but I didn't expect to fall in love like this.'

A host of emotions flitted across Susannah's face, but hope was quickly replaced by doubt.

176

'What are you saying?'

He moved to Dolly's side. 'I didn't mean to deceive you, Susannah. It was love at first sight, which sounds trite, I know, but that's how it happened. I saw Dolly and I fell in love with her. I've asked her to marry me.'

Susannah sank down on the sofa next to her mother. 'But that's ridiculous. You can't marry a servant. What would your father say?'

Dolly broke away from Rupert and ran from the room.

'He will probably react like you and your mother, Susannah. Angel is the only one here who has a grain of humanity in her make-up. I love Dolly and that's an end to it. I'll marry her and she'll accompany me wherever I'm posted. She'll make a brave and wonderful army wife, and I consider myself a lucky man.' Rupert stormed out of the room, slamming the door behind him.

There was a moment of stunned silence before Susannah burst into tears.

'I blame you for this, Angel Winter,' Eloise said angrily.

Angel was about to protest but Susannah raised her head. 'If anyone is to blame it's Rupert. He made me think I was the one he came to see, when all the time he was spooning with one of our servants. Sir Eugene needs to know about this. He'll put a stop to it.'

'Sukey,' Angel said aghast. 'You can't mean to interfere.'

'Can't I? We'll see about that. Do you realise that I'll be the laughing stock of the county if this gets about? Last night at the ball everyone assumed

177

that Rupert was my beau.'

Angel shook her head. 'You danced with his father more often than with anyone else.'

Eloise was suddenly alert, holding her head on one side like an inquisitive bird. 'Is this true, Susannah?'

'I suppose so,' Susannah said sulkily. 'But he's old, Mama. He must be forty-five or more.'

'Sir Eugene Westwood is a handsome, eligible widower.' Eloise rose to her feet, holding out her hand. 'Come, dear. You must gather yourself together, wash your face and change into your new cream-sprigged muslin. I knew it would be worth spending all that money on such a fine gown. Angel will put your hair up for you.'

'What are you talking about, Mama?' Susannah said tearfully. 'My heart is breaking and all you can think of is sprigged muslin.'

'Appearances are very important, Susannah. I will also go and change into something more suitable. Angel, send for the carriage. Susannah and I are going to Westwood Hall to pay a call on Sir Eugene.'

'Am I to accompany you?' Angel asked dazedly. This was a turn of events she had least expected.

'I think I can manage this without your assistance, my girl, but when you've sent for the carriage I want you to come upstairs to do Susannah's hair. Make haste now.' With a surprising burst of energy, Eloise shooed Susannah from the room.

Angel was supposed to go to the stables and pass on the message, but instead of obeying Eloise's instructions she went to the kitchen, where she

178

found Dolly in tears and Rupert attempting to explain the situation to a startled Cook and Lil. Meg and Flossie, the scullery maid, looked on open-mouthed.

'What's to be done?' Lil demanded brusquely. 'You've got the girl in this state, sir. So what are you going to do about it?'

Angel held her breath. It was almost unheard of for servants to challenge their betters and Lil was risking the wrath of both Sir Eugene and Aunt Eloise if Rupert chose to complain.

'You're quite right, Miss, er ... I'm sorry, I don't know your name.'

'Miss Heavitree, sir, but you may call me Lil.'

'Well, Lil, I intend to ride to London and obtain a special licence so that Dolly and I can be married properly, in church, as I would wish. This isn't a hole-and-corner affair, and my wife will receive the respect due to her.'

Angel hugged Dolly. 'Don't cry, dear. Captain Westwood will make everything all right.'

'B-but where am I to go now?' Dolly raised a tear-stained face. 'Mrs Devane has just given me the sack and I'm to leave immediately.'

Cook sat down heavily on a stool and it almost toppled over beneath her considerable weight. 'Lawks, I never heard of such a thing. You should think yourself lucky, my girl. A gentleman doesn't often take up with such as you.'

Rupert eyed her coldly. 'Dolly is as good a person as I've ever met, and she's better than most.'

'I never meant no harm, sir. I was just saying what everyone else will think.'

'Quite so, Cook,' Lil said hastily. 'But you do

see the problem, sir? Where will Dolly go while she waits for you to make other arrangements?'

'I can't imagine that Aunt Eloise will allow her to remain here.' Angel fished a hanky from her pocket and passed it to Dolly. 'But we'll sort something out, even if I have to smuggle you into my room and keep you hidden for a day or two.'

'Madam won't like that.' Meg moved towards the doorway. 'I can't be party to this. If Mrs Devane were to discover that I condoned such a thing I'd lose my position as well.'

'Just pretend that you know nothing.' Angel waited until Meg was out of earshot. 'I have an idea. There's Uncle Dolph's house in Naked Boy Court. Dolly knows it well enough and Baines looks after everything while the colonel is away. You could both stay there.'

Rupert frowned. 'That wouldn't do at all, Angel. I've only met Sir Adolphus on a couple of occasions and I wouldn't want to do anything to compromise Dolly's good name. I'll book into an inn for the night.'

'Sergeant Baines took a liking to Dolly,' Angel said thoughtfully. 'I'm certain he'd be only too pleased to help.'

Dolly wiped her eyes. 'Will you come too, Angel? I don't fancy sleeping in that creepy house without you there.'

'Of course I would come, if I could, but I think Aunt Eloise would object strongly and she might try to prevent you from going if she discovered your plans, Dolly. This must be done secretly and quickly.'

'I'll go with her,' Lil volunteered. 'No one could

make anything of it if Dolly has me as her chaperone, and I'll knock the daylights out of anyone who tries to stop us.' Lil flexed her muscles and clenched her jaw as if to demonstrate her undoubted powers.

'That's right,' Cook said approvingly. 'You go, Lil. Keep young Dolly safe until she's got the ring on her finger.'

Rupert placed a protective arm around Dolly's shoulders. 'No one will harm Dolly. I'll see to that, but you're most welcome to come with us, Lil. I want Dolly to be treated like the lady she is, and we'll call in at the vicarage on the way to London. I want us to be married in the village church with everyone welcome, and the landlord at The Plough will provide the wedding breakfast.'

Dolly broke away from him, her face ashen and her lips trembling. 'I can't do this to you, Rupert. Your father and sister will never forgive you, and they'll hate me.'

'You mustn't think like that,' Angel said quickly. 'Tell her it's not true, Captain Westwood.'

He wrapped his arms around Dolly, holding her close, and Cook uttered a sentimental sigh, which was echoed by Flossie, who hovered, quite forgotten, by the sink. Cook rounded on her. 'Get on with them dishes, you lazy slut. This has nothing to do with you.'

Rupert held up his hand. 'I want to thank you all, including you, young lady,' he smiled and winked at poor Flossie, who was herself close to tears. 'You've all been marvellous, and Dolly and I thank you from the bottom of our hearts.' He

181

held Dolly at arm's length, giving her a gentle shake. 'My father and Blanche will love you as I do, but it will take them time to get used to the idea that I've married, as they think, beneath me. It's a stupid, outdated notion and we will prove them wrong.'

'Well said, sir.' Lil slapped him on the back, almost knocking him over, but he regained his balance with a good-natured grin, and Cook led a round of applause.

Angel kissed Dolly on the cheek. 'Go and pack. Take my valise, the one that Sir Adolphus gave me. I have to go upstairs now and do Susannah's hair so I can't help you, but I'll cover for you, Lil. I'll say that you're unwell and have to remain in bed for a few days. I don't want to see you put out on the street.'

'No, I should hope not.' Lil grabbed Dolly by the hand. 'Come on, love. I can see that you're at sixes and sevens. I'll give you a hand and I'll pack a few necessities for myself.'

'Remember me to Sergeant Baines.' Angel left them making plans, but she could not help feeling a little envious. She tried not to think of it too often, but, although she loved the countryside, part of her missed the streets of London. She had happy memories of her childhood in Spitalfields, and she had done her best to forget her experience in the workhouse and how she came near to starvation before she met Dolly. She wished that she could accompany Dolly and Rupert on the first part of their great adventure, but that was impossible. For one thing, there was much to be done at home, and for another, she wanted to be there when Hector returned. She ran upstairs to Susannah's room.

Later that day, finding herself alone and with little left to do, Angel decided to take the ageing grey-hounds for a walk. The sudden turn of events had shaken everyone, even Humphrey, who had re-turned from London unexpectedly just as Rupert and Dolly, accompanied by Lil, left for the city in the Westwoods' carriage. Humphrey had pro-mised to say nothing to his mother or Susannah, but Angel knew that the affair would not remain a secret for long. Toby was still sleeping off the after-effects of over-indulgence the previous evening, but although he liked to pretend that he thought about nothing other than field sports, Angel knew that he had a keen intelligence and a probing mind that would one day make him a lawyer to be reckoned with. He would most certainly have something to say about his sister's humiliation.

She left the house wearing a straw bonnet to protect her face from the blazing summer sun, and a simple cotton print frock, and she set off with Juno and Thor at her heels, heading for the wide sweep of the marshes. She had walked these paths often and knew the safest way to negotiate the boggy ground, but that afternoon there was a sudden change in the weather. Clouds began to bubble up like giant puffballs, blotting out the sun. It started to rain, slowly at first, but then it seemed as though the skies had opened, throwing a downpour at her with physical violence. The warm ground steamed, creating a thick mist, which developed so suddenly that she became disorientated. Angel knew that she had come too far to make it home before the paths became waterlogged and dangerous, and the only thing to do was to keep going in what she hoped was the right direction. The dogs kept close to her, looking up with beseeching eyes as if pleading with her to stop the constant pounding of the rain on their sleek coats. She herself was soaked to the skin, her straw bonnet hung limply around her face and, to make matters worse, she was chilled to the bone. The rain eased a little, leaving a thick white mist in its place, and Angel had to test the ground before each step. A mistake could leave her stranded and sinking into the boggy morass, and the thudding of her heart was the only sound she could hear apart from the panting of the two dogs.

She was becoming exhausted and losing hope when she saw the faint grey outline of habitation not far ahead. The ground beneath her feet felt firmer and she quickened her pace until she came to a fence that separated the marsh from the market gardens. Her spirits soared as she recognised the cottage on the far side of the plot filled with lavender. The scent of it made her dizzy with anticipation as she opened the gate and let herself into the neatly kept area gardened by Jack Wicks. It felt like coming home and she hurried down the path to the back door.

'Mrs Wicks, are you there? It's me, Angel Winter. Can I come in?'

A moment later the door opened. 'Angel, is it really you?' Sally Wicks stared at her in disbelief.

'Come in, my dear. You're soaked to the skin and that pretty bonnet is all but ruined.'

An invitation had never sounded more tempting and Angel almost fell over the threshold. 'But what about the dogs, Mrs Wicks? They're very wet.'

'Bring them in too, poor creatures. Stumpy is getting old so he won't bother them. He tries to get about like he used to, but he's a bit arthriticky, poor old man.'

The kitchen was just as Angel remembered it from all those years ago. A fire burned in the range, which was most welcome even though it was midsummer, and Angel's clothes began to steam as she sat close to the hearth, sipping a cup of hot, sweet tea. Sally's hair was a little greyer and her hips were slightly wider, but her brown eyes still shone with kindness and her smile of welcome was genuine. She pulled up a chair and sat down beside Angel.

'We heard that you'd had a stroke of good fortune, my dear. It was the talk of the flower girls that you and Dolly had been adopted by a rich gentleman and taken to live in his mansion.'

'Good heavens,' Angel said, chuckling. 'That's unbelievable. It's not entirely true, but it's close enough. How on earth did they find out?'

'A girl called Maisie, who shared a room with you at Mother Jolly's, started the rumour.' Sally reached out to finger the material of Angel's print gown. 'That cost a bob or two; you must have fallen on your feet.'

Angel could see that Sally would not be satisfied until she knew everything and she described, as briefly as possible, all the events that led up to the present day. Sally listened with rapt attention, uttering oohs and aahs at suitable intervals.

'So that's the whole story,' Angel said, taking the opportunity to drink the remainder of her tea, which by now was tepid.

'Who would have thought that such a thing could happen? Marrying a handsome young man who will inherit a fortune sounds like a fairy tale for young Dolly, but what about you, dear? Will you have a happy ending with your young man?'

Startled, Angel covered her confusion by getting up to put her cup on the table. 'I haven't got a young man, Mrs Wicks.'

'Call me Sally, dear. We don't have to stand on ceremony here.' Sally cocked her head on one side, eyeing Angel curiously. 'I didn't mean to offend you, but the way you spoke of Captain Devane made me think there might be something between the two of you.'

Angel shook her head. 'I'm very fond of Hector, but I doubt if he's ever thought of me as a woman. I'm still a little girl to him.' Her cheeks burned and it was not just the heat from the fire that brought the colour to her face.

'I'm sorry, my dear. I won't pry into your affairs. It's none of my business, but I'd like to see you happy. You've had more than your share of ill fortune.'

Angel glanced out of the window as a ray of sunshine filtered through the small panes. 'It's stopped raining. I ought to start back for Grantley. It's a long walk and they'll be wondering what's happened to me.'

'Won't you stay for supper, dear? I know that Jack and Danny would love to see you. They'll be home any minute now.'

'I'd like to see Jack. He was very kind to me and it was because of the mistletoe that I met Sir Adolphus. I might not have had the courage to approach him if I hadn't been desperate to earn a few pennies.'

'As I recall it was Danny who took you back to St Giles with the mistletoe.'

'I'm not sure he enjoyed the experience,' Angel said, laughing. 'He didn't think much of me.'

Sally jumped to her feet at the sound of the door opening. 'Well, we'll see if he's changed his mind. That'll be them now.'

Stumpy raised himself from his blanket by the fire and staggered over to meet his master as Jack Wicks strode into the room bringing with him a gust of fresh air. Thor and Juno had been asleep but they jumped up and went over to him. Jack bent down to make a fuss of Stumpy.

'What have we here?' He patted the two greyhounds on their heads and his leathery skin creased into a broad grin as he caught sight of Angel. 'Why, if it isn't my little friend, all grown up.' He pushed his cap to the back of his balding head. 'Aren't you a fine young lady now?' He turned to his son as Danny walked into the kitchen. 'Look who's here, Dan, my boy. You remember Angel, don't you?'

Angel stood up and held out her hand. 'Mr Wicks, it's good to see you again.' She shot a wary glance at Danny. 'And you too, of course.'

Danny Wicks came to a halt, staring at her. He

187

was no longer the callow youth who had treated her with such disdain. He had matured into a good-looking fellow; tall and broad-shouldered, his face and arms tanned nut brown by exposure to the elements. He had inherited his father's even features and firm chin, and a look of his mother about the eyes. Altogether he was a personable young man and Angel found her prejudices melting in the warmth of his wide smile.

'It's good to see you again, Angel. I'm afraid I wasn't very nice to you when we last met.'

She nodded. 'I'm surprised you remember.'

'What's this I hear, Danny?' his mother said sternly. 'I can't believe you were unkind to a little girl.'

'I could have been nicer, Ma. But that was then. I'm grown up now and I apologise for my young self, Angel Winter.' He held out his hand and Angel took it in a warm clasp.

'It was a long time ago, Danny. I expect I was a bit of a pest.'

Jack took off his hat and threw it with an expert twist of his wrist so that it landed on a peg at the back of the door. 'We heard of your good fortune, Angel. If anyone deserved a stroke of good luck it's you.'

'I've just been telling Sally that selling mistletoe changed my life.' Angel turned to Danny with a smile. 'That was your doing, even if you didn't know it at the time.'

'Well, I'm glad I'm good for something.' Danny shrugged off his jacket. 'What's for supper, Ma? I'm starving.'

He sounded so much like Toby that Angel wanted to laugh, but she managed to keep a straight face. 'I mustn't intrude,' she said hastily. 'I'd love to stay and talk but I should start back over the marsh in case it rains again. I know the pathways well, but it's a different matter when the mist comes down.' Thor and Juno took their cue from her and went to stand by the back door, wagging their tails.

'Are you sure you won't stay for supper?' Sally lifted the lid on a saucepan and a savoury aroma wafted round the kitchen. 'There's plenty here.'

'Maybe another time, if you'll have me.' Angel made a move towards the doorway. 'By the way, Jack, I was very impressed by the amount of lavender you have grown.'

He was at her side in an instant. 'Let me show you round my plot. It's not huge, but I'm hoping to rent the one next to it when the present tenant retires. I can sell lavender all year round, green in summer and dried in winter.'

'I make small muslin bags and stuff them with the flower heads,' Sally said proudly. 'They fetch a good price on Jack's stall. If I could make more I could supply shops, but I do quite well as it is.'

'Yes, I remember you telling me that all those years ago.' Angel kissed Sally on the cheek. 'It's been lovely to see you, and I'll come again soon, if that's all right?'

'Yes, dear, please do, and you must stay longer next time.'

Jack opened the back door and stepped outside. Angel followed him with Danny close behind. A quick walk round the perimeter of the lavender beds revealed the extent of Jack's planting, and the scent filled her nostrils, bringing back some of the happier memories of Covent Garden.

'You've done so well,' she said admiringly. 'The plants look very healthy.'

'We keep them trimmed so that the stems don't become woody,' Jack said knowledgeably. 'We've done well enough for ourselves, I'm glad to say.' He shot a sideways glance at his son. 'But young Dan isn't interested in carrying on the trade. He has other ideas.'

'Don't start that again, Pa.' Danny slapped his father on the back. 'You love your plants but if we get a bad winter or a late frost it can ruin a whole crop. We need to expand and consider growing fruit and vegetables in greenhouses, like the toffs do, only on a more commercial basis.'

'Maybe, son, but that would take money we haven't got. It's not something I would even consider.'

Angel could see that an argument was about to ensue, and she did not want to become embroiled in a family squabble. 'I could stay here all day, but I really must go on my way.' She called the dogs to her side. 'It's been lovely seeing you all after such a long time.'

Jack nodded and smiled. 'You must come again, if you can, but we understand that your life is different now. You're a young lady and you belong at the big house. I'm glad for you, Angel.'

'Just because I live at Grantley Park doesn't mean that I'm a different person, Jack.'

'I think you'll find it does make a difference,' Jack said gently. 'We're plain and ordinary people, and I dare say your poor ma was a lady, who found herself in trouble. You never were a common girl, Angel.'

'I try not to think about it.'

'I'll set you on the right path,' Danny said. 'Let's see if Stumpy can outrun your hounds.'

The suggestion was so ridiculous that it brought a smile to Angel's face, banishing the sad thoughts about the mother she would never know. 'All right, but I don't want to keep you from your meal.'

'Don't worry about that. Ma will keep me a plateful. She won't let me go without.'

'Goodbye, Angel. Come again very soon and we'll talk about the bad old days,' Jack said, grinning. 'See her safely home, Dan. The ground will be even more treacherous than usual after that rainstorm.'

With the dogs hobbling on ahead, Angel and Danny set off across the marsh. The sun was low in the sky and Angel had not realised how long she had spent in the cottage, but it must have been several hours as her clothes were bone dry. Her bonnet was past repair and she had not bothered to put it on, but had tied the ribbon around her belt and it hung at her waist.

'You have changed a lot,' Danny said gravely. 'But for the better. You were a spiky little thing.'

'And you thought you were so much better than me.'

'I've apologised for that.'

'Yes, you have, and I expect I was a bit of a nuisance, but I've always loved mistletoe. It grows freely on the apple trees in our orchard.'

He shot her a sideways glance. 'You have an orchard?'

'No, of course I don't. It belongs to Sir Adolphus. I just live there, Danny. I'm part of the
family.'

'Are you?'

'Do you doubt it?'

He thought for a moment. 'I can't say I've had
much to do with the nobs, but it seems to me
that they look down on the rest of us. I hope they
do treat you like family, but when it comes down
to it I reckon they're all the same. They stick
together like burrs, and if things went wrong you
might find yourself out on your ear.'

'Even close families fall out,' Angel countered.
'It sounded earlier as though you'll be leaving
your father to carry on his trade without you.'

'I don't want to hawk mistletoe and lavender
round the city streets for a living. I've heard that
people in the Channel Islands are beginning to
cultivate tomato plants in greenhouses heated by
steam boilers. I don't see why we can't do that
here.'

'It sounds like a wonderful idea, but wouldn't it
cost a great deal of money to set up?'

'You sound like my pa,' Danny said ruefully. 'I
know it would, but I intend to go into it further.
I'm sure it's the way to progress.' He took Angel
by the arm as they reached a particularly soggy
patch of ground. 'A storm like the one we had
earlier can do no end of damage.'

Angel allowed him to guide her to a safer path.
'You don't have to convince me, Danny. I can see
your point, but it's your father you have to win
over, not me.'

'I'm sorry. I get on my high horse sometimes,

192

and I'm not a patient man.'

She laughed. 'You don't have to remind me of that, Danny Wicks. You were a horrible boy.'

'And you were a suspicious little girl,' he said, chuckling.

Angel glanced over her shoulder at the sound of hoofbeats thudding on the turf behind them. 'There's someone coming.'

'Only a madman would ride across the marsh,' Danny said angrily.

'Or someone who knew it like the back of his hand.' Angel shielded her eyes from the sun. 'It's Hector.'

'Who is he?'

'Captain Devane. He's the head of the household while Uncle Dolph is abroad.'

They stopped, standing very still as Hector drew his horse to a halt. 'Angel, what are you doing out on the marsh at this time of evening? It will be dark soon.'

'Not for an hour or so,' Danny said with a belligerent lift of his chin. 'She's with me and I know the safe pathways.'

'And who are you?' Hector demanded, scowling.

'This is an old friend of mine, Hector. Danny's parents were very good to me when I was a child.'

'Well, I suppose I should thank you for looking after Angel,' Hector said grudgingly. 'But I'll take her home, and you'd best find your way back across the marsh while there's still some daylight.' He leaned over, holding out his hand. 'Hannibal can take two of us, Angel.'

'You'll do better on horseback.' Without waiting for a reply Danny hoisted Angel onto the saddle. 'Come and visit us again.' He saluted and backed away.

'I could have walked,' Angel said crossly as Hector put his arms around her to take up the reins.

'Walk on.' Hector clicked his tongue against his teeth and Hannibal moved forward, picking his way across the boggy ground.

'And you were very rude to Danny. He was doing me a favour, although I could easily have found my way home.' Angel turned her head to see Danny standing where they had left him.

'I'm sorry if I appeared uncivil,' Hector said reluctantly. 'But the fellow looked as though he was being overfamiliar, and you were alone with him. What do you think my mother would say to that?'

'You are not your mother, Hector, and I am not your sister. I'm sorry if my behaviour offends your code of conduct, but what do you expect of the girl snatched from the streets?' She could feel his warm breath on her cheek, and the familiar scent of him made her feel ridiculously safe.

'I refuse to be drawn into an argument. I've said I'm sorry, and there's an end to it. I've got more things to worry about than offending a fellow I don't know and will probably never see again.'

She glanced at his stern profile, and relented. 'What's wrong, Hector? Why did you have to dash off to London in such a hurry?'

'It will wait until we're all together, Angel. I really don't want to go through it over and over again, but it's not good news. To put it simply, our affairs are a mess and, what's worse, I've been recalled to duty and will be leaving tomorrow, as will Westwood. I don't know what Susannah will make of that.'

Angel leaned her head against his shoulder. 'This is awful. Coming on top of everything else, I don't know how your mama will cope.'

'What do you mean? What can have gone wrong in the few hours since I left the house this morning?'

Chapter Eleven

'I suppose you'll find out soon enough,' Angel said with a sigh. 'Rupert and Dolly are in love. He's going to marry her by special licence.'

'The bastard. I'm sorry, Angel, but I'd like to wring his cheating neck. Does Susannah know?'

'Yes, well, in part. Your mother took her to Westwood Hall this morning. I think she planned to tell Sir Eugene, although I'm not sure what good that would do because Rupert and Dolly have gone to London taking Lil with them as chaperone. Dolly and Lil are going to stay at your uncle's house until Rupert gets the licence.'

'The devil they are.'

'Aunt Eloise told Dolly to leave immediately, and I didn't think you'd mind if she went to Naked Boy Court,' Angel said hastily. 'I know that she's just a servant in your eyes, but she's my friend.'

'If Westwood wants to ruin his career, that's his

195

business, but I do care about my sister. If he's been leading her on I'll have more than a few words to say to him.'

They rode on in silence, with only the soft thud of Hannibal's hoofs on the boggy turf and the panting of the dogs as they trotted along at their side, keeping them company. Dusk had fallen by the time they reached Grantley and Hector dismounted first. He lifted Angel to the ground and handed the reins to a groom, who had come running from the stables.

The front door was open and a shaft of light spilled onto the stone steps. Eloise was there to meet them, pale-faced and frowning. 'Where have you been, Angel? I thought you had run away with that wretched servant girl.'

'I went for a walk, Aunt Eloise, and got caught in the rain.'

Hector kissed his mother on the forehead. 'She's safe and well, Mama. But I need to talk to you and the rest of the family. I've something to say that concerns us all.'

Eloise stared at him wide-eyed. 'That sounds ominous, Hector. What is it?'

'I ought to go and change.' Angel made a move towards the staircase, but Hector caught her by the hand.

'No, this concerns you as much as anybody.' He turned to his mother. 'Are the others in the drawing room?'

'Yes, and we didn't wait dinner for you because I had no idea whether or not you would return this evening.' Eloise shot a sideways glance at Angel. 'As for you, miss, I'll thank you not to go wandering off like that. I was about to send out a search party. My brother would never forgive me if I allowed anything to happen to you.'

The meaning of this was clear, but Angel was used to Mrs Devane's barbed comments, and she had always known that her adoptive aunt merely tolerated her presence. Eloise headed for the drawing room with her head held high and her silk taffeta petticoats swishing as she glided across the highly polished floor.

In the drawing room Toby and Hector were sprawled in chairs on either side of a crackling log fire. Even though it was high summer, a chill always seemed to rise from the marshes by late evening and a fire was more than welcome. Susannah perched on the window seat, gazing out into the twilit garden. She turned her head to give Angel a cursory glance and then looked away.

'Hector has something momentous to tell us,' Eloise said flippantly. 'After the disasters of today I can't think what could be worse.' She sank down on the sofa and patted the empty space at her side.

'Take a seat, Hector. Don't keep us in suspense.'

Toby took a sip from the glass he cupped in his hand. 'I hope our spirit merchant hasn't cut off our credit. This is an excellent Armagnac.'

'Is that all you can think about?' Hector demanded angrily. 'I can tell you now that the account has been closed. I settled it today, as well as the one you had with Fortnum's, Mama. We can no longer afford to live in the same style.'

'What are you talking about, Hector?' Eloise

197

unfurled her fan and used it vigorously. 'Is this some kind of joke?'

'It's worse than any of mine,' Humphrey said, chuckling. 'Come on, Hector, you'll be telling us next that we have to sell Grantley.'

Susannah leaped to her feet. 'Stop it, all of you. My heart has been broken and all you can do is talk about food and wine and make silly jokes.'

'Don't be upset, Sukey,' Angel said gently. 'You wouldn't have been happy with Rupert.'

'How do you know that?' Susannah's eyes flashed and her lips tightened. 'It's all your fault for bringing that harlot into our house. See what happens when you try to be kind to the poor and needy – they turn on you and ruin your life.'

'That's enough.' Hector's sharp reprimand silenced Susannah and she sank back on her seat, pushing Angel away as she tried to comfort her.

'Tell us what you have to say, Hector,' Eloise said wearily. 'It's been a long and trying day and I feel one of my heads coming on.'

'To put it bluntly, we're in financial difficulties.' Hector picked up a decanter and poured a measure of brandy into a glass. He raised it to his lips and took a sip. 'Luxuries like this will have to be forfeited. We'll have to manage with fewer servants and cut down on the outdoor staff as well.'

'Why, darling?' Eloise asked anxiously. 'What has brought about this ghastly state of affairs? Surely there's been some mistake?'

'No, Mama. I'm afraid it's even worse. Uncle Dolph made some investments that have failed spectacularly. He'd taken out a large mortgage on Grantley in order to purchase the shares and it

198

has to be repaid, which might mean putting the whole estate and the house up for sale.'

Toby dropped his glass and it shattered on the brass fender. 'There must be something we can do, Hector.'

'I spent the day with our solicitor, and he can't see any other way out of this mess.'

'Surely not, darling?' Eloise clutched her hands to her cheeks. 'Why weren't we told of this sooner? I can't believe that Freddie Beauchamp would let us down so badly.'

'Mr Beauchamp died two months ago, Mama. Apparently a letter was sent to Uncle Dolph informing him that Beauchamp's partner was to take over from him.'

'It must be on his desk. I never open Dolph's post. It wouldn't be seemly for me to pry into his affairs.' Eloise closed her eyes and leaned back against the silk cushions. 'This is a nightmare. I'll wake up in a minute and find it was just a bad dream.'

'Who is the new man?' Toby asked anxiously. 'Do we know him, Hector?'

'He's the senior solicitor now. His name is Galloway.'

Angel's breath caught in her throat as a vision of the workhouse flashed before her eyes. 'Geoffrey Galloway?'

'Yes, I believe so.' Hector gave her a searching look. 'Do you know him, Angel?'

'How would a girl from the street know a solicitor?' Susannah demanded bitterly.

'Allow her to answer.' Hector lowered his voice. 'Are you all right, Angel? You look as though you've seen a ghost.'

'If it's the same Geoffrey Galloway, he's the man who separated me from Aunt Cordelia and placed me in the workhouse.' The words came out in a horrified whisper.

'Don't be silly, Angel,' Eloise said crossly. 'I'm sure our solicitor is above reproach.'

'I must say I didn't take to the man.' Hector downed his drink in one gulp. 'But there's not much I can do in the short time I have left at home. The fact remains that we are virtually bankrupt, and I have to return to my regiment tomorrow. I wish I could stay and see you through this difficult time, but I'd be shot as a deserter if I didn't return to Natal Province.'

Susannah rose to her feet with a gasp of annoyance. 'That's right, Hector. Do what you always do and run away. Go back to playing soldiers and leave us to face losing our home and everything we treasure.' She fled from the room, slamming the door behind her.

'I don't always agree with Susannah when she has a tantrum,' Eloise said, sighing heavily, 'but this time I do think you could put us first, Hector. I'm sure the army would understand.'

Hector opened his mouth to reply but Toby spoke first. 'I'm afraid he's right, Mama. Hector is a professional soldier and he has to leave, but perhaps I can do something.'

'I'd help if I could,' Humphrey said sadly. 'But I wouldn't know where to start.'

'We can all do something.' Angel had kept quiet until now, but she was not going to stand by and say nothing when Hector was being unfairly criticised. 'I don't know much about the army, but I do know that Hector would stay if it were possible. I'll do anything I can to save Grantley Park. You took me in, Aunt Eloise, even though you didn't want to, and for that I'll always be grateful. You are my family and I love you all.'

Hector took her hand in his and his dark eyes shone with gratitude. 'Thank you, Angel. I've arranged for my salary to be paid into Mama's account at the bank, and with a bit of luck we might be able to persuade our creditors to give us more time. The unrest in Natal Province can't go on for ever, and might yet be resolved with diplomacy, and then I'll return and resign my commission.' He turned to his mother with a pleading look. 'If you can keep going until then, putting the necessary economies in place, I'll give up my career in the military and devote myself to running the estate. We might have to sell some of the land, but I hope we can keep Grantley.'

'I'll leave Rugby,' Humphrey said eagerly. 'I'll stay at home and work in the stables or in the garden.'

Hector nodded. 'It might come to that, old chap. Galloway is coming here tomorrow to go over the figures with me.' He glanced at Toby. 'There's no question of you leaving Oxford before you take your finals, and we might need a good solicitor if this chap Galloway is the same person who treated Angel so despicably.'

'I'd take great pleasure in suing the bounder.' Toby raised himself from his chair and went to pour himself another drink. 'Might as well enjoy the stuff if we're going to forgo it in the future. I suppose my allowance will dry up, Hector?'

'You'll just have to get used to frugal living,' Hector said with a wry smile. 'Or you could find gainful employment. I believe others less fortunate than we are have to work their way through university.'

Eloise rose to her feet. 'Stop it, both of you. I feel quite unwell and I'm going to my room. I trust you to sort matters out tomorrow, Hector.'

He hurried to open the door for her. 'Good night, Mama. Try not to worry. I'm sure we'll find a solution.' He turned to Angel with an encouraging smile. 'I don't know about you, but I'm starving. I haven't eaten all day.'

'I'm hungry too. I'll go to the kitchen and find something for us to eat.'

'You could try ringing the bell,' Toby said lazily. 'We have servants to do that, Angel, or have you forgotten?'

'Lil and Dolly are in London, and Cook and Flossie will have retired for the evening. I'm not helpless like you boys.'

'Quite right,' Hector said approvingly. 'I'll come with you, Angel.'

'I'd be surprised if you know where to find the kitchen,' Angel said over her shoulder.

'That's where you're mistaken. I used to know when Cook had made jam tarts or mince pies and I'd hang around the kitchen until she relented and gave me one or two. I'm used to bivouacking, so I'm not entirely helpless.'

'We'll see.'

Half an hour later Angel and Hector were seated

at the kitchen table finishing their meal of fried ham and eggs. 'That was excellent. Thank you, Angel.' Hector sat back in his chair, sipping a cup of tea. 'Who taught you to cook?'

She replaced her knife and fork, smiling. 'There's not much to frying a couple of slices of ham and adding some eggs to the pan, but like you, I used to loiter in Aunt Cordelia's kitchen and watch Cook, although she had no time for children. But Lil would always stand up for me and Cook was scared of Lil.' She laughed. 'Who wouldn't be? If you'd ever seen Lil in a temper you'd know what I mean.'

'Lil Heavitree would make a wonderful sergeant major. She'd put the fear of God into the enemy as well as the troops.'

'But she's a good friend, and she's taking care of Dolly. You don't mind them using your house in London, do you?'

'It belongs to Uncle Dolph, but he's far away and you said they'll be returning in a couple of days' time, so no harm done.'

Angel toyed with her knife, avoiding meeting his gaze. 'If your Mr Galloway is the same man who abandoned me in the workhouse, what will you do?'

'Describe the man you knew.'

'He was tall and thin. He was going bald but he had mutton-chop whiskers and a bushy ginger moustache and a little beard. I used to think he was nice when I was small because he always had a poke of sweets in his pocket for me, but he changed completely after he had sent Aunt Cordelia to live with his sister.'

Hector frowned as he replaced his cup on its saucer. 'Then it must be the same fellow. His whiskers are grey now, but your description fits him perfectly.'

'What will you do?'

'Are you willing to face him again?'

'Yes, most certainly.'

'Then leave him to me, Angel. I won't allow anyone to hurt you ever again.'

Geoffrey Galloway rose from the leather chair in Hector's study as Angel entered the room, and his oily smile was replaced by a shocked expression that might, in any other circumstances, have made her laugh.

'Yes, this is the man, Hector,' she said evenly. Her heart was pounding and memories of their last encounter threatened to overwhelm her, but somehow she managed to remain poised and calm. 'This is the person who lied to my aunt and left me in the workhouse.'

Galloway's cheeks flooded with colour, which faded instantly, leaving him pallid and sickly-looking. 'You misread my motives, Angel, my dear. I left you in the care of the workhouse master and his good wife, because I was living in bachelor rooms with no facilities to look after a young girl. I fully intended to take you to the country...'

'I don't believe you,' Angel said hotly. 'You promised Aunt Cordelia that you would look after me.'

'You must understand that Mr Wilding's demise was sudden and unexpected,' Galloway said cautiously. 'We were all thrown into a state of confusion.'

'I've heard enough.' Hector stood up and walked slowly round his desk to face Galloway. 'I don't want you handling my family's affairs.'

Galloway made a swift recovery. 'It's not your decision, Captain Devane. My firm represents Sir Adolphus and only he can terminate our agreement. I am now senior partner in the business, so I fear you will have to deal with me. The alternative is to allow the creditors to foreclose on the mortgage.'

Angel stifled a gasp of dismay, but Hector's expression remained impassive. He might as well have been carved from marble for all the emotion he showed.

'You are a crook and a mountebank, Galloway. My uncle will hear of this when I return to Natal Province. In the meantime I expect you to conduct the matter befitting a man of your profession. If you fail me I'll report you to the Law Institution or whatever the governing body of lawyers and barristers is now called.'

Galloway smirked visibly and resumed his seat. 'I'm glad you see it my way, Captain Devane.' He shot a sideway glance at Angel. 'Am I to infer that this young woman is part of your household?'

Angel clenched her hands at her sides. She was not a violent person, but at this moment it would have given her great satisfaction to wipe the stupid smile from Galloway's face with a sharp slap.

'Miss Winter was discovered barefoot in the snow, selling mistletoe in an attempt to keep herself from starvation. My uncle brought her here on Christmas Eve seven years ago, and she is a much-loved member of our family. You will treat her with the respect she deserves.'

'You realise, of course, that she was a foundling, abandoned in Angel Alley, Whitechapel as an infant, her parentage unknown.'

'That is none of your business, Galloway,' Hector said sharply. 'Miss Winter's background has nothing to do with our present dilemma, and you might find yourself dealing with her when my mother is indisposed, as is all too often the case. My brothers will be returning to Rugby School and Oxford at the beginning of the Advent and Michaelmas terms, but until then Tobias will be here to help and give advice. He is studying law, so he knows what he is talking about.'

'Really, Captain Devane, you seem to think I am an out-and-out villain, but you are mistaken. What happened in the past is now history, and I have earned my position through diligence and the goodwill of my clients. You have nothing to fear.' Galloway turned to Angel with a smile that did not reach his eyes. 'I am at your service, Miss Winter. I hope that misunderstandings will be forgotten and we will get along splendidly. My one aim will be to save Grantley Park from ruin, I can assure you of that.'

'I certainly hope so, Mr Galloway,' Angel said coldly.

'I second that.' Hector went to sit behind his desk, resting his elbows on the leather top. 'Now then, Galloway, what is your plan of action? Remember that I have only a short time at home and then I leave for Natal Province.'

'I have not forgotten, Captain. With that in mind I have arranged to meet with your creditors this afternoon.' He produced a sheaf of papers from a document case and laid them in front of Hector. 'If you read and approve of these terms upon which repayment would be made, you must sign them and I will take them with me, but I have to leave within the hour.'

Angel went to stand behind Hector, making an attempt to read the documents over his shoulder, but she found the legal terms daunting and it seemed unnecessarily complicated. Galloway sat on the edge of his chair, smirking, but Angel concentrated on the papers, avoiding his gaze.

'Is this the best you could do?' Hector demanded, raising his head to glare at Galloway. 'Are these really the most favourable terms you could achieve?'

'Are you doubting my probity, Captain Devane? I have worked tirelessly in conjunction with the creditors' lawyers to produce an agreement that is fair to both parties.'

'Then your idea of fairness does not equate with mine,' Hector said angrily. 'The amount they expect to receive each month is extortionate.'

'But, Captain Devane,' Galloway said silkily, 'your uncle lost a great deal of money, and he put the estate up as equity. You can hardly blame the creditors for demanding a just return. Perhaps we should consider the benefits of selling the land, which might save Grantley, although I can't be certain of that.'

Hector's eyes narrowed. 'What are you getting

out of this, Galloway?'

'I'm deeply offended that you should even think that of me, sir. I am now the senior partner in the firm, and I am highly respected. Don't believe everything that Miss Winter tells you.'

'That's enough, Galloway. If matters weren't desperate I would throw you out for making a remark like that.'

'I apologise, of course. Perhaps I spoke out of turn, but I urge you to sign the agreement, Captain Devane. Otherwise I fear that you will lose everything.'

Hector hesitated for a moment, gazing down at the document, his brow knitted in a frown. 'At any other time I would fight this.' He sighed heavily. 'But I really have no choice.' Picking up a pen, he dipped it in the inkwell, signing his name with a flourish. 'Take it to them and be damned.'

Galloway stood up, holding out his hand. 'It was the only way. You can rest assured that your interests will be well looked after in your absence.' He shot a sideways glance at Angel. 'You will find me a valuable ally, Miss Winter, but a dangerous enemy.' He snatched up the documents and placed them in his tooled leather case. 'Good day to you both.'

'I still don't trust him,' Angel said as the door closed on him. 'And he threatened me. Did you hear that, Hector?'

'Yes, but he won't get away with it for long. When I see Uncle Dolph I'll tell him everything that has transpired in his absence. Galloway will find himself in serious trouble if he steps out of line, and we'll be changing solicitors at the first possible opportunity.' He sat back in his chair, steepling his fingers. 'I'm so sorry to leave you with all this, Angel. I realise that the burden will fall on your shoulders and that you'll be facing an uphill struggle.'

'You know that I'll do anything I can to save Grantley. I'll take in washing, if necessary.'

Hector's troubled expression was wiped away by a smile. 'Can you imagine my mother's face if that were to happen?'

'It would be a picture,' Angel said, laughing. 'But I meant what I said.'

'I know you did, and I love you for it.'

To Angel's relief, Hector rose to his feet and went to look out of the window. His words had made her heartbeat quicken and she knew she was blushing. There was nothing remotely lover-like in his tone, but it was the first time he had ever spoken to her so fondly. His next words, however, brought her back to earth with a thud.

'Damnation. It's Westwood. He's got a confounded nerve.' Hector rushed to the door. 'I'll have a few words to say to him.'

Angel ran after him. 'He's trying to do the right thing, Hector. Give him a chance.'

'Keep out of this, Angel. I won't stand for anyone taking advantage of my sister.' He came to a halt in the entrance hall, turning to face Angel. 'He came here to see Susannah, but his intention all along was to meet secretly with one of our servants. Do you deny that?'

'No, of course not, and he knows it was wrong, but–!'

'But, nothing. Don't interfere, Angel. This is my

209

business.' He wrenched the front door open and stepped outside.

Despite his warning Angel followed him, but she kept her distance as Rupert drew his horse to a halt and leaped from the saddle.

'I know what you must think of me, Devane, but I've come to offer my apologies for the way I've behaved.'

'It's my sister who is the injured party,' Hector said stiffly. 'I think Susannah deserves an explanation and an apology. You abused our hospitality, and you led my sister to believe that you were calling on her when all along you were courting one of our servants. It was underhand, Westwood. Underhand and unworthy of you.'

Rupert bowed his head. 'I accept all that, and I am truly sorry, but we can't always pick and choose when it comes to matters of the heart.'

'Oh, come on,' Hector said scornfully. 'You sound like a character out of one of my sister's novelettes. My brothers and I used to tease her about them when we were younger.'

'I'm not making any excuses for falling in love, Devane.'

'Dolly Chapman is a servant. How do you think she'll be received by the other officers' wives? She is likely to find herself ostracised.'

'Hector.' Angel had heard enough. She hurried to his side and laid her hand on his arm. 'That's not fair and it's unworthy of you. Dolly is a sweet girl and she'll make a loving wife. She might not have the benefit of a well-to-do family and a good education, but she is willing to learn and she is better able to follow the drum than many a gently bred girl.'

Rupert took her hand and raised it to his lips. 'Thank you, Angel. Never was a truer word spoken.' He turned to Hector, his smile fading. 'Say what you like about me, but don't insult my bride-to-be.'

'Perhaps I overstated my case, but she won't have an easy time, Westwood.'

'I'll be there to love and protect her, and the main reason for my calling on you today is to invite you all to the wedding this afternoon. I bought a special licence and the vicar is happy to oblige. I'm afraid there won't be a wedding breakfast because there wasn't the time to arrange one, but you are all welcome to attend the church.'

'Thank you,' Hector said stiffly.

'Will your family be there?' Angel asked. 'And who will give Dolly away?'

Rupert's grey eyes darkened. 'I was hoping my father would oblige, but he's decided to stay away.'

'But surely Blanche will be there?'

He shook his head. 'Blanche has also declined. She has taken Susannah's side, and I suppose it's only natural.'

Angel tugged at Hector's sleeve. 'You're the head of the house, Hector, and Dolly was part of Grantley until yesterday.'

'What are you suggesting?' Hector's grim expression was not encouraging but Angel was determined to give Dolly a day to remember.

'Rupert is a fellow officer, and you will be leaving later today. Surely the past could be put behind you, if only for a day. Will you give Dolly away, Hector?'

211

Chapter Twelve

Wearing one of Angel's silk taffeta afternoon gowns in a delicate shade of green that made her eyes sparkle like emeralds, Dolly walked up the aisle on Hector's arm. Angel had had to use all her powers of persuasion, but eventually he had agreed to give Dolly away, and he looked impressive in his dress uniform, as did Rupert, who was waiting at the altar. The village church was eerily silent as there was no music to herald the bride's arrival. Miss Creedy, who ran the village shop and post office, usually officiated as the organist but there had not been enough time to secure her services, and the choirboys were out in the cornfields, helping with the harvest.

Despite the fact that the wedding arrangements had been rushed, Angel could have wished that there were more well-wishers to see Dolly and Rupert take their vows. Humphrey was the only member of the family, apart from Hector, who had felt able to attend. When Eloise learned of their plans she had sent for the carriage and taken Susannah to Westwood Hall. No doubt they would be taking tea with Blanche and Sir Eugene, who had also chosen to ignore their invitations, and poor Dolly would be the object of their combined anger. Even so, Blanche could have made an effort, Angel thought, angrily. Rupert was her brother and his only crime was to have fallen in love with a girl who was not from his social class. The couple were genuinely in love, it was apparent for all to see as Dolly joined Rupert at the altar.

There were sentimental sighs from Lil, Cook and Meg, who were in the pew behind Angel and Humphrey. Angel stepped forward to take the posy of moss roses from Dolly as the vicar intoned the words of the marriage ceremony. Having done his bit, Hector came to sit beside her. She glanced at his strong profile and a sudden shiver ran down her spine. He would be leaving that afternoon, as would Rupert, and they would be embarking on a long sea voyage that would take them to South Africa and a war that seemed inevitable, although far removed from their daily lives. Angel took a deep breath and forced herself to concentrate on the bride and groom as the vicar announced that they were now man and wife.

Outside the church Dolly and her new husband were showered with scented rose petals, which Angel and Meg had collected from the garden that morning. Cook wiped away tears, and Lil blew her nose loudly, while Meg gazed, misty-eyed at Dolly.

'You are such a beautiful bride.'

'It'll be your turn next, Meg, and I'll dance at your wedding.' Dolly's face glowed with happiness as she hugged her friend. 'Thank you all for coming.'

'Yes,' Rupert added, shaking hands. 'Thank you from me, too. I promise to look after Dolly, and we'll come and see you when we return from Natal Province.'

Cook and Meg both curtsied, but when Lil attempted to copy them she almost toppled over and she righted herself with a grunt and a lop-sided grin. 'Never was much good at being lady-like.'

Humphrey gave Dolly a hug. 'I hope you'll both be very happy, and come home safely.'

'Congratulations.' Hector shook Rupert's hand. He turned to Dolly with a genuine smile. 'I hope you'll be very happy.'

'Thanks, Devane,' Rupert said, slipping his arm around his wife's tiny waist. 'I appreciate what you've done for us.'

Angel glanced at Lil, Cook and Meg, who were huddled together with expectant looks on their faces. 'Would you like to come back to the house for some light refreshments?'

Rupert shook his head. 'You'll have to excuse us, I'm afraid. We're leaving for Southampton as soon as we've changed into more suitable clothes. What about you, Devane?'

'I'll be off soon, too. I'll probably see you at Waterloo Bridge station.'

'I've hired a carriage. You are most welcome to come with us.'

A wry smile curved Hector's lips. 'I don't think I'll play gooseberry to the newlyweds, but thank you, Westwood.' He bowed to Dolly. 'Mrs West-wood.'

Dolly stared at him and then burst into laughter. 'That sounds ever so strange. Mrs Westwood. Who would have thought it?'

That was Angel's cue to rush over and give her a hug, closely followed by Lil and the others. Rupert had to prise his bride from their embraces, and they walked arm in arm to the inn, which was only a few paces away.

Humphrey slapped his brother on the back. 'I'll miss you, Hector. I wish I was coming with you.'

'No, you don't, Humpty. It's not going to be a picnic over there, and as for taking a woman to face camp life, it's not what I would wish for someone I loved.' Hector proffered his arm to Angel. 'I'm going home to finish packing, and I'd like to go over a few things with you before I leave.'

'Yes, of course.' Angel tucked her hand through the crook of his arm. 'You can trust me to do the best for Grantley.'

'I know I can. I'm depending on you to keep everything together, Angel.'

'I'll leave Rugby and stay here to help run things,' Humphrey said, falling into step beside them.

'It might come to that, old chap. It all depends on how much extra Uncle Dolph can contribute to the repayments, and I won't know that until I've had a chance to talk it over with him. His old lawyer knew the family business inside and out, but I don't trust Galloway, and neither does Angel. I want you to do all you can to help her, Humpty, and I'm going to say the same to Toby.'

'I'll do my best,' Humphrey said seriously. 'Mama has no head for business and I'd as soon put a cat in charge of things as trust Susannah. She'd spend every last penny on new gowns and shoes, if she had a chance.'

'I don't think that's fair.' Angel tried to sound severe, but she could not help laughing – it was exactly what Susannah would do.

The sun was shining and the air was filled with birdsong and the intoxicating scent of summer flowers and warm grass. It was a beautiful day for a wedding, and, as Angel walked homewards, arm in arm with the brothers, she realised she had never felt happier than at this moment, but she dare not think about what was to come; her near-perfect life was being threatened by outside forces. She would have to be strong and she could not allow herself to think of what could befall Hector when he returned to Natal Province. The possibility that he might not return hovered above them like a bird of ill omen, and she resolutely pushed it to the back of her mind. Besides which, she had her old enemy to contend with now. She did not trust Galloway an inch, and she would fight him to the last drop of her own blood if it meant she could keep Grantley for the family she had come to think of as her own.

'Why so silent?' Hector asked as they reached the tall wrought-iron gates that protected Grantley from the outside world. 'I did what you asked and gave your young friend away, even though my mother and sister will never forgive me.'

'Don't tease her.' Humphrey gave his brother a playful punch in the ribs. 'Mama and Sukey never remember anything for more than five minutes, unless it's the latest Paris fashion or the prospect of a ball.'

Hector feinted with his right, as if sparring with his brother. 'Don't let either of them hear you saying things like that, brat.'

'Don't squabble,' Angel said, trying hard not to giggle. Their boyish behaviour came as a relief after the tensions of the past couple of days. 'I have a better idea. Let's go indoors and raise a toast to the happy couple. I think there might be a dusty bottle of champagne left in the cellar.' She wanted to hold on to this moment for ever, but she knew that it would pass quickly and then Hector would be off to war, while the future of Grantley was hanging in the balance.

Eloise and Susannah returned in time to change for dinner and Angel met them in the entrance hall.

'Hector left an hour ago,' she said bluntly. 'Didn't you think it important to say goodbye?'

'Don't be impertinent.' Eloise thrust her parasol into Angel's hand. 'I suppose the girl has left and we're without a chambermaid.'

'Dolly and Rupert were married this afternoon.' Angel controlled her temper, although she was seething inwardly. 'It was a pity his father and sister didn't think fit to attend.'

Susannah tossed her parasol onto a chair. 'I suppose the gardener or one of the grooms gave the little trollop away.'

Angel glanced over her shoulder at the sound of footsteps as Humphrey appeared from the direction of the drawing room, coming to a halt at her side.

'As a matter of fact it was Hector who gave the bride away,' he said casually, 'and a fine job he did of it, too.'

217

Eloise sniffed the air suspiciously. 'Have you been drinking, Humphrey?'

'I had a glass or two of champagne to toast the happy couple and to wish Hector *bon voyage*, if that's appropriate for a man who might be facing war.' Humphrey curled his fingers around Angel's hand. 'You could have come home in time to see him off. We might never see him again.'

'Don't say things like that.' Susannah's bottom lip trembled. 'Haven't I suffered enough without you adding to my troubles?'

'You always were selfish, but I thought better of you, Mama.' Humphrey strolled off, leaving his mother and sister open-mouthed.

'Come back here this minute, Humphrey,' Eloise cried, stamping her foot like a spoiled child. 'You cannot speak to your mama in that tone of voice. I won't stand for it.'

Susannah placed her arm around her mother's shoulders. 'This is all your fault, Angel. You encouraged that girl to think she was our equal, and now Humphrey is being objectionable and you've allowed him to drink. Shame on you.'

Angel could see that neither of them was open to reason and she turned away. 'Dinner will be served in an hour,' she said coldly.

'Susannah, help me upstairs.' Eloise leaned heavily on her daughter's arm. 'And as we have no chambermaid you will have to bring hot water to my room, Angel Winter. You will work to pay back the hospitality that has been lavished upon you since my brother foisted you on us.'

'That's not very fair, Mama,' Susannah protested as she helped her mother to ascend the

218

wide staircase. 'It's not Angel's fault that we have to make economies.'

'Is it not? It's strange how bad luck has come upon us since her arrival. We were a happy and united family until she was forced upon us.'

Angel did not wait to hear Susannah's answer. She sighed, but she was used to Aunt Eloise's barbs, and in that respect nothing much had changed. She made her way to the kitchen to ask Lil to wait on table that evening, and she sent Flossie upstairs with a pitcher of hot water.

'I can't wait on table,' Lil said stonily. 'You know how clumsy I am, Angel. Like as not I'll tip soup into Madam's lap.'

'Serve her right.' Cook slammed a lump of dough down on the table top. 'I know I shouldn't say it of my betters, but the housekeeping has gone awry since Mrs Kerslake retired and no replacement was found. How can a house of this size be managed with just the three of us? It's impossible, that's what it is.'

'We know there's something going on, Angel.' Lil gave her a searching look. 'Out with it. Tell us the worst, and don't pretend that things are normal, because I saw that villain, Galloway. What did he want here?'

Angel could see that they were not going to be fobbed off with platitudes. 'The truth is that the family are in trouble financially. Sir Adolphus has lost a lot of money and his creditors are threatening to bankrupt him. It's possible that Grantley and the estate might have to be sold.'

Cook slumped down on a three-legged stool, leaving just the top of her head and her white mobcap visible above the table. 'Heaven help us all.'

'I wouldn't trust anything that Galloway fellow says.' Lil folded her bony arms across her chest. 'You remember what he did to you and to poor Mrs Wilding.'

'Of course I do. I've told Captain Devane everything, but he had no choice other than to sign an agreement to repay the creditors a monthly sum.'

'Can we afford it?' Lil's sandy eyebrows knotted over the bridge of her nose. 'Has her ladyship upstairs got a private income?'

Angel shook her head. 'I don't think so.'

'What does it mean for us?' Cook demanded angrily. 'Are we going to be dismissed?'

'Not if I can help it.' Angel moved to the doorway. 'I'm going to do everything I can to ease the situation, and I know you'll help me, even if it means putting up with extra work.'

Lil and Cook exchanged weary glances. 'I'll wait on table,' Lil said gloomily, 'but don't blame me if it goes horribly wrong.'

'I can't work any harder.' Cook rose stiffly to her feet and began attacking the bread dough. 'But I'll do me bit, Angel.'

'Thank you both. I knew I could count on you. But please don't say anything to the outside staff, not yet anyway. I'm going to London tomorrow to see Galloway in his office and find out exactly how we stand. We're none of us going to give in easily.'

The firm of Beauchamp and Quelch had offices in one of the terraced four-storey houses in Lincoln's

Inn Fields that had once been the homes of lords and ladies, but were now inhabited almost entirely by the legal profession. Angel arrived there with Lil in attendance. The clerk in his green-tinged black suit, worn shiny at the elbows and knees, gazed at them suspiciously.

'Mr Galloway sees nobody other than by appointment.'

'I think he'll see me,' Angel said confidently. 'Please tell him that Miss Winter wishes to speak to him on an urgent matter.'

Lil leaned over the desk, fixing the nervous man with a hard stare. 'And if you value that skinny neck of yours you'll come back with a satisfactory answer. Do you understand me?'

He stood up and backed away, keeping a wary eye on Lil until he was able to escape into a narrow corridor.

'Galloway will see me,' Angel said firmly.

'If he refuses I'll break the door down.' Lil cracked her knuckles, making an impressive sound that echoed off the wainscoted walls. 'Don't think I won't do it, Angel. I'm not in a mood to be thwarted by a mealy-mouthed clerk.'

They waited for nearly an hour with Lil growing more and more impatient as the minutes ticked by. She sat, flexing her fingers and glaring at the clerk, who was becoming increasingly anxious, and had started twitching nervously. Angel was also losing patience and she was about to demand an explanation when she heard the sound of footsteps and Galloway appeared in the doorway.

'I'm sorry to keep you waiting, ladies,' he said with an ingratiating smile. 'Come with me, if you please.' He hesitated, turning his head to give Lil a sly look. 'Not you. I don't deal with old lags.'

Lil drew herself up to her full height, bristling and baring her teeth. 'No need to bring that up, guv. I'm a respectable woman now and I'm here to look after Miss Angel.'

'I have no secrets from Miss Heavitree.' Angel controlled her voice with difficulty.

'You do know the history of the woman who suckled you as a baby, don't you, Angel?'

His tone was offensive, but Angel realised that he was being deliberately provocative and she forced her lips into a smile. 'Of course I do, sir. We have no secrets from each other. Now might we get on with our business? You've kept us waiting long enough.'

He shrugged. 'Follow me.'

His office was at the far end of a dark and narrow corridor, and its interior was just as gloomy, with a strong smell of musty books and town gas. Galloway motioned them to sit on upright wooden chairs while he enthroned himself comfortably behind his desk.

'Now what can I do for you, Angel?'

'It's Miss Winter to you, mate,' Lil said angrily. 'I remember how you wormed your way into poor Mrs Wilding's good books. I reckon it was you who caused Mr Wilding's financial ruin while feathering your own nest. I blame you for both their deaths, you scoundrel.'

Galloway leaned forward, eyes narrowed and lips pulled back in a snarl. 'I could have you up in court for slander, Lumpy Lil. Do you think a magistrate would believe the word of a fallen woman?' His bark of laughter echoed round the room. 'I could lay my hands on your police record if I wished, so don't try to be clever.'

Angel laid her hand on Lil's arm. 'Ignore his taunts, Lil. You're better than that.' She met Galloway's cynical grin with a straight look. 'And don't try to frighten me, Mr Galloway. I'm here today to find out the extent of Grantley's financial problems, and I want straight answers from you.'

'I can see that you have grown up, Miss Winter,' Galloway said, nodding. 'Well, since you ask I could show you the mortgage agreement that Sir Adolphus signed two years ago, and the demands for payments that have not been met, but as Captain Devane went through them so recently I don't think it appropriate.'

'I need to see them for myself.'

'Surely this is none of your business,' Galloway said silkily. 'After all, Mrs Devane is head of the family in the absence of her brother and her eldest son.'

Lil rose to her feet and leaned over the desk. The muscles in her forearms stood out cord-like beneath the thin cotton sleeves of her grey frock. 'You will do as Miss Winter asks, Galloway. I learned a few tricks in prison and I ain't afraid to use them on you.'

He stood up abruptly, and for a moment Angel thought that he was going to strike Lil, but he snapped his fingers in her face instead. 'Sit down, you silly bitch. I could have you up before the magistrate for making threats on my person, but you're not worth the bother.' He sat down again and opened a drawer, taking out a sheaf of papers, which he slammed down in front of Angel. 'I represent the family and you are an interloper, taken in by Sir Adolphus on a whim. By the same token the Devanes could throw you out and refuse to have anything more to do with you. Read these and then get out of my office. If you return I'll give my clerk instructions to have you forcefully ejected. Do you understand, Angel Winter?'

She bent her head over the papers, holding up her hand for silence. 'This is all I need. I wouldn't think of coming here again, but your days as the family's solicitor are numbered, I promise you that, Mr Galloway.' She could hear him spluttering, but she ignored his mumbled insults and concentrated on the documents, which seemed genuine enough. When she was satisfied that she had understood their contents she rose to her feet.

'I can do nothing about you. That will be for Sir Adolphus to settle, but he knows how you treated me when I was a child and he will not take kindly to learning that you've taken over from the late Mr Beauchamp.' She joined Lil, who had already risen and was holding the door open. 'Good day to you, Mr Galloway. I hope we never meet again.'

Outside in the sunshine Angel took a deep breath. Even though the air was fetid with the stench from the river and festering privies and drains, it was still cleaner than the smell of corruption that surrounded Galloway in a nimbus cloud.

'That man is a villain,' she said, sighing. 'But I couldn't see anything to suggest that he was lying about Grantley's financial position.'

Lil mopped beads of sweat from her forehead with an already damp hanky. 'I could have wrung his neck, the old toad. Men like him should be strung up and left for the crows to feast on.'

'He seems to be enjoying Grantley's difficulties,' Angel said thoughtfully. 'You'd think that it would be in his interests, as the Devanes' lawyer, to save the estate from bankruptcy.' Angel waved to attract the attention of Russell, the Devanes' coachman who had been waiting in the shade of the huge plane trees. 'I can't bear to see everything lost, even though none of it belongs to me.'

The carriage drew up at the kerb and Lil opened the door before the coachman had a chance to leap down and oblige. 'I ain't helpless, cully,' she said, giving him a gap-toothed grin. 'Take us back to Grantley, away from the city stench.' She bundled Angel unceremoniously into the carriage and climbed in beside her. 'Drive on.' Her strident tones caused the pigeons and sparrows that had been pecking at the ground in their constant search for food to fly up into the branches with squawks of alarm.

Angel leaned back against the worn squabs and closed her eyes. She needed to think, but try as she might she could see no easy way out of the problem. Hector had promised to talk things over with his uncle, but they were both far away and the creditors were obviously pressing hard for repayment of the mortgage. That was clear from the demands she had just seen.

They travelled on in silence and Lil fell asleep, her head lolling to one side and her mouth open. Angel gazed out of the window at the mean streets, the filthy, ragged children running round barefoot, and the slatternly women leaning in doorways with babies in their arms and toddlers hanging on their skirts. The stench of the gasworks and the soap factory mingled with the smoke and heat from the iron works as they headed east towards the River Lea. Having crossed the river, Leyton marshes stretched out on either side of the main road. Soon they would be home.

Then, without warning, the carriage came to a halt, almost throwing Lil from her seat. She awakened with a start.

'Lord bless us!' Lil righted her bonnet, which had slipped over one eye, and leaned across Angel to peer out of the window. 'What's happened?'

Angel opened the door and climbed down to the ground. She had seen a girl in an obvious state of distress, leaning against a tall young man. Their luggage was strewn about the road and a coachman and a footman were in the process of unharnessing the two horses, as the carriage tilted dangerously to one side.

'Is there anything I can do to help?' Angel asked anxiously. 'Are you hurt?'

The young man managed a smile but it was obvious that he was shaken. 'Thankfully, no. But as you can see, my sister is very upset.'

'What can we do to help them, Russell?' Angel asked urgently.

'Leyton is only a short distance away, miss. But Grantley is nearer, although they'd need a tow to get there.'

The worried young man turned to the coachman, who was leading one of the horses. 'You'd best ride to the nearest village for help, Atkins.'

Atkins glanced at the sturdy carriage horse and paled beneath his tan. 'I – I never rode bareback before, sir. I've driven plenty but I ain't no rider. Smith will have to go.'

The footman shook his head. 'I can't ride. I never had a chance to learn, sir.'

'What's the matter with you lily-livered cowards?' Lil demanded angrily. 'Help me onto the brute's back and I'll go. I'm good with horses, even though I never sat on one.'

'That won't be necessary,' Angel said hastily. 'I'm sure one of the others will be brave enough to try.'

'It's all right, Mr Montgomerie, sir. Smith will go and I'll give him a leg up.' Atkins tethered his animal to one of the shafts. 'Come on, Smith. There's nothing to it, boy.' He tossed the unfortunate footman onto the horse's back and slapped the animal's rump, causing it to break into a trot that almost unseated the nervous footman.

'Will he be all right, Atkins? Smith doesn't look too confident on horseback.' The young man watched anxiously as the footman clung to the horse's mane.

'Smith will be fine, sir, but I can't say the same for this here vehicle.' Atkins surveyed the damage, shaking his head. 'I'm afraid the axle is broken, sir. This can't be fixed in a hurry.'

The young lady lifted her head, tears streaming from her large blue eyes. 'Oh, Percy, what will we do?'

'Calm down, Belle. No one is hurt and the horses are unharmed. The carriage can be

227

mended; it just means a delay of a few days.' The young man turned to Angel with a winning smile on his pleasant features. 'How do you do, ma'am? As there is no one to introduce us formally please allow me to present my sister, Belinda Montgomerie, and I'm Percival, although everyone calls me Percy.'

'I seem to have lost my hanky,' Belinda said, sniffing.

Lil stepped forward, taking a slightly damp handkerchief from her reticule. 'Use this one, miss. It's quite clean, just a bit soggy. It was hot as hell in the city.'

Angel shot her a warning look as she stepped forward, holding out her hand. 'I apologise for my maid's colourful language, but it was exceedingly warm. However, that's by the bye. I'm Angel Winter and I live at Grantley Park, which is just a few miles east of here.'

Belinda wiped her eyes and blew her nose before handing the hanky back to Lil. 'Thank you, Miss Winter. I'm only upset because we're going to miss our cousin's wedding in Colchester, and I was so looking forward to being a bridesmaid. I wish now that we'd taken the train.'

'Just be thankful that you're in one piece,' Percy said severely. 'It could have been so much worse.' He turned to the coachman, who was holding the reins of the second horse. 'How long do you think it will take to repair the damage, Atkins?'

The coachman scratched his head. 'I dunno, sir, and that's the truth of it. Out here in the wilds it might take any amount of time to get the vehicle towed to a coach builder or a smithy.'

'What do we do in the meantime, Percy?' Belinda's bottom lip began to tremble ominously.

'Here, miss. You'd better keep hold of this,' Lil said, handing her the crumpled hanky.

Angel laid her hand on Belinda's shoulder. 'If you would like to come with us you can stay at Grantley until your carriage is roadworthy. Would that be a help?'

The Montgomeries exchanged glances and nodded in unison.

'That is very kind.' Percy's worried frown was replaced by a smile. 'It looks like rain and I wouldn't want my sister to suffer from exposure. She's quite delicate and easily takes a chill. But,' he added thoughtfully, 'we will only accept if you allow us to pay for our accommodation.'

An idea struck Angel with the suddenness of a summer thunderstorm. It was so obvious that she wondered why she had not thought of it before. 'Yes,' she murmured. 'Come with us and we'll talk about that later.'

Chapter Thirteen

'What?' Eloise's voice rose to a shriek. 'Turn Grantley into common lodging house? Over my dead body.'

'A hotel, not a lodging house. There's a big difference.' Angel handed her aunt the silver vinaigrette containing a sponge soaked in sal volatile, and Eloise inhaled deeply, her blue-

229

veined eyelids fluttering.

Susannah sank down on the sofa, fanning herself vigorously. 'You must be mad, Angel. What will you think of next?' she said angrily. 'You're upsetting Mama with such talk.'

'Where are these people now?' Eloise rose from her chair and started pacing the floor, wringing her hands. 'They could be thieves or murderers and you expect me to welcome them into my home?'

'You do me an injustice if you think I would be foolish enough to bring anyone like that to Grantley. At the moment they're in the morning parlour, and I told Lil to take them tea and cake. You must meet them and decide for yourself, Aunt Eloise.'

'This is ridiculous.' Susannah rose to her feet, glaring at Angel. 'You've really gone too far this time.'

'I'm sorry, but you need to face facts,' Angel said with a determined lift of her chin. 'I went to see Galloway this morning. The creditors will take possession of the estate if the mortgage repayments aren't received. Hector is going to try to sort matters out with Uncle Dolph, but that will take time, and there are a pile of unpaid accounts in the study. I don't think you showed them to Hector, Aunt Eloise, so he doesn't know the full extent of our financial troubles.'

Eloise sat down again, wafting the vinaigrette under her nose. 'I meant to give them to him, but the ghastly business with Rupert and the maid put everything else out of my mind. The tradesmen will wait for their money – they always do.'

'The accounts are very much overdue, Aunt.'

'My brother is responsible for the family finances. He won't allow us to lose our home.'

'Mama is right,' Susannah said carelessly. 'Don't interfere. We'll get by, we always do.'

Angel bit back a sharp retort. It was obvious that neither her aunt nor Susannah was taking the matter seriously. They appeared to live in a world where everything would turn out all right in the end, regardless of what they were told.

'It's not quite as simple as that,' Angel said patiently. 'Uncle Dolph doesn't know the full extent of the problem, and by the time Hector reaches him and explains things it could be too late to save Grantley. We have to do something, and to be honest I can't see any other way than to make use of what we have – the house and its beautiful parkland.'

'But we would be a laughing stock,' Susannah protested. 'What would Sir Eugene say if he discovered that we took in paying guests?'

'He would probably congratulate you on your enterprise.' Angel looked from one to the other. 'The Montgomeries are not common people, Aunt Eloise. They are what Miss Creedy would call "carriage trade" and quite charming.'

'Then, of course, we must offer them our hospitality,' Eloise countered, 'but I wouldn't dream of taking money from them.'

The faint hope that she might make her aunt see sense vanished like morning mist. Angel knew when she was beaten, but there was someone closer to Aunt Eloise who had a stronger grasp on reality. She backed towards the doorway. 'Will

231

you excuse me a moment, please? Don't go away because I'll return shortly.' She let herself out of the drawing room and went in search of Toby.

She found him in the gun room where the fishing tackle was kept alongside the twelve-bore guns he used when out hunting. 'Toby, thank goodness I've found you.'

'I'm just off fishing,' he said casually. 'Thought I'd see if I can catch our supper tonight.'

'We have guests,' Angel said warily.

'Really?' Toby's eyes were alight with curiosity. 'That sounds interesting. Who are they?'

'A brother and sister by the name of Montgomerie. Their carriage lost a wheel and I've asked them to stay until it's fixed.'

'Splendid. Is she young and pretty?'

'Both of those,' Angel said firmly.

'Then I'll catch twice the number of trout or maybe a few eels. It's time we started entertaining, even if we are all but bankrupt.'

'That's what I wanted to talk to you about, Toby.'

He closed the lid on his wicker fishing basket. 'Not now, Angel. Maybe after supper when I've had a couple of brandies and I'm feeling mellow.'

'No, now.' Angel spoke sternly and was rewarded by a startled look. 'I'm sorry, but I don't think that any of you understand quite how serious this situation is.'

'Come on, Angel. You know that Hector will sort it out when he's had a word with Uncle Dolph. Leave it to the men in the family, my dear.'

'Things are more serious than you imagine. We need to find the money ourselves or Grantley will be lost for ever, and you'll have to leave university and look for work.'

'By golly, is it as bad as all that? I thought Hector was sorting things out.'

'It's extremely serious, and the Montgomeries have offered to pay for their accommodation while they wait for their carriage to be mended.'

He shrugged. 'Then that's all right. Take the money and put it towards the mortgage repayments, if it makes you happy. I see nothing wrong with your idea.'

'But your mama disagrees. I can't make her see sense, Toby, but she always listens to you. Please speak to her and make her realise that if we don't do something quickly we will all be out on the street, and it's not a nice place to be. I know, because I've been there.'

'You really are serious, aren't you? Is it that bad, Angel? I thought that Hector was just exaggerating things in order to keep me in line.'

'It's worse than bad. Galloway is thoroughly dishonest. I don't know why he wants to cheat your family, but I can assure you that he's not on our side. If you can convince Aunt Eloise that our only hope of saving Grantley is to make it pay for itself we might stand a chance.'

'Uncle Dolph won't let it happen, Angel. He loves Grantley.'

'He was the cause of this mess in the first place. Are you going to back me up, Toby? Or do we sit back and allow the estate to sink into bankruptcy?'

'Leave it to me. I can handle Mama, but I hope this works, Angel.'

She breathed a sigh of relief. 'There's only one way to find out.'

That evening at dinner, the family and their guests sat down to eat in the dining room. Cook's watercress soup had been a success and Lil had managed to serve it without dropping the tureen or emptying the ladle into anyone's lap. Toby had eventually gone fishing and the second course of grilled trout was followed by pigeon pie accompanied by peas that Angel had picked in the kitchen garden.

'It is so kind of you to entertain us so royally,' Belinda said, pouring cream over a bowl filled with ripe red strawberries, also plucked from the walled garden and still warm from the sun.

'Indeed it is,' Percy added. 'Please offer my compliments to your cook.'

Eloise smiled and inclined her head graciously. 'We do pride ourselves on our table at Grantley.'

'And everything tastes so much better here in the country,' Belinda said eagerly. 'We live in London and I'm sure that produce sold in the markets doesn't have nearly as much flavour.'

Percy raised his glass. 'A wonderful meal and excellent wine. We can't thank you enough for your hospitality.'

Toby puffed out his chest. 'I pride myself in knowing a fine wine from one that's merely palatable.'

'So that's why your allowance never lasts a term.' Eloise gave him a fond smile. 'My son is studying law. One day he'll be a High Court judge.'

Humphrey opened his mouth to make a

comment but a warning glance from Angel was enough to silence him.

Susannah treated Percy to an arch smile. 'Would you like some more strawberries, Mr Montgomerie?'

He shook his head. 'Thank you, no. I couldn't manage another mouthful, but we've dined like royalty.'

'You've been so kind, inviting us into your lovely home, Mrs Devane,' Belinda said shyly. 'We were so lucky to have been rescued by Angel.'

'Indeed we were,' Percy said, nodding. 'I think you must be our guardian angel, Miss Winter.'

Eloise's lips pursed into a semblance of a smile, and she rose to her feet. 'We will withdraw and leave you gentlemen to enjoy your cigars and brandy.' She eyed the almost empty decanter on a side table. 'Or I believe we have a fine old port wine in the cellar. Humphrey dear, maybe you could find a bottle. We had to dismiss the butler quite recently, for reasons I won't go into now,' she added hastily. 'Go now, there's a good fellow.'

Angel waited by her chair until Eloise had left the dining room, followed by Belinda and Susannah. With Humphrey having gone in search of the port wine Angel took the opportunity to broach the subject of money. She grasped the back of the chair with both hands and cleared her throat.

'Might I have a few words with you, in private, Mr Montgomerie?'

Percy gave her a searching look and a slow smile crinkled the corners of his hazel eyes. 'I think Miss Winter is anxious because she knows

235

I will insist on making a contribution towards our stay here, which is only fair. If we had put up at the inn we would have had to pay for our bed and board, and I refuse to take advantage of Mrs Devane's generous hospitality.'

'That's exactly the case,' Angel said hastily. 'This is hard to admit, but Grantley is in danger of repossession, Mr Montgomerie, and we have to take drastic measures in order to keep it in the family.'

'That's a bit harsh,' Toby protested. 'I'm sure we can afford a bit of supper and a bed for a night or two.'

'That's just it – we can't. I'm sorry, Toby, I thought you understood.'

Percy cleared his throat. 'Please don't be embarrassed, Devane. I understand completely.' He took a wallet from his pocket and handed a crisp five-pound note to Angel.

'No, really. That's far too much.' Startled, she tried to give it back to him, but he put his wallet away, shaking his head.

'Not at all. My carriage is in your coach house waiting for the blacksmith to do the necessary, and my sister and I are being treated royally. Let's say no more about it.'

'That's damned good of you, Montgomerie,' Toby said with a tipsy grin. 'More than generous.'

Angel folded the money and tucked it down the front of her bodice for safekeeping. 'I say thank you a million times, sir.'

'I'll demand it back if you continue to call me sir.'

'Then, thank you, Percy,' Angel said, chuckling.

'It is very good of you, and we'll make sure that you enjoy your stay at Grantley.' She glanced over her shoulder as Humphrey burst into the room brandishing a crusty bottle of port.

'This is definitely the last one, Toby.'

Toby leaped to his feet and took it from him, treating it as gently as if it were a newborn baby. 'If you've shaken it I'll skin you alive, Humpty Dumpty.'

'Now I really feel at home,' Percy said, laughing. Satisfied with her own efforts, Angel left them to drink their port and made her way to the drawing room. The five-pound note was just the beginning – she planned to show it to Aunt Eloise at the first opportunity. If that did not convince her there was money to be made by entertaining wealthy guests, nothing would.

Encouraged by Percy Montgomerie's munificence, Angel was up early next morning and went straight to the kitchen to discuss the menus for that day. Cook was flattered by the favourable comments she had received from their guests, but Lil was not so enthusiastic.

'We need more help, Angel,' she said flatly. 'There's only the three of us to do everything. You can't count Meg because she's a lady's maid and she don't get her hands dirty.'

Cook nodded vigorously. 'That's right, Angel. In the old days we had a dozen or more indoor servants and a housekeeper, not to mention the butler. Then there was the gardeners and the stable boys, grooms and two coachmen. You can't expect us to manage on our own.'

Angel took a deep breath. She had been expecting this sort of argument. 'Of course you need more help. I don't expect you to do it all.'

'Are you going to roll your sleeves up and set to?' Lil stood, arms akimbo, and her chin outthrust, but there was a twinkle in her eyes and her lips twitched as if she were about to burst out laughing.

'Yes, I am,' Angel countered. 'I'm not afraid of hard work. I'll be housekeeper, chambermaid and scullery maid too, if necessary. I don't think my aunt would like it if I waited on table, but we can get a girl in from the village to take Dolly's place.'

Lil and Cook exchanged wary glances. 'If you say so, love,' Lil said doubtfully.

Cook wiped her hands on her apron. 'Well, then, Miss Angel. You could start by fetching me some vegetables from the kitchen garden. I've got a boiling fowl and I'm making soup for luncheon, so I'll need onions and carrots and some herbs. Then there's dinner tonight. Perhaps Mr Toby could bag me a couple of rabbits.'

Angel made a move towards the door. 'Leave it to me, Cook.' She paused, frowning. 'Maybe you could make some of those dainty fairy cakes for dessert and I'll pick some raspberries to go with them.'

Angel's first task was to rouse Toby from his bed, but she found him already up and dressed and looking forward to a day's hunting and fishing, his favourite pastime. It was more difficult to rouse Humphrey, but in the end she managed to persuade him to ride into town to settle the vintner's bill and give him an order for wine and brandy. Having satisfied herself that she had done all she could do for the moment, she went to fetch a couple of trugs from the potting shed.

It was still early and the dew sparkled on the grass as Angel made her way to the walled garden. A cloudless azure sky held the promise of another fine day and it was going to be hot, but a light breeze fanned her cheeks and played with her blonde curls as she worked in the walled garden. A robin followed her movements as she used a trowel to dig up carrots and ease onions from the warm soil. She cut lettuce and picked tomatoes, and having filled one trug she concentrated on the raspberry canes, popping the occasional succulent fruit into her mouth as she worked. It was hunger that made her remember she had not had any breakfast, but by then the trugs were overflowing with fruit and vegetables, and Cook would be waiting. She let herself out of the walled garden and was taking a short cut across the lawn when she saw Percy Montgomerie striding across the grass towards her.

'You're up early, Angel.'

She was suddenly conscious of her dishevelled appearance. Raspberry juice had stained her apron and hands and her hair had escaped from the snood at the back of her neck and was curling wildly about her face and shoulders. 'I've been to the kitchen garden,' she said lamely.

He took the trugs from her hands. 'Allow me. These are heavy. Where are you taking them?'

'To the kitchen. We're rather short staffed so I'm helping out.'

239

'Do you often help out?'

'Not really.'

'Forgive me for saying so but it seems to me that you're being taken advantage of. I'm sorry if that seems impertinent, but this is servants' work.'

'As I told you last night, Grantley is in financial difficulties. My uncle and cousin are far away, in Natal Province, or they would be taking charge.'

'And your aunt is too much a lady to dirty her hands.'

'You are very blunt, Percy.'

He met her angry look with an apologetic smile. 'I'm sorry. It's a failing of mine, but I hate to see someone like you put upon by others, especially when that person is part of the family.'

'But I'm not, you see.' Angel could have bitten her tongue out. The surprised look he gave her made it impossible to leave it at that. 'I am not related to Sir Adolphus or to Mrs Devane. It's a long story, and I really have to get these vegetables to Cook, and then there's breakfast...'

He stopped outside the scullery door. 'Shall I take these in, or will I make your life even more difficult if I do so?'

'I'll take them. Thank you for your help but I mustn't keep you.'

'You mentioned breakfast. Come to think of it I haven't had mine yet. Shall I see you in the dining room? Or will you be waiting on table?'

She shot him a suspicious glance. 'Are you laughing at me, Percy?'

'That's better. No, Angel, I'm not laughing at you, but I find it distressing to see a lady being treated like a servant.'

She opened the door. 'Thank you for carrying the trugs.'

'I'll see you at breakfast.'

Percy, Belinda and Susannah were halfway through their meal when Angel joined them in the dining room.

'What's the matter with your hands?' Susannah stared pointedly at Angel's fingers, which were stained red.

'You have a very productive kitchen garden,' Percy said smoothly. 'If the raspberries Angel picked are half as delicious as the strawberries we enjoyed last evening, I can't wait to taste them.'

Susannah's eyes widened in surprise. 'Er – quite so.'

'You must have been up early, Percy,' Belinda said curiously. 'I knocked on your door several times and received no answer.' She turned to Susannah, smiling. 'I thought he must still be asleep. Do your brothers lie in bed until noon?'

'Yes, they're lazy devils.' Susannah shot a sideways glance at Percy. 'Did you enjoy your early morning walk?'

'As a matter of fact I went to the stables to find out if anything had been done to mend the broken axle, and I was walking back across the park when I met Angel.'

A frown creased Susannah's brow. 'I see.'

'I'd just come from the walled garden,' Angel said hastily. 'I'd been picking fruit and digging up vegetables for Cook.'

'Oh, heavens! I've just remembered that

241

Blanche and her papa are coming to luncheon today.' Susannah leaped to her feet, spilling coffee on the white damask tablecloth. 'Have you told Cook to prepare something special?'

'I didn't know they were coming,' Angel said, shrugging. 'I'll let Cook know, although I'm sure there'll be plenty of chicken soup.'

'Is that all we're having? They're used to finer fare than that.'

'I love chicken soup,' Belinda said stoutly. 'Your cook is excellent, Susannah. I'm sure you have no need to worry.'

'I've never enjoyed a better meal than the one we had last night,' Percy added firmly.

'Nevertheless I must go to the kitchen and tell Cook to make an extra effort. Mama would want me to do so.'

'Is Mrs Devane unwell?' Belinda asked innocently.

'Mama never rises before eleven.' Susannah mopped ineffectually at the puddle of coffee with her napkin.

Angel had not had a chance to help herself to the rapidly cooling buttered eggs and crisp bacon, but Cook and Lil were in enough of a panic without Susannah adding her twopenn'orth, as Dolly would have said. 'Don't worry, Sukey. I'll go and talk to Cook, and I'll send Meg up to Aunt Eloise's room with some hot chocolate.' She turned to Belinda and Percy with an apologetic smile. 'If you'll excuse me, I have rather a lot to do, but I'll see you at luncheon.'

'Don't worry about us,' Belinda said cheerfully. 'It's such a lovely day that I rather fancy a walk.

What about you, Percy?'

He shook his head. 'I need to be on hand at the stables to make sure that work is started on the carriage. We have to be in Colchester on Friday at the latest.'

Susannah sank back onto her chair. 'Pour me another cup of coffee before you go, Angel, there's a dear.'

'Allow me.' Percy had reached for the silver coffeepot and refilled Susannah's cup before Angel had a chance to move. He looked up and gave her a wry smile. 'Don't worry about us, Belinda and I can look after ourselves.'

'I'm sure you can, but you're our guests and while you're here I intend to see you have every comfort we can provide.' Angel had the satisfaction of seeing Susannah for once at a loss for words. She left them to finish their breakfast and returned to the kitchen.

'That's all I need, Miss Angel,' Cook said bitterly. 'The mistress will expect me to produce a meal fit for a king, even though it's only Sir Eugene and Miss Blanche, and I've only got this scraggy boiling fowl.'

Lil stopped chopping onions to wipe tears from her eyes. 'They'll have to like it or lump it. We can't perform miracles.'

'I'm sure the soup will be delicious, as always,' Angel said tactfully. 'If you'll clear the table after breakfast, Lil, I'll set it for luncheon. I'll put Meg in charge of laundry and Flossie is now a tweeny. She'll have to do the fires and empty the chamber pots and all the things that Dolly did.'

Flossie popped her head round the scullery door. 'I heard that, miss. Am I really going to be a tweeny?'

Angel smiled with relief. At least someone was happy. 'Yes, Flossie. I'll show you what to do, and from now on your duties are mainly upstairs, but you'll still need to help in the kitchen until I can find someone to replace you.'

'Such comings and goings,' Cook grumbled. 'I suppose we'll be having dukes and duchesses to stay soon.'

Lil tossed an onion skin at her. 'Shut up, Eudora. Be thankful we ain't homeless, because that's what will happen if we don't do all we can to help Angel with this plan of hers.'

'I know you'll all do your best,' Angel said hastily. 'And so will I. We'll get through this together.'

Angel had just finished setting the table in the dining room, and was adding a bowl of freshly picked tea roses and sprigs of lady's mantle as a final touch, when she heard the Westwoods' carriage draw to a halt outside. She took off her apron and hurried to open the door. If they thought it odd that a member of the family was doing the work of a servant they were either too polite to say anything or they simply did not notice.

Eloise appeared at the top of the staircase and descended to meet her guests with a regal smile. Once again Angel noticed that her aunt had taken extra-special care with her toilette and was wearing her newest afternoon gown. The pink-

and-white striped polonaise basque over a frilled white underskirt was the latest fashion, and Eloise wore it with style. She extended her hand and Sir Eugene raised it to his lips.

'How kind of you to join us for luncheon.' Eloise flashed him a smile before turning to Blanche. 'And dear Blanche, you look so lovely in that muslin gown. Do come into the drawing room. Susannah is dying to seeing you again.'

Blanche acknowledged her effusive greeting with a nod and a smile as she handed her parasol to Angel without as much as a glance in her direction. Angel had known what it felt like to be invisible when selling flowers on street corners, and that feeling came back to her now. She took Sir Eugene's hat and gloves, but his attention was firmly fixed on Eloise, and it occurred to Angel that bringing Blanche to see Susannah was merely an excuse for him to become better acquainted with Eloise Devane. There were, she decided, definite advantages to being a servant. Having completed her task as parlour maid, Angel went to join the family in the drawing room and was greeted warmly by Sir Eugene and Blanche, as if seeing her for the first time that day.

She took a seat by the window, sitting quietly and listening to Sir Eugene giving advice on how to run the estate, when a movement outside caught her eye and she saw Percy hurrying across the terrace. Moments later he entered the room and she stood up, sensing that something was amiss.

'I'm sorry to intrude,' he said breathlessly, 'but has anyone seen my sister? Belinda went out for

245

a walk after breakfast and she hasn't returned. I've ridden round the estate and as far as the village, but there's no sign of her.'

Chapter Fourteen

Eloise was adamant that nothing bad could have befallen Belinda either on Grantley land or in the village, but despite her protests Sir Eugene gallantly offered to join the search, and even Susannah had the grace to look a little worried.

'But, Mama,' she protested, 'Belinda might have fallen and twisted her ankle, or she could have become confused and lost her way.'

'Exactly,' Sir Eugene said firmly. 'I'll join you, sir. We haven't been introduced but my name is Westwood, and I know the countryside round here like the back of my hand.'

'How do you do, sir? Percy Montgomerie, and it's my sister who's missing. I wouldn't worry normally if she was a bit late back from a walk, but she left soon after breakfast and she's unfamiliar with the area.'

'In that case I suggest we start right way.' Sir Eugene strode from the room and Percy hurried after him.

'Well, really,' Eloise said, falling back on the sofa and fanning herself vigorously. 'This is too much.'

'Don't upset yourself, Mama.' Susannah went to sit beside her mother. 'I'm sure they'll find her safe and sound.'

'I'll go with the search party.' Angel left them grumbling about the inconvenience caused by Miss Montgomerie's thoughtless actions, and she went to join Sir Eugene and Percy on the carriage sweep where they were discussing the best plan of action.

Percy looked up and smiled. 'Are you coming with us, Angel?'

'Yes, of course. I'll do anything I can to help find your sister. Did Belinda say where she was going?'

He shook his head. 'No, merely that she wanted some fresh air, but it's not like Belle to wander off.'

'We need horses,' Sir Eugene said firmly. 'On foot it will take hours and we could easily miss her.'

'We'll send the stable boy and the groom to comb the woods.' Angel tried to put herself in Belinda's place. 'I'm trying to think where she might have gone.'

'She was fascinated by the marsh,' Percy said slowly, 'but I doubt if she would have been rash enough to go there on her own.'

A shiver ran down Angel's spine as she re-membered the day when she had been lost in the mist and rain. 'It's quite treacherous, even in summer. I'll take the dogs and walk that way.'

'I don't know, that sounds dangerous.' Percy hesitated. 'Why don't you stay in the grounds and leave the marsh to us? I'll enlist Atkins and Smith. They're doing nothing while we wait for the blacksmith to finish his work.'

'Surely she wouldn't have gone so far? Anyway, we're wasting time,' Sir Eugene said impatiently. 'Come on. The sooner we find your sister the sooner we can sit down and enjoy the excellent food that is always on offer at Grantley.'

Despite her worries Angel had to hide a smile. If only he knew to what lengths they had gone in order to provide the most basic meal, but Sir Eugene had been born to wealth and privilege and she doubted if he had ever experienced the gnawing pangs of hunger and the debilitating weakness caused by near starvation. She picked up her skirts and ran after them as they strode towards the stables.

Thor and Juno greeted her ecstatically and, despite their ageing bones, they were eager to join her for a walk. She had set off for the marshes when the temperamental English climate took a sudden turn for the worse. Ominous black clouds blotted out the sun, followed by a sudden down-pour that quickly soaked Angel to the skin. The dogs huddled at her side, looking up at her with sad brown eyes as if pleading with her to make it stop. She patted their heads absently, looking round for anything that might give them shelter, but visibility was almost nil and she could only keep walking and hope that it was just a shower. The only good thing was that the rain itself was relatively warm, but her cotton print gown was sodden, as was her hair. Water dripped down her face and neck and she wished that she had stopped to put on a bonnet and shawl.

Then, just as suddenly, the rain ceased and the sun broke through the clouds that dispersed as quickly as they had gathered, leaving a cerulean sky and steam rising from the wet ground. Both dogs were suddenly alert and rushed on ahead, and Angel shielded her eyes from the sun's glare. Through the haze she saw two figures walking towards her and a small dog that bounced up and down barking at Thor and Juno. Even though they were far away Angel recognised Danny, and the smaller figure, leaning heavily on his arm, was distinguished by her elegant although extremely dishevelled appearance. Belinda Montgomerie was safe and in good hands. Angel broke into a run.

'Belinda, are you all right?' she asked breathlessly as she came to a halt.

'I might have been sucked down into the bog if it hadn't been for Danny.' Belinda's voice broke on a sob. 'I couldn't free myself, Angel. It was a terrifying experience. I've heard of people being swallowed up in a morass of black mud and never seen again.'

Danny grinned, shaking his head. 'There wasn't any danger of that, miss. You just panicked and struggled too hard, making it worse.'

'But I could have been stuck there for ever,' Belinda insisted. 'I didn't see another soul until you heard my cries for help and came to my rescue.'

'Well, I never thought of you as a hero, Danny,' Angel said, laughing. 'But thank you anyway. I'm sure that Percy will be very relieved. He's had everyone out looking for you, Belinda.'

'Oh dear, he'll be so cross with me.'

'I think he'll be more relieved than angry.'

Angel met Danny's amused gaze with a smile. 'It's a good thing you were around. She could have been stuck there for ages.'

'Well, let's get you girls home. You're both soaking wet.'

'And so are you.' Angel eyed him critically. 'You're muddy too. You'd best come to Grantley and dry off.'

'I'm not the sort of person they'd welcome as a guest. I'll see the young lady safe and then I'll be on my way. A bit of water never hurt anyone.'

'You are a stubborn brute,' Angel said affectionately, 'but you'll do as you're told, for once. Lil and Cook will welcome you and you can dry off by the kitchen range.'

'I'm truly grateful to you, Danny.' Belinda gazed up at him admiringly. 'Thank you for rescuing me.'

Angel walked on as the path was too narrow for three abreast, and the dogs gambolled ahead of her. Forgetting their age, they played like puppies, and bad-tempered Stumpy seemed to have regained some of his youthful zest for life. They reached Grantley to find that Sir Eugene and Percy had arrived before them and had dismounted in the stable yard.

'Belinda!' Percy's shocked tones echoed round the mews. He handed the reins to Sir Eugene. 'What happened?' he demanded anxiously, looking Belinda up and down. 'Are you hurt?'

'I strayed off the path and I was sinking in a bog when this man saved my life.' She glanced up at Danny, smiling shyly. 'I might have been stuck there for hours if it hadn't been for him.'

'She was scared, sir, but unharmed. She wouldn't have sunk much further, but she couldn't free herself.' Danny tipped his cap, backing away. 'I'll be off now.'

Percy slipped his arm around his sister's waist. 'I haven't thanked you yet. You must have some recompense for your trouble. I don't even know your name, sir.'

'This is Danny Wicks,' Angel said smiling. 'He's an old friend.'

'Well, I'm very pleased to make your acquaintance, Wicks.' Percy shook Danny's hand. 'You did my sister a great service today.'

'I'd have done the same for anyone. The marsh isn't the place to roam freely.' Danny was about to walk away but Angel ran after him.

'I can't let you go home in that state. What would your ma say?' She lowered her voice. 'Besides which, I need your advice, and I have an idea that might benefit both you and your family as well as Grantley.'

A slow smile lit Danny's eyes. 'You always were an independent spirit, Angel.'

'I don't know about that.' Angel glanced over her shoulder to see Susannah and Blanche fussing around Belinda. She tucked her hand in the crook of Danny's arm. 'I'm just as wet as you are and I'm shivering in spite of the sunshine. Will you do as I ask, or have I got to beg?'

'You don't give me much choice. Lead on, girl.'

Having left Danny in the capable hands of Cook and Lil, Angel went to her room to change out of her wet clothes. She brushed her hair and scraped it back into a chignon, although it was impossible to tame it completely. Tendrils curled around her forehead and tickled her ears, but this was not the time to worry about looks. There were more important matters on hand, and speaking to Danny was one of them.

She returned to the kitchen to find that Lil had managed to serve the broth without scalding herself or any of the guests, and Humphrey had returned from the vintners with enough wine to keep their guests happy. Cook had baked a cherry pie that looked tempting, its crust glistening with sugar crystals, and it smelled delicious. There was also a handsome sherry trifle studded with almonds, although Cook made it clear that she was extremely put out as she thrust the cut-glass bowl into Angel's hands.

'It's mortifying to offer a choice of only two desserts. In the old days there would have been more courses, even at luncheon, as well as sorbets and ice cream. I don't know what Sir Eugene will think of us.'

Danny looked up from the bowl of broth he had almost finished and was just about to mop up with a chunk of bread. 'I'd say he was a lucky chap to be offered pie and trifle. We wouldn't have that choice in a month of Sundays.'

'You aren't a Devane,' Cook said, sniffing. 'This family used to pride itself on keeping a good table.'

Lil picked up the pie and a jug of cream. 'They should think themselves lucky, that's what I say. We'll be stuck with bread and scrape if the mistress doesn't do something quickly.' She shot a sideway glance at Angel. 'Can't you do something more, love? You always was a good one for ideas.'

'I've plenty of those,' Angel said eagerly. 'But will they work? That's the crux of the matter.' She turned her head to give Danny an encouraging smile. 'Don't go until we've had our chat. I'll be back in a moment or two.'

'I might just wait to see if there's any of that cherry pie left. I reckon I could eat a whole one of them all by myself.'

The party in the dining room seemed to be going well. Angel served the trifle, leaving Lil to cut the pie and offer it round the table.

'Aren't you going to join us, Angel?' Percy shook his head when she brought the trifle to him. 'I see that there's a place set for you.'

'We haven't found a replacement for a maid who left recently, so for today I am taking her role.' Angel put the fact as tactfully as she could, but she could feel the tension in the room. Eloise grasped the stem of her wineglass so tightly that her knuckles whitened and Sir Eugene stiffened, staring straight ahead. Susannah bit her lip and stared down at her plate, and Blanche shot a wary look in her father's direction.

Eloise recovered first. 'It's so hard to find good servants these days.'

'We don't seem to have a problem,' Belinda said happily. 'But, of course, we live in London and that makes a difference.'

Percy did not look convinced. 'Even so, I wouldn't expect to be served by a member of the family. I hope we will have the pleasure of your company at dinner, Angel.'

Lil sniggered audibly and received a look from Eloise that would have turned an ordinary mortal to stone.

Belinda continued to smile happily, seemingly oblivious to the fraught emotions seething beneath a veneer of good manners. 'May I have some cherry pie? It looks so tasty.'

Her naïve remark seemed to ease the tension and everyone began speaking at once. Angel took the opportunity to return to the kitchen and was relieved to see that Danny had waited for her, even though his clothes had dried out and he was ready to leave. She took off her apron and laid it over the back of a chair.

'Come on, Danny. I'll walk part of the way with you.'

'What is it you wanted to say?' he asked as they cut across the park.

'The family are all but bankrupt,' Angel said bluntly. 'I've persuaded Aunt Eloise to take in paying guests, but we have very little money, and if we don't satisfy the creditors the house and land will be forfeit. That's why the Montgomeries were invited to stay – they offered to pay for their keep.'

'Are you saying that you intend to turn the old house into a lodging house?'

'More or less, and this is where you come in. You said you wanted to expand your business, and we have plenty of land. We need fruit and vegetables and you could supply those to us free, in lieu of rent. It's a chance for all of us to benefit from the estate, or else it will be sold to the highest bidder in order to pay off the creditors.' She stopped and encompassed the gardens and park with a wave of her hand.

'It's true that I was thinking along those lines,' Danny said doubtfully, 'but this is something different.'

'I don't see why, Danny. The walled garden produced enough to feed the family and servants when we had gardeners, but now there's only one old man who does his best, and you can see the size of the problem. There's a greenhouse, although it's never used these days. You could grow tomatoes and cucumbers in there and do us all a favour at the same time. What do you think?'

He scratched his head, frowning. 'I need a bit of time. I have to say I like the sound of it, although if it doesn't work we'll all be in Queer Street.'

She smiled. 'At least we'll be there together. I owe you this chance, Danny. If you hadn't given me a sack of mistletoe to sell I wouldn't be here today. I don't forget my friends.'

They had arrived at the gates and Danny stopped, reaching out to clasp Angel's hand. 'I'll speak to my dad and let you know what he thinks.'

'Yes, please do. I think it would benefit us all.'

His grasp tightened and he held her gaze, his lips curved in a smile. 'You're quite a girl, Angel Winter.'

The warmth in his eyes brought a blush to her cheeks and, for a moment, she allowed herself to enjoy being the object of someone's admiration, but then she withdrew her hand. 'Goodbye,

Danny. Let me know soon.'

'I will.' He walked off, whistling a popular tune as if he had not a care in the world.

As she watched him stride homewards Angel felt more optimistic about Grantley's future. There was a spring in her step as she made her way back to the house, and she braced herself to face Aunt Eloise's displeasure; after all, it was nothing new. It was not that Eloise had ever been overtly unkind, but when things had gone wrong in the past Angel had always been the one most likely to suffer the consequences. Toby was his mother's favourite with Humphrey coming second, and Susannah a close third, and Angel had been the scapegoat. Nothing much had changed over the years, and probably never would.

Angel headed for the stables, hoping to have a few quiet words with Percy. She caught up with him as he was about to enter the coach house. The sounds of hammering and sawing were encouraging, but when the carriage was roadworthy it would mean the Montgomeries would be on their way. Angel called out to him and he came to a halt.

'Angel, have you come to view the blacksmith's progress?'

'Not exactly. I wanted to ask a favour of you.'

'Of course. Anything within my power – consider it done.'

'You know that Grantley is in financial difficulties.'

He nodded. 'Yes, and it's such a pity.'

'You've enjoyed your stay here?'

'Most certainly. We couldn't have wished for more.'

256

'All I want you to do is to spread the word amongst your friends that Grantley is somewhere they can stay in comfort and safety, away from the putrid air in the city.'

'So you do intend to run Grantley as a hotel?'

'Yes, I do. At least until Sir Adolphus returns home. We have to pay the bills somehow.'

Percy's smooth brow creased into worried lines. 'I am so sorry, Angel. I know I speak for Belinda when I say that we've enjoyed your hospitality, even though we could see how difficult it must be to run such a large house with the minimum of staff. I'll do everything I can to put business your way.'

She stood on tiptoe to kiss his cheek. 'Thank you, Percy. I had a feeling I could rely on you.'

He smiled ruefully. 'I wouldn't want to see you back on the streets selling flowers.'

'Who told you about that?'

'Susannah told my sister. It must have taken courage to survive on the city streets, and I admire that.'

Angel faced him squarely. 'Did Susannah also tell Belinda that I was a foundling, abandoned in Angel Alley, Whitechapel one Christmas Eve?'

'Only a fool would hold that against you.' Percy held her hand, giving her fingers a comforting squeeze. 'You are a remarkable young lady, and it was a stroke of good fortune that caused our paths to cross. I'm proud to know you, Angel Winter, and I promise I'll do my best to send custom your way.'

Angel was in a buoyant mood as she returned to the house, but her feeling of euphoria evaporated at the sight of Eloise pacing the floor in the entrance hall.

'I've been waiting for you, miss.'

'Is anything wrong, Aunt?'

'Wrong? How dare you ask that when you've humiliated us all by waiting on table at luncheon like a common lackey. What were our guests to think?'

Angel forced herself to remain calm. 'The Montgomeries are paying guests and they enjoyed a splendid meal that Cook made out of almost nothing. If you visited the kitchen occasionally you'd realise what hard work went into creating such a feast.'

'You behaved like a servant. It was utterly embarrassing.'

'A servant gets paid for their services. I did what I did out of love and loyalty to my family. I know it's not what you're used to, but if we don't act now you'll find yourself living on charity, as I have done since I was a child of twelve. I can tell you that it's not nice to be constantly reminded of your obligations.'

Eloise clutched at the newel post. 'I feel faint. No one talks to me in that manner.'

'Perhaps it's time they did. There's a harsh world outside Grantley's gates. I've experienced it – you haven't – and I wouldn't want you to either. But if you want to keep Grantley I suggest you allow me to try, because I don't see anyone else coming up with ideas.'

Eloise held her hand to her head. 'Help me up to my room, Angel. I'm having one of my turns.'

'No, you aren't,' Angel said coldly. 'You're

perfectly well, and you use these megrims in order to get your own way. Shout at me if you like, send me away if that's what you want, but if you've got a shred of sense you'll let me do things my way and then you might keep a roof over your head.'

Eloise snapped into an upright position, her face ashen and her eyes blazing. 'You are a very impertinent girl, but what can one expect from a foundling? Your mother was no better than she should be and I dare say you'll turn out the same. I'm going to my room and you must do what you like, but Sir Adolphus will hear of this when he returns from South Africa. We'll see what he has to say.' She ascended the stairs with her head held high and no sign of the weakness that often accompanied one of her fits of pique.

'So be it,' Angel said loudly. 'Uncle Dolph deserves our support. He has mine and I won't let him down, even if I have to beg, borrow or steal enough money to keep Grantley in the family.'

Percy and Belinda left early next morning for the wedding they were to attend in Colchester, but they booked rooms for an overnight stay in order to break the journey on their return to London. Angel went to the village and purchased a diary, and Miss Creedy let her have one for less than half price as there were only a few months left of the year. She was on the way home when she saw Danny striding towards her and she came to a halt, crossing her fingers beneath the folds of her cotton print gown.

'Well?' she asked breathlessly. 'Have you come

to a decision?'

He fell into step beside her. 'That's not much of a welcome, but yes, we have, and Pa and I want to take you up on your offer. Working together we can produce more, and Pa will sell the excess on his stall in the market.'

'That's wonderful. When can you start?'

'I'll come with you now, if that's all right. I want to get the measure of the greenhouse and work out what we can plant and when, although the growing season is almost over. We might be able to force things along in the greenhouse if we can heat it during the cold winter months.'

'I believe there's a coal stove, but it's fallen into disuse and covered with ivy. I came across it one day when I was a child.'

'That's what I was hoping, and if we can get it working again we might be able to go into business much sooner.'

They came to a halt inside the gates. 'I've got our second booking,' Angel said, holding up the diary. 'The first of many, I hope, so do whatever you have to do, Danny.'

He gave her a mock salute. 'Yes, General Winter.'

'Very funny, but you're not far wrong. Trying to convince the family that this is the only way to survive would be a challenge for the Iron Duke himself.' Angel left Danny to go about his business and she took the diary to her room, where she sat down at the small escritoire beneath the window and entered the Montgomeries' booking for one night.

'It's a start,' she said out loud, addressing a

startled pigeon that had landed on the sill and then flew off in alarm.

The money from the Montgomeries, together with the allotments Eloise received from her brother and Hector, were just enough to cover the next mortgage repayment, although it left virtually nothing for the family to exist on, and the servants would have to wait for their wages. Not to be beaten, Angel did a deal with the farmer whose land abutted the Grantley estate, allowing him to use the five-acre field for pasture, in return for milk, butter, cream and cheese. Similarly, the kitchen waste was kept in a bin and used to feed the farmer's pigs in return for cuts of pork and bacon when they became available. These measures, together with the produce from the kitchen garden, kept the family and servants fed, with enough fruit and vegetables left over to store for the winter or make into preserves.

The kitchen was the hub of Angel's small empire and she worked alongside Cook and Lil, pickling vegetables and bottling fruit according to the recipes in *Mrs Beeton's Book of Household Management*. The aroma of raspberry jam, simmering on the range, filled the house with the scent of autumn, and Angel managed to persuade Susannah to help her gather blackberries from the hedgerows. They returned from a particularly successful foray carrying baskets overflowing with ripe berries, their lips stained purple from sampling the fruit. Susannah complained that her skirts were muddied and her hands were ruined, but her cheeks were flushed and her eyes bright with laughter. Angel was satisfied that, for once, Susannah had forgotten that she was an elegant young lady and had enjoyed herself without worrying about what her mother might think. Humphrey also spent most of his time out of doors, either helping the aged gardener or working in the stables. In fact he showed more aptitude for estate management than either of his older brothers, and his latest project was building a hen house on the far side of the walled garden where he intended to keep chickens and supply the family with freshly laid eggs. Angel encouraged him, although Eloise said it was a passing phase and Humphrey would return to Rugby at the start of the new term and forget all about wanting to work the land.

'You will go into the Church if you cannot think of another profession,' Eloise said one day at breakfast. 'I didn't raise my sons to become farmers. Just look at your hands and fingernails, Humphrey. You look like a common labourer, and your skin is as swarthy as that of a gypsy. It won't do. It simply won't do. What would Sir Eugene say?'

'What has he got to do with anything, Mama?' Humphrey said crossly. 'He's not my father.'

Bright colour flooded Eloise's pale cheeks. 'Well, my dears,' she said, looking round at her children's startled faces. 'That's the thing. Sir Eugene has proposed marriage, and although naturally I didn't give him an answer straight away, I fully intend to accept.'

'I say, Mama, that's a bit sudden, isn't it?' Toby dropped his knife and fork on his plate with a loud clatter.

Humphrey sniggered, receiving a warning look from Angel, but Susannah pushed back her chair and leaped to her feet. 'Mama! How could you? I thought you had him in mind for me, not for you. You're too old to remarry.'

'I am not old,' Eloise said angrily. 'I'm forty-seven, two years younger than Sir Eugene – an ideal age. As for you, my girl, you made it plain that you thought he was far too senior in years to be your suitor.'

'So you decided to marry the richest man in Essex. I'll never forgive you, Mama.' Susannah stormed out of the room.

Toby rose to his feet. 'I suppose you realise what this means? You will go and live at Westwood and give up any claim you might have to Grantley. Sir Eugene has an heir and I doubt if he would want your family foisted upon him.'

'Really, Tobias, you're being ridiculous,' Eloise said faintly. 'Of course you would be welcome at Westwood Hall, but you would still have a home here.'

'I very much doubt it. You might take Susannah with you, but what about Humphrey and me, not to mention Angel? We don't know if we will be able to keep Grantley, and if it were sold where would we go?'

'But I've almost finished the hen house,' Humphrey protested. 'I was going to market to buy some pullets.'

'You're all being ridiculous,' Eloise stormed, tears flowing. 'Don't you want your mama to be happy?'

263

Toby threw up his hands. 'Happy? Will you be content when you know that you've ruined your children's lives?'

'You're being unreasonable. Your uncle won't allow Grantley to be sold.' Eloise stood up, shaking visibly as she faced them. 'I can't see why anything would change.'

'He can't afford to keep the estate going, Mama,' Toby said bluntly. 'We're only hanging on because Angel is running it like a business.' He turned to Angel, holding out his hand. 'Tell my mother how many bookings have come our way so far.'

'We have three couples booked in so far this week, with another two next week, and the sign that Humphrey made should attract the carriage trade. It's taking time but we're gradually building up the business.'

'And you wonder why I can't stand seeing the old house, my ancestral home, turned into a common lodging house?' Eloise's voice broke on a sob. 'I refuse to live like this. I want my old life back and when I marry Eugene I'll be a lady again.' She hurried from the room, sobbing into her hanky.

'Look what you've done, Toby,' Angel said angrily. 'That was uncalled for, and you don't know what Uncle Dolph plans to do. Why did you have to spoil her announcement?'

Toby put his hand in his pocket and took out a crumpled sheet of paper. 'This came yesterday. It was addressed to Mama but as head of the house, in the absence of Uncle Dolph and Hector, I opened it. Read it for yourself.'

'What does it say?' Humphrey demanded nervously. 'You've gone awfully pale, Angel. Is it bad news?'

Chapter Fifteen

It was very bad news, and once again, Angel travelled into London to see Galloway, but this time she had Toby with her. Galloway refused to see them at first but Toby lost his temper and threatened to break down the door, and eventually they were admitted to Galloway's dingy office.

Angel noticed that a snarling stuffed fox's head had been added to the trophies hanging from the wainscoting, and a pair of antlers hung precariously over a portrait of Galloway himself. It was crudely executed and unflattering, but he stood beneath it, thumbs tucked in the lapels of his expensive pinstriped jacket, glaring at them with an expression a little less friendly than that of the unfortunate fox.

'Well?' he snapped. 'What do you want? I could have sent for a copper to arrest you for disturbing the peace and assault, but I'm a generous man. Say what you have to say and then get out.'

'You, sir, are no gentleman.' Toby clenched his fists at his sides.

'What do you expect, Galloway?' Angel said angrily. 'You've threatened us with eviction, even though we're up to date with the repayments on the mortgage.'

Galloway sauntered over to his desk and sat down. 'But you've ignored the conditions of the agreement by letting rooms to travellers. It's clearly stated that the residence is for private use only.'

'I read the document and I don't recall seeing any such clause,' Angel said suspiciously. 'What proof have you got?'

Galloway opened a drawer and pulled out a sheaf of papers. 'It's clearly written here. Your uncle signed the document so it's legal and binding. Either you cease trading or court proceedings will be instigated.'

'Surely you can't do that,' Angel protested. 'You are supposed to be my uncle's solicitor, but you seem to be representing the creditors.'

'I'm merely offering you my advice,' Galloway said smoothly. 'As your lawyer I can only give you my opinion based on many years' experience and my extensive knowledge of legal matters.'

'I happen to be studying law, sir.' Toby leaned over the desk, his face close to Galloway's. 'I suspect that you have an ulterior motive and you want us to lose Grantley.'

'Prove it if you can.'

'I want a copy of that document,' Angel said firmly. 'We need to study it in detail.'

'Impossible. Has Sir Adolphus given you authority to handle his affairs?'

Angel and Toby exchanged anxious glances, and Galloway uttered a bark of laughter.

'Precisely my point. Go home and enjoy Grantley while you have a roof over your heads.

Stop this ridiculous attempt to turn the old house into a business and you might be able to remain there for a while longer, but continue as you are and you will lose your uncle's home for ever. Do I make myself clear?'

'You, sir, are a villain.' Toby slammed his fist on the desk, causing the glass inkwells to rattle on their silver stand. 'My uncle will hear of this.'

Galloway's eyes narrowed to slits. 'I'll say this once more – you have to cease trading immediately or the creditors will foreclose on the mortgage under the terms and conditions of the agreement. I'm only doing my duty as your uncle's legal representative.'

'You can't do this to us,' Angel cried passionately. 'Grantley has been in the family for generations.'

'But not your family,' Galloway said smoothly. 'You don't know where you came from, Angel Winter. Continue the way you are and you will be the one to find yourself back where you belong, on the streets of Whitechapel.' He rose from his seat. 'Now get out, both of you, or do I have to get my clerk to send for the police?'

Toby was about to argue but Angel grabbed his hand. 'We're wasting our time here.' She met Galloway's cynical grin with a defiant stare. 'I don't know what you hope to gain by this, but it's not over yet. We're not giving up easily.'

Outside the sun shone on the dusty pavements and the London plane trees were showing signs of autumn, their leaves turning colour in shades of yellow, gold and bronze, but the beauties of nature were far from Angel's mind and Toby was visibly seething with rage.

'I'd like to throttle that bastard,' he said, curling his hands into fists. 'I apologise for the language, Angel.'

She shook her head. 'There's no need. I feel the same way, but what can we do? He has all the documents and he's right in that none of us has Uncle Dolph's permission to make decisions about the estate. I don't suppose he imagined we would need it.'

'Galloway is up to no good – I'm certain of that – but without proof there's nothing we can do.'

'Perhaps Aunt Eloise is doing the right thing,' Angel said slowly. 'She's taking care of herself, and, although she's upset, I'm sure that Susannah will come round eventually.'

'I know what I must do.' Toby clutched her by the shoulders. 'I'm the man of the house and it's up to me. I'm going to Natal Province to find Uncle Dolph and tell him exactly what's going on. If necessary he can get a local lawyer to draw up a document giving me power of attorney so that I can put a stop to Galloway's game.'

'You could send a telegram,' Angel suggested dazedly. 'It would get there quicker.'

'But there's no certainty it would reach him, or that he would be able to reply, let alone sort out the legalities.'

'But how will you raise the money for the fare? It's a long journey.'

'I'll think of a way. I could sell my guns. They're Purdeys and they'll fetch a decent amount. I'll sell the family silver, if necessary, but Galloway isn't going to get his hands on Grantley. I'd give my life if it meant saving the old place from him.'

'Sell the silver?' Eloise stared at Toby as if he had gone mad. 'You can't do that. It doesn't belong to you or to me.'

'Mama,' Toby said patiently, 'you must try to understand the seriousness of our situation. Galloway is a villain, but I can't prove it without seeing the document he says Uncle Dolph signed. I don't know what game Galloway is playing, but he's not on our side, of that I'm certain.'

'But, Toby, my darling boy, it would be sheer madness for you to travel all the way to South Africa, and term begins soon. You must return to your studies.' Eloise turned to Angel, who had been sitting quietly, biding her time. 'Tell him, Angel. You pride yourself on having common sense.'

'It's the future of Grantley that's at stake, Aunt Eloise. I can't see any other way. Toby needs to have Uncle Dolph's permission before he can do anything.'

Eloise shook her head. 'I won't sanction it, Toby. Your uncle would never forgive me if I allowed as much as a teaspoon to be sold off to pay for such a jaunt. Write to him, or go to the War Office and ask them to contact Adolphus.'

'But, Mama—'

'No, Toby. I don't want to hear another word. Do as you please, but you are not going to sell a single family heirloom.' She swept out of the drawing room, leaving Angel and Toby staring after her in disbelief.

'She doesn't realise how serious this is,' Angel said, after a pause. 'Will you do as she says and visit the War Office?'

Toby strode over to the window and stared out at the sun-drenched gardens. 'All this could go, simply because my mother refuses to face the truth.'

'She doesn't know Galloway.' Angel walked over to join him. 'The gardens are so beautiful and the house has stood here for centuries. I can't bear to think of it falling into the hands of people who don't love it as we do.' She ran her fingers down the stone mullion that separated the leaded-light casement windows. 'We can't allow Grantley to be taken from the family, Toby.'

He slipped his arm around her shoulders. 'I don't intend to. Tomorrow, first thing, I'll take my Purdeys to London and I'll visit the War Office to find out if they would contact Uncle Dolph on our behalf, although I doubt if they'll be much help. I don't know if it's possible to send cablegrams all that way, but at least I can tell my mother that I've tried, and if I get a good price for my guns it might be enough to get me to South Africa. It's the signed power of attorney we need.' He frowned thoughtfully. 'In the meantime we'd better not take any more bookings.'

'The Montgomeries are arriving tomorrow, but they're friends and I won't accept any money from them, so Galloway can't use that against us.'

Toby gave her a searching look. 'Could it be that Percy Montgomerie has an ulterior motive for his frequent visits?'

'Maybe he comes to see Susannah.'

'Or maybe it's someone who is standing not a mile away from me at this moment,' Toby said, chuckling. 'Don't look so shocked, Angel. You're a very pretty lady, and clever too.'

'Don't talk nonsense.'

He shrugged and his smile faded. 'Whatever his reason for coming here, I'm grateful to him for his help, and now it's up to me. The more I think about it the more I'm convinced that I must travel to Natal Province if we're to save Grantley. I'll find Uncle Dolph if it's the last thing I do and I'll tell him exactly what's been occurring in his absence.'

'I wish I could come with you,' Angel said wistfully.

'Where I'm going is no place for a woman.'

'Dolly went there. She'll be living in camp with the other army wives.'

He shot her a sideways glance as he headed for the door. 'But Dolly isn't a lady – you are.'

Angel opened her mouth to reply but he had already left the room.

The next morning Angel was about to go to the kitchen to talk over the menus for the Montgomeries' visit, when she spotted Danny heading across the park in the direction of the kitchen garden. Until this moment she had not given any thought as to how their changed circumstances might affect the Wicks family, but she had unintentionally involved them in what could turn out to be a financial disaster.

Danny took the news with a degree of fatalism. 'I suppose it was too good to be true,' he said, shrugging. 'Pa and I have got the greenhouse tidied up and replaced the broken panes of glass. The boiler is in remarkably good shape, all things considered, and we were about to start planting seeds for an early crop of tomatoes, given that there's plenty of wood in the spinney to keep the fire going without spending money on coal.'

'I'm sorry I can't be more optimistic, Danny, but it doesn't mean you have to stop what you're doing. I'm hoping that we can get to Uncle Adolphus in time to stop Grantley being lost to us. I don't know what Galloway is playing at, but I don't trust him and it seems that he's working against us when it should be the reverse.'

Danny rolled up his sleeves, exposing muscular forearms bronzed by the summer sun. 'I'll sort him out for you, Angel.'

She met the humorous gleam in his eyes with a smile. 'I might hold you to that one day, but for now we'll have to muddle along as best we can.'

'I'll still keep the kitchen garden tidy for you and I've made a clamp to store the potatoes, carrots and beetroot for the winter.'

'A clamp?' Angel stared at him, puzzled.

He pointed to a mound at the far end of the garden. 'My pa always stores roots that way. It's a drainage trench and then layers of straw and soil to protect the vegetables.'

'Very clever,' Angel said, nodding. 'Thank you, Danny.'

'My pleasure, miss.' He doffed his cap, grinning widely. 'Now if there's nothing else to say, I'd best get on.'

'Of course. I'll leave you in peace then.' She

hesitated. 'Would you really take Galloway on?'

'Just say the word. I'd like to get my hands on the man who left you in the workhouse. Nothing would give me more pleasure than to bloody his nose and black his eye.'

'I hope it won't come to that, but thank you, anyway. It's good to know I have friends.'

'More than friends, I hope. You mean a lot to me, Angel.' He turned away and began sifting soil into wooden seed trays.

She had no reply for his last remark and she let herself out of the greenhouse. A chilly breeze fanned her hot cheeks and a shower of golden leaves scattered on the ground in front of her as she walked through the kitchen garden and out into the park. Danny's vehement statement had come as a surprise. She supposed that his response was based on gratitude for allowing him and his father to resurrect the old greenhouse. It was comforting to know that she had such staunch allies, but she was also a little uneasy. She hoped that she had not given him the wrong impression when she asked for his help. Keeping Grantley supplied with fruit and vegetables was purely a business arrangement and nothing more. She quickened her pace, heading for the house, but she could not forget the look in Danny's dark eyes, nor the cajoling tone in his voice.

Angel reached the house just as the Montgomeries' carriage drew up outside. She hurried to greet them as their footman leaped down to open the door. Percy climbed out first, holding out his hand to help Belinda to alight.

'Angel,' she cried, delightedly. 'It seems such a

273

long time since we were last here.' She rushed over to give her a hug. 'How well you look, but no wonder when you live in such a beautiful home with all this lovely parkland and fresh air.'

'This is your third visit in two months, Belle,' Percy said, smiling. 'We might as well live here.'

'Oh, that would be splendid,' Belinda clapped her hands. 'I'd love to live in the countryside. Charles Street is very fine in its own way, but in summer it's stifling and I long for green fields.'

'You're here now.' Angel returned the hug. 'Come inside and rest after your journey.'

'We've only travelled seven miles or so,' Percy said with a wry smile. 'It's hardly an overland trek.'

'Nevertheless, carriage rides are tiring, and I'm sure that Belinda would like some refreshments, and so would you, if you're being honest.'

'I'm always honest, and I see you've been working again.' Percy looked her up and down and Angel's hand flew automatically to smooth her hair, which had been ruffled by the wind. She realised then that the hem of her gown was damp and stained green from trailing over the dewy grass.

'I've been to see Danny in the kitchen garden,' she said hastily. 'I'll change before luncheon.'

'I suppose you'll be waiting on us yourself?'

She hesitated at the foot of the stone steps, giving him a searching look. 'You're being very critical, Percy. It's not like you. What brought this on?'

Belinda linked her hand through the crook of Angel's arm. 'Let's go indoors. Just ignore my brother. He's like this when he's worried about something or someone.' She glanced over her shoulder, pulling a face at Percy. 'Angel will wish we'd stayed at home if you keep picking on her.'

He followed them into the house. 'I'm sorry, Angel. I didn't mean to upset you. It's just that I don't like to see you living like this. I feel somewhat responsible for the hotel idea and I'm beginning to think it was a terrible mistake. It's too much responsibility to put on your shoulders.'

Angel led them to the morning parlour and closed the door out of habit, although there was no danger of servants eavesdropping. She waited until they were seated. 'I'm glad you're here because I count you both as my friends.'

'What's the matter?' Belinda asked anxiously. 'You look so serious, Angel.'

'Sit down and tell us what it is,' Percy said firmly. 'You know that we'll do anything we can to help.'

Angel faced them, clasping her hands tightly in front of her, and she explained why they must not offer her any money for their stay, and Toby's reasons for visiting the city. Belinda's expression mirrored her thoughts, but Percy remained stoically calm. He waited until she finished speaking.

'It sounds as though your lawyer is working against you,' he said slowly. 'The Society of Attorneys would be very interested in this case, but that doesn't help you at this moment.'

'Toby intends to go to South Africa to ask Uncle Dolph for the power of attorney so that we can demand to see the documents that Galloway is withholding, but I'm afraid it might take too long. We – I mean the family – could lose every-thing, Percy.'

'I'd put you in touch with my solicitor,' Percy said thoughtfully, 'but I'm sure that Galloway is too cunning to be caught out at this stage. At the moment it's all subtle threats and he would deny any suggestion that he was acting dishonestly.'

'What can they do?' Belinda jumped to her feet and wrapped her arms around Angel. 'I have a little money. I'll give it all to you, Angel, if it will help.'

'Thank you, Belle, but I wouldn't dream of taking it, and to be honest I think it would take a great deal of money to settle this problem.'

'I suggest we wait for Toby to return from London,' Percy said calmly. 'We can't do anything until we know what his plans are.'

Angel eyed him curiously. 'Does that mean you intend to help us, Percy?'

'If I can, but South Africa is far away. In a rough reckoning it would take three months to get there and back, maybe more. Could you hold out for that length of time?'

Angel shook her head. 'I can just about scrape up enough money to pay the mortgage this month, but that leaves us with nothing to live on, and the servants haven't been paid since last quarter.'

'I could lend you the money,' Percy said slowly, 'but even if Toby gets to see the actual agreement that Sir Adolphus signed, he might find that it's legal and binding. If so, there's nothing that will save Grantley, and perhaps you ought to face that fact.'

'Don't say things like that.' Belinda's bottom lip wobbled and her blue eyes filled with tears. 'Can't you see you're upsetting Angel?'

'I'm sorry, and I know it's hard, but you and Toby have to be realistic,' Percy said firmly. 'This predicament is due to the reckless investments that Sir Adolphus made, which virtually bankrupted him and the estate. It might be too late to do anything about it, Angel. I'm sorry, but it's true.'

'We'll wait for Toby to come home,' Angel said stubbornly. 'Anyway, where are my manners? I'll go to the kitchen and ask Cook to make some coffee for you.'

'Why not ring the bell?' Percy asked, chuckling. 'You have a few servants left.'

'Lil and Flossie are in the laundry room and Meg is helping Aunt Eloise to dress. She's been invited to lunch at Westwood Hall. You do know that she's engaged to be married to Sir Eugene, don't you?'

'It was in *The Times*,' Belinda said excitedly. 'It's so romantic.'

'How does Susannah feel about it?'

'We're all very happy, of course.' Angel opened the door and came face to face with Susannah. 'Oh, we were just talking about you, Sukey. Percy wanted to know what you thought about your mama marrying Sir Eugene.'

Susannah sailed into the room and embraced Belinda like a long-lost sister. She held her hand out to Percy. 'I'm delighted that Mama has found happiness again,' she said, intoning the words like a child repeating its catechism. 'How lovely to see you both. Are you staying long this time?'

Angel left them and hurried to the kitchen to make a pot of coffee. Cook was never in a good mood these days and the tensions in the family seemed to have permeated the whole house.

Toby returned from London in time to join everyone in the drawing room where they had gathered before dinner. Angel had changed into a gown more suitable for entertaining guests, but she was still flushed from the heat of the kitchen where she had helped Cook to prepare the food. Eloise had sent word that she would be staying at Westwood for dinner, and Susannah had taken over the role of hostess, which she was obviously enjoying, although she was using the freedom to flirt outrageously with Percy.

Angel waited impatiently for Toby to settle down with a glass of sherry. 'Well?' she said eagerly. 'Did you have any luck in London?'

'Why did you go there anyway?' Susannah demanded. 'Nobody tells me anything.'

Toby exchanged wary glances with Angel. 'We didn't want to worry you, Susie. There's nothing you can do about the situation.'

'What situation?' Susannah looked from one to the other, shaking her head. 'I'm not a child, Toby. Why do you confide in Angel and not in me?'

'What happened in London, Toby?' Percy asked curiously. 'Did you get anywhere with the War Office? Angel told us what's happened.'

'I was fobbed off with a junior clerk who said he'd look into the matter, but it was all top secret and he doubted if anything could be done to get in touch with Uncle Dolph, at least not quickly.'

'So what will you do?' Angel asked. 'Did you sell your guns?'

Toby nodded gloomily. 'Yes. They fetched a good price, as I knew they would.'

'You sold the Purdeys?' Susannah stared at him, her eyes wide with shock. 'But they were your most prized possession. They belonged to Papa and he left them to you in his will.'

'Don't rub it in, Susie. It was a last resort, but at least I have the fare to Durban.'

'Why would you want to go there?' Susannah rose to her feet and filled a glass with sherry. She sat down again and sipped her drink. 'What's going on? You are all in it together, quite obviously, so please tell me before I scream.'

Angel was seated next to her and she reached out to pat Susannah's hand. 'We're in a fix, Sukey. Toby didn't want to worry you, but it's possible we might lose Grantley even though we've been repaying the mortgage.'

'I don't know why you include yourself,' Susannah said spitefully. 'Grantley doesn't belong to you.'

'It's not yours either.' Toby slammed his empty glass down on a drum table at his side. 'The estate belongs to Uncle Dolph and if anything happened to him it will go to Hector, but it's Angel's home just as much as it's ours. This is why we don't tell you things, Susie. You only think of yourself.'

Percy held up his hands. 'Wait a minute, Toby. Susannah has a point in that the present situation affects all of you. Angel told me everything and,

279

in my opinion, for what it's worth, I doubt if simply getting a power of attorney is going to save Grantley from grasping creditors. It seems to me that this man Galloway is in league with the people who want to get their hands on the estate, for what reason I've no idea, but it smacks of collusion and dirty dealing.'

Toby glared at him with a belligerent set to his jaw. 'Then what would you advise? Do we just sit back and allow it to happen?'

'We can't do that,' Angel cried passionately. 'We've fought so hard, we can't just give up.'

'I think I'm going to cry,' Belinda said tearfully. 'It's so sad.'

'Well, I'm not giving in so easily.' Toby rose to his feet. 'I'm tired and dusty after a long ride, so I'll go and change before dinner, but this isn't over, Percy. I'm not going to let Grantley go without a fight.' He stormed out of the room, leaving the door to slam of its own accord.

'I'm going to tell Mama and Sir Eugene,' Susannah said, pouting. 'If he's going to marry her the least he can do is save Grantley for her children.'

Angel was about to say something soothing when the door opened and Lil stomped into the drawing room, wiping her reddened hands on her apron. 'Dinner's served.'

'Toby has just gone upstairs to change,' Angel said tactfully. 'We'll have to wait until he comes down.'

Lil stood, arms akimbo. 'You try telling that to Cook. She's worked herself into a state and been throwing knives around – one of them almost sliced Flossie's ear off. We've all had enough of trying to make proper meals out of what Master Toby brings down with his gun and what's left in the vegetable garden.' She glared at Percy and Belinda. 'You started this daft business of running the house like a hotel. Well, you should try doing it with a handful of servants and nuppence in the bank.' She turned to point her finger at Susannah. 'If you peach on me and tell your ma what I just said, you'll find yourself without any servants. We're all looking for other positions and if I go I take Angel with me. I ain't leaving my baby girl in a sinking ship.' She flounced out of the room leaving everyone in stunned silence.

'You're her daughter?' Belinda said dazedly.

'No. I'm not.' Angel rose to her feet. 'But I'd be proud to have someone as kind and loving as her for a mother.'

'I'm sorry,' Belinda said hastily. 'I did know you were a foundling – I didn't mean to upset you. It must be awful having nothing to connect you to your real family.'

'I doubt if I'll ever find out who my mother was, but I'm sure she had a good reason for abandoning me.' Angel traced the outline of the ring beneath the ruched silk of her pale-blue gown. She was tempted to show it to them, but it was her secret and hers alone – the only thing that linked her with the woman who had given her up, for whatever reason.

Percy cleared his throat noisily. 'You shouldn't make personal remarks, Belle. It's not done.'

'I've said I'm sorry.' Belinda was on the verge of tears but the door flew open and this time it was

Humphrey who rushed into the room.

'A messenger arrived with this. It's for Toby and I think it's from the War Office.'

Susannah was first on her feet and she snatched it from him. 'It must be about Uncle Dolph. Maybe he's coming home.'

'It's addressed to Toby,' Angel said hastily. 'You should wait until he comes down.'

'It'll be for all of us,' Susannah said, breaking the seal. 'Oh, no!' she murmured, and sank to the floor in a dead faint.

Chapter Sixteen

The news that Sir Adolphus had died of a fever in camp had come as a shock and had left the family in deep mourning. Even though they had never been close, Angel felt his loss deeply. Sir Adolphus had been her saviour and her mentor, but Eloise was his sister and she had taken the news badly, retiring to her room and refusing to come out, even though Susannah, perhaps surprisingly for someone so self-centred, was in no fit state to be of any practical use. Their inability to do anything constructive made it necessary for Angel to accompany Toby to the solicitor's office in an attempt to sort out the late colonel's affairs.

It was the third time she had been to see Galloway, and although he pretended to be sympathetic it was obvious that he was far from sincere in his condolences, and Angel had difficulty in containing her anger.

'Your brother is the heir to the estate.' Galloway addressed himself to Toby. 'I have your uncle's will here and he leaves everything to Hector Devane, with a few minor bequests, which sadly will not be fulfilled because there are insufficient funds.'

'What are you saying, sir?' Toby demanded.

Angel could see that Galloway was enjoying their discomfort. His beady eyes glittered with malice and she felt a shiver run down her spine. This was not going to end well.

'The mortgage agreement is null and void now that your uncle is deceased. It will be up to Captain Devane to renegotiate the terms.'

'But Hector is in Natal Province,' Angel protested. 'You know that well enough.'

Grinning broadly, Galloway sat back in his throne-like chair. 'Indeed I do, and if the creditors are not prepared to await his return, they will demand immediate repayment of the entire sum.' He scribbled some figures on a sheet of paper and slid it across the table. 'Can you find this amount of money quickly?'

Toby gulped and swallowed. 'But this is more than my uncle borrowed in the first place.'

'Naturally interest has been added, which is only to be expected.'

'You're enjoying this, aren't you?' Angel said angrily. 'Who are these creditors, and why are you taking their side. What's in it for you?'

Galloway laid his hand on his heart. 'I'm hurt that you think so little of me. I abide by the rules of the society that governs my profession.'

'I don't believe you, Galloway.' Toby thumped

his fist on the desk, sending the inkwell skittering across the tooled-leather surface. 'What do you gain from our misfortune?'

Galloway rose to his feet and leaned across the desk, glaring at Toby. 'You can't pay, can you? I know your family finances and you haven't got two ha'pennies to rub together.'

'So what happens if we can't get my brother home in time to sign a new contract, even supposing the creditors agree to such a thing?' Toby faced him angrily and his voice shook with emotion.

'The creditors will foreclose and take possession of the estate.' Galloway resumed his seat, a triumphant smile replacing his belligerent scowl. 'You might not have noticed, but the area where you live is rapidly becoming a dormitory for the City of London. The railway makes it possible for workers to travel into town each day, and quite soon Grantley and the surrounding land will be criss-crossed with streets crammed with yellow-brick two-storey terraced houses. Hundreds of families will form communities where once only the rich and privileged lived, and you and your kind will be forced to earn your money like the rest of us.'

Angel glanced anxiously at Toby and for a moment she thought he was going to punch Galloway's smug face, but the touch of her hand on his arm restrained him.

'What do you get out of this?' Toby growled.

'A handsome bonus, enough to allow me to retire to the country where I already own a decent-sized property.'

'You, sir, are a dishonest man and a disgrace to

your profession.' Toby made a move towards the door. 'Don't think you can get away with this. We're not done for yet.'

Angel followed him out of the office and along the now-familiar dark passage. The clerk glanced anxiously at them but they passed him without saying a word. It was only when they reached the – street outside that Toby vented his feelings. He uttered a loud yell that sent pigeons and sparrows flying for the safety of the trees.

'If I was qualified now I'd sue him for client conflict and own-interest conflict and anything else that I could get him for, the thieving b–' He broke off, grimacing. 'Sorry, Angel, but I'm so bloody angry.'

'I know, I feel the same, but we need to think clearly. Let's go home.' She waved to the Montgomeries' coachman, who was waiting for them on the far side of the gardens. 'Maybe Percy has some ideas, or we could ask Sir Eugene.'

'This is Devane business now. I'm not going cap in hand to Sir Eugene. He'll take care of Mama, which is one worry less, but the rest of us will have to find our own way out of the mess Uncle Dolph foisted upon us.'

'I wish Hector were here,' Angel said wholeheartedly. 'It's bad enough having lost Uncle Dolph, without Hector risking his life thousands of miles away.'

'My brother can't help us out of this hole. He has only his army pay, and you heard Galloway: there's no money for him to inherit.' Toby stepped forward as the carriage drew to a halt, and he opened the door. 'It doesn't look good for any of

285

us, Angel.' He handed her into the vehicle and leaped in after her.

They arrived home to be greeted by Humphrey.

'They've been waiting for you for hours, Toby. I had to come outside because I couldn't stand it any longer.' He took the steps two at a time and opened the front door. 'Sir Eugene wants us to sell Grantley, and Mama agrees with him. You've got to stop them.'

'I'm not sure there's anything I can do.' Toby strode into the hall, tossing his hat and gloves onto a chair. 'Come on, Angel, this concerns you as much as it does the Devanes.'

'I feel somewhat to blame for all this,' Angel said guiltily. 'I'm sure Galloway bears a grudge against me, although I don't know why he should. I've done nothing to him.'

Humphrey grasped her hand. 'Don't say things like that. You're one of us and it's not your fault.'

'Thank you, Humpty Dumpty. If only that were true.'

They entered the drawing room to find Sir Eugene and Eloise waiting for them, with Percy, Belinda, Blanche and Susannah looking as though they were about to witness a trial by jury where the accused was a serial killer.

'What news, Toby?' Sir Eugene demanded sharply. 'I can tell by your expression that it didn't go well.'

Toby glanced round at their expectant faces and he shook his head. 'No, it's not good, sir.'

Angel went to sit beside Susannah, listening quietly while Toby repeated what Galloway had told them. She loved Grantley, but she realised that the feeling went even deeper with Eloise, who had been born in the old house and whose entire way of life was under threat. Her heart ached for the family that had adopted her, and for Hector, who was too far away to do anything to save his home and protect those he loved.

Eloise clutched Sir Eugene's arm. 'What will happen now? I can't bear the thought of Grantley being razed to the ground, and the beautiful gardens torn up to be covered in brick and concrete.'

He patted her hand. 'I'm not sure that there's anything to be done, my dear. I'm afraid your brother left his affairs in such a parlous state that losing Grantley is more or less inevitable.'

Percy nodded. 'I know it's nothing to do with me, but I was going to offer financial help until Toby informed us of the facts. Even if this man Galloway is in collusion with the creditors, that would appear to be a separate matter. The family could take him to court for misconduct, but the costs incurred would be prohibitive and the outcome uncertain.'

'I could have run it as a hotel,' Angel said passionately. 'I'm sure I could have made it pay.'

'I don't doubt it,' Sir Eugene said kindly. 'I'll consult my solicitor to see if there's anything we can do to save the estate, but the real reason I came here today was to tell you that Eloise and I have named the day. We're to be married by special licence in three days' time.'

A murmur of congratulations rippled round the room, although it was hardly a joyous chorus. 'That's wonderful news.' Angel nudged Susannah, who nodded and murmured something unintelligible.

Eloise blushed and smiled. 'Of course we want you all to come to the wedding, including Percy and Belinda. You might have come into our lives through an accident on the highway, but you are now valued friends.'

'Thank you,' Belinda said, smiling.

'Of course we would be delighted to attend,' Percy added, nodding.

'Congratulations, sir,' Toby said stiffly. 'I hope you will both be very happy.'

'You will be welcome to reside with us at Westwood Hall,' Sir Eugene said, encompassing the brothers and Susannah with a wave of his hand. 'That includes you too, Angel. We will be one family.'

Angel could tell that Susannah was not delighted by the generous offer, and Blanche did not look too pleased either. Humphrey and Toby retreated to the window seat, saying nothing, but it was clear that the Devane siblings did not take too kindly to the idea.

'Might I make a suggestion?' Percy rose from his seat and went to stand in front of the fireplace. 'I agree with Sir Eugene that independent legal advice should be sought in the hope of delaying the repossession of Grantley. Maybe an application to the War Office on compassionate grounds might be enough to bring Hector home so that he can challenge the agreement signed by his uncle. It's a slim hope, but there may be by-laws that would prevent the land being used for housing, and local authorities would have to approve the plans for new buildings.'

'Well said, Percy.' Toby sprang to his feet. 'I remember studying the Local Government Act of 1858 in one of my law classes, although I'm blowed if I can recall any details.'

Blanche clapped her hands. 'I think that's a wonderful idea, Percy. You are so clever.'

Susannah gave her a withering look. 'And you are so obvious.'

'I don't know what you're talking about,' Blanche said, blushing. 'I know how I'd feel if Westwood was about to be sold.'

'There is one thing I insist upon,' Sir Eugene said firmly. 'Eloise and I have talked it over at length. Toby must return to Oxford to complete his studies, and Humphrey will continue at Rugby.' He fixed Toby with a stern stare. 'As your stepfather I will be willing to foot the bill and it would make your mother very happy.'

'That's very generous of you, sir.' Toby nudged Humphrey, who nodded dutifully, although Angel suspected that he was far from pleased. She knew that he still hankered after a life on the stage, but would not dare admit it to his elder brother or his mother, let alone his prospective stepfather. Sir Eugene was not the sort of man who would take kindly to a son of his treading the boards.

'And Susannah and Blanche will be sisters,' Eloise continued happily. 'I'll be devastated if we lose Grantley, but life must go on and I'm sure we'll all be very happy at Westwood Hall.'

Angel could see that Susannah had her doubts and she squeezed her hand. 'There's always the house in London if you are desperate,' she whispered.

'What did you say, Angel?' Toby came to life, leaping to his feet.

'Galloway didn't say anything about the house in Naked Boy Court. Maybe Uncle Dolph didn't mention it in his will.'

'I always hated that house,' Eloise said, shuddering. 'I'm sure it's haunted.'

Sir Eugene slipped his arm around her shoulders. 'Would the sale of it raise enough money to save Grantley?'

'I can't say, Eugene. Anyway, it would be up to Hector to make that decision. He must come home to sort out his affairs. You'll have to tell the War Office in the strongest terms that we need him, my dear.'

'You mustn't worry, Eloise. I'll put my solicitor to work and you must concentrate on our wedding. You and the girls have only a few days in which to make ready.'

'That means a shopping trip to the West End,' she said excitedly. 'We will all go, Susannah, Blanche and Angel.' She turned to Belinda with a persuasive smile. 'I'd be delighted if you would accompany us.'

Angel glanced at the clock on the mantelshelf and realised with a start that it was almost four o'clock. Lil and Cook would be working frantically below stairs in an attempt to make a meal fit for their guests, and she would be needed to help. 'If you'll excuse me, Aunt Eloise. I must go and change.'

'It's too early to dress for dinner,' Susannah

said pointedly.

'There won't be any dinner if I don't give them a hand in the kitchen. You might be living in the past, Sukey, but some of us have to get on with things, no matter what.' Angel stood up, flashed an apologetic smile in her aunt's direction and hurried from the room.

The shopping trip went well, but the amount of money that Eloise spent at the House of Worth in Regent Street both surprised and shocked Angel. The cost of one dress alone would have been enough to pay the servants' wages for the last quarter. Sir Eugene might be funding everything, but given the choice, Angel would have chosen to wear an old gown and put the princely cost of the new outfit to better use. As it happened she had no choice in the matter and somewhat reluctantly, and under pressure from Susannah, she chose a raw-silk polonaise dress in turquoise with a ruffled neckline and beaded embroidery. It was the simplest of all the gowns modelled for them and paled into insignificance when compared with Eloise's blush-pink silk wedding dress, embellished with crystals and frills trimmed with lace. Susannah and Blanche chose equally extravagant gowns and, not to be outdone, Belinda picked a striking outfit in French ultramarine tussore with a dashing feathered hat that threatened to put everyone in the shade. The gowns, all of which fitted without the need for alteration, were to be delivered by carrier, but Angel returned to Grantley feeling depressed and guilty. Hector might soon be risking his life, fighting for his country, and it seemed wrong to fritter away Sir Eugene's fortune on garments that might be worn once or twice, and then consigned to a trunk in the attic for the moths to feast on. She had no idea of the total cost, but surely it would have gone a long way to pay off the debt on Grantley. It was frustrating, but it was out of her hands.

Even though the reception was to be held at Westwood Hall, Angel felt that Grantley deserved some share in the festivities, and she filled the entrance hall and reception rooms with vases of chrysanthemums, late dahlias and greenery from the garden. It had fallen to Angel to break the news that the wedding breakfast was to be prepared and served by Sir Eugene's army of servants, a task she was dreading, and Cook's reaction was exactly what she had been expecting, only a little more colourful. As usual it was Lil who came to her rescue. She told Cook to think herself lucky that the work was being done elsewhere and now they wouldn't have to scratch their heads thinking up a menu that would please all the toffs that Sir Eugene would invite. But Cook's pride was hurt and the good name of Grantley was, in her mind, tarnished beyond repair. Lil had thrown up her hands in despair and gone outside to smoke the last of her baccy, leaving Angel to pacify Cook. After a failed attempt she had given up and gone to find Danny to break the news that their plans for turning the greenhouse into a going concern were about to come to nothing.

Danny was cleaning the glass panes with vinegar and water when Angel found him. His smile of welcome faded. 'What's up? Something's wrong, I can tell by the look on your face.'

She sighed. 'Is it so obvious?'

'It's about Grantley, isn't it? I was in the village yesterday and they're all talking about it. They're saying that Sir Adolphus is dead and the whole estate is to be sold. Is that true?'

'Our last hope has gone. He died penniless and it seems that Grantley is going to be buried, beneath brick and concrete. I am so sorry, Danny.'

'It's not your fault, girl. You gave me fair warning, and anyway Dad and me knew it was a risk.'

'Jack will be disappointed and so will Sally.'

He shook his head. 'My mum and dad are old hands in the growing game. They've had their ups and downs and they'll deal with this one. Is it definite?'

'I think it would take a miracle to get us out of this mess.' She turned her head away, unable to look him in the eye, but with a swift movement he took her in his arms and kissed her hard on the lips. It was a clumsy but passionate embrace that took her by surprise, and yet it seemed the most natural thing in the world to respond to the urgency of his embrace, but it was over as suddenly as it had begun. He released her with a murmured apology.

'I'm sorry, Angel.'

She stood there, unable to move away from the comforting nearness and warmth that exuded from his strong frame. He seized her by the shoulders, his fingers pressing into her flesh.

'No, I'm not sorry. I've wanted to do that ever since we met that day on the marshes, but you've grown into such a lady, I was afraid you'd be offended by a coarse, common sort of fellow like me.'

She met his intense gaze with a straight look, holding on to her dignity even though she was shaken to the core by the sudden change in their relationship. 'Don't say that, Danny. You're none of those things and I'm just the same person I was when we first met.'

'I took advantage of you just now. I shouldn't have kissed you.' His serious expression melted into a boyish grin. 'But I'm glad I did. It was worth a slap in the face, except that you're too well-mannered to stoop so low.'

'I'll slap you if it will make you feel better,' Angel said, smiling.

'You're not angry with me?'

'Danny, we're friends. Let's keep it that way.'

'You're saying that you don't have feelings for me.'

'I don't know, and that's the truth.'

'But you kissed me back, Angel. You must have some affection for me.'

'Everything is so confused at the moment that it's difficult to think straight. Maybe when matters are clearer–' She broke off, unable to finish the sentence without giving him false hope. It was true, she had responded to his unexpected embrace, and, if she were being honest, she was left wanting more. She could not look him in the eye.

'Does that mean I have a chance with you, Angel? If you tell me no, I'll never bother you again.'

'I have to go now. The wedding is tomorrow and

there's so much left to do.' She hurried from the greenhouse, but she sensed that he was watching her and she could still feel his arms around her, and the taste of his mouth lingered on her lips like vintage wine.

She had calmed down a little as she left the walled garden. The hazy sunshine of early autumn turned the piles of leaves beneath the oak trees into mounds of molten gold and squirrels clambered amongst the branches gathering acorns to store away for the coming winter. There was a hint of a chill in the breeze and Angel had the feeling that it was not only summer that was coming to an end – it was the way of life that the family at Grantley had enjoyed for centuries that was coming to a close. She shivered, despite the warmth of the sun on the back of her head, and she found herself making for the rear entrance in case Aunt Eloise should look out of the window. If she saw her bareheaded and without gloves there would be the inevitable lecture on how a young lady must conduct herself. But well-bred young ladies did not behave as she had in the greenhouse. They did not allow young men to kiss them in the way that Danny had just kissed her, and, above all, they did not allow themselves to enjoy the experience.

Angel pushed such thoughts to the back of her mind. There were problems enough without adding complications, and her main concern should have been to prevent the Wicks family from losing business. She came to a sudden halt, wondering why she had not thought of it before. Sir Eugene owned most of the land that stretched to the edge of the marshes. Maybe he could be persuaded to let some of it to Jack and Danny at a reasonable rent. She decided to ask him at the first possible opportunity, but now there was a nervous bride to deal with and a depressed Susannah, who was still piqued because Sir Eugene had chosen a more mature woman. Angel was not looking forward to the wedding next day. There would be tears before bedtime, as Lil had always said when Angel was small, only this time it would be Susannah who had the tantrum.

Eloise walked up the aisle on Toby's arm. He was leaving for Oxford later that day, but he had agreed, somewhat reluctantly, to give his mother away. Humphrey had offered but Eloise had refused without hesitation. 'Thank you, Humphrey dear, but I'm afraid you would forget what you were supposed to be doing and leave me standing outside the church, or you would tread on my train and ruin my beautiful new gown. You are a sweet boy, but you are a disaster when it comes to the social graces, and you haven't got a morning suit. You can't plod down the aisle in corduroy and tweed, even if it would elicit a laugh from the congregation.'

Humphrey had retired hastily to the kitchen where Cook, who had always had a soft spot for him, allowed him to sample some of the rock cakes she had made for the servants' party that evening. Angel was already there, checking the provisions that Sir Eugene had insisted on providing for those below stairs, which included a crate of champagne and another of ale. Lil had her eye on the beer, but Cook said she fancied a glass or two of bubbly, although Meg and Flossie were more interested in the huge iced cake that had been sent from the Westwood Hall kitchens. Cook said it was an insult to her abilities, but Angel had caught Flossie pinching a bit of the icing and she had a feeling that Cook would be outvoted on this occasion.

But for the moment there was accord in the Devane family. Humphrey was seated in the front pew with Angel, Susannah, and Blanche; Percy and Belinda were directly behind, while Cook, Lil, Meg, Flossie and the outdoor staff sat in the back row. The small church was crowded and it seemed that the whole village had turned out to witness Mrs Devane become Lady Westwood. Angel was touched to see Danny and his parents amongst the congregation dressed in their Sunday best, and it made her even more determined to speak to Sir Eugene at the first opportunity.

With the ceremony over, the newlyweds left the church to the vibrant sound of Mendelssohn's 'Wedding March', played with gusto by Miss Creedy, who was resplendent in a purple dress and a bonnet decorated with an ostrich feather that kept time with every nod of her head and tickled her nose. Angel had been mesmerised by it during the ceremony, especially when Miss Creedy had to keep moving her head from side to side in order to read the music. How she had managed to perform without sneezing continuously was little short of a miracle, but she had soldiered on and had not hit too many wrong notes.

Outside the church one of the Westwood Hall footmen stood by the waiting landau, which had been decorated with swags of greenery and white roses, and the four-in-hand tossed their heads as if eager to start off on the road home to their comfortable stable. Rose petals were thrown, and the crowd cheered as the bride and groom walked slowly towards the vehicle, but Eloise hesitated as she drew level with the family.

'Toby, my dear, are you sure you cannot stay for the wedding breakfast?'

He kissed her on the cheek. 'No, Mama, we've been through all this. I've arranged to travel with one of my friends, and we're meeting at Paddington Station at four, so I can't be late.'

'You will come home for Christmas, won't you, Toby?'

'Of course, and I'll ride over to Westwood every day to call on you.'

Sir Eugene cleared his throat. 'That might not be possible, my boy. I wasn't going to broach the subject until after the reception, but I received a letter from my solicitor this morning. He's been in touch with Galloway and although he didn't say as much, I gather that he shares our opinion of the fellow.'

'What are you saying, Eugene?' Eloise demanded querulously. 'This surely isn't the time to talk about such things.'

He glanced over his shoulder at the villagers who were watching at a respectful distance. 'This is exactly the time, my love. I can't allow your sons to return to their studies in ignorance of the situation. It seems that the creditors have agreed to a temporary stay of execution as regards the repossession of Grantley, but only if the house is vacated immediately and remains in that state until matters are settled.'

'Are they willing to wait until Hector returns?' Angel asked breathlessly. 'According to the newspapers there is still peace in Natal Province.'

Sir Eugene nodded. 'For the time being, it seems, but I wouldn't be surprised if there weren't all-out war with the Zulus and the Boers before long. However, that's not our problem. We can only hope that Hector and Rupert are on their way home. I've made representations to the War Office, but so far I haven't had a response.'

'Hector will sort things out.' Toby shook Sir Eugene's hand. 'Goodbye, sir. I trust you to take good care of Mama. She's very precious to those who love her.'

'Don't make me cry on my wedding day,' Eloise implored, her eyes misting. 'I haven't got a hanky with me.'

Angel produced one from her reticule and handed it to her. 'It's good news, I think.' She glanced anxiously at Sir Eugene.

'Of course it is, silly,' Susannah said dismissively. 'Hector will take charge. Anyway, part of this is his fault. He should have discussed financial matters with Uncle Dolph and made certain that Grantley was safe before he went cavorting off on his steed, and acting the hero.'

'That's not fair.' Angel faced her angrily. 'He couldn't have foreseen what would happen.'

Susannah shrugged. 'Maybe, but I'm glad I agreed to move to Westwood. Where will you go, Angel Winter? I believe you're homeless once again. How very sad.'

Chapter Seventeen

'That was mean,' Blanche said angrily. 'You'd better not make trouble when you live with us, Susannah, because I won't put up with it.'

'That's enough,' Sir Eugene snapped. 'You're upsetting your mama, and I mean that to include you, too, Blanche. As for you Angel, of course you are welcome at Westwood Hall, as well as the indoor staff from Grantley. Westwood is large enough to house everyone, at least temporarily. According to my solicitor the outdoor staff are to be kept on by the creditors in order to prevent the estate falling into disrepair. Does that clarify matters sufficiently?' He looked from one to the other, and when no one had anything to say he handed his bride into the carriage. 'For heaven's sake smile, my dear. Wave to the villagers and try to look happy. We don't want them thinking they're attending a wake and not a wedding.'

Eloise smiled valiantly as she settled herself in the landau and Sir Eugene climbed in beside her. The crowd waved and cheered as a second carriage drew up to take the rest of the family to Westwood Hall, except for Toby, who kissed his sister and gave Angel a fond hug.

'There's always the town house,' he said in a low voice. 'Hector would want you to go there, and I think you should take the servants with you. I doubt if Cook would fit in with the staff at

Westwood and I'm fond of the old girl, even if she is a bit of a tartar at times.'

Susannah's spiteful words had shaken Angel, as had Sir Eugene's announcement that Grantley was no longer to be her home. 'What would Hector say?'

'He'll be furious when he finds out what's been going on, and he'd want you to be looked after. Go to Naked Boy Court and stay there until he returns. In the meantime I'm going to study my law books and speak to my professors to see if there's anything more that can be done. We're not giving up Grantley without a fight. Are you with me?'

'Of course I am.'

'Oh, do come along, Angel.' Susannah was already in the carriage seated beside Blanche, who was pouting ominously.

Percy had been chatting with a group of well-wishers, but he broke away from them and strolled over to join Toby and Angel. 'My carriage is over there, Angel. Would you like to travel with Belinda and myself? Humphrey seems to have taken your place with the girls.'

'There'll be fireworks before evening, Percy, old man,' Toby said, chuckling. 'I wish I could hang around to see it happen, but one of our grooms is waiting with my horse and I'm off to the railway station.'

Percy turned to his sister, who had come to join them. 'Here's someone who is excellent at letter writing. Belinda has an eye for details that would make the great Miss Austen green with envy.'

'Oh, Percy, you do exaggerate so.' Belinda's

301

cheeks flushed a delicate shade of pink. 'Don't listen to him, Toby.'

'Nonsense, Belle, the poor fellow is leaving us to bury himself in the hallowed halls of Oxford. You will correspond and keep him up to date with everything, won't you?'

She smiled shyly. 'Would that be all right, Toby? I wouldn't want to take you away from studies.'

'It would be splendid.' Toby raised her hand to his lips. 'I'll look forward to hearing from you. Humphrey will give you my address, but now I really must go.' He turned to Angel, giving her a last hug. 'Remember what I said. Don't let them get the better of you; you're worth ten of them.' He strode off, heading for a spot beneath an orange-berried rowan tree where the groom was waiting with his mount.

The carriage containing Susannah, Blanche and Humphrey had already left and the Montgomeries' barouche took its place. Percy helped Belinda to mount the step but Angel caught sight of Danny standing with his parents. 'Would you mind waiting just a second?'

'Not at all, Angel. Take your time.'

She hurried to join the Wicks family and was greeted warmly by Sally and Jack, but Danny acknowledged her with a wary smile. 'I have to be quick because my friends are waiting for me,' Angel said breathlessly. 'I just wanted to tell you that Grantley is to be closed for the time being, but I've had an idea that might help you.'

Jack shook his head. 'You mustn't feel obligated to us, girl. Danny explained the situation and we understand.'

'I still might be able to help,' Angel insisted. 'I'm going to speak to Sir Eugene and ask if he'll rent you some of his land near the marsh. You told me that you needed to expand your business.'

Jack pushed his best bowler hat to the back of his head. 'I suppose I did, but it's not your problem, Angel. Although more land, at the right rent, would be just the thing.'

'You and Sally were good to me when I was younger and I've never forgotten it. If I can help you now then it will make me very happy.'

Sally clutched Angel's arm. 'But, my dear, you don't owe us anything. Just look at you now, you're living in that beautiful big house, and your gown must have cost a fortune. You're a proper young lady.' She glanced at her son. 'Isn't she beautiful, Danny? You'll remember what a skinny little scrap of a girl she was when you took her back to London with the mistletoe.'

'Aye, Ma. I do.'

Angel shot him a sideways look and the memory of his kiss brought a blush to her cheeks. 'There's plenty of mistletoe in the orchard at Grantley,' she said hastily. 'If things go well I'm sure you'd be more than welcome to it. After all, it's not too long until Christmas.'

'I will, but only if you'll help me to pick it this time.'

'Yes, maybe.' Angel could see from the alert look on Sally's face that the warmth in Danny's smile and the teasing tone in his voice had made her suspicious. 'I have to go, but I'll let you know if Sir Eugene agrees.' She left them without looking back and went to join the Montgomeries.

The reception at Westwood Hall was a grand affair although Angel knew hardly any of the hundred or more guests. She had hoped to have a few quiet words with Sir Eugene, but he was fully occupied introducing his new bride to those who had not yet had the pleasure of her acquaintance. It was all very formal and well-mannered, and the servants kept everyone supplied with champagne, moving amongst the elegantly dressed notables and their ladies and melting away like well-trained ghosts when their services were not required. The scent of hothouse lilies and jasmine mingled with the expensive French perfumes worn by the ladies, and the equally expensive pomade and cologne used by the gentlemen. Strains of music from an orchestra in the ballroom created a gentle background to the chatter and laughter of the guests.

Angel spent most of the time with Belinda, who was shy in company, a complete opposite to her brother, who seemed to be enjoying himself hugely.

'Percy gets on well with everyone,' Belinda said, sighing. 'I wish I was as much at ease with people.'

'He's a good few years your senior, isn't he, Belle?'

Belinda nodded. 'Yes, he's thirty-one, ten years older than me. His mother died when he was born and Percy was eight when father remarried.'

'I'm sorry. I had no idea. That must have been very difficult for Percy.'

'I think so, but he never speaks of his early childhood, although I believe he had a series of nannies and then a governess, who was very strict. I think he was fond of my mother, but I don't remember her.'

Angel looked up as a waiter hovered in front of them with a tray of champagne. She took a glass for herself and one for Belinda. It was hot in the orangery where they had escaped from the crush in the ballroom, and the air was humid. They found somewhere to sit and Angel flicked open her fan, wafting it to and fro. 'Did your mama die, too?'

Belinda did not answer immediately. She gulped down a mouthful of champagne. 'It's a family scandal,' she said in a whisper. 'No one speaks of it.'

'Then I won't ask questions.' Angel leaned back in the rattan chair, closing her eyes as she listened to the melodious strains of a Viennese waltz.

'I want to tell you,' Belinda insisted. 'You're my friend, Angel, and I have very few of those. Percy takes care of me, but sometimes I wish he wouldn't be so protective. I'm not made of glass.'

Angel turned her head to give Belinda a searching look. 'Whatever it is, I'm not in a position to judge anyone for their past.'

'My mama was just a girl when she married our father. She was seventeen, barely out of the schoolroom, and Papa was in his fifties. I think it must have been an arranged marriage because Percy told me that Mama was very unhappy. After I was born she tried to run away, taking me with her, but she was forced to return. Then she fell in love with someone else.'

'My goodness! What happened then?'

'They were discovered and there was a terrible scene. Percy saw it all.'

'Poor boy, it must have been awful for him.'

'Papa threw her out.'

'Did her lover stand by her?'

Belinda's blue eyes filled with tears and she drained the glass of champagne in one swallow. 'I don't know; I wish I did.'

Angel's hand flew to the ring that lay close to her heart. 'What happened to her and her baby?'

'A lighterman found her body floating in the Thames on Christmas Day nineteen years ago. I knew nothing of that until Percy told me. He waited until he thought I was old enough to understand, but since then I've never felt the same about Christmas. If I ever marry and have a daughter I'm going to call her Jane Elizabeth, in memory of my mama.'

'Her name was Jane Elizabeth Montgomerie?'

'Yes, that's right.'

Angel unclipped the chain and slid the ring onto her cupped hand. 'This belonged to my mother,' she said softly. 'It has initials engraved on it.'

'Where did you get that ring?' Percy's voice had a sharp note that made both Angel and Belinda look up, startled.

'You made me jump,' Belinda complained, sniffing.

'May I see?' Percy's expression was grave as he held out his hand to take the ring. He held it up to the light. 'I've only seen one other exactly like this.'

'You recognise it, don't you?' Angel sprang to her feet. Her heart was thudding against her ribs and she could hardly breathe. 'You know who owned it.'

'It's probably a coincidence.'

'What's the matter, Percy?' Belinda demanded anxiously. 'What do you know about the ring?' She shot a curious glance at Angel. 'How did you come by it?'

'I was abandoned as a baby,' Angel said breathlessly. 'This ring was left with me, and I've always assumed that it belonged to my mother. It's inscribed with the initials J E M.'

Belinda's voice shook and she grasped Angel's hands in hers. 'Are you thinking what I'm thinking?'

Percy stared at the ring as it nestled in the palm of his hand. 'My stepmother was wearing a ring exactly like this the last time I saw her. The claw setting and the entwined ruby hearts are unmistakable.'

'Are you sure, Percy?' Angel said urgently.

'It's not something I would forget easily. I'd been sent to bed early – I suppose to get me out of the way because I'd witnessed the scene between Papa and my stepmother. It was a hot and sultry evening and the sky was the sort of yellow you get before a thunderstorm. The air was thick and smelled of sulphur. I knew something terrible was about to happen and I was scared. Then the door opened and Mama rushed in and flung her arms around me. I remember that she smelled of violets and her eyes were reddened from crying. She told me that she had to leave and I begged her not to go, but even as I clung to her I knew it was no use. As she raised her hand to stroke my cheek a flash of lightning made the rubies in her ring gleam like drops of blood against her white skin. Her last words to me were, "Look after your little sister, Percy. I know I can rely on you." Then Father burst into the room and dragged her out, calling her names I can't repeat. I never saw her again.'

'What became of her?' Angel asked urgently.

'On the day I was due to leave for boarding school, Papa called me into his study and told me that my stepmother had run off with her lover and that he had abandoned her. She had thrown herself in the river and drowned.'

'Are you really my sister?' Belinda asked eagerly.

Angel was desperate to believe that she had found her family at last, but it seemed too good to be true. 'I don't know, Belle. All I do know is that the ring was found in the blanket that had saved me from dying from cold. It was Christmas Eve and the snow was falling. I might have died or ended up in the Foundling Hospital, but for the kindness of the Wildings. The rest you know.'

'You *are* my sister,' Belinda cried, flinging her arms around Angel. 'It was fate that led us to meet on the highway. I knew I had a reason to love you, and now I know why.' She held her hand out to her brother. 'We have a sister, Percy.'

A scowl darkened his handsome features and he backed away. 'It's supposition – a coincidence. Perhaps the woman who abandoned Angel was a thief who had stolen the ring. Just because it was found with you doesn't prove anything.'

'But she could be our sister,' Belinda insisted urgently. 'She has blue eyes and fair hair. We even have the same sort of nose, if you look closely.'

'Many people are blond and blue-eyed; it doesn't mean that they are related. You've read too many romantic novels, Belle. It's a coincidence, plain and simple.' Percy turned to face Angel. 'I'm sorry, but it's a complete taradiddle.'

'Why are you being like this, Percy?' Angel demanded angrily. 'Would it be so terrible if we were brother and sister? I thought we were friends.'

'Yes, we're good friends, but not brother and sister. It's too much of a coincidence.' He turned on his heel and strode into the ballroom.

Angel was shaken by his reaction, but Belinda burst into tears, clinging to Angel and sobbing against her shoulder. 'H-how c-could he be so hateful? You are my sister, I know it's true.'

'Perhaps he's right, Belle,' Angel said gently. 'It isn't proof and the ring could have been stolen.'

Belinda released her and sank back onto the chair. 'You're as bad as he is. And, anyway, if whoever abandoned her baby was a thief she wouldn't have left a valuable ruby ring with the baby she didn't want. Answer that if you can.'

'I can't,' Angel said tiredly. 'You know it's impossible to prove it one way or the other. I still don't know who I am, or where I belong.' She kissed Belinda's damp cheek. 'Never mind Belle. We can still be friends, but now there's something I have to do – a promise I have to fulfil.'

'Go on then. Leave me if you must, but if you see Percy tell him I want to go home, and I don't mean Grantley. It's high time we returned to London.'

'I'll tell him.' Angel sighed heavily. Her moment

of elation had ended in dejection and disappointment. She went in search of Sir Eugene.

It was the early hours of the morning by the time the carriage deposited Angel, Susannah and Humphrey on the steps of Grantley. Percy and Belinda had opted to stay at Westwood Hall overnight, and that saved Angel from making polite conversation. She was hurt and baffled by Percy's sudden change in attitude. He had ignored her for the rest of the evening and Belinda had been too upset to join in the dancing after supper. Humphrey had partnered Angel, but she was glad when at long last Susannah could be persuaded to return home. The only good thing to come out of the evening was the fact that Angel had managed to snatch a quiet moment with Sir Eugene, who was in a benevolent mood and quite happy to grant the Wicks family permission to rent some land. They were to contact his estate manager and make the necessary arrangements. It seemed as though their luck had changed.

The Devanes were not so fortunate. Sir Eugene's solicitor had advised the family to leave Grantley as soon as they had packed their belongings, and that left Angel with a decision to make.

Humphrey was up early next morning, his trunk packed and ready to be taken to the station.

'I don't know how you can look so fresh, Angel. I feel terrible,' he said, rising from the breakfast table, his food left untouched.

She smiled as she reached for the marmalade. 'I only drank a couple of glasses of champagne,

310

maybe that's why.'

'You're right, I shouldn't have drunk so much, but I'll sleep it off on the train.' He leaned over to kiss her on the cheek. 'I wish I could stay and help you to move everything to London. I could easily put off my return to Rugby.'

'Yes, I know that, but your mama wants you to continue your studies and that's more important than moving house. I've got plenty of help and the stable boys will load everything into the carriage. Russell is going to make several journeys, taking us last so that we can make certain that nothing is left behind. I wouldn't want any of the family heirlooms to fall into the wrong hands.'

'Hector would be so proud of you if he could see the way you're handling such a difficult situation, but I feel useless.'

She rose to her feet and gave him a hug. 'Don't be silly, Humpty Dumpty. You've given me all the encouragement I need and you've always been on my side. Now I'm able to do something for you, so let's not hear any more talk like that.'

He dashed his hand across his eyes, looking suddenly very young and defenceless. 'I must go.'

'I'll come and see you off.'

'No. Please, stay and finish your meal. I don't want to blub in front of Russell. He'll think I'm a big baby.'

Angel resumed her seat. 'You're the man of the house, so don't let anyone treat you differently. Take care of yourself, Humpty, and we'll see you in London at Christmas.'

He murmured something inaudible and hurried

from the room.

Angel sighed and pushed her plate away. The full impact of leaving the home she loved hit her like a slap in the face. They were being forced out and there was no going back. She turned her head at the sound of approaching footsteps, thinking that Humphrey must have forgotten something, but it was Lil who appeared in the doorway carrying the silver coffeepot.

'What's going to happen to us?' She filled Angel's cup and added a dash of milk. 'Are we to lose our jobs?'

'No, definitely not while I have a breath in my body.' Angel took a sip of coffee and reached for the sugar, adding a small lump and stirring. 'I spoke to Sir Eugene last evening. Aunt Eloise has left everything to him, so until Hector returns you might say he's the head of both households. He agreed with me when I suggested that we remove as many of the valuables from Grantley as possible and take them to the town house. If things go badly the Devanes could lose everything, including the paintings and the silver and all the things that mean so much to them.'

'Some of us have got on well enough in our lives without owning such things.'

'I know that, Lil, but we've been treated well here at Grantley. Sir Adolphus didn't have to take us in, but he did, and I'll be forever grateful to him. Now it's time to repay some of his kindness.'

'Well, the lady of the house wasn't so generous. She's treated you more like a servant than a member of the family. I've not been able to do anything other than watch how she's used you to keep house and wait on the young madam, Miss Susannah. I suppose she came back with you last night?'

'Susannah is going to live at Westwood Hall. She came home last night to make sure that Meg packed everything she needs and the rest of Mrs Devane's belongings – I mean, Lady Westwood's belongings.'

'I thank the Lord that my lady has moved house. Mrs Devane was bad enough, but Lady Westwood will be unbearable.'

'Now you're being prejudiced,' Angel said, laughing. 'I'll come to the kitchen when I've finished breakfast and I'll speak to Cook, Meg and Flossie. They can all come to London with us, but Sir Eugene isn't prepared to pay their wages. We'll all have to find work if we're to keep body and soul together, at least until Hector returns home.'

Lil eyed the gleaming array of silver on the sideboard. 'I suppose I could start packing this lot up if I can find a tea chest or two in the attic.'

'Anybody would think you were eager to see London again.'

Lil tossed her head. 'I was born and raised in Whitechapel. I've got Thames water in me veins instead of blood, so of course I want to go home, but you're my girl, Angel, and that's more important to me than anything. Where you go, I goes too. It's as simple as that.'

Angel jumped to her feet and threw her arms around Lil. 'I love you, Lil. You've been more than a mother to me.'

Lil's sallow cheeks were tinted with pink, but she pushed Angel away. 'Get on with you. Don't

313

talk soft.' She hurried from the room, wiping her eyes on her apron.

Left to herself, Angel glanced at the empty chairs set about a table that could seat twenty-four. Memories of happier times flashed before her eyes. Christmas dinners with Uncle Dolph taking his rightful place at the head of the table, the aroma of roast goose and plum pudding and the giving and receiving of gifts. There had been birthday parties and celebratory dinners when the boys came home from school or university, and then Hector's last meal before he left to re-join his regiment. It seemed as though a long shadow passed through the room as she remembered his hasty departure. She had missed him more than she was prepared to admit, even to herself, and she wished with all her heart that he were here to save Grantley from the grasping hands of the developers. It would give her much satisfaction to see the look on Galloway's face if the matter could be resolved in a manner that prevented him making money from the family's misfortune. She was just about to sit down again when a flurry of activity in the entrance hall made her rise hastily from the table. She opened the door and for a moment it felt as though, by thinking of him, she had summoned up the devil.

Galloway strode towards her, his beetle brows drawn together over the bridge of his bulbous nose. 'What's going on here?' he demanded, indicating the tea chests.

'What does it look like?' Angel countered angrily. 'Who gave you the right to barge into my home uninvited?'

'This is no longer your home, Angel Winter. It belongs to your late uncle's creditors, and that means the contents as well.' Galloway swaggered into the dining room. 'The silver is worth a pretty penny, and that will go towards paying me for my part in the deal.'

'You can't take the silver or the paintings. They're family heirlooms.'

'And they remain in the house.' Galloway turned to face her, eyes narrowed. 'Don't try to be clever, Angel Winter, because you won't win. Sir Eugene's solicitor may have bought you some time, but don't imagine that will save Grantley. You will leave the house today and take nothing other than your personal effects. Do I make myself clear?'

Angel drew herself up to her full height, meeting his arrogant gaze with a steady stare. 'Perfectly clear, but one thing I don't understand is your reasons for behaving in this manner. You could be struck off for what you're doing.'

He shrugged. 'I'm looking after my own interests as well as those of Grantley. The creditors could have taken possession of the estate without giving you the chance to repay what you owe.'

'You speak as though this is personal to me. I own nothing, largely thanks to you. I believe that you played a part in Uncle Joseph's downfall, and you hoped that Aunt Cordelia would marry you, but she had more sense.'

'You were just a child. You don't know what you're talking about, and anyway, I don't have to listen to you. I am in charge now and you will do as I tell you.'

She held her ground as he made a move towards

her. 'Why do you hate me? What did I ever do to you?'

'Do you really want to know why I want to see you suffer?'

'Yes, I do. It doesn't make sense.'

He took a seat at the head of the table, putting his feet up on the nearest chair. 'Is there any coffee left in the pot? I had a damned uncomfortable ride in a donkey cart from the station.'

Angel poured him a cup of strong black coffee, resisting the temptation to tip it over his head as she placed it in front of him. 'Well, go on. I'm listening.'

He sipped the coffee. 'It's cold.' He pushed the cup and saucer away. 'Ring for a fresh pot. I have something to tell you that will put you in your place for ever. You ruined my life and I intend to ruin yours.'

'That's ridiculous,' Angel protested. 'What could I have done to harm you?'

Chapter Eighteen

'You were born,' Galloway leaned his elbows on the table, eyeing her with contempt. 'But it was your conception that led to me losing the only woman I've ever loved.'

Angel stared at him in disbelief. 'I don't understand.'

'I was a talented musician, and I could have studied anywhere in Europe.' Galloway had a far-

316

away look in his eyes and a smile hovered on his lips, which Angel found more frightening than his scowl. 'I could have become a great pianist, but my father was a solicitor and he insisted that I follow in his footsteps, although he had retired by the time I was old enough to leave school. He forced me to accept a position as an articled clerk with Beauchamp and Quelch. I was paid a pittance and I eked out my wages by teaching the piano. My first pupil was a young girl called Jane Elizabeth Malone.'

The initials were the same as those on her ring and Angel's hand flew to her mouth to suppress a gasp of surprise. The mere idea of having him for a father was enough to sicken her, and a wave of dizziness threatened to overcome her and she sat down, unable to speak.

'Jane was on the verge of womanhood, fresh as a rose and just as beautiful,' Galloway continued, seemingly oblivious to her distress. 'She was very talented and she had a wonderful sense of fun – she was always on the brink of laughter, and she brightened up a dreary world. I fell hopelessly in love with her, but her strict father would never have consented to a humble clerk paying court to his daughter. Jane returned my love and we planned to elope, but her father had other plans for her.'

Galloway spoke like a lovelorn youth, but Angel could find no pity in her heart for the man who had caused her so much pain and distress.

'What has this got to do with me?'

'Shut up, and you'll find out.' Galloway's eyes narrowed and his lips tightened into a thin line.

'Her father had arranged for her to marry a much older man who was extremely wealthy. Despite her protests the wedding went ahead and there was nothing I could do to prevent my Jane being tied for life to a man more than twice her age.'

'So you gave up without a fight,' Angel said acidly. 'Why doesn't that surprise me?'

He gave her a withering look. 'We continued to meet in secret until she told me that she was in the family way, and we parted. I vowed never to see her again, but almost a year later I had to deliver a writ to a house close to where she lived. I walked up and down her street, hoping to catch a glimpse of her and I realised that she still held me captive, despite being a married woman and a mother. I forced myself to change my route and I went to Green Park to clear my head of the torment that raged in my soul, and it was there I met her again. She was accompanied by a nursemaid pushing the infant in a perambulator, but the moment I saw Jane again I was lost.'

'Who did she marry?' Angel demanded, clenching her hands in her lap. 'What was her married name?'

His glance flicked over her with reptilian coldness. 'Montgomerie. A man who made his fortune importing Peruvian guano – a man who dealt in muck for a living – but that's by the bye. As I was saying, we met in the park and it was obvious that she wasn't happy. The fine house, elegant clothes and servants to wait on her were no substitute for true love. We arranged to meet at Gunter's for tea, and after that we saw each other almost daily, finding some excuse to meet, as if by accident.'

'So you were the man she ran off with.' The words escaped Angel's lips on a breath, but her heart was pounding and the blood drummed in her ears. It was a question she had to ask even though she dreaded the answer. 'Are you my father?'

He leaped to his feet, dragging the tablecloth with him and sending crockery and glassware flying. Coffee spilled onto the white cloth, spreading in a dark stain like blood oozing from a wound. 'No, dammit. She was already with child when she left her husband, although she swore that she did not know it at the time. But I wasn't going to have a cuckoo in the nest. She had a choice between you or me, and she chose you. I left her.'

Angel stood up. She was shaking, but with anger, not fear. 'You abandoned her. You took her away from her home and the child she had borne her husband, and then you walked away.'

'I returned some months later to find her living in a dosshouse, about to give birth. I offered to take her back, but only if she gave you up. There is the Foundling Hospital and there are orphanages aplenty, but she refused my help. She was thin and gaunt and had lost her looks, but I wanted to stand by her. Once again she chose you over me, and yet you wonder why I hate you.'

'So you left her penniless and unable to care for her baby. She threw herself into the Thames and drowned. Doesn't that prey on your conscience?'

'She could have made a different choice, but she was stubborn and she cared more for a squalling infant than she did for me. One of the

319

old hags in the dosshouse told me that Jane had left you in Angel Alley that Christmas Eve. It was easy to trace you then, and pure coincidence that Joseph Wilding was one of my clients. When I learned of Jane's death I knew who was to blame. I made it my business to follow your progress so that one day I could make you as miserable as you've made me.'

'You're mad,' Angel said breathlessly. The manic flame in his eyes and the twisted look of hatred on his face were enough to convince her that he was quite insane. 'You're the one who was at fault for abandoning the woman you said you loved. You caused her death, not me. Get out of here or I'll have you thrown out.'

'No, my dear. You're the one being thrown out. You will leave this morning. I'm due a tidy sum when the developers take possession of the estate. It will go some of the way to mend a broken heart.'

'You have no heart,' Angel said bitterly. 'You are a monster and I hope you rot in hell.' She could not bear the sight of him a moment longer and she left the room, heading for the kitchen and Lil, the only person who had been a constant in her life so far.

Meg and Flossie had, at the last moment, decided to return to their families in the village, and it was Angel, Lil and Cook who arrived at the house in Naked Boy Court.

Sergeant Baines was older, greyer and even less agreeable than he had been years ago, but he let them in with a sigh of resignation. 'Are you sure

I've got to put up with all them women?' he demanded as Cook and Lil helped Russell to unload their luggage from the Devanes' carriage.

Angel met Baines's stern look with a smile. 'It's not for ever, Sergeant Baines. I'll explain everything, but I'm sure we could all do with a nice hot cup of tea.'

He glared at Lil, who had struggled into the entrance hall hefting a heavy case. 'I don't want no interference in my kitchen. It's bad enough having lost the colonel without being invaded by petticoats.'

Lil glanced over her shoulder. 'A gent would help a lady.'

'I ain't a gentleman and you certainly ain't a lady,' Baines said dolefully. 'I suppose you'll do what you want whatever I say, just like last time.' He stomped off in the direction of the kitchen.

'Try not to get on his bad side,' Angel whispered. 'We haven't anywhere else to go.'

'Huh! Men, they're all the same.' Lil went outside the collect more of their luggage from the yard.

Angel picked up her valise and carried it upstairs to the bedroom that she had shared with Dolly. Nothing had changed, except perhaps the layer of dust was a little thicker and the heat was stifling, having built up during the long hot days of summer. She opened a window, stretching a lacy cobweb until it gave way and the agitated spider swung to safety on a silken thread. The familiar stench of the city wafted into the room. It was putrid, but in a strange way it was comforting. Angel had grown up with the odours of the river and the exotic smells emanating from the ware-houses that clustered around the docks. The rich aromas of roasting coffee and molten sugar, wine and spices had always struggled for supremacy over the rank stench of sewage, animal dung, soot and smoke, but that was the price city dwellers paid for living at the throbbing heart of the Empire. She left her case on the bed, intending to unpack later, and went downstairs to keep the peace between Lil and Baines.

Later, after a meagre supper of bread and cheese, washed down by some of the sergeant's beer, there being no tea left in the caddy, Angel remained at the table with Baines while Lil and Cook went upstairs to make up the beds. It was the opportunity for a quiet chat that Angel had been waiting for.

'You already know why we've had to leave Grantley so suddenly,' she said earnestly. 'But you were close to Sir Adolphus, is there anything you can think of that might help save the estate?' She met his quizzical gaze with a hint of a smile. 'I'm not asking for myself, Baines. The colonel took me in and treated me like one of his own. I owe it to him to do everything I can to keep Grantley from being buried beneath roads and streets of new houses.'

'People have to live somewhere,' Baines said gruffly. 'But I seem to recall the colonel telling me that part of the Grantley estate is Lammas Land.'

'What is Lammas Land?' Angel asked urgently.

'I think it means common land, and has some-thing to do with the local parishioners having

322

rights to graze animals after the hay harvest until the following spring. I can't remember the exact details, but there's a chest filled with the colonel's papers in his study. You might find something in it that would help.'

'If it is common land does that make a difference?'

'I can't say, miss. But there's only one way to find out.' Baines put his hand in his pocket and took out a bunch of keys. 'I never let these out of me sight, but I trust you.' He handed it to Angel with a nod. 'That solicitor fellow came here one day not long after I heard that the colonel had died. He wanted to know if the colonel kept any papers here, and I said I had no knowledge of the colonel's private business. As far as I know, I says, everything is dealt with by the colonel's lawyer and that ain't you, sir.'

'And what did he say to that?'

'He looked away, muttered something and left. I didn't take to the fellow and I certainly didn't trust him, and from what you told me earlier, it seems I was right.'

Angel rose to her feet, clutching the keys in her hand. 'I can't wait until morning. I won't get a wink of sleep until I know what's in that chest.'

'It'll be cold in the study.' Baines swallowed the last of his beer. 'I'll bring the chest back here so that you can go through it in comfort.' He stood up and Angel heard his bones creak as he flexed his muscles, but she was not about to refuse his offer.

He picked up the lamp and led the way through the draughty passages to the study, which was equally dank and cold. The smell of musty books and rising damp added to the sombre atmosphere in the shuttered room. Angel could not quite dispel the feeling that Sir Adolphus still inhabited the place where he had spent many hours, poring over his books with his two greyhounds for company. Thor and Juno had been left with Russell and his wife, who lived in a cottage behind the coach house at Grantley, and Angel had the satisfaction of knowing that they were loved and well cared for. She was certain that Sir Adolphus would have approved of such an arrangement, and, as if in answer to her unspoken question, a draught of cold air rushed through the room, creating flurries in the dust and rattling the shutters. A superstitious shiver ran down Angel's spine, but Baines remained calm and unruffled as he picked up the wooden chest.

'Reckon I'd best light a fire in here tomorrow,' he said gruffly. 'The colonel wouldn't want his books to be ruined by damp.' He gave Angel a sympathetic grin. 'Come on, miss. Let's get back to the warmth. He wouldn't want you coming down with a chill.'

Angel nodded, too choked with emotion to speak.

The contents of the chest were disappointing: mostly household accounts, newspaper cuttings reporting the various skirmishes that the colonel's regiment had been involved in, and bills for his uniform and accoutrements. It was not until she took out a scroll of parchment, tied with red tape, that she discovered what appeared to be the original deeds. She unrolled the fragile document and spread it out on the kitchen table, peering at the spidery writing. 'Do you think this is what Galloway was looking for, Baines?'

He leaned closer. 'I dunno nothing about legal matters, miss. But I'd say it's a fair chance that this is important or he wouldn't have made such a fuss about searching the master's study. I thought I might have to throw him out bodily, but lucky for him he decided to retreat.'

'He'll be back,' Angel said thoughtfully. 'I need to know what to do with this, and I want to find out more about Lammas Land. I think there's someone who might be able to help, and if not I'll go to Sir Eugene.'

'Maybe you should wait for Captain Devane's return, miss.'

'I've a feeling it will be too late by then.' Angel rolled the document carefully and secured it with the tape. 'Tomorrow morning, first thing, I'm going to Hackney and then on to Westwood Hall. Promise me that you won't fall out with Lil and Cook, Baines. We have to stick together or we'll lose everything.'

It was late morning by the time Angel arrived at the Wickses' cottage and Sally greeted her warmly, as did Stumpy. The dog jumped up and down, attempting to lick Angel's hand, and he kept on until she bent down to make a fuss of him. The scent of dried lavender wafted from the tiny front parlour and the kitchen was filled with the savoury aroma of cooking and loaves of freshly baked bread, cooling on the table.

'Jack and Danny are working on the plot,' Sally said, wiping her hands on her apron. She eyed Angel curiously. 'Danny told us about the trouble at Grantley. Is there anything we can do to help, love?'

Angel took off her mantle and bonnet and laid them on a chair. 'That's why I'm here, although it's a good excuse to come and see you as well.'

'Sit down, dear, and I'll call the men in. We'll have a nice cup of tea and you can tell us all about it.'

Sally bustled to the door, opened it and stepped outside to call to her husband and son.

They arrived, moments later, ruddy-cheeked and smelling of wet earth and fresh air. Jack beamed at Angel, but Danny held back, eyeing her warily.

'This is a pleasant surprise,' Jack said warmly. 'How are you keeping, Angel?'

She smiled. 'I'm well, thank you.'

Sally gave her son a straight look. 'Have you nothing to say, Danny?'

'Is there any news about our strip of land?' he said gruffly.

'That's not much of a welcome.' Sally moved to the range and picked up the kettle. 'Sit down both of you and have a cup of tea. I think Angel has something she wants to tell us.'

Angel pulled up a chair and sat down. She explained the reason for her visit as briefly as possible. 'I thought you would know about Lammas Land, Jack,' she concluded. 'It's mentioned in the deeds to Grantley and the deer park is included in the curtilage, whatever that is.'

Jack scratched his head. 'I dunno about curtilage, but Lammas Land is common land, and I don't think the developers would get permission to build on it, but you'd have to get proper legal advice.'

'You won't be using Galloway again, will you?' Danny asked anxiously.

'No, certainly not. I'm going to see Sir Eugene at Westwood Hall. He's been very helpful so far, and naturally Lady Westwood is eager for Hector to claim his inheritance.'

Sally gave her an anxious look as she passed a cup of tea to her husband. 'Surely you're not going to attempt the walk across the marshes today, Angel? The mist is coming in already, and you know how treacherous the ground is at this time of the year.'

'I've come this far and I have to see Sir Eugene as soon as possible. Galloway has already been to the house in Naked Boy Court, looking for the deeds. I have them in my reticule and I must get them to Sir Eugene so that he can put them before his solicitor.'

'I'll take the donkey cart and see her safe across the marsh, Ma,' Danny said, rising from his chair. 'Can you manage without me for an hour or two, Pa?'

Jack shrugged. 'It's more important to look after Angel, but don't loiter. I want you back before dark.'

A white mist swirled around them as the donkey plodded along the well-worn path across the marsh. Visibility was down to a few yards and there was a chill in the air. 'Don't worry,' Danny said, giving the reins a gentle flick. 'Dash knows his way blindfold.'

'I suppose he must do. You used to come this way every day when you were working in the greenhouse at Grantley.'

'If there's anything I can do to help get it restored to the family, you know I will.'

'This is help enough, Danny. It would take me a long time to cross the marsh on foot and I'd probably get lost, especially with the fog closing in as it is.'

Danny cleared his throat. 'I think you know how I feel about you, Angel. I wouldn't have said anything while you were living with the Devanes, but now you're free of them I think I have the right to speak.'

'I might have been living in the big house, but I'm still the same girl I was when I first knew you.'

'No, you're not. You're a lady, and I'm just a gardener sharing Pa's stall in Covent Garden market, but I love you, Angel. I reckon I always have, only I didn't know it until that day in the greenhouse when I kissed you, and you kissed me back.'

Angel felt the blood rush to her cheeks and she turned her head, unable to look him in the eyes. 'That was a mistake, Danny.'

'I won't have that. Can't you see that I'm asking you to marry me, Angel? I'm a clumsy fellow and I'm not good at making romantic speeches, but I really do love you, and I'd do everything in my power to make you happy.' He reached across to take her cold hand in his. 'Marry me, Angel. I'll look after you and do my best to make a good life for us.'

She forced herself to look at him and her heart swelled with sympathy. There was no doubting the sincerity in his gaze and she struggled to find the right words, but there was no easy way to tell him that she was in love with another man. 'Oh, Danny, I can't marry you. I wish I could say yes, but...'

He released her hand and took up the reins, jerking at Dash's head so that the donkey broke into a startled trot. 'There's someone else, isn't there?'

'Yes, I mean, no. At least he doesn't know how I feel and I doubt if he's ever thought of me in that way.'

'Is it that toff Montgomerie? I've only seen him briefly with his sister. His sort doesn't mix with the likes of me.'

'Stop it, Danny. Don't talk about yourself like that, and it isn't Percy. As a matter of fact it's possible that Percy is my half-brother.'

'Your brother?'

'No, he's my half-brother, or so it seems. Galloway, the man who left me to rot in the workhouse, was in love with my mother, who was forced into marriage with Percy's father. She gave birth to Belinda but she was still in love with Galloway, although it's hard to believe, and she left her husband to be with him. Then she realised that she was expecting another child, which was me. Galloway abandoned her and she committed suicide. He firmly believes that I was the cause of all his misfortunes and that's why he wants to ruin my life.'

Danny whistled between his teeth. 'That's some story. I can't take it all in.'

'I've always thought of myself as Angel Winter, but I suppose I'm Angel Montgomerie. It sounds very odd.'

'And it puts you even further above me,' Danny said gloomily. 'You really are a lady.'

Angel was about to reply when Dash stumbled and Danny had a struggle to keep the cart steady. He leaped to the ground and went to soothe the frightened animal.

'Is he all right?' Angel asked anxiously.

'I think so, but I'll lead him until we reach the edge of the marsh, it's not too far now.'

Angel sat back, breathing a sigh of relief. She was very fond of Danny and that kiss in the green-house had stirred up emotions and unnamed desires, but that was not enough. She loved his family, but marriage was out of the question, and it had nothing to do with her birth. She had had little time to think about her relationship with Belinda, but now, wrapped in a moist cloak of mist and apparently detached from the outside world, it dawned on her that having a real flesh-and-blood sister would be the most wonderful gift of all. And then the chill from outside wound its way around her heart – Percy had rejected the idea that they were related, and had walked away. Angel shivered and wrapped her mantle closer around her body. It was all too complicated and she was confused and emotional, but she must put personal problems aside and think of Grantley, her home and Hector's birthright.

To her intense relief they left the marsh and the sun forced its way between the clouds as they reached the gravelled road. Danny climbed onto the cart and took the reins without saying a word, and they drove on in silence until they were about to pass Grantley Park.

'I hope you won't let this come between us,' Angel said softly. 'I do care for you, Danny. I'd want us to be friends.'

He shot her a wary glance. 'Easy to say, but if what you say is true, you're related to the Montgomeries and surely they'll want you to live with them. Whatever happens to Grantley, your time there will come to an end.'

'That's why I'm doing this, Danny,' Angel said earnestly. 'Hector should inherit Grantley and I'm hoping that the document I'm taking to Sir Eugene will help in some way.'

'He's the one, isn't he?' Danny said suspiciously. 'You're in love with Captain Devane.'

'Don't be ridiculous. We were brought up as brother and sister. Of course I care what happens to him, and all the family.' Angel fixed her attention on the road ahead. 'I don't want to talk about it, Danny. Just drive, please.'

He flicked the reins and encouraged Dash to move at his usual plodding pace, and they lapsed into silence.

By the time they reached Westwood Hall what had begun as light drizzle had turned into a downpour, blotting out the landscape and soaking Angel to the skin. Her teeth were chattering and she was shivering as Danny reined Dash in and the cart ground to a halt. The front door opened and a liveried footman ran down the steps to help Angel alight, but he looked askance at the conveyance and its driver.

'Shall I pay the fellow, Miss Winter?'

Angel found herself blushing despite the cold. 'Mr Wicks is a friend, James. He was doing me a kindness and I'll be leaving again as soon as I've seen Sir Eugene.'

'Take the cart to the coach house and you'll be looked after until Miss Winter is ready to leave,' James said frostily.

Angel shook her head. 'Send for a stable boy to take care of the animal, James. Mr Wicks is with me.'

'It's all right, I'll wait in the coach house,' Danny said hastily. 'I want to make sure that Dash is rubbed down.' Without waiting for a response he urged the tired animal to move on.

Reluctantly, Angel allowed James to usher her into the hall. 'I need to see Sir Eugene urgently.' She shed her sodden mantle and took off her ruined bonnet, handing them to a maidservant.

'I'll see if the master is at home, Miss Winter.' James bowed and walked off with a measured gait, reminding her of a well-trained circus horse she had seen as a child at Astley's Amphitheatre. She paced the black-and-white marble-tiled floor as she waited for him to return. The elegant entrance hall with its Corinthian columns and sweeping staircase adorned with family portraits and paintings of chubby-cheeked cherubs seemed suddenly cold and uninviting. On previous visits she had been a welcome member of the Devane family, but now she felt very much an outsider. She turned at the sound of someone calling her name and saw Belinda hurrying towards her, arms outstretched.

'Angel, I thought it was you. I happened to be looking out of the library window and I saw you climb down from such a comical contraption. Where have you been since the wedding? We've missed you.' She gave Angel a warm hug. 'Come into the library, there's a roaring fire and it's nice and private. We can have a talk without fear of interruption. Blanche never enters that particular room. I don't think she's ever read a book in her whole life, and Susannah is too busy flirting with Percy to think about anything else.'

Breathless from all the information that Belinda had flung at her, Angel shook her head. 'I'd love to, Belle, but I am here to see Sir Eugene.' She paused, taking in Belinda's flushed appearance. 'Why are you here, anyway? I thought you'd returned to London after the wedding.'

'We did, but Percy made an excuse to come here.' Belinda lowered her voice to a whisper. 'I think he rather fancies his chances with Susannah, but don't say I told you so. She flirted outrageously with him at the wedding.'

'I still don't understand why he was so upset when he discovered that we're related. I know it was a shock to all of us, but he seemed quite angry.'

Belinda put her head on one side. 'Are you so naïve, Angel? He had taken quite a fancy to you, and he was ashamed. Do you understand now?'

'I didn't know, Belle. I really had no idea, but it's natural for brothers and sisters to care for

333

each other.'

'Don't worry about our brother, he's recovering nicely and looking elsewhere for romance. I think Blanche has always had a soft spot for Percy and he seems quite taken with her. As for myself, I couldn't be happier to find I have you as my sister.' A frown creased Belinda's smooth forehead. 'But why are you here? And what made you travel in this awful weather?'

'I've found the deeds to Grantley. I think there might be a way to prevent the developers from building on the estate, so I must see Sir Eugene. I certainly can't trust Galloway.' Angel turned her head at the sound of footsteps and saw James striding towards them. She patted Belinda's hand. 'I'll tell you everything later, but first I must speak to Sir Eugene.'

'In that case I'm coming, too,' Belinda said, taking Angel by the arm. 'They're in the drawing room.'

Angel had hoped to speak to Sir Eugene in private, but Eloise, Susannah and Blanche were seated by the fire in the drawing room with their silk skirts spread out around them, flowerlike and in delicate pastels.

Sir Eugene rose from his chair. 'Come and join us, Angel,' he said, smiling. 'You know you're always welcome at Westwood.'

Belinda gave Angel a gentle push in his direction and sat down, folding her hands primly in her lap.

Eloise nodded graciously, but Susannah did not look pleased, and Angel was instantly aware of the reason when she turned her head and saw Percy standing by one of the tall windows that over-looked the parterre garden. He acknowledged her with a smile, and she took that as a good sign.

'What brings you here today?' Eloise demanded. 'You looked like a drowned rat. Did you walk all the way from Ludgate?'

'Come and sit by the fire,' Blanche said graciously. 'Move up, Susannah. You're taking all the room on the sofa.'

Angel shook her head. 'Thank you, but I haven't come to stay. I need to ask Sir Eugene's advice on a legal matter.'

'Perhaps a change of clothing might be in order,' Percy suggested, eyeing Angel with some concern. 'You look as though you're soaked to the skin.'

'I'm sure my maid has something that would fit her,' Susannah said spitefully.

Percy turned on her, frowning. 'That was un-generous, Susannah. Angel will be treated with the respect that is due to a Montgomerie.'

'What are you talking about, Percy?' Susannah's pretty mouth drooped at the corners. 'That's not funny.'

'No, indeed,' Eloise added acidly. 'It's a poor joke.'

'It's no joke, Lady Westwood.' Percy placed his arm around Angel's shoulders. 'We've only recently discovered the truth, but Angel is Belinda's sister and my half-sister.'

'What nonsense is this?' Eloise demanded angrily. 'If spoken in jest, it's in very poor taste. I don't believe a word of it.'

Chapter Nineteen

Belinda leaped to her feet and moved swiftly to stand beside Angel. 'It is true, Lady Westwood, and we can prove it. Show them your ring, Angel.'

'This is nonsense.' Eloise rose to her feet. 'It's a clumsy attempt to rise above your station in life, Angel Winter. You had your cap set at my eldest son from the moment you set foot in my home.'

'That is simply not true,' Angel protested. 'How can you say such a thing, Aunt Eloise?'

'I am not your aunt. You were foisted upon me by my soft-hearted brother, who was also a simpleton when it came to women's wiles. I know nothing about your ring, but it cannot possibly prove anything other than the fact you were a foundling, and your mother was probably a common thief. You will pack your bags and you will return to the streets where you belong. I want you out of my house now.'

'That is both cruel and unfair,' Percy said angrily. 'I admit I was sceptical at first, but when I looked at the facts I realised that I was wrong.'

'We believe that Angel is our sister and she will always have a home with us,' Belinda said, blushing furiously. She shot an anxious glance at her brother before averting her gaze and staring down at her hands, clasped tightly in her lap.

Susannah tugged at her mother's sleeve. 'Mama, perhaps you ought to apologise. If Percy and

Belinda are taken in by the story it's their business.'

'I think Angel and Belinda look like sisters,' Blanche added shyly. 'All three of you could easily be related. I agree with Belinda and Percy.'

Susannah tossed her head. 'You would agree, Blanche Westwood. You'd do anything to curry favour with Percy.'

'That's unfair, Susannah.' Percy moved to Blanche's side, taking her hand in a firm grasp. 'Blanche is the kindest, nicest lady I have ever known, and she deserves better from you.'

Susannah's eyes widened in surprise. 'Is there something going on between you two? If there is it's been conducted in a very underhand manner.'

'This has gone far enough,' Sir Eugene snapped. 'That remark was uncalled for and you will apologise to my daughter, Susannah.'

'Why am I always the one in the wrong?' Susannah leaped to her feet. 'I have a headache, Mama. I'm going to my room.'

'Really, Eugene,' Eloise said plaintively. 'Did you have to be so hard on her?'

'Susannah needs to curb her tongue,' Sir Eugene said angrily. He turned to Angel and his expression softened. 'Why did you come here today? It doesn't matter to me if you are a foundling or if you are a Montgomerie; as far as I'm concerned you have always been a part of the Devane household and you seem to have held the whole family together since Sir Adolphus passed away.'

Percy nodded in agreement. 'Well said, sir.'

Angel opened her reticule and took out the

parchment, which was creased but otherwise undamaged. 'This is why I came. I walked all the way from Ludgate Hill to Hackney, and I might have been lost on the marsh if a friend hadn't taken pity on me and given me a lift on his cart. I don't want anything from the Devane family, but I love Grantley and I want to help save it for future generations. This deed might be the key, but it needs an honest solicitor to handle the case and that excludes Galloway.' She handed it to Sir Eugene, who studied the document in silence.

'I stand by what I said.' Eloise rose from the sofa. 'You are a sly minx, Angel Winter, and I want nothing more to do with you.' She tossed her head and left the room, following in her daughter's wake.

Blanche was the first to react. 'She's upset. Someone should go with her.'

'She's always like that,' Angel said, shaking her head. 'She'll join Susannah and they'll comfort each other.'

Sir Eugene folded the document and raised his head. 'Yes, Blanche, don't let them upset you. I'll have a word with my wife later.'

'May I see the deed, Sir Eugene?' Percy asked eagerly. 'I studied law at Cambridge, although I never took up the profession as I decided to devote my time to running the family business.'

Sir Eugene handed it to him. 'A second opinion is always useful, but it does appear that part of the estate is common land, and the deeds clearly state that it should be held for the commoners in perpetuity. Whether that would be enough to stop the developers building new roads and houses is another matter, but if true, they might be willing to negotiate a settlement and look for land elsewhere.'

'I know I can speak for Hector and the boys,' Angel said slowly. 'They can't keep up the repayments, and they most definitely wouldn't be able to raise sufficient funds to pay off the mortgage, even if they sold all their valuables.'

'You've worked so hard to keep the family together, Angel.' Percy patted her on the shoulder. 'I'm proud to call you my sister.'

'And so am I,' Belinda added, speaking up for the first time.

Percy rewarded her with a smile. 'Angel has had a hard time and she's come through it bravely. Lady Westwood should be more considerate towards her.'

'Be careful, Percy.' Sir Eugene sent him a warning glance. 'You're speaking about my wife, but I do think she has undervalued Angel, and I'll seek to remedy that. In the meantime I'll go into town tomorrow and give this to my solicitor. That man Galloway should be exposed as the charlatan he is.'

'Thank you, Sir Eugene. I knew I could rely on you,' Angel said, breathing a sigh of relief. 'I'll leave the deeds with you, but now I really must go. Danny will be waiting for me and we don't want to be out on the marsh after dark.'

'Nonsense,' Sir Eugene said sternly. 'You must stay for a day or two, while I try to sort out this matter.'

'Thank you, sir, but I have to return to Ludgate Hill or they'll wonder what's happened to me.'

'Surely we can send a messenger?' Percy said, frowning. 'Belinda and I are returning to London in the morning, Angel. You could come with us. Besides which, we need to talk about the future. You're a Montgomerie and you deserve to be treated as such.'

Angel had no doubt that Percy and Sir Eugene meant well, but they were trying to run her life, and it was not what she had planned or wanted. She must find her own way and that did not include marriage to Danny or living on her half-brother's charity. She made a move towards the door. 'I must leave now. Danny is waiting for me.'

'I won't allow you to wander across the marsh at dusk.' Sir Eugene reached for the bell pull. 'My coachman will take you back to London tonight, if that's what you wish, and I'm sure your friend can find his own way home.'

No matter how much Angel argued the point, both Sir Eugene and Percy were adamant that she must not be allowed to risk travelling across the marsh, let alone undertake the walk from Hackney to Ludgate Hill after dark. In the end she had to agree and Danny was sent on his way without giving her a chance to say goodbye or to thank him. After taking her leave of everyone, Angel was ensconced in the Westwoods' barouche with a foot warmer filled with hot ashes to keep her warm, and a woollen blanket to cover her knees. Such luxury was a treat in itself, but she could not help worrying about Danny. The last thing she had wanted was to hurt his feelings: it was bad enough having had to reject his offer of marriage, let alone sending him home, no doubt thinking the worst.

Despite her worries, the warmth and comfort of the padded leather squabs was gently lulling her off to sleep when the carriage lurched suddenly and she opened her eyes with a start. The horses had slowed from a spanking trot to a walk, but the vehicle was swaying and creaking ominously. Something was wrong and Angel leaned forward to peer out of the window. It was dark now but she could see the flickering light of flambeaux and the outline of a large house at the end of a long carriage sweep. As the barouche came to a halt it took her a few seconds to realise that they had stopped outside the gates of Grantley Park. She opened the door without waiting for the coachman to alight from the box.

'What happened?'

Trubshawe was puffing with exertion as he hurried to put down the steps and hand her to the ground. 'We hit something, miss. It's too dark to see properly, but it looks as if someone has put a boulder on the road, deliberate like. I think we broke an axle, but luckily we're outside Grantley. I've heard that Russell and a couple of the grooms are still there.'

'They are,' Angel said thoughtfully. 'Who would do a thing like this?'

'I dunno, miss. But it's going to take some time to fix. We'd best get you to the house so that you can have shelter for the night.'

'But there's no one there. It's closed while the wrangling over the estate goes on.'

Trubshawe glanced over his shoulder. 'There's lights outside as if they was expecting guests, so someone must be at home. Maybe it would be

341

best if you stay here until I find out who's there, miss. We've all heard about Grantley's troubles and it might be someone up to no good.'

Angel could think of only one person who might have gained access to the house. Hector would know nothing of the events that had led to the abandonment of his home. No one had heard from him since his last letter, which had arrived in the middle of September. It had not been clear when he would be free to travel home, but he had hoped it would be soon. The thought that he might be there at this moment, wondering where everyone had gone, put everything else from Angel's mind.

'Robbers would hardly advertise their presence with flaming torches. I'm coming with you, Trubshawe.'

Despite his protests she kept pace with him as he marched up the drive towards the house. She stopped at the bottom of the stone steps. The flickering flames added to the feeling of expectancy – perhaps Hector had wanted the whole neighbourhood to know of his return.

'Let me find out who's there, please, miss.' Trubshawe stood at her side, looming over her like a guardian angel in a caped greatcoat.

She was touched by his concern, but she wanted to be the first face that Hector saw and the first person to welcome him home. 'It's all right, Trubshawe. Go and get help, I'll be quite safe.' She waited until he had stomped off in the direction of the stables and her feet barely touched the ground as she raced up the steps to hammer on the door.

The sound of approaching footsteps made her pulse race even quicker as she waited, hardly daring to breathe. The hinges squealed as the door was wrenched open and Angel was momentarily blinded by the glare from a lamp held close to her face. A hand shot out and she was dragged over the threshold, and the door slammed shut.

'You think you're so clever, don't you?' Galloway's voice was unmistakable and, judging by the odour he exuded, he had been drinking and was sweating copiously. 'You can't get the better of me, Angel Winter. I'm far too clever for you.'

She wrenched her arm free and flung herself at the door, but it was locked and he held the key in his free hand, laughing and waving it drunkenly in her face. 'You won't get away that easily, my pet.'

'Let me go. You can't keep me here against my will. Trubshawe will come back for me, and Russell, too.'

He held the lamp high above her head, staring at her with a grim smile. 'They'll be too busy fixing the carriage. As far as Russell is concerned I'm your lawyer and I've come here to help you.'

She leaned against the door, taking comfort from the solid feel of the ancient oak panels. Grantley would protect her, no matter what Galloway said or did. This was her home and she knew every nook and cranny of the old house. It would be impossible for him to keep her prisoner. 'You put that rock on the road, didn't you?' she said boldly. 'How did you know I would be in the carriage?'

'I've had you followed. I know that you left

343

Naked Boy Court and walked to Hackney; then that poor besotted gardener's boy took you to Westwood Hall. My man came here hotfoot to tell me that you were stupid enough to insist on travelling back to London tonight, so the rest was easy.'

'I might not have come to the house. What would you have done then?'

'What choice did you have, darling? You could hardly spend the night in the carriage and I knew that curiosity would get the better of you. You're so much like your mother that you could be Jane returned from the grave.'

'I'm not my mother, but for her sake, and if you really loved her, let me go. I've done nothing to you.' She held up her hand as he opened his mouth to argue. 'Don't go through all that again. How could an innocent child be responsible for your failure as a man?' She braced herself as he raised his fist, but the blow never fell, and he dropped his hand to his side.

'You're a little bitch, but you won't be so full of yourself when I've finished with you.'

The vicious look on his face and the tone of his voice scared her, but she was determined not to let him see she was afraid. 'You'll have to let me go. They'll come looking for me as soon as they realise I'm missing. Russell and his wife will know that something is wrong if you keep me locked up here.'

Galloway's derisive laugh echoed off the wainscoting, coming back again and again like a ghostly chorus. 'I've thought of that, darling. As far as Russell and that stupid wife of his are concerned

344

I've come to save Grantley, and you'll be in good hands.'

'Trubshawe will return to Westwood and tell Sir Eugene what's happened. He knows that you're a criminal. He's on to you, Galloway, and soon the authorities will know what you've done.'

'Don't underestimate me, darling. I laid my plans so that they're foolproof. You might as well face the fact that you're spending the night alone with a man who isn't your father, your brother or your husband. Your reputation will be ruined and no decent man will want to marry you. I couldn't have your mother, but I'm going to have you, and I'm going to take my time and watch you suffer as I suffered.'

'You're insane.' Anger took the place of fear, but even so, Angel could see that he was hell-bent on revenge and she was to be his victim. She looked round, calculating the best way to escape. If she caught him unawares she could outrun him and head for the maze of passages that led to the servants' wing at the back of the house. The window in the still room had never closed properly due to a broken latch, and the laundry-room door opened out into the courtyard. Unless Galloway had made a thorough search of the house, he was unlikely to have found the spare key that was kept under the soap jar. 'You can't keep me here against my will,' she added defiantly.

'We'll see about that.' With the speed of a spitting cobra, Galloway grabbed her arm and twisted it behind her back, causing her to cry out. 'Upstairs now, and if you make another sound I'll break your arm.'

Dazed by the pain and unable to break free, Angel could do nothing other than obey.

'This room will do,' he snarled, giving her arm a savage jerk.

Several years ago she had been given a bedroom of her own, but only because Susannah had reached her fourteenth birthday and had protested that she was now too old to share. Angel had discovered on her first day at Grantley that Susannah always got what she wanted, and the large, elegantly furnished bedchamber overlooking the formal garden at the back of the house had been swiftly made ready for her. New curtains and bed coverings had been ordered and the room had been redecorated with wallpaper of Susannah's choosing. Angel had been left in their old room, with a view of the deer park and a particularly lovely old magnolia grandiflora outside her window. Its leathery leaves tapped on her window at night when the wind rustled the branches, and the lemon-scented flowers seemed to capture the moonbeams, the large waxy white petals reflecting the silvery light.

Galloway gave her a final shove, sending her sprawling onto the carpet. 'I'll be up later to take what I want, so don't think you're getting off lightly. Tidy yourself up, girl. You look like a skivvy and I'm very particular about the women I take to my bed.' He slammed the door and the key grated in the lock.

If she had had any doubts as to his intentions, they had been dispelled by his last words. Angel scrambled to her feet, nursing her sore arm. She flexed her fingers and uttered a sigh of relief – at least nothing was broken. Galloway had taken the lantern with him, leaving her in almost total darkness apart from a sliver of moonlight that squeezed through a gap in the curtains. She made her way slowly across the floor and drew them back, welcoming the starlit scene like an old friend. Night after night, as a young girl, she had sat on the window seat, gazing at the view made mysterious and mystical in the moonlight. In summer she had inhaled the scent of roses and honeysuckle and the whispering breeze had caressed her hot cheeks. The distant bark of a dog fox and the cries of barn owls calling to their mates mingled with the chatter of the stream as it flowed over rocks and pebbles on its journey to merge with the River Lea.

At first she had missed the city with its noise and bustle, but gradually she had fallen in love with Grantley in all its moods and seasons, and accepted it as her home. Despite Galloway's threats she felt safe in familiar surroundings, although the holland covers on the furniture added to the feeling that she was in the middle of a bad dream and might, at any moment, awaken to find herself in the four-poster at the house in Naked Boy Court. Then a cold shiver ran down her spine as she remembered the look on Galloway's face and the steely intent in his eyes. The kindly man who used to give her sweets when she was a child had changed beyond all recognition, and she suspected that he was on the verge of madness. He had laid his trap as a spider spins its web and she had walked into it. Now she must think of a way to escape, but as she opened the window a cold wind whipped her hair into a tangle around her face and sent her shivering. Looking down, she realised that it was a long drop to the gravel path below. The sturdy trunk of the magnolia was out of reach, and any attempt to climb to the ground would almost inevitably lead to disaster. It would be pointless to shout for help as the stable block was too far away for anyone to hear, and the only living things close enough to pay attention were the deer grazing in the park. She sat there transfixed, barely able to move as she struggled to think of a way to escape from the maniac who had made his intentions crystal clear. Time ceased to have any meaning as her mind raced, but she was at a loss and chilled to the bone. She was about to close the window when she heard footsteps coming nearer and nearer.

Angel leaped to her feet, looking round for a weapon of any kind that she might use against a drunken man intent on rape, and the only thing that came to hand was the ewer on the wash-stand. She snatched it up and moved swiftly to stand behind the door, arm raised ready to strike. The handle rattled as if someone was trying the door, and someone was calling her name. Her breath hitched in her throat as she recognised Danny's voice.

'Danny, I'm locked in.'

'I haven't got the key. I'll have to break it down. Get away from the door, Angel.'

She moved to a safe distance as the door shook on its hinges, but the first attempt failed and the second, then a third blow had the wood splintering and the door fell to the floor with a loud crash. Danny staggered into the room, coming to a halt as he wrapped his arms around her.

'Are you all right? Did he hurt you?'

She drew away, caught between tears and laughter. 'I'm so glad to see you. How did you know I was here?'

'Poor old Dash isn't a match for the Westwoods' matched bays. He was plodding along at his normal pace when we came across the barouche with its broken axle. I saw the lights outside Grantley and I knew immediately that there was something wrong. Anyway, explanations later. Let's get you out of here. Russell will have harnessed the horse to the chaise and he's going to take you back to Ludgate Hill.'

'But what about Galloway?' The full enormity of her position overtook her and she began to tremble uncontrollably. 'He made terrible threats and I believe he was capable of anything. What have you done with him?'

Danny gave her a comforting hug. 'I didn't come alone. Trubshawe and Russell accompanied me. Let's say that Galloway was outnumbered. He's not going anywhere other than the village lock-up. Russell sent one of his boys for the local copper, and tomorrow Mr Galloway will find himself up in front of the beak. I don't think he'll be able to talk his way out of this one.'

'And the magistrate happens to be Sir Eugene,' Angel said with a wry smile. 'He knows all about Galloway and his crooked ways. He's gone too far this time.' She reached up to kiss Danny's cheek. 'Thank you. I owe you my life – I think he would have killed me if I'd resisted, but I wasn't going to give in without a fight.'

'He'll be sent for trial at the Assizes, no doubt, and I want to be there to see the villain sentenced.' Danny brushed a stray lock of hair back from Angel's forehead. 'Never mind him now. Try to forget what happened tonight.'

'I just want to get away from here, Danny.'

'I'd take you home with me, but I think you'd be better off with Lil to take care of you. I'll be working the market stall for the rest of the week. The dried lavender goes well in the winter and in a few weeks it'll be holly and mistletoe.'

She reached up to brush his cheek with a kiss. 'As I told you before, there's plenty of it growing on the fruit trees in the orchard, and Grantley is still owned by the Devanes. We'll pick what we want and sell it as we did before. Christmas is coming – things must get better.'

'Always the optimist.' He slipped her hand through the crook of his arm. 'Let's get you on your way home. I'll stay here until the constable takes Galloway into custody. I don't trust that fellow not to try and make a bolt for it.'

Angel had no wish to see Galloway, even though he was apparently bound hand and foot and being watched closely by Trubshawe. Danny handed her into the chaise and tucked the blanket from the Westwoods' barouche around her as tenderly as a nursemaid. Russell flicked the reins and the horse moved forward at a trot. Angel turned and waved to Danny and then lay back against the squabs, exhausted and relieved to have escaped from a terrifying ordeal. She would never be able to repay Danny for what he had done – he was a true friend. She closed her eyes and allowed herself to drift off into a deep and dreamless sleep.

The noise of the city was tumultuous after the peace and quiet of the countryside and Angel awakened to find the chaise tooling along Ludgate Street in the direction of Ludgate Hill. Russell drew the horse to a halt at the entrance to Naked Boy Court and climbed down to help Angel alight.

'Are you all right, Miss Angel?' he asked anxiously. 'That fellow didn't hurt you, did he?'

Ignoring the pain from her bruised arm, Angel shook her head. 'No, and I have you and Trubshawe to thank for that.'

'I'll leave you here, miss. Will you be all right walking down that dark alley on your own?'

'I'll be fine, thank you, Russell. I'm used to London ways, so don't worry about me, and thank you for bringing me home.'

He tipped his hat and climbed back onto the box. 'I'll wait here a while, just in case you need me, miss.'

Angel smiled and nodded. The dark, dank alleyway held no fear for her. What she had just gone through had been far more terrible, and she entered Naked Boy Court eager to reach home and safety. As she lifted the latch on the tall wooden gate she was reminded of that first day when she had escaped the boys who were tormenting her and she had seen Sir Adolphus in the yard, feeding the dogs. She could hear Thor barking, with Juno joining in, and it was the most welcoming sound in the world. Almost immediately the front door opened, sending a beam of

351

gaslight onto the cobbles and Angel walked into Lil's open arms.

'You waited up for me. You shouldn't have.'

'I ought to box your ears for stopping out so late and frightening us all to death,' Lil said crossly, but her eyes were moist as she gave Angel a hug. 'Come in and get warm. Where have you been all this time?'

Angel bent down to stroke the two dogs, who nuzzled her hands, looking up at her with shining eyes in mute welcome. 'It's a long story. I'd love a cup of tea, Lil.'

'Cook and Baines are waiting in the kitchen and the kettle's been on the hob for so long it's probably boiled dry.'

Angel ignored Lil's testy tone, knowing that her agitation was caused by worry and not anger. The warmth of the kitchen enveloped her as she entered and she was greeted by smiling faces. Even Baines managed to crease his walnut features into the semblance of a grin.

'Sit down, Angel,' Lil said gently. 'There's someone waiting to see you.'

Chapter Twenty

Angel turned to see Hector standing in the doorway. Surprise, exhaustion and a jumble of emotions turned her to stone, and she could not move a muscle.

'What's the matter with you, Angel?' Lil demanded. 'It's Captain Devane – he turned up out of the blue this morning. Aren't you pleased?'

Hector stepped forward, taking Angel's limp hand in his and raising it to his lips. 'I'm sorry. It was unfair to spring this on you.' He scanned her face, frowning. 'You look tired and you're very pale. Are you ill?'

They were all staring at her as Angel struggled to find the right words.

'Hector. I...' she swallowed convulsively. 'What a lovely surprise.'

The tension in the room eased and suddenly everyone was talking at once. Hector pulled up a chair. 'Sit down, Angel. You really do look done in.' He turned to Lil, who had picked up the kettle and was filling the teapot. 'A tot of brandy might help.'

Baines rose to his feet. 'I'll fetch the bottle, Captain.' He disappeared into the scullery.

'Crafty old devil,' Cook said crossly. 'He hides it in a different place every time he takes a nip. You'd think he didn't trust us.'

'I don't, and that's the truth.' Baines emerged from the scullery with a bottle clutched in his fist. 'I mark the level so I know if anyone's been tippling. I paid for this meself, so don't look daggers at me, Eudora Jones. You might have been queen of the Grantley kitchen, but you're a guest here, and don't forget it.' He drew out the cork and placed the brandy on the table. 'You can help yourself, of course, Captain.'

Recovering from her shock, Angel smiled. 'Nothing changes, but it is good to have you home, Hector. How did you know we were here and not at Grantley?'

'I disembarked from the troop ship this morning, and I stopped off to leave Uncle Dolph's campaign trunk with Baines.' He poured a measure of brandy and handed it to him. 'The colonel was buried with full military honours.'

'I wouldn't expect anything less, Captain.' Baines raised his glass in a toast before tossing back his drink. 'It's getting late so I'll take the dogs out, if you'll excuse me, Captain.' He stood up and the dogs raised themselves from the floor, eyeing him expectantly. At a single command they followed him out of the room.

'So you understand the reasons for our being here,' Angel said slowly. 'You know, of course, that we're in real danger of losing Grantley.'

Hector nodded. 'I would have come home sooner had it been possible, but I'm here now and things are going to change.'

'Galloway is an even bigger crook than we thought, Hector,' Angel said urgently. 'You'll hardly believe it when I tell you the full extent of his wickedness, and it was his intention to ruin my life.'

'I hope they hang the old bastard.' Lil shot a wary look in Cook's direction. 'And I ain't apologising for me language.'

Cook tossed her head. 'I don't normally condone the use of bad words, but in this case I think you may be forgiven.'

Hector's lips twitched as he exchanged amused glances with Angel. 'I think we all share your dislike of the man, Miss Heavitree.'

'If you could bring yourself to call me Lil, it

would please me greatly, Captain.' Lil gazed at him expectantly. 'It really would.'

'Well then, Lil, it would be my pleasure. I know how important you are to Angel.' Hector turned to Cook with an apologetic smile. 'You, too, Cook. But then you've been part of the family ever since I can remember.'

'You used to love my chocolate cake, Captain. If I can get to grips with this old-fashioned lump of rust that Baines uses to heat his food, I'll make one especially for you.'

'I look forward to it,' Hector said, smiling. 'We will get Grantley back, I promise, and tomorrow I'm going to visit Quelch, who was my father's solicitor and senior partner in the firm until he retired. He would be furious if he knew what Galloway had been doing since he took over, but he won't get away with it for much longer. I'm home now and I can't wait to get my hands on that gentleman.' He added a dash of brandy to Angel's tea and passed it to her. 'This should help. You can tell me everything when you're rested.'

'That's all very well, Captain, but I want to know where she's been all day,' Lil said firmly. 'Anything could have happened to you, my girl.'

'There'll be time for explanations in the morning.' Hector laid his hand on Angel's shoulder. 'A good night's sleep is what you need, and then you can tell me everything.'

His kindness and understanding brought tears to Angel's eyes and her delight at seeing him again, combined with the effects of the brandy, was making it difficult to maintain her com-

355

posure. 'You don't have to worry about Galloway – he's been arrested.' The words came flooding out before she could stop herself.

'Why?' Hector demanded. 'How did that happen?'

'It's a long story. I'll explain in the morning, but I can tell you that he'll be up before Sir Eugene tomorrow, and then he'll be sent to the Assizes, that's what Danny said.'

'Danny?' Hector's slanting eyebrows snapped together over the bridge of his aquiline nose. 'Who is Danny?'

Angel sighed. She was not feeling up to a cross-examination. 'You know who Danny is. His father, Joe Wicks, helped me when I was living on the streets. You've heard me talk about them many times in the past.'

'Are you still seeing that fellow?' Hector said sharply. 'I thought you'd grown out of your fascination with market traders.'

Stung by the unfairness of his comment and the harsh tone of his voice, Angel stood up, swaying unsteadily on her feet. 'I was one of them, Hector, or have you forgotten? I am a common flower seller, as your mother and Susannah never fail to remind me.' She could have chosen that moment to tell him that she was a Montgomerie, and their pedigree was equal to, or even more illustrious than that of the Devanes, but she had her pride.

'I'm sorry, Angel,' Hector reached out to take her hand, but she snatched it away.

'So you should be. We were raised as brother and sister, and you knew everything about my

356

past, so why throw it in my face now?'

Lil and Cook exchanged worried glances. 'You're overtired, love,' Lil said hurriedly. 'I'll fill a stone bottle with hot water and bring it up to your room. Why don't you go to bed and get some rest? Captain Hector will be here in the morning.'

'I'm not a baby, Lil. Thank you, but I don't need cosseting, but I am tired so I'll say good night.' Angel nodded in Hector's direction and hurried from the room, managing to hold back the tears until she had closed the door and turned the key in the lock.

She was awakened by the sound of someone tapping gently on her door. At first she thought it was part of the dream she had been having, but then the urgency increased and she sat up in bed, brushing her tumbled curls back from her forehead. 'Come in.'

The door opened and to her horror it was Hector who strode into the room. 'I'm sorry if I woke you, Angel, but I have to go out and I wanted to speak to you in private.'

She pulled the coverlet up to her chin. 'What is so important that it can't wait until I'm up and dressed? And why are you in uniform?'

'We got off on the wrong foot last evening. It was my fault and I apologise for being boorish, but I was tired and shocked to see you looking so ill. Am I forgiven?'

'I suppose so. I'd had a very bad day, and I was surprised to see you.'

Hector perched on the edge of the bed. 'You

357

look like you did when you first came to Grantley,' he said, smiling. 'You were ready to take on
anybody who challenged your right to be there,
and you looked daggers at me, just as you're
looking now.'

His smile disarmed her completely and the
anger she had felt the previous evening disappeared like morning mist. 'You were very unfair
to Danny. He went out of his way to help me.' She
shuddered at the memory of Galloway's leering
face. 'You have no idea what I went through
yesterday.'

'No, but Lil told me that Galloway had been
making a nuisance of himself.'

'You could say that, but he really overstepped
the mark yesterday.'

'Then tell me, Angel. Tell me everything and
then I'll give you my news.'

She leaned forward, modesty forgotten as the
bedcovers slipped to reveal her white cambric
nightgown, trimmed with broderie anglaise. 'You
first. You can't leave me in suspense.'

'All right, you win, as always.' He reached out
to clasp her hand. 'When Uncle Dolph was on
his deathbed he wrote a will that cancels out the
one held by his solicitor. He left Grantley to me
in its entirety, but he bequeathed this house to
you.'

Angel snatched her hand away 'Are you serious?'

'Never more so. He was very fond of you, and I
think he saw more of what went on at home than
he let on. He wanted you to be independent and
that's why he bequeathed this house to you and

you alone.'

'Are you sure?'

'I have the will in my pocket and I'll make certain it goes to probate as soon as possible.'

'The family will contest it,' Angel said guardedly. 'They won't be happy.'

'Mama and Susannah always have something to say about everything, but they'll come round eventually. As to my brothers, they wouldn't want to be saddled with this old place. They both love the country and I'm sure they would be happy to spend the rest of their lives at Grantley.'

'But, Hector, you're in very real danger of losing your home. I thought you understood that. Unless you can pay off Uncle Dolph's creditors, you'll lose Grantley for ever.'

'I do know that, and that's why my second mission this morning is to go to the solicitors and find out exactly what has gone wrong. I want to know why Galloway was allowed to rob his clients, and I'm going to put a stop to his antics for ever. I'll do whatever I have to do, Angel, but Grantley stays in the family.'

'I hope you're right, but at least Galloway is under lock and key. That must make things easier. But what is your first mission? It's nothing good, judging by the look on your face.'

'I'm going to The London Hospital to visit Rupert. He was thrown from his horse and badly injured. It's doubtful if he'll ever walk again.'

'Oh, no. How awful. Is Dolly with him?'

'We all came home on the *Orontes*. Dolly nursed him devotedly during the voyage, and she's with him now. I want to make sure they're both being looked after and have everything they need.'

Forgetting everything other than the desire to help and support her friends, Angel threw back the covers and swung her legs over the side of the bed. 'Go downstairs and wait for me, Hector. I'll be ready in two shakes of a lamb's tail. I'm coming with you.'

He took one look at her set expression and rose to his feet. 'All right, I'm going. But be quick. I have a lot to accomplish today, and then I'm going to Grantley to open up the house. We're not finished yet, and you still haven't told me everything.'

Angel pushed him towards the door. 'I'll tell you in the cab on the way to the hospital. Now go, please, and let me get dressed.'

Rupert was in a side ward with Dolly seated at his bedside. Her ashen face flushed with colour at the sight of Angel and she leaped to her feet.

'You came, Angel. I knew you would.'

Angel hugged her fondly. 'It's good to see you again, Dolly.' She turned to Rupert, who was pale beneath his tan with dark shadows etched below his eyes. 'I am so sorry.'

'But at least I'm alive,' Rupert said grimly. 'That's what everyone tells me, but I've heard it a million times. They're wrong, though – if I can't walk again I might as well be dead. What use is a cripple?'

'Don't say things like that,' Dolly cried passionately.

'You'll feel better when you're at home.' Hector

glanced round the sterile room with a wry smile. 'Hospitals are depressing places at the best of times.'

'That's right,' Dolly said hastily. 'Good food and country air will work wonders, Rupert.'

He turned his head away. 'You know better than anyone why we wouldn't be welcome at home. Father might have a new wife, but that won't alter the fact that he disapproved of our marriage. I can't put you through that, my darling. Especially now.'

'I'm in the family way,' Dolly said, blushing. 'It's wonderful, but we haven't told anyone else. I don't know what we'll do or where we'll go.'

'Everyone loves babies.' Angel spoke with more conviction that she was feeling. She might speak for herself, but somehow she could not imagine Eloise in the role of grandmother. Unless, of course, Susannah married well; then it would be a different matter.

'A child needs a proper father.' Rupert raised his arm to cover his face. 'I'm finished, Hector. I'm a bloody useless mess.'

'I never had you down as a coward,' Hector said angrily.

'Don't say things like that to him.' Dolly's pretty mouth drooped at the corners and her eyes filled with tears. 'Can't you see how he suffers?'

'Of course we can.' Angel put her arm around Dolly's shoulders. 'But giving in isn't going to help.' She turned to Rupert, facing him angrily. 'Hector's right. You're a brave man, you have a loving wife and soon you'll be a father. Of course you're needed, and giving up isn't going to help

361

anyone, least of all the people who truly love you.'

'I can't go home like this,' Rupert murmured. 'I don't want to be an object of pity.'

Dolly threw herself down onto the chair and laid her head beside his on the pillow, and their tears mingled.

Hector drew Angel aside. 'I'd take them to Grantley, but I daren't chance that until this business is settled. I think I have the answer, but I don't want to say anything yet.' He looked down at the husband and wife united in grief. 'Rupert obviously needs to be here for a while, but she's the one I worry about.'

'I agree.' Angel leaned over to stroke Dolly's hair back from her forehead. 'You must come home with me. I need your help to make the house in Naked Boy Court beautiful.'

Dolly raised her head. 'I – I can't leave Rupert on his own.'

'He's in good hands,' Hector said firmly. 'He'll have the best treatment that money can buy.' He glanced at Angel, shrugging. 'Sir Eugene has a bottomless purse and I'll make sure he does the right thing.'

'There, you heard what Hector said, and you must think of your child.' Angel helped Dolly to her feet. 'You need looking after just as much as Rupert, and you'll have Lil and Cook as well as me, and there's Baines, too. When Rupert is well enough to leave hospital Baines can be his batman. He's an army man through and through, and nothing would suit him better than to have another officer to care for.'

Dolly managed a watery smile. 'You've got it all worked out.'

'You looked after me when I was in need. We stuck together in the old days, Dolly, and that's what we're going to do now.' She patted her on the cheek. 'You can visit Rupert as often as you please.'

'Are you happy with this arrangement, Rupert?' Hector leaned over the bed, lowering his voice. 'You want what is best for your wife and child, don't you?'

Rupert nodded. 'Of course. Do as they say, Dolly. Hector's right – I'm in good hands here, and you must take care of yourself and my son.'

'Good man.' Hector stood aside as the door opened and a nurse entered the room, giving them a disapproving look. 'I know the drill, Sister. We're just leaving.'

Outside the hospital Hector tried to hail a cab. 'Take Dolly home, Angel. I have business in the City and then I'm going to Westwood Hall to have a word with Sir Eugene. I'll stay the night at Grantley.'

'How will you manage without any staff?'

A smile curved his generous lips. 'I'm a soldier, used to bivouacking anywhere. I'm sure I can manage in my own home.'

'You will let me know what happens with the solicitor, won't you?'

'Don't worry. I'll keep you informed of my every move.' He succeeded in attracting the attention of a cabby and stepped forward to help Dolly into the hansom, but when it came to Angel's turn Hector's fingers curled around hers and he held her hand for longer than was strictly necessary. 'You've held my family together, Angel. I couldn't have had a better sister, and I can never thank you enough for what you tried to do.'

She climbed into the cab and settled down beside Dolly, but she could still hear Hector's voice, thanking her for what she had done out of love for her home and adopted family, and she could feel the warmth of his grasp as he had held her hand.

'I don't like leaving Rupert on his own in hospital.' Dolly's voice intruded on Angel's thoughts, bringing her rapidly back to the jolting, stale-smelling interior of the hansom cab.

'He'll be well cared for,' Angel said automatically. 'You can visit him every day, but more importantly we must look after you and your son and heir.'

'It might be a girl.' Dolly leaned back against the shabby leather squabs, a dreamy expression on her face. 'It would be lovely to have a daughter, but I don't mind either way.' Her smile faded and she sat forward, clutching Angel's hand. 'What's to become of us? Rupert might never walk again, and how will we live if Sir Eugene won't take us in, or if he stops Rupert's allowance? We could have managed nicely on his army pay, but that's stopped now and I can't support us by selling flowers. It might mean the workhouse.'

'Stop it, Dolly. I'm sure that Sir Eugene will come round eventually, and until then you will always have a home with me in Naked Boy Court. Uncle Dolph left me the house in his will.

I still can't believe it, but it's true and it's large enough for all of us. It just needs somebody to love it and make it into a proper home.'

'Do you really mean it, Angel?'

'You and I might not be related, but I love you like a sister.' A sudden vision of Belinda's face brought Angel back to the real world. 'I have such a lot to tell you, Dolly. I've discovered who I really am.'

Dolly shrank back into, the corner of the seat, eyeing Angel with genuine concern. 'Does that mean you'll be different from now on? Who are you?'

'I'm just the same person I ever was, you noodle. It was Galloway, the crooked solicitor, who told me the tale. Just wait until I tell you everything that's happened since you went away.'

'You make everything sound so exciting. I have missed you, Angel. The other army wives were nice enough but I had a feeling that the officers' ladies looked down on me, and the camp followers scared me to death. They were even tougher than Lil, and that's saying something.'

Angel chuckled at the thought of women who were beefier and stronger than Lumpy Lil Heavitree. 'I'd pitch Lil against them any day. But we're almost home, so my news will have to wait until we're tucked up in bed. You can share my room until we've got one ready for you. It will be like old times, swapping stories and talking half the night.'

Hector returned later that day to find Angel in the parlour, swaddled in one of Lil's large pinafores and a scarf tied around her head. She was balancing precariously on a chair as she attempted to brush cobwebs from the cornice.

'I thought you were going to stay the night at Grantley, Hector?'

'I've only come to collect a few things I'll need to keep me going,' he said cheerfully. 'Are you all right up there, Angel? You look as if you're about to topple over.' He held up his hand. 'Come down before you break your neck. Anyway, Lil should be doing that, not you.'

Angel climbed down without needing his assistance, although the temptation to leap into his arms had almost got the better of her. The memory of their recent parting was still fresh in her mind, but such thoughts would only lead to heartbreak. Hector would need to think carefully before he chose a wife, and marriage to an heiress would secure Grantley's future for ever. She brushed the dust from her skirts, avoiding his direct gaze. 'I've sent her to market, and Dolly is helping Cook to prepare supper. Have you got to go right away? It's a good seven miles to Grantley and you could set off first thing in the morning.'

'I'm not leaving Grantley unoccupied any longer. I've hired a hack from the livery stables, so it won't take too long.'

'Did you get anywhere with the solicitor?'

'Quelch said that as Galloway was acting against our interests the agreement he entered into isn't binding, but it's a pity that Uncle Dolph chose to borrow from a company whose only interest is to acquire land for building. They won't give up easily.'

'Sir Eugene's solicitor said that part of Grantley is common land and has to be kept as such.'

'That's interesting, I'll ask him about it when I visit Westwood. I must see my mother and sister, and I intend to put Rupert's case to his father, all of which means that I have a lot to accomplish in as little time as possible.'

'Does that mean you only have a short leave?'

'I've resigned my commission, Angel. When Uncle Dolph was dying he begged me to leave the army and concentrate on Grantley. He said that he regretted his cavalier attitude to the estate and the people who depend upon it for their living, and he wanted me to make amends for his neglect.'

'That's a heavy responsibility to put on your shoulders, Hector. Are you sure it's what you want?'

He met her anxious gaze with a smile that melted her heart. 'If you'd asked me that a few years ago I would have answered differently, but now it's what I want most in the world. I've seen enough war and destruction to know that I wasn't cut out to be in the military. Grantley and the land around it has come to mean more and more to me. I can't imagine either of my brothers working to restore the estate to its glory days.'

'That's fine talk, but you will have to find the money first. Perhaps you should consider marrying an heiress?'

'Who knows?' He gave her a whimsical look. 'Have you anyone in mind?'

'I'm not a matchmaker. Perhaps you should consult your mother. I'm sure Aunt Eloise has a whole list of eligible young ladies lined up for you.'

Hector laughed and brushed a cobweb off her forehead with the tip of his forefinger. 'Now why didn't I think of that? But maybe I have other plans.'

The mere touch of his hand was enough to send her senses reeling, but she fought against the emotions that threatened to overcome her. Hector had been her childhood hero, but she was certain that his love for Grantley was deeper than he realised. If marrying a rich woman secured its future he would have little choice other than to follow the tradition that had kept the estate in the family for centuries.

'You'd best go now,' she said briskly. 'You'll want to get there before dark. The road through the marshes is treacherous at this time of year, as well you know.'

His smile faded. 'You're right, of course. I'll be back as soon as I can.'

'Good luck,' Angel said faintly as the door closed behind him. The room seemed suddenly cold and empty without his presence and she shivered. She was sending him to war, but not the kind that would be lost or won on the battle-field. He had to fight to keep his birthright and he would have to stand up to his mother. Aunt Eloise was a determined woman, and Angel suspected that she had long ago chosen a suitable bride for her eldest son, and she would not be a penniless foundling, but that was not the full extent of her worries. Uncle Dolph had left her his London home, but without a steady income it would be impossible to maintain the establishment. Dolly had promised to pay for her keep, and Baines had his army pension, but that left Angel with Cook and Lil to provide for, and their wages to find. Angel's initial euphoria was fading by the minute. She would have to find work, or Dolly's fears might be realised – the shadow of the workhouse was still very real.

Chapter Twenty-One

The old house in Naked Boy Court echoed with the sound of women's voices as they worked from room to room, dusting, sweeping, scrubbing floors and polishing. The scent of beeswax, turpentine and lavender oil wafted around the house, together with the smell of lye soap that Lil concocted over a brazier in the back yard. Curtains were taken down, washed and hung out to dry, although some of them fell apart before they reached that stage, and others were so moth-eaten that they had to be torn up and used as rags. Windows were cleaned with vinegar and water, and the attics were raided for anything that could be taken to the second-hand furniture shop in Blue Boar Court. Dolly did her best to help, but she spent most of her waking hours at the hospital, returning home pale and exhausted after her efforts to keep Rupert from a pit of despondency.

The days were growing shorter, and still there was no word from Hector. Then, on a bitterly cold November day, Rupert was discharged from hospital. He had been given strict instructions to rest and regain his strength. Baines carried him from the hackney carriage to the parlour where Angel had used some of their dwindling supply of coal to light the fire, and they made Rupert as comfortable as possible on the horsehair sofa. He was pale and exhausted after the bumpy journey from the hospital, and they left him to take a nap.

'The doctors say he mustn't overexert himself,' Dolly whispered as she followed Angel to the kitchen. 'But he needs fresh country air and good food. I'm not being ungrateful, Angel, but he ought to be at home where he can be properly looked after.'

'I agree.' Angel hesitated outside the kitchen door. 'But don't say anything to the others, it will only make them feel uncomfortable. They've worked so hard to get everything ready for his homecoming.'

Dolly nodded tearfully. 'I know, and I'm truly grateful, but Sir Eugene could see that Rupert gets the best doctors and medicines. Even if I have to remain here, I want Rupert to go home.'

'That's ridiculous, Dolly. You're his wife and the mother of his child. You are part of the Westwood family now.'

'I don't think Sir Eugene will agree, and as to Lady Westwood, you know what she's like. She'll never see me as anything other than a housemaid.'

Angel could not argue with that, even though it hurt her to admit that Dolly was right. Eloise Westwood was a hard woman, and she had set

370

ideas. 'I can see that there's something on your mind, Dolly. Is there anything I can do to help?'

'I'd like you to go to Westwood and have a word with Sir Eugene. Tell him how poorly Rupert is and ask him to help his son. Beg him on your knees, if that's what it takes.'

'All right, but please don't upset yourself. Think of the baby and try not to worry.'

Dolly's eyes brightened. 'You'll do it? You'll go today?'

'I will. I can't promise anything, but I'll do my very best.'

'You're a true friend and I love you.' Dolly was about to hug her but she clutched her belly.

'What's the matter?' Angel asked anxiously, but Dolly's face creased into a smile.

'My son kicked me. He's a proper little fighter, Angel. He'll make his father proud.'

'For both their sakes look after yourself. I'll pack a bag, but the quickest way to get to Leyton is by train and I haven't enough money for the ticket.'

Dolly opened her reticule and took out a purse. 'Rupert wanted you to have this. Use it as you think fit.' She tipped some coins into Angel's outstretched hand.

'You're not to worry. I'll do my very best.'

It was early afternoon when Angel alighted from the train at Lea Bridge Station. Low Leyton Marsh was white with frost and grey clouds threatened heavy rain or even snow; it was certainly cold enough. Angel wrapped her woollen muffler around her neck, picked up her bag and

371

started walking along the road that led to Westwood Hall. A biting wind snatched spitefully at her bonnet and slapped her cheeks, bringing tears to her eyes, but she put her head down and continued on her way.

As she neared Grantley the first flakes of snow began to float down from a pewter sky and she hesitated, wondering whether to call at the house first, in the hope of seeing Hector. He had been gone for a few days and she was becoming anxious. The ornate wrought-iron gates were padlocked, but the side entrance was unfastened and she let herself into the grounds. The green grass of the deer park was rapidly disappearing beneath the snow, which was settling fast, but the house appeared to be shuttered and there was no sign of life.

She trudged up the carriage sweep and knocked on the door, but there was no answer and she retraced her steps, heading in the direction of the stable block. The familiar smells and sounds were a comfort and reassured her that at least one part of Grantley still existed. She could remember a time when the stalls had been filled with horses, and the family had employed grooms and stable boys as well as Russell and an under-coachman. The mews had always been a hive of activity, but now it was eerily silent, apart from the odd snicker from one of the two remaining horses. Then, as she came to a halt, she thought she could hear someone moving about in the coach house.

'Is anyone there?' Her voice echoed eerily around the stable yard, and a head popped out of one of the stalls. She recognised Parry, a boy from the village who was training to be a groom.

'Is that you, Miss Angel?' He squinted against the driving snow.

'Yes, Parry. I'm looking for Captain Hector. Have you seen him recently?'

'No, miss. He came here a while ago, but he didn't stay long.' He jerked his head in the direction of the coach house. 'Mr Russell is at home, miss. He might know more.'

'Thank you, Parry.' Angel headed for the back of the building and the cottage where she hoped to find Russell.

Mrs Russell opened the door and her mouth dropped open in surprise. 'Oh, Miss Angel, what are you doing out and about in this weather? Come in, my dear.'

Prissy Russell had been one of Angel's favourites when she was growing up at Grantley. In the early days, when she had felt lost and lonely, especially when Susannah had been spiteful, Angel had made for the stables and Prissy had often taken her in and allowed her to help knead the dough when she was baking, or peel the carrots and potatoes when she was making a stew. Childless herself, Prissy Russell loved children, and Angel had always been sure of a welcome. A second cousin to Miss Creedy from the post office, Prissy was her complete opposite. She could not play the organ, but she had a rich contralto voice and when she sang the whole congregation hushed and listened in rapt silence. She often sang while she worked and had encouraged Angel to join in the chorus of popular songs, urging her to hum the tune, even if she did not know the words.

'I can't stay long,' Angel said as she stepped over the threshold into the main living room and kitchen. 'I'm on my way to Westwood Hall, but I wanted to see Captain Hector. I thought he had returned to Grantley.'

'Sit by the fire for a while, and dry your clothes. You're blue with cold, my dear.'

Angel took off her gloves and her muffler and hung them over the brass rail on the range. 'Captain Hector? Have you seen him recently?'

'He was here yesterday, but then he left. We don't know what's happening or if we'll be able to stay here. It's very worrying and my poor husband hardly gets a wink of sleep. He tosses and turns and then he gets up and walks round the room, keeping me awake, too. Do you know anything, Miss Angel?'

'I wish I did, Mrs Russell.' Angel rose from the chair; if she stayed a moment longer she would not want to go outside and face the long walk in the snow. 'I'm going to Westwood Hall now, and if I find out anything that will give you comfort I'll be sure to let you know.'

'Won't you stay for a cup of tea and a bite of my seed cake? You need something inside you before you brave the weather.'

'I would love to, but I must get there before dark.'

Prissy picked up the teapot. 'Russell will take you in the chaise. That's his job, miss. You must allow him to do it.'

Angel sat down again. She knew when she was beaten and she loved Prissy's seed cake.

Angel alighted from the chaise. 'Thank you, Russell. I'll be sure to let you know if I find out what's happening to Grantley.'

He tipped his hat. 'Thank you, Miss Angel. I'm very anxious, as you might understand. We'll be homeless if the party buying the estate turns us out on the street.'

'I'll do my very best to prevent that happening.'

'I'll wait for you here, miss.'

'I can't ask you to do that, Russell. I might be a long time, depending on what Sir Eugene has to say and if Captain Hector is here.'

'Send word if you're invited to stay, miss. I'll wait just in case you want to return to Grantley.'

Angel turned and saw the footman silhouetted in the doorway and she hurried up the steps. If James was surprised to see her, he was too well trained to make any comment.

'I must see Sir Eugene immediately and in private,' Angel said firmly.

'I believe he's in the library, Miss Winter. Lady Westwood is in the drawing room with Miss Susannah.'

'Thank you, but I wish to speak to Sir Eugene.'

James snapped his fingers and a maid hurried over to take Angel's damp mantle and bonnet. 'Please wait here, Miss Winter.' He strolled off at a leisurely pace, and returned minutes later with an equally irritating lack of urgency.

'Follow me, please.'

Angel could not wait a moment longer to put Rupert and Dolly's case to Sir Eugene, and she followed close on his heels as he led her to the study.

Sir Eugene was seated by a log fire, reading a book, which he closed with a snap and set down on the low table in front of him. His smile seemed genuine and he motioned Angel to take a seat. 'It's good to see you again, my dear. James said you wanted to see me urgently. Is something wrong?'

Angel sat down, clasping her, hands in her lap in an attempt to appear calm and collected, although inwardly she was quaking. So much depended on the outcome of this interview. 'You've heard that Rupert was badly injured?'

'Yes, and I'm saddened to hear it.'

'He was discharged from hospital this morning, and he is now at Naked Boy Court, but he needs proper care and medical attention, which we cannot give him.' There was no point beating about the bush. She had to make him understand.

'By *we* I assume you mean yourself and the servant girl he married against my wishes.'

'Dolly is no longer a servant, sir. She's a loving wife and soon to be a mother.'

'I see.'

'Rupert doesn't know that I've come here to plead their case, Sir Eugene. But the doctors say he's unlikely to walk again. He needs his family around him at a time like this.'

Sir Eugene rose to his feet and walked over to the window, standing with his back to Angel. 'And you braved the snow to come and tell me this?'

'I did what any friend would do in the circumstances.'

'When is the infant due?'

A glimmer of hope gave Angel the courage to go on. 'In March or early April. Dolly is well, but tired after the long sea voyage and she's spent every day at Rupert's bedside. I think he might have given up had she not been so devoted.'

He turned to face her, his expression grave. 'Even if I were to accept the girl into my home I know that my wife would never acknowledge her, and I fear that Susannah would follow suit.'

'Blanche might feel differently.'

'I have hopes for my daughter. According to Eloise there is a strong chance that Blanche will become mistress of Grantley before long.'

Angel stared at him, too stunned to speak.

'You may look surprised,' Sir Eugene said casually. 'But I have to think of my daughter's future and it's a match that I would encourage wholeheartedly.'

'Hector and Blanche?' Angel's mouth was dry and the words stuck in her throat.

'Yes, indeed. Their union would please me greatly.'

'But I had the impression that Blanche and Percy had an understanding.'

'I think I nipped that romance in the bud. With due respect, Angel, your brother is a fine man, but Grantley land abuts mine and I would like to see our two estates united by marriage.'

Angel bit back a sharp retort. The idea was old-fashioned and outlandish. 'Is Hector here now?' she asked, forcing herself to remain calm.

'He had only just arrived at Grantley when he received a telegram ordering him to return to his regiment.'

'But he told me that he'd resigned his commission.'

'That's true, but apparently this was a summons he could not ignore. He left for Transvaal almost immediately.'

'I don't understand why he didn't let me know. I've been imagining all manner of things that might have prevented him from returning to London.'

Sir Eugene gave her a searching look. 'Is there an understanding between yourself and Hector? If there is he kept it very quiet.'

'No, sir. Not at all.'

'I'm glad for your sake, Angel. You must understand that families like ours do things quite differently from those lower down the social scale.'

'What are you trying to tell me?'

'I promised Hector that my solicitor would take the case from Galloway, who is now languishing in prison, and will be there for some time to come. I have offered to repay the mortgage on condition that it would be my dowry for Blanche.' He held up his hand as Angel opened her mouth to protest. 'I want my daughter close by so that I can be sure she is happy and well cared for.'

'Did Hector agree to this?' Angel demanded, keeping a tight rein on her emotions. She understood Hector's desire to keep Grantley at all costs, but to sacrifice his future happiness seemed too high a price to pay.

'He said he needed time to think about it, but I told him that Percy Montgomerie is a frequent visitor here and it's obvious that he has feelings for Blanche.'

'Maybe Blanche returns my brother's affection, sir. Perhaps you ought to find out how she feels?'

'My daughter will do as she is told, and I'm hoping that Montgomerie might turn his attention to Susannah. It would make Eloise very happy to have such a wealthy son-in-law.'

'It sounds as though you are selling the girls off to the highest bidder,' Angel said angrily.

Sir Eugene gazed at her dispassionately. 'I don't wish to sound unkind, Angel, and I like you well enough, but someone with a background like yours could not be expected to understand the need for keeping up tradition, and the importance of lineage.'

'My mother came from a respectable family, and my father was a Montgomerie. My pedigree, even if I wasn't aware of it until recently, is as good as yours or any member of the Devane family – and you're right – I don't understand how anyone could coerce their child into an arranged marriage. A similar contract, forced upon my mother, ended in tragedy.' Angel rose to her feet and was about to walk out of the room when Sir Eugene called her back.

'Wait a minute.'

She came to a halt, turning slowly to face him. 'Well?'

'You may tell Rupert that he's welcome here, but for her own sake I think it best if his wife remains with you, at least until the child is born.'

'For her own sake?' Angel could hardly bear to repeat the words.

'You know very well what I mean. Do you really think that the girl would find it easy or even

379

bearable to live here, knowing that my wife would find her an embarrassment? The girl, if I remember rightly, speaks like a common person and doesn't know how to behave in society.'

'And that is your last word, Sir Eugene?'

'It is. Give Rupert that message and the rest is up to him. You will stay here tonight, of course.'

'Russell insisted on waiting with the chaise. I think it best if I return to Grantley. Thank you, Sir Eugene, I can find my own way out.'

At Angel's request the flustered maidservant scurried off to fetch Angel's mantle and bonnet. James stood to attention, staring straight ahead and Angel knew that she had offended his sense of propriety, but that was of little importance compared to the shocking news that Hector might be prepared to marry Blanche in return for a handsome dowry. She would never have believed it of him, but he must have been desperate if he had agreed to consider such an arrangement. Neither he nor Blanche deserved to be trapped in a loveless union in order to keep their parents happy, and if Percy really had fallen in love with Sir Eugene's only daughter that would mean another heart would be broken. Angel hurried down the steps, wrapping her damp muffler around her neck, and she climbed into the chaise before Russell had a chance to get down and assist her.

'Drive on,' she said sharply. 'I'll spend the night at Grantley.'

'You'd be more than welcome to stay in the cottage with me and Mrs Russell,' he said gruffly. 'I know it's not what you're used to, but the house is locked up.'

'Thank you, Russell. I appreciate the offer but I want to make sure that everything is as it should be, and tomorrow I'll need the carriage to take me to London.'

Russell unlocked the door leading into the entrance hall at Grantley. He struck a match and lit the oil lamp kept for welcoming guests when they arrived after dark. 'Are you sure you want to stay here on your own, Miss Angel?'

'If there are ghosts in Grantley they're friendly ones,' Angel said, smiling. 'I've never felt afraid in this house.'

'We aren't supposed to be here.' Russell glanced round anxiously as if expecting to be arrested for trespass at any moment.

'Don't worry about that,' Angel said confidently. 'I have a plan, and tomorrow, weather permitting, I'm going to London, but I'll be back later with Dolly and the others. What's more, I'm going to send telegrams to the boys to come home for Christmas. We aren't beaten yet, Russell.'

'Tell you what, miss. I'll fetch the dogs. They'll keep you company tonight.'

'Thank you, that's very thoughtful of you.' Angel went round lighting candles while she waited for Russell to return with Thor and Juno. The house smelled damp and musty and it was bitterly cold, but Angel was determined to see the night through. It was more a gesture of defiance than anything else, and a way of claiming back the property that belonged to the Devane family, but there were ghosts of her own to conquer and they were not associated with long-dead ancestors.

Galloway's attack on her person was still very real to her, and the rank odour of sweat and stale alcohol that had hung round him in a miasma still tainted the air. Galloway was safely incarcerated in prison, but she needed to free herself from the memory of that night, and the horrors he had threatened to inflict on her.

Her happy childhood had ended when Galloway had separated her from Aunt Cordelia. She could only imagine what her aunt's life must have been like when she went to live with Galloway's sister. Perhaps that had led to her early demise? She would never know, but the memory of the workhouse was still fresh in her mind. The fears and privations of existing on the savage streets of Seven Dials were forever carved on her heart, and yet that had not been enough for the man who had driven her mother to suicide. Galloway had known her true identity all along, but he had kept the knowledge to himself, depriving her of the love of a brother and sister, and now the people she had come to love might lose everything. Galloway had had a hand in that, too. The man was evil and Angel needed this long cold night to fight the demons that he had created.

She turned with a start as the door opened and Russell let the two elderly greyhounds loose. She kneeled down and put her arms around them as they licked her face and nuzzled her hands. 'I'll be fine now, Russell. With two such stalwart bodyguards I'll be quite safe until morning.'

'If you change your mind you can still come to the cottage, miss. It's stopped snowing, so with a bit of luck I'll be able to take you to London tomorrow. You'd best lock up after me, miss. I've seen off prowlers several times since the house has been empty. Word gets round.' He let himself out and Angel locked and bolted the main entrance.

'Come along, dogs. We'll go to the kitchen and I'll light a fire. We don't want to freeze to death, do we?'

Thor and Juno looked up at her, wagging their tails.

It was only when she had succeeded in getting a fire going in the range that Angel realised she had not eaten since enjoying a slice of cake in the Russells' kitchen, and she was very hungry. She filled the kettle from the pump in the scullery and set it to heat on the hob. There was a spoonful of tea left in the caddy, but a search of the cupboards proved fruitless. Cook and Lil had been thorough when they packed the contents of the larder, but just when she thought she would have to go hungry for the rest of the night, Angel discovered a bag containing enough oats to make a bowl of porridge.

A full stomach and the warmth of the fire gave Angel the courage she needed to check the rest of the house, and the company of Thor and Juno made her even bolder. With the lamp clutched in her hand she went from room to room. The furniture lay hidden beneath holland covers glowing eerily in the cold light of the moon, but the only sound was that of her own breathing and the pitter-patter of the dogs' paws on the polished wooden floor. Occasionally the scrabble of rodents behind the skirting boards made her stop and hold the lamp higher, but otherwise the downstairs rooms slumbered in total silence. She found nothing untoward upstairs and, having explored the attics, she returned to the comparative warmth of the kitchen, but this time she was armed with blankets and a pillow. She made herself comfortable in the rocking chair by the fire and laid a blanket on the flagstone floor for the dogs. Exhausted after the physical and emotional turmoil, she fell asleep.

Angel was awakened by the sound of someone tapping on the kitchen window. She opened her eyes, and for a moment she could not understand why she had been sleeping in a chair by the kitchen range, but the sight of Russell standing outside in the snow brought her back to the present with all its attendant problems. She got up hastily and went to open the back door. Thor and Juno rushed outside as fast as their arthritic limbs would take them, and Russell stepped into the scullery, pausing to stamp the snow off his boots before he followed her into the kitchen.

'You're all right then, miss?'

She smiled. 'A bit stiff from sleeping in a chair, but otherwise I'm perfectly well.'

'My Prissy has cooked sausages for breakfast and she's frying eggs as I speak. She would be honoured if you'd share our meal.' He glanced at the sticky saucepan that Angel had left in the sink. 'We was both worried that you didn't have no supper.'

'I made some porridge and I had tea without milk, but I would love to share your breakfast.

I'm starving!'

'Then I suggest you put your coat on and come with me. I just need to harness the horse, and we can leave for the city as soon as you're ready.'

Angel hesitated, frowning. 'We have another carriage horse, don't we?'

'Yes, miss.'

'Hector taught me to handle the reins when I was a child. I'll take the chaise and you can bring the barouche. I intend to bring everyone here when I return later today.'

'You're moving back to Grantley, miss? I thought we'd lost it for ever.'

'We'll be living here unlawfully to begin with, but I think I can change that and I'm prepared to risk it. The only question is, can I persuade the others that I'm doing the right thing?'

Chapter Twenty-Two

'You're going to sell this house?' Baines's voice rose to a shout. 'The colonel would turn in his grave, miss.' He leaned against the kitchen wall, folding his arms across his chest in an uncompromising manner that left Angel in no doubt as to his opinion.

'Sir Adolphus left it to me, Baines,' she said patiently. 'He must have known that Grantley was in a perilous position, but he obviously thought he would survive long enough to pay off his debts. The sad fact is that the estate's future is hanging in the balance.'

'But this is your house.' Lil pulled up a chair and sat down, scowling ominously. 'You'll have nothing if you sell up and give the money to the Devane family.'

'Would you be the new owner of Grantley?' Cook asked. 'If that's so, then I say go ahead.'

Angel shook her head. 'I don't know about the legal side of things. I just feel I must do something. Hector has had to return to South Africa and someone needs to take his side.'

'Maybe he should have sorted matters before he went,' Lil said gloomily. 'What are the other two Devane boys doing to help? Nothing, that's what. They're spoiled brats, if you ask me. What do you say, Eudora?'

Cook shrugged. 'It's not for me to criticise my betters, but if they were my sons I'd send them out to work.' She pushed back her chair and stood up. 'I'd better see to the soup or we'll be left with bread and scrape for our midday meal.' She waddled over to the range, snatched up a wooden spoon and began stirring the contents of the pan as if she were beating it to death.

'Put the young fellows in the army,' Baines muttered. 'That would make men of them.'

Angel could see that she was getting nowhere. She turned to Dolly, who had been sitting quietly at the table, listening to the argument. 'What do you think? I told you what Sir Eugene said, so this decision will affect you and Rupert.'

'I want what's best for my husband, of course,' Dolly said seriously, 'but I think I am the best person to nurse him back to health. I say we should move back to Grantley, even if it means that I have to take on my old duties.'

'There's no chance of that,' Angel said, nodding. 'I want everyone to agree, or my plan won't work. I suggest that we reclaim the house and estate. If we give up now we're allowing Galloway to get the better of us, and the mysterious people who want to bury Grantley under bricks and mortar will have won.'

Lil leaned forward, fixing Angel with a hard stare. 'You've got a brother and sister living in London, and they're filthy rich. If it was me I think I'd have a word with them before I gave up what's legally mine.'

'You've given me an idea,' Angel said slowly. The thought of asking Percy for money was abhorrent, but he was a businessman and he might be able to help in other ways. She stood up. 'Pack what you need and Russell will take you to Grantley. I have an errand to do before I follow on.'

Lil leaped to her feet. 'I hope you're not intending to drive round town unaccompanied.'

'I can handle the reins as well as any man, Lil.'

'The colonel wouldn't approve, miss,' Baines said firmly. 'It's not proper for a young lady to be seen driving unaccompanied. I'll get me hat and greatcoat and I'll bring the chaise round from the livery stable.' He stomped out of the kitchen.

'He may be a grumpy old devil, but he's got the right idea,' Lil said, sniffing. 'Don't refuse his help, Angel. I know you and your independent spirit, but he needs to feel useful.'

'Lil Heavitree, don't tell me you're going soft in

your old age.' Angel smiled as she plucked her reticule from the table. 'I'm ready to go into battle for Grantley. I'm going to find a solution that will make everyone happy, and that's a promise.'

Angel pretended not to notice the curious stares of the pedestrians, but she realised that they must present an odd sight seated side by side in the chaise. Baines had donned his old uniform, which was greenish with age and a couple of sizes too small. With his mop of greying sandy hair sticking out at all angles beneath his cap, and his mutton-chop whiskers that merged with his drooping moustache, he looked oddly out of place, but he knew how to handle the reins and, despite her proud boast, Angel had no experience of driving in the mad mêlée of cabs, carriages, handcarts and costermongers' barrows, let alone the seemingly suicidal pedestrians who hurled themselves across the street in a desperate, and occasionally unsuccessful, attempt to reach the other side.

Angel was glad to reach the Montgomeries' mansion in one piece and she instructed Baines to walk the horse, but as she waited on the doorstep it struck her that she would have had a wasted journey if Percy was not at home. The door opened and to her relief the footman asked her to wait in the vestibule. He returned quickly and led her to a reception room on the ground floor. Minutes later she was joined by Percy, who greeted her with genuine warmth.

'Angel, you've been on my mind a great deal recently, and I'm so sorry we've neglected you.'

'Not at all. I'm just as remiss.' Angel hesitated,

eyeing him warily. 'Percy, I haven't time to waste on small talk so I'll come straight to the point. I need your advice.'

'Sit down and tell me what's troubling you. I'll do anything I can to help.'

Angel perched on the edge of the damask-covered sofa. 'I expect you've heard about Galloway.'

'Yes, and I was shocked when Blanche told me what had happened.' Percy's lips curved in a tender smile. 'She's a wonderful girl.'

'Sir Eugene led me to believe that you have feelings for Blanche, which is in part why I'm here today.'

'What's the matter? Has something happened that I don't know about? I saw her only a few days ago and that's when she told me about Galloway. That man deserves to hang for what he did to my stepmother and the way he treated you.'

'Discovering that I have a family of my own has turned everything upside down, but in a good way, of course. You were always kind to me, Percy.'

A dull flush coloured his cheeks and he looked away. 'I was attracted to you from the first, Angel. I admit that freely, and now I realise it was because we're related.'

'I felt the same, and now I know you're my brother it makes sense.'

'I admired your spirit and your courage when you were facing problems that were not of your making. You did your best to keep Grantley from financial ruin, and I respect that. I'm only sorry I've been so little help to you lately, but I've had business matters to deal with.'

'You can help me, Percy, but I have something to tell you first and you're not going to like it.'

'What is it? There should be no secrets between us, Angel. We're family.'

'Sir Eugene told me that he sees Hector as his future son-in-law. He's thinking of paying off the mortgage on Grantley in place of a dowry.'

Percy's smile faded. 'This is the first I've heard of it. Blanche and I have an understanding, which is partly why I've neglected you, and I'm truly sorry for that. Blanche has no interest in Hector. I can say that categorically.'

'I think Aunt Eloise is to blame for Sir Eugene's interference. I can understand why she wants to save Grantley for the Devane family, but an arranged marriage isn't the way.'

'You speak passionately, Angel. Has Hector been toying with your emotions? I can tell you now that I won't stand for such behaviour. No one treats my sister in such a manner.'

Angel met his angry gaze with a smile. 'You really do mean that, don't you?'

He seized her hand and raised it to his lips. 'Yes, I do. As head of the family I should have made you feel more welcome. I've failed you and it seems that I've failed Blanche also.'

'There's plenty of time to remedy that,' Angel said firmly. 'You need to tell Sir Eugene that you want to marry Blanche, and you love each other – that's the most important thing.'

'You're right. It's something I should have done from the outset, but Blanche was afraid of upsetting her father. He's done his best to keep us apart, but now I know his plans I'd say that he needs to be put straight.' Percy gave her a searching look. 'But that's not the main reason for this visit, is it. What did you want to ask me?'

'Sir Adolphus left me the house in Naked Boy Court and I plan to sell it so that I can pay off the mortgage on Grantley. The trouble is that I don't know how to go about it, and I know you're a businessman, so I was hoping you could tell me what steps I should take.'

'You would do that for Devane?'

'For the whole family. Toby and Humphrey are involved as well as Hector. I grew up with them, Percy. Grantley was my home until recently and I love the house and the whole estate. I was happy there, even though Aunt Eloise made it quite clear that I was an interloper, and Susannah resented me.'

'Everything you say tugs at my heartstrings, Angel. All those wasted years when you could have been brought up with Belle and me, and we didn't know you existed. Our father was a monster and I don't mind admitting it, but your mother was a lovely lady and she deserved better than Pa. Galloway took advantage of her youth and unhappy situation. I feel I owe it to her to do something to make amends.'

'No, Percy, I didn't come here to ask you for anything other than advice.'

'I'm a rich man. I inherited a fortune, but I've also worked hard, so hard that I've been in danger of neglecting those I love, but things are going to change. How much do you need to repay the mortgage?'

She stared at him in disbelief. 'I don't know exactly, but Sir Eugene's solicitor could tell you. Why would you want to help Hector?'

'I don't, but I want you to keep the house that you inherited from Sir Adolphus. I think I know how much it means to you to possess something that is yours and yours alone, and from a purely selfish point of view, if Grantley is back in the hands of the Devane family I doubt if Hector would even consider offering for Blanche. That leaves the field clear for me, and I intend to act now. Belinda and I were planning on a visit to Westwood Hall anyway, so perhaps you'd like to accompany us?'

Dazed by the sudden turn of events, Angel stared at him. 'Did I imagine it, or did you say that you would redeem the mortgage on Grantley without me having to sell up?'

'I said it, and I meant it. When you get to know me better you'll realise that I don't make idle promises. It will take a while to make the necessary arrangements, but I think I can safely say that Grantley will be back in the hands of the Devane family before Christmas.'

'It is already,' Angel said chuckling. 'Or it will be very soon. Baines is waiting for me in the chaise as we speak. It might be illegal, but I've staked our claim on Grantley and we're planning to move in today, regardless.'

He threw back his head and laughed. 'I believe our ancestors were privateers; it seems you have inherited some of their piratical tendencies.'

Angel and Baines arrived at Grantley in time to

see Lil and Cook alighting from the barouche, both of them complaining loudly of cramp and aching muscles. Dolly climbed down unaided and was clearly agitated as she watched Russell attempting to lift Rupert from the carriage. Baines drew the tired horse to a halt and leaped to the snowy ground with surprising agility for a man of his age, his own infirmities apparently forgotten as he went to assist Russell. Angel alighted more slowly and as she mounted the steps she was greeted by Prissy, who stood in the doorway, holding a lantern.

'I was worried you might not make it home tonight,' Prissy said urgently. 'I was afraid it was going to snow again, but I've lit the fire in the range and in the main bedrooms.'

'Thank you, Prissy,' Angel said, forcing her cold lips into a tired smile. 'You've saved our lives. We're all chilled to the bone and very weary.'

'There's a pan of rabbit stew on the hob, miss. I thought it might be welcome.'

'You are a wonder.' Angel kissed her on the cheek. 'Thank you.'

Prissy handed her the lantern. 'I'll be off then, miss. But I must say it's good to have you home. I know I can speak for the tenants and the whole village if it comes to that.'

'Grantley will be saved,' Angel said firmly.

'You really are an angel.' Prissy grabbed Angel's hand and kissed it. 'You was heaven-sent to keep us all from losing our jobs and our homes.'

Russell appeared from the dark depths of the entrance hall. 'Stop prattling, woman. We need to get the horses stabled and fed. I'll see to the barouche and you can take the chaise. That's if you can remember how.'

'I can handle a carriage and pair, let alone an old nag pulling a chaise,' Prissy countered.

Russell took her by the hand. 'That's my girl.'

Angel closed the door behind them and stood for a moment, taking in the familiar surroundings softened and mellowed by lantern light. She had never given it much thought, but the house seemed smaller than it had when she first stood on the same spot, but she had been a child, and now she was a woman. She had fallen in love with Grantley then, and looking back she realised that she had hero-worshipped Hector as a girl and gradually that emotion had deepened. She could not imagine life without him, but he was once again facing the difficult situation in the Transvaal, and she prayed silently that matters would not escalate into war and that he would return soon.

'Angel, what are you doing?' Lil bustled into the hall. 'Prissy has left a pan of stew that would feed a small army, but Baines has his eye on it already and you know how much he can put away in one sitting.'

'Coming,' Angel said, chuckling. Minor squabbles might erupt, but they were quickly forgotten. She followed Lil in the direction of the kitchen. 'Is Rupert all right?'

Lil glanced over her shoulder. 'We've made him comfortable in the morning parlour, and Dolly is with him. Baines will carry him upstairs at bed-time.'

Angel caught up with her. 'Don't say anything

to the others, but I'm going to drive myself over to Westwood Hall tomorrow. If I can persuade Sir Eugene to come here and see how Dolly cares for Rupert he might change his mind and acknowledge her as part of their family.'

'He's like all men,' Lil said grimly. 'Stubborn, pig-headed and stupid. Even Baines has his moments, although he's a better specimen than most.'

Angel was too surprised to say anything to this last remark. Lil's opinion of men was well known and often expressed, but to hear her say something nice about Baines came as a shock, albeit a pleasant one. Perhaps Lil was mellowing with age... Angel smiled to herself as she entered the kitchen and was assailed by a waft of savoury-smelling stew, hot bread and a gust of warm air. The house had come to life again, and she was happy.

Next morning the sun shone, turning the crystalline whiteness of the park into molten silver as Angel drove through the gates of Westwood Hall. The branches of the beeches that lined the avenue were heavy with snow, which slid to the ground at intervals with soft thuds. It was too much to hope that a thaw had set in, and despite the sunshine there was an icy bite in the air. Angel drew the horse to a halt beside the elegant Victoria carriage that she recognised as belonging to the Montgomeries. Their coachman was seated on the box, keeping a tight rein on the pair of matched greys that were pawing the ground and eager to be on their way.

Angel alighted from the chaise, tossing the reins to a groom who had come hurrying to her aid. She was about to mount the steps when the door opened and Percy emerged from the house followed by Belinda. His angry expression sent a chill down Angel's spine as she hurried to meet him.

'What's the matter?'

He came to a halt, holding his hand out to Belinda. 'You may well ask, Angel. Sir Eugene is an obstinate, stiff-necked fool. He can't see that he's making his only daughter miserable. He doesn't seem to care about anything other than combining his land with Grantley.'

Belinda's eyes were red-rimmed and the tip of her nose was suspiciously pink, as if she had been crying. 'Please don't leave like this, Percy,' she cried passionately. 'You've left Blanche broken-hearted. What is the poor girl to do if you desert her?'

'I'm not deserting her,' Percy snapped. 'I'm leaving because her father doesn't want anything to do with us. He's made it crystal clear that he considers a fortune made in trade is little better than one created through a life of crime. I'm not staying another minute in that house.'

'We haven't even had breakfast,' Belinda said tearfully. 'I do hate unpleasant scenes.'

'You must go to Grantley.' Angel gave her a hug. 'I can't promise you the spread you would have had here, but Lil has raided the chicken run and we have eggs. You'll be assured of a warm welcome and I'll be back as soon as I've had a word with Sir Eugene.'

'I wouldn't bother,' Percy said grimly. 'He's not in the sort of mood to accommodate anyone. You'd be wasting your time if you wanted to put Rupert's case to his father.'

Angel hesitated. She could see James hovering in the doorway and she had been rehearsing her speech all the way from Grantley. 'I'm here now so I must try.'

'The best of luck,' Percy said abruptly. 'Come on, Belle. We'll break our journey at Grantley, but I still say you're wasting your time, Angel.' He helped his sister into the carriage and was about to climb in beside her, when he turned and retraced his steps. 'I didn't tell Sir Eugene of my plans to redeem the mortgage, and it would be better if you didn't mention it either.'

'Why not? I'd have thought it would show him what a good, kind person you really are.'

A glimmer of a smile softened Percy's stony expression. 'I don't think Sir Eugene would see it that way. He'll be furious when he finds out that I'm paying off the mortgage on Grantley, especially as I make no claim to the land.'

Angel eyed him thoughtfully. 'Percy, I know you're doing this for me, but if you go ahead with this plan it means that you are the real owner of Grantley, and Sir Eugene would allow you to marry Blanche.'

'I don't intend to buy my bride. If Blanche comes to me it will be because she loves me, and not because her father wishes it. I could have your name put on the deeds, but I don't think you'd want that.'

'Heavens, no,' Angel said, shocked by the sug-

397

gestion. 'Hector is the rightful heir.'

'And he is most fortunate to have secured your love and loyalty.' Percy leaned over to kiss Angel on the forehead. 'I'm doing this for you, and you alone, Angel Montgomerie. You suffered because of our father and because of Galloway. I'm trying, in a small way, to make amends.'

'Angel Montgomerie,' Angel said dazedly. 'I suppose that's right, although I hadn't really put it into words until this moment.'

'I doubt if you'll keep that surname for long. Good luck, dear sister.' He turned and walked towards the waiting carriage.

Angel entered the house feeling more than a little nervous, but she had made up her mind to challenge Sir Eugene's views on his son's marriage to Dolly, and nothing was going to stop her.

Sir Eugene was clearly out of sorts and agitated. Angel realised that she should have listened to Percy, but she had come this far and she put her case as simply as she could, although she forgot most of her carefully rehearsed speech.

Sir Eugene stood with his back to her as he stared out of his study window at the white expanse of parkland punctuated by bare trees, their branches silhouetted against an azure sky like black lace. He turned slowly as she stopped speaking.

'What have I done to deserve such ungrateful offspring?' he demanded.

Angel could think of nothing to say, and he did not seem to require an answer.

He met her anxious gaze with an unsympathetic

frown. 'You should have left well alone, Angel. My son is perfectly capable of speaking up for himself and that dollymop he married against my wishes. And now your brother wants to marry Blanche and take her away from me.'

'Oh, no, sir. I don't think that was Percy's intention. He loves Blanche and I believe she loves him, too. They might not be living on your doorstep, but that doesn't mean you will lose your daughter.'

'What do you know about such things?' Sir Eugene slumped down at his desk, holding his head in his hands. 'Go away, Angel. You mean well, I know, but I am not ready to accept that girl into my home. Rupert has made his choice and he must go his own way. The fact that he was thrown from his horse and badly injured is neither here nor there.'

'Do you wish him to remain a helpless cripple, sir?'

He looked up, his brow darkening. 'That is both uncalled for and impertinent. Of course I don't wish him harm, in fact I'll pay for the best physicians to attend my son, but while he wishes to remain with that woman he is not welcome here. The same goes for your brother. I have plans for Blanche and I won't allow them to be thwarted. Percy Montgomerie must look elsewhere for a bride because he will never marry my daughter.'

'I'm sorry you feel like that, Sir Eugene.'

'You should go now, Angel. We've said all there is to say.' Sir Eugene picked up a sheaf of documents and began sorting them into a neat pile.

Angel realised that she had been dismissed. She had failed to help either her brother or Rupert, although if Sir Eugene was prepared to pay for his medical treatment that was a step in the right direction. She let herself out of the study, and was about to cross the wide expanse of the entrance hall when the sound of light footsteps pitter-pattering across the marble floor brought her to a standstill. She turned to see Blanche hurrying towards her. If Belinda had looked upset, Blanche appeared to be distraught.

'You've seen Papa,' she breathed. 'Did you speak up for Percy? Did you make Papa change his mind?'

Angel shook her head. 'I'm sorry. I tried, but he wouldn't listen.'

'He never does,' Blanche said bitterly. She shot a wary glance at James, who was hovering in the background, clearly curious, but trying hard to appear uninterested. Blanche lowered her voice. 'Will you give Percy a message?'

'Of course.' Angel drew her aside. 'It's obvious that your footman is trying desperately to hear what you have to say. You'd better whisper in my ear.'

Blanche leaned closer. 'Tell Percy that I'll do as he asked.'

'Are you planning to elope?'

'I didn't want to upset my family, but now I think it's the only way.'

Angel nodded. 'All right, I'll tell Percy.' She hugged Blanche. 'Good luck.'

Percy received the message with a curt nod.

'Thank you, Angel. Now I know what I must do, but not a word of this to anyone, not even Belle.'

'You're not telling your sister? Surely you must, Percy?' Angel had managed to get him on his own, for once, but it had not been easy. She had made an excuse to take him to the library, and as there was no fire in that particular room it was not the most inviting place to be on a bitterly cold day. Belinda was in the parlour with Dolly and Rupert, Cook and Lil were in the kitchen, preparing food, and Baines had gone out with a shotgun, hoping to bag something for the dinner table.

Percy shook his head. 'Belle is the loveliest girl imaginable, but she can't keep a secret, and she'll get so nervous that everyone will know something is wrong. I'll leave a note with you, Angel. You must give it to her first thing in the morning.'

'You're going so soon?'

'I was expecting this, and I've planned accordingly. I'm taking Blanche to London tonight and we'll be married by special licence in the morning. It's best if you don't know the exact details.'

'I won't tell anyone.'

'I know that, but I don't want to put you in a position where you have to lie to your family and friends. It's best if Blanche and I slip away quietly. Once we're married there's nothing her father can do about it.'

'Oh, Percy, are you sure about this? He's disowned his own son. Rupert and Dolly married for love, but look at them now. They're homeless and very nearly penniless.'

'Luckily for me I can afford to provide handsomely for my wife. I'll take good care of Blanche, and, if her father truly loves her, he'll come round eventually, as I think he will with Rupert.'

'I hope so,' Angel said softly. 'I do hope so, for all your sakes.'

'I've persuaded Belle that she ought to stay here tonight, as I have to return to town on urgent business,' Percy continued eagerly. 'It wasn't difficult to convince her. She thrives on new experiences, and reclaiming the house for the Devanes in such a flagrant manner appeals to her sense of the dramatic. Anyway, I don't want to leave her on her own in London, so I'd be grateful if you would look after her while I'm away.'

'Of course, I will. She's my sister, as I have to keep reminding myself, and it's time we got to know each other better.' Angel put her head on one side, regarding him with interest. 'Are you taking Blanche on honeymoon?'

'Yes, to the Italian lakes. I can tell you that much, and by the time we return I hope things will have settled down a little, and that Sir Eugene will be resigned to the idea.'

'I don't want to seem mercenary, but what will happen to Grantley if you go away? Will I have to sell the house in Naked Boy Court after all?'

'Of course not, Angel,' Percy said firmly. 'You mustn't worry about a thing. I'll see my solicitor first thing tomorrow, and I'll leave everything in his hands. My man of business will handle the financial side of things, so you need not worry about Grantley. I promise you that everything will be done to arrange matters to our mutual satisfaction.' He produced a leather pouch from his pocket and placed it in Angel's hand. 'This will help your finances while I'm away and pay for Belle's keep.'

'Thank you, Percy. I really appreciate everything you're doing for me, but Belinda will be upset when she finds out that you eloped without telling her.'

'I know, and I wish I could have done otherwise, but Belle is a sweet-natured girl and she'll forgive me when she sees me happily married to the woman I love.'

Angel stood on tiptoe to kiss him on the cheek. 'I wish you all the happiness you deserve, Percy. I'll make sure that Belle understands.'

'Understands what exactly?' Belinda stood in the doorway, staring from one to the other. 'What's going on, Percy?'

Chapter Twenty-Three

Belinda was angry at first but, having grown up with Susannah's mercurial temperament, Angel knew how to smooth ruffled feathers, and Belinda's sunny nature did not allow her to sulk for long, whereas Susannah's moods could last for days. If Susannah was a tigress, then Belinda was a kitten, and, as Angel discovered, much more lovable.

Westwood Hall was in uproar, according to Susannah, who rode over to Grantley the next day to spread the news that Blanche had eloped. Looking elegant in a new riding habit and top hat, its severe outlines softened by a flowing veil, Susannah paced the floor in the morning parlour, waving her riding crop as if conducting an orchestra.

'Life there is unbearable. I feel like a poor relation.'

Angel and Belinda exchanged wry smiles. 'You look very well on it,' Angel said drily. 'I'd have thought you had everything you ever wanted.'

Susannah stopped, fixing Angel with a hard stare. 'Would you now? I'm the poor relation – the unmarried daughter who will end up an old maid – the sort of person who is tolerated, but ignored by the rest of the family.'

'Why would you think that?' Belinda asked innocently.

'Don't speak to me. I'm sure you were party to your brother's deception, you little worm. I dare say you've been laughing at me behind my back when Rupert chose Dolly instead of me.'

Angel recognised the militant sparkle in Susannah's eyes. 'Stop it, Sukey. For heaven's sake put the crop down before you hurt someone. This behaviour won't wash with me and you're scaring Belinda.'

'Don't call me Sukey. You know I hate it.' Susannah abandoned the crop and sank down on a chair by the fire, her bottom lip trembling. 'I thought that Percy came to Westwood to see me. It's not fair, he used me as an excuse to pay court to Blanche. I'm the one who's been slighted, but nobody pays me any attention. I might as well be invisible. That servant girl stole Rupert from beneath my nose, and Blanche, with her simpering ways, has trapped Percy, who should have been my beau.'

'I'm sure Percy didn't mean to give you the wrong impression.' Belinda looked to Angel for confirmation. 'He's not like that, is he, Angel?'

'No, I'm sure it wasn't deliberate,' Angel said earnestly. 'Percy is a kind man, and you ought to be grateful to him.'

'What for?' Susannah demanded angrily. 'He used me.'

'Nonsense. I don't believe that for one moment.' Angel was angry now, and in no mood to placate Susannah, who was teetering on the edge of a full-blown tantrum. 'You're only twenty, you are beautiful and no doubt Sir Eugene will give you a generous dowry. You have plenty of time to find the right husband.'

'It might be different if I was still Susannah Devane of Grantley, but now I'm just the step-daughter at Westwood. Everyone knows that Sir Eugene is desperate to marry me off. I wouldn't be surprised if he put an advertisement in *The Times* offering a huge dowry to any slavering old roué who would take me off his hands.'

'I'm sure that's not true,' Belinda said softly.

'Of course it isn't.' Angel experienced a sudden pang of sympathy. She knew only too well what it was like to feel alone and unwanted. 'Are you really unhappy at Westwood?' She met Susannah's mutinous gaze with a steady look. 'Do you miss living at Grantley, or is this one of your megrims?'

Susannah's eyes brimmed with tears. 'This is

my home, and it's going to be destroyed. I don't know why you're here, because Sir Eugene says that the bailiffs will come in and force you out, but I wish I could turn back the clock and have things as they were.'

Angel leaned over to grasp Susannah's hand. 'We've made a stand, Sukey. We're not supposed to be here, but Percy has promised to repay the mortgage and secure Grantley for the family, and that means you as well as Hector and the boys.'

'Why would he do that?' Susannah asked suspiciously. 'You aren't a Devane. You're only his half-sister, if Galloway is to be believed, and we all know that he's a villain and not to be trusted.'

Belinda jumped to her feet. 'You are a mean girl, Susannah Devane. Mean and ungrateful. Angel is doing this for your family and if you can't see that, then you are a very stupid girl as well.' She flounced out of the room and slammed the door.

'You asked for that,' Angel said, chuckling.

'Who would have believed that the kitten has claws?' Susannah met Angel's amused look with a wry smile. 'I suppose I did go too far, but life has been unbearable with Mama taking sides with Sir Eugene. Everything I do or say is wrong.'

'Come home, Sukey.'

'What did you say?'

'Grantley is still your home. It belongs to the Devane family – I'm just looking after it until Hector returns. You have more right to be here than I do, and Uncle Dolph left me the house in Naked Boy Court.'

'Do you really mean it?'

'Sukey, we've had our ups and downs, but in the end we've managed to scrape along together. I don't think you'll end up an old maid, but this is still your home. I'm certain that Hector would agree with me.'

'But we have no money. Will we have to let rooms to travellers as we did before?'

'That was just a temporary solution, and it will be up to Hector to make decisions when he returns from the Transvaal. Percy has given me enough money to keep us going until he returns from his honeymoon, but we will have to do without servants. Maybe you ought to consider that before you make your final decision.'

'As long as I don't have to cook or wash dishes, I don't mind. I can do without a lady's maid, and I'll even do a little light dusting, but don't expect me to scrub floors.' Susannah rose gracefully to her feet. 'I suppose I'll have to put up with Dolly, too.'

Two days later Dolly burst into the parlour where Angel was struggling with damp kindling in an attempt to get the fire going. 'Come quick. You must see this for yourself.' She hurried from the room.

Curious and eager to be diverted, Angel followed Dolly into the hall where she was looking out of the window that overlooked the carriage sweep. The thaw had set in, leaving the gravel drive covered in slush, but the deer park was still swathed in an icy white blanket and a pale, buttery sun had edged its way between the clouds.

'My goodness. Would you believe it?' Angel

stared at the procession, headed by the West-woods' carriage drawn by the pair of matched bays, followed by a cart laden with trunks and valises, and behind that a brougham. 'I think we're about to be invaded.' She went to open the door, and a blast of cold air caused the temperature in the hall to drop by several degrees.

Sir Eugene was the first to enter. He acknow-ledged Angel courteously, but when he saw Dolly his expression froze and he turned away.

'I wish to see my son,' he said abruptly.

'He's still in bed, Sir Eugene.' Angel sent a warning look in Dolly's direction. 'I was attempting to light the fire in the parlour, but it's too cold to bring him downstairs at the moment.'

'Barbaric,' Sir Eugene said coldly. 'The house is a mausoleum and in my opinion should be consigned to history. Show me to his room, if you please, Miss Winter.'

'It's Miss Montgomerie, if you insist on being formal, Sir Eugene,' Angel said firmly. 'I understand that you're angry with my brother, but please don't take it out on me.'

'Don't mention that person's name in my presence. He seduced my daughter.'

'They are married now, Sir Eugene.' Angel forced herself to speak calmly, but she was inwardly seething. 'They are honeymooning in Italy, and Blanche will have every luxury that money can buy.'

'I don't wish to know that.' Sir Eugene turned to greet a man dressed entirely in black who entered the house carrying a large leather medical bag. 'Dr Sellers has come to examine Rupert. Take us to him, if you please.'

Angel was about to mount the stairs when Susannah swanned into the hall, followed by a retinue of servants hefting trunks and suitcases. 'I take it that I still have my old room?'

'Of course.' Angel continued up the stairs. Susannah was perfectly capable of organising the delivery of her considerable wardrobe, but she would have to unpack and put everything away on her own. That would be interesting.

Angel decided to leave them all to their own devices, and, having shown the doctor to Rupert's room, she returned to the parlour, closing the door behind her with a sigh of relief. She had just succeeded in persuading the kindling to burn when Dolly joined her.

Angel gave her a cursory glance. 'Judging by the look on your face it didn't go well between you and Sir Eugene.'

'He barely spoke to me, and then it was only to tell me to leave the room so that the doctor could examine Rupert. I felt like a naughty child, and goodness knows what the doctor must have thought.'

Angel used the bellows to good effect and the flames shot up the chimney. The scent of damp apple wood filled the room, and Angel rose to her feet. 'Sir Eugene must be worried about his son. He might pretend to be hard and unfeeling, but I'm sure he loves Rupert as much as you do.'

'I suppose so, but I'm Rupert's wife. He can't ignore that fact for ever.'

'Give him time, Dolly. I'm sure that when he sees how devoted you are Sir Eugene will come round. He's lost Blanche as well.'

Dolly wrapped her arms around her swollen belly, as if cradling her unborn child. 'I hope he'll change his mind when the baby arrives. It would be so sad if Sir Eugene rejects his grandson.'

'Or granddaughter,' Angel added, smiling.

Dolly was about to answer when the door opened and Sir Eugene walked into the room. 'I heard voices,' he said stiffly. 'We're leaving now.'

'What did the doctor say?' Dolly asked anxiously. 'Can he do anything for Rupert?'

Sir Eugene ignored her, addressing himself to Angel. 'Dr Sellers has a clinic in Highgate where he specialises in spinal injuries. He has agreed to take Rupert as his patient.'

Dolly eased herself out of the chair. 'I must go with him.'

'Out of the question,' Sir Eugene snapped. 'Rupert will receive the best treatment possible. He will be there for several months at considerable expense.'

'But she's his wife,' Angel protested. 'Surely she has the right to visit him in hospital?'

'Dr Sellers insists that his patients must adhere to a strict routine, and visitors only serve to upset and unsettle them.' Sir Eugene faced Dolly with an uncompromising expression on his lined face. 'My son married you against my wishes, but I am a man of honour.' He took a purse from his pocket and thrust it into her hand. 'You are not welcome in my house, but this money will keep you and your child for a while.'

'You can keep your money, Sir Eugene. I'd rather go back to selling flowers on street corners than accept anything from you.' Dolly flung the purse at him and fled from the room.

Sir Eugene picked up the purse and handed it to Angel. 'Blood will out, as they say. But I think you are more practical than your young friend. I'm well aware of Grantley's financial situation, so take the money and put it to good use. My conscience is clear.'

Angel nodded and pocketed the money. 'Your conscience is your affair, sir. But you're right, I can't afford grand gestures.'

'Susannah has opted to live here. God alone knows why, but she has an allowance from me, which will continue. I'm not a monster, Angel, whatever you might think.' Sir Eugene opened the parlour door and a wave of sound echoed round the room.

'What's going on?' Angel asked anxiously.

'You'll have to restrain the girl. She's creating a scene.'

Angel hurried into the hall, but it was Lil who put a stop to Dolly's ill-judged attempt to prevent Rupert from leaving. Lil scooped her up in her arms and stomped off in the direction of the kitchen, despite shrieks of protest from her wriggling burden.

'Look after her for me,' Rupert said weakly as the footmen carried him from the house.

'Of course I will. You mustn't worry about Dolly,' Angel said earnestly. 'I'll take good care of her.' She stood by the front door, ignoring the bitter cold as she watched him being lifted gently into the carriage, the doctor standing by. Sir Eugene climbed in after him and Dr Sellers

411

made his way to his own vehicle. Angel closed the door, with a sinking feeling. The next few weeks were not going to be easy.

Susannah settled in, but very quickly her attitude to Angel changed. It did not happen overnight, but she began to challenge everything that Angel said and did. She had always disliked Lil and made a point of criticising her efforts at waiting on table and even the food that Lil had helped to prepare. Lil was seething and Angel knew it was only a matter of time before she exploded and put Miss Devane in her place, although Susannah's position in the household was open to debate. It was apparent that Susannah considered herself to be mistress of Grantley and had no intention of undertaking menial tasks. Moreover, she expected to be waited on hand and foot, as she had been all her life. Angel could stand so much, but by the end of the first week her patience was wearing thin, and Dolly was a pale shadow of her former self. She wandered about the house, doing what was asked of her, but it was obvious that her thoughts were with Rupert and she seemed to be in danger of pining away. Lil was unsympathetic, Cook kept trying to tempt Dolly to eat for two, and Susannah was openly impatient. Angel struggled to maintain a middle course, but it was becoming increasingly difficult.

Matters came to a head when Toby and Humphrey arrived home for the Christmas holiday. Susannah greeted them like the lady of the manor, ordering Baines to carry their cases upstairs to their rooms, although she had taken no part in getting the bedrooms ready. It was Angel who had lit the fires and Dolly had helped to air and make up the beds. Lil and Cook had spent two days baking and preparing the food that the boys loved, and Baines had been out with his shotgun to provide game for the table.

Toby greeted Angel warmly and congratulated her on having the courage to stand up for Grantley. Humphrey hugged and kissed her, although he merely acknowledged his sister with a grin and a cheerful insult. Susannah was clearly put out, and even more so when Toby tried to include Dolly in their conversation as they sat in the drawing room, drinking tea and eating the gingerbread that Cook had made, knowing it was Humphrey's favourite.

Dolly eyed Susannah warily as she picked up the teapot. 'It's empty,' she said vaguely. 'I'll make a fresh brew.'

'You don't have to do that,' Toby said casually. 'That's what servants are for, and you're one of us now, Dolly.'

'Thank you, Toby, but I know they're busy so I'll go.' Dolly left the room before Susannah had a chance to make a cutting remark.

'We're not supposed to be living here,' Angel said hastily. 'I was afraid that we'd lose Grantley if the company who loaned Uncle Dolph the money decided to take possession of the house. It's taken longer than I'd hoped, but when the deal is done you'll have to thank Percy for paying off the mortgage.'

Toby leaned back in his chair, frowning. 'I know he's your half-brother, but why would he

413

care what happens to us?'

'I was going to sell the house in Naked Boy Court so that I could repay the debt, but I didn't know how to go about it, so I asked Percy for his advice. He didn't want me to lose my inheritance, but he knows how much Grantley means to me and that's why he's putting matters straight.'

'Grantley belongs to my family,' Susannah said sulkily. 'You might have been adopted by the Montgomeries, but that doesn't make you one of us.'

'That's a bit harsh, Sukey.' Humphrey was sitting beside Angel on the sofa and he moved a little closer. 'Angel is part of our family and you know it. Why are you being so mean?'

'I think what Percy is doing for Grantley is absolutely splendid, Angel,' Toby said, enthusiastically. 'Don't take any notice of Sukey – it was a good day for us when Uncle Dolph brought you to live here.'

'I second that.' Toby reached for another slice of cake. 'Where would we be without you?'

'Maybe Hector would be at home now if she hadn't frightened him away,' Susannah said slyly. 'He resigned his commission, you know, because he intended to run the estate, but someone not a million miles from here set her cap at him and suddenly he retreated. I wonder why...'

Angel stared at her, too shocked to speak.

'Don't talk rot, Sukey,' Humphrey said with his mouth full. 'Hector's always had a soft spot for Angel. We all knew that, and he's never run away from anything in his whole life.'

'That was unkind, Susannah.' Angel found her

voice, although Susannah's spiteful remark had made her feel physically sick. 'We don't know exactly why Hector had to leave so suddenly, and I wasn't even here.'

Susannah tossed her head. 'Who knows what went on between you? Do you deny that you are sweet on my brother?'

'I say, Sukey, that's not fair.' Humphrey slipped his arm around Angel's shoulders. 'This girl has saved Grantley. It's her brother who is paying for Uncle Dolph's mistakes, and I think that's a gallant gesture.'

'Yes, you've gone too far this time,' Toby added angrily. 'What are you doing here, anyway? I thought you were living in luxury at Westwood.'

'This is my home.' Susannah rose to her feet, her face contorted with rage. 'Uncle Dolph should have left the London house to me, and not this street urchin.' She pointed a shaking finger at Angel. 'Look at her, sitting there as if she owns the place. You'd think that butter wouldn't melt in her mouth, but she's devious. Can't you see what she's doing? Her brother will be Grantley's owner and we'll be thrown out of our own home.'

Angel stared at her dumbfounded by such a vitriolic attack. 'That's not true,' she protested. 'Why are you being like this?'

'She's jealous,' Humphrey said angrily. 'Don't take any notice.'

'She's got you wrapped round her little finger already.' Susannah's eyes narrowed and her pretty lips contorted with fury. 'Well, I'm the head of the household in Hector's absence, and I'm telling you to go back to your coven, you witch. You

415

might have cast a spell on my brothers, but I can see right through you. Get out of my house and take your common friend with you.'

Angel stood up, clenching her hands at her sides. Susannah's attack was uncalled for and had come as a shock. She had known that resentment was simmering beneath the surface, but something had triggered it into a malicious volcanic explosion.

'This is as much my home as yours, Susannah,' Angel said with as much dignity as she could muster, although she was trembling with pent-up emotion.

Humphrey and Toby both rose to their feet, but Susannah was beyond reason. She made a move towards Angel, clawing her fingers as if she was about to attack. 'I've had just about enough of you. You're nobody. You were found in the gutter and that's where you belong. You'll leave now and Dolly goes with you, and that uncouth creature who follows you wherever you go. I don't want to see any of you again, and I know that Mama would agree with me.'

Toby stepped between them. 'Hold on, Sukey. I'm the man of the house when Hector is absent and I say they stay.'

'So do I,' Humphrey said, nodding. 'You should apologise to Angel.'

Susannah ignored him, concentrating her attention on Toby. 'You know nothing of the way we've been living these past few weeks. You live a life of luxury at Oxford while we have to fetch and carry and look after ourselves.'

Toby faced up to her, his jaw set and his fingers

416

twitching as if he would like to revert to childhood and slap his sister or pull her hair. 'You always were a bully, Susannah. I say that Angel and Dolly are part of the family and I want them to stay.'

'Me too,' Humphrey said eagerly. 'Why don't you go back to Westwood, Sukey? We'll look after Grantley and Angel will help us.'

'You are still a child, Humpty Dumpty,' Susannah said icily. 'You and Toby are little more than schoolboys and have no say in the matter.' She fixed Angel with a hard stare. 'I'm going to speak to Mama and she'll make Sir Eugene responsible for the mortgage on Grantley. You'll never get your hands on the estate, Angel Winter, and you'll never see Hector again. I'll make sure of that.'

'Stop this, Susannah.' Toby took a step towards her. 'You're hysterical.'

'I won't let you throw Angel out,' Humphrey said tearfully. 'She's like a sister to me and I love her more than I love you.'

Angel held her breath. For a moment she thought that Susannah was going to lose control altogether and strike her younger brother. 'Stop this now.' Angel forced herself to sound calm although she was inwardly quaking. 'I will leave, if that's what you really want, Susannah. I won't allow you to tear this family to shreds simply because you dislike me.'

'Dislike?' Susannah's eyes narrowed to slits. 'I've always hated you, Angel Winter. You were Uncle Dolph's favourite and you turned my brothers against me. I want you to pack your things and get

417

out. Russell will take you to London.'

'It will be dark in less than an hour,' Toby protested. 'Why not leave it until tomorrow, Sukey. Maybe when you've calmed down...'

Susannah picked up the milk jug and hurled it at him. 'If you don't like it, you can go, too.'

'That's enough,' Angel said furiously. 'I wouldn't stay here if you begged me, Susannah Devane. You are mean and spoiled, and heaven help the man who is fool enough to marry you.'

She stormed out of the room, slamming the door behind her, but it opened almost immediately and Humphrey rushed out. 'Angel, wait, please wait. Don't go like this...'

Chapter Twenty-Four

Christmas was drawing nearer, but the house in Naked Boy Court was far from festive. Baines had insisted on returning to London with Angel, Lil and Dolly. He grumbled about the disruption and claimed to miss his hunting expeditions, but Angel suspected that he was secretly glad to be back in the city. He continued to spar with Lil, although their arguments invariably ended with them sharing a pipe of baccy and enjoying a glass of ale by the fire.

Susannah had insisted that Cook must remain at Grantley, leaving Lil to take over kitchen duties in London. She lacked Eudora's delicate touch with pastry, but when it came to kneading bread dough her strength and energy produced tasty loaves that were so light in texture they almost floated off the table, and her cakes were a delight. Dolly moved silently among them, pale as a ghost and uncomplaining, but Angel was concerned about her friend's welfare. It was clear that separation from Rupert was bringing Dolly to a low ebb and Angel decided to enlist her sister's help.

Belinda was only too pleased to offer the use of the Montgomerie barouche for a trip to the private clinic, but she insisted on accompanying them.

'I must say I'm glad you're back in London,' she said as the luxuriously appointed carriage tooled along the streets in the direction of Highgate. 'Of course, I'm sorry that Susannah behaved so badly when you were trying to help, but I never really liked her.'

'She's jealous of Angel.' Dolly looked from one to the other. 'Well, that's the truth, isn't it?'

Angel shook her head. 'I think you're wrong. Susannah is everything I am not.'

'Thank goodness for that.' Dolly leaned back against the velvet squabs, a rare smile playing on her lips. 'I don't think the world is big enough to take two Susannah Devanes. She's spoiled rotten, Angel. Anyone can see that. She's selfish and she's eaten up with jealousy because she knows that her brothers love you more than her.'

Angel let this pass. She knew that Dolly was teasing her, which was infinitely better than Susannah's malicious barbs.

'I think we've arrived,' she said as the carriage

came to a halt outside the gates of a building half-hidden behind a high brick wall. The gate-keeper emerged from his lodge and after a brief conversation with the coachman the gates were unlocked and opened. Angel heaved a sigh of relief. 'I was afraid we wouldn't be allowed in.'

An impish smiled curved Belinda's lips. 'I took the liberty of sending a letter to Dr Sellers, delivered by hand this morning, suggesting that my brother and I were interested in his work and might be persuaded to make a donation.'

'You naughty girl,' Angel said, chuckling. 'I couldn't have done better myself.'

Dolly's smile faded. 'But what will he do when he finds out that he's been tricked? I won't be allowed to see Rupert.'

Belinda leaned over to pat Dolly's hand. 'It's not entirely false. Percy does subscribe to worthy causes, and if Dr Sellers is genuine and he's actually helping cripples to walk again, I think Percy would be very happy to support his work.'

'I'm impressed.' Angel looked out of the window. 'And it's an imposing building. Someone has invested heavily in Dr Sellers' project. Let's hope that it's benefiting Rupert.'

The carriage drew to a halt outside the front entrance and the footman climbed off the box to open the door and put the step down.

Belinda was first to alight and was greeted by Dr Sellers himself. He did not appear to recognise Angel and Dolly and they hung back to give Belinda a chance to impress. Whatever she said obviously worked, and Dr Sellers invited them into the building. He showed them round, giving them detailed accounts of the treatments available, ending the tour in a waiting room that was strictly functional. The grey walls were unadorned and added to the cold, clinical atmosphere. The furniture was upholstered in black leather that might have looked smart in a gentleman's study, but the austere setting did not show it off to advantage, and the seats were hard and slippery. A few shiny copies of the *Illustrated London News* were set out on a side table, and were as pristine as the day they had come off the printing press.

'Do you allow the patients to have visitors?' Angel asked innocently. It seemed obvious from the state of the waiting room that very few people passed this way, but she could tell that Dolly was becoming agitated, and at any moment might demand to see her husband.

'No, it's not our policy,' Dr Sellers said gravely. 'We find that it upsets the strict routines that the patients need, and sometimes the mere sight of a family member is enough to unsettle the more sensitive souls. They become homesick and might even go into a decline.' He smiled benevolently. 'May I offer you ladies some tea and cake? We have an excellent cook, and patients are fed on the best of everything.'

Dolly opened her mouth to speak but Angel forestalled her. 'Thank you, Doctor. That would be most acceptable.'

He nodded. 'If you'll excuse me for a moment I'll get one of my staff to organise it.' He disappeared into the corridor, leaving the door ajar.

'I must see Rupert,' Dolly whispered urgently. 'He's not going to agree to it, is he?'

421

Belinda glanced round the waiting room. 'No clues here, but I thought I saw a list at the foot of the stairs. Perhaps it tells you which rooms the patients occupy.'

'Leave it to me,' Angel said in a low voice. 'Keep him talking, Belle. Mention money and he'll be your slave. I'll say that Dolly is feeling faint and needs fresh air–' She broke off as Dr Sellers entered the room, smiling benevolently.

'Make yourselves comfortable, ladies. Refreshments will be with us shortly.'

'My friend is feeling a little unwell,' Angel said urgently. 'If you don't mind, I'll take her outside for a breath of fresh air.'

'Of course, but perhaps a young lady in her condition ought to be at home, resting?' Dr Sellers peered at Dolly over the top of his silver-rimmed spectacles. 'I speak as a physician, you understand.'

'I'll be perfectly all right. I'm just rather hot.' Dolly fanned herself with her hand, and Angel slipped her arm around her waist.

'Come, my dear. I'll look after you.' She led Dolly from the room, leaving Belinda to keep the doctor occupied with even more questions about his work.

The list that Dolly had mentioned not only contained patients' names but also included the room numbers, and a plan of the building.

'Obviously they don't expect people to break the rules and come here,' Angel said in a whisper as they made their way to Rupert's room. She stood aside as Dolly walked in, and the look on Rupert's face made all their efforts worthwhile.

Angel stood guard at the door, tactfully turning her back on the young couple. It all seemed too easy, but then she heard footsteps and a nurse appeared at the far end of the passage. Angel stepped back into the room, peering round the door and praying silently that the woman would not come this far. It seemed as though her prayers were answered as the nurse was apparently doing her rounds and checking on each patient in turn.

'We have to go now, Dolly,' Angel said reluctantly. 'I'm sorry, Rupert, but a nurse is heading this way and she'll be here any minute now.'

He raised Dolly's hand to his lips. 'It was wonderful to see you, my darling, but you mustn't come again. I'm doing well, but you must look after yourself and the baby.'

'But I hate leaving you all alone,' Dolly said tearfully. 'I'll get in somehow.'

He shook his head. 'My father came to see me yesterday. I don't know if it's because of the season, or if his conscience is troubling him, but he's arranging to have me moved back to Westwood. Dr Sellers has agreed to supply a nurse to take care of me, and I can continue my treatment at home.'

'That's wonderful. I'll see you there.'

He shook his head. 'I'm afraid not. I tried to persuade Papa to allow you to live with me at Westwood, but he's a stubborn man.'

'Why can't you have your treatment in London?' Dolly whispered. 'I'm sure Angel wouldn't mind if you stayed with us.'

'It's not practical, darling. You must be patient and leave it to me. I will win my father round, and I promise you that we'll have Christmas together.'

'The nurse is coming,' Angel whispered urgently. 'She's in the next room now. Hurry up, Dolly or we'll be caught and thrown out.'

Dolly leaned over to kiss her husband on the lips. 'It would be the best Christmas present in the world, Rupert. I'll live for that day.'

'Come on, Dolly,' Angel urged. 'You'll ruin everything if you linger.'

Dolly obeyed reluctantly, pausing in the doorway to blow a kiss to Rupert. Angel had to drag her away, and they only narrowly missed being caught.

Belinda rose to her feet when they entered the waiting room. 'You look a little better, Dolly. However, the doctor is right. I think we should get you home as soon as possible.' She extended her hand to Dr Sellers, smiling graciously. 'Thank you so much, for the tour of your clinic. I'll speak to my brother when he returns from his honeymoon.'

Dr Sellers bowed over her hand. 'Might I enquire who put you in touch with me, Miss Montgomerie?'

'I forget now,' Belinda said vaguely. 'But your fame is spreading.' She swept out of the waiting room, leaving Angel and Dolly to follow more slowly.

When they were safely ensconced in the carriage, they burst into fits of the giggles.

'I don't know why I'm laughing,' Dolly said, wiping her eyes with her hanky. 'Sir Eugene will never accept me as his daughter-in-law.'

Belinda was suddenly serious. She put her head

on one side, giving Dolly a searching look. 'You're a very pretty girl, but you lack polish, and that gown doesn't do you justice.'

'What are you saying, Belle?' Angel was suddenly alert. 'You're planning something, I can tell.'

'Would you like to spend a few days with me, Dolly?' Belinda leaned forward to grasp Dolly's hand. 'I'm all alone in that huge house while Percy is away. We would keep each other company and I could give you a few tips on dress, and how to deal with difficult people like Sir Eugene. You lack confidence, that's all.'

'Are you trying to make a lady of me?' Dolly stared at her in amazement. 'Can you make me like you and Angel? You was always a toff, Angel, even when we was selling flowers on street corners.'

'Even when we *were* selling flowers on street corners,' Belinda said, smiling. 'It's the little things that give you away. You've already lost most of your cockney accent, and you only need a little polish to make you shine like a bright star. Sir Eugene will forget his prejudices and welcome you into his home.'

Dolly turned to Angel. 'What do you think?'

'Anything is worth a try, and you couldn't have a better mentor than my sister.' Angel squeezed Dolly's gloved hand. 'Think of the baby. He or she should be born in the family home. It will be Rupert's one day, and Blanche is your sister-in-law. You have a rightful place at Westwood, Dolly. If I were you I'd grab it with both hands.'

Dolly moved in with Belinda, and, although Angel was sad to lose her companionship, she knew that it was the best thing for her friend. As Belinda had pointed out, all Dolly needed was a little town polish, some elegant clothes and a boost to her confidence, and she could take her place in society.

Her humble origin was nobody's business but her own.

Dolly's move to the house in Mayfair left Angel in a difficult financial position. Without Dolly's contribution to the housekeeping, Angel was finding it even harder to make ends meet. Christmas was a week away and she had only a few coppers in her purse. She could have asked Belinda for money, but she knew from previous conversations that her sister had a generous allowance, and that she spent it lavishly. Percy held the purse strings and there was no word as to when he and his bride would arrive home.

After a sleepless night, Angel was in the kitchen trying to coax the fire back to life when she heard someone hammering on the front door. She grabbed the lantern and hurried along the passage, wiping her hands on her apron.

'Hold on,' she called. 'Don't be so impatient.' She drew back the bolts, turned the key in the lock and dragged the heavy door open. 'Good heavens! Danny. You're the last person I was expecting to see.'

'That's a nice welcome. Can I come in?'

'Of course.' She stepped aside, holding up the lantern to light his way. 'What's in those sacks?' she asked, staring at the dark shapes stacked against the wall.

He stamped his feet on the mat as she closed the door. 'What do we sell this close to Christmas?'

'Mistletoe?' She led the way to the kitchen and was relieved to see flames licking round the coal. 'Where did you get it from?'

'I'll give you two guesses.' He unwound his muffler and took off his cap, laying them carefully on the table.

'You didn't steal it from the orchard at Grantley, did you?'

'We heard that you're the owner now, and I did it for you, so it wasn't theft.'

'News certainly gets around, but it's not true. Percy has paid off the creditors because he wanted to help me, but Grantley will always be Hector's home. The family took me in and I'll be forever grateful.'

'And the same people threw you out. I know all about it, Angel. Cook told Prissy Russell and she told Ma. They were at school together so they share all the gossip. That Susannah is an ungrateful bitch and she's always been jealous of you.'

Angel placed the kettle on the hob. 'You're entitled to your opinion, but why are you here?'

'Aren't you pleased to see me?'

He moved a little closer and she could smell the frosty air on his clothes, and the earthy scent that clung to his boots. Tall, broad-shouldered and muscular, Danny was the epitome of the outdoors, and as strong and dependable as nature itself. She was ridiculously pleased to see him and the temptation to hug and be hugged back was almost too much to bear.

'Of course I am,' she said, turning her attention to the tea caddy, which was almost empty.

He covered her hand with his. 'I'll treat you to a mug of coffee and a ham roll at the stall down the road.'

'What about the mistletoe? You'll need an early start if you're going to take it to Covent Garden.'

'It's yours, Angel. It didn't take a genius to work out that you'd been sent packing without a penny to your name. That seems to be the way the gentry treat people like us. We're disposable, like the rubbish they put out for the dustman.'

'That's not fair, Danny. I've been well treated, apart from Susannah.'

'And Mrs Devane,' Danny added. 'You were little more than a servant in her eyes. But never mind them. Come with me now. We'll have breakfast and then I'll help you sell the mistletoe. If Dolly wasn't in the family way she could have joined us.'

'Do you know everything that's been going on at Grantley?'

He picked up his cap and muffler. 'Prissy keeps Ma well informed. They meet up once a week for tea and cake and gossip. Get your coat and bonnet, girl. We've got work to do.'

A fresh coating of snow had fallen during the night, and, despite the footprints of early risers, there were patches of virginal white sparkling in the gaslight like a sequin-encrusted ball gown. The sky seemed darker just before dawn, and the hard-packed snow muffled the sound of horses' hoofs, and the crunch of wooden wheels on the cobblestones. It was bitterly cold and cabbies and carters were muffled up to their eyes, while steam billowed from the horses' bodies, and their breath curled into clouds above their heads.

Angel clutched Danny's arm as they made their way to the coffee stand. The stallholder huddled close to the brazier, and stopped work every now and then to blow on his numbed fingers. The tip of his nose was bright red and his teeth were chattering, but he greeted them cheerfully enough.

Danny purchased two ham rolls and two cups of coffee, laced with sugar. They leaned against a shop window while they ate in companionable silence and sipped their hot drinks. Angel glanced at Danny, who was watching her with a look that made her breath catch in her throat. The boy had grown into a man, and she knew at that moment that his feelings towards her were the same, if not stronger. She drank what was left in the mug and replaced it on the stall.

'Ta, mate,' she said, smiling. 'That's given me a good start to the day.'

The man peered at her bleary-eyed. 'I'm glad someone is happy. I got ten kids to feed and clothe.'

Danny flipped a coin in his direction. 'Merry Christmas, mate.'

The man caught it and stuffed it into his pocket. 'Same to you, sir.'

'Let's go to work.' Danny hefted a sack of mistletoe over his shoulder. 'Let's get this lot sold first.'

Angel fell into step beside him. 'How can you afford to give away a silver sixpence, Danny?

429

Have you robbed a bank?'

'We've been working hard all year, and I've got ambition. Pa might be happy with his stall in Covent Garden, but I intend to expand the business.'

'How would you do that?'

'I'm not depending on Devane to let us have use of the greenhouse, and I've got my eye on a piece of land I want to buy. Before you know it I'll be supplying fruit and vegetables to Covent Garden.'

'That's wonderful, Danny. But perhaps we'd better start selling the mistletoe or Christmas will be over.'

'I know I talk too much, but I have ideas tumbling about my brain. One day I'll be a rich man and own a big house. My wife and family won't want for anything.'

'Let's start small, shall we? A halfpenny for a big bunch?'

Danny pulled a sprig of mistletoe from the sack and held it over her head. 'Mistletoe fresh from the countryside. Gentlemen, it's the only time you can kiss a girl without getting your face slapped.' He leaned over to plant a kiss on Angel's lips, much to the enjoyment of a group of young men in city suits, who were about to enter a bank building.

'I'll have a bunch, cully.' One of the men, slightly younger than the others, handed over a penny. 'Now I'll have twice as much chance,' he said, chuckling. 'May I kiss the young lady, too?'

'Not a chance, mate,' Danny said, grinning.

A small crowd had gathered and Danny

repeated the act several times. Angel had never been kissed so often in her whole life, but she responded gamely, and to her surprise she found she was enjoying the experience. They sold the first sack easily enough, and had to return to Naked Boy Court to fetch the remainder. Danny changed his line of patter to suit the passers-by. Shy young men walking with their sweethearts needed gentle humour to give them the courage to buy, but plump housewives, bustling to market, needed more charm and the promise of receiving a kiss from their husbands or lovers. Danny did not disappoint – he seemed to have a natural gift for selling, and Angel could not help but be impressed.

By mid-afternoon they had sold all the mistletoe. Gaslights flickered in shop windows as they made their way along Fleet Street, heading towards Ludgate Hill, and naphtha flares on costermongers' barrows sent long shadows dancing across slushy cart tracks on the street surface. Bunches of red-berried holly hung in shop doorways and the windows were filled with pyramids of rosy red apples and oranges stuck with cloves. The scent of citrus peel and cinnamon wafted from bakers' shops and game of all types dangled outside the butchers, with plump turkeys centre stage.

'You must be hungry,' Danny said, taking Angel's hand and tucking it in the crook of his arm. 'There's an eel pie and mash shop not far from here.'

'I haven't tasted eel pie since I was a child,' Angel said eagerly. 'Uncle Joseph was fond of eel pie but

Aunt Cordelia thought it was only common, vulgar people who frequented such places.'

'She didn't know what she was missing.' Danny guided her into a narrow court and the savoury smell of pie and mash, laced with parsley liquor drifted in tempting waves from the open door. The café was small, poorly lit and crowded with working men, but Danny found them a table close to the window and he returned from the counter carrying two steaming plates piled high with mashed potato and a glistening golden pie.

Angel had not realised how hungry she was and she tucked in, savouring each tasty mouthful.

'I like to see a girl with a good appetite,' Danny said, chuckling. 'There's only one person who can cook better than this and that's Ma.'

Angel nodded, licking a crumb of pastry from her lips. 'You're right, of course. I haven't seen your parents for a while. Are they keeping well?'

'They're just the same as ever, but working hard.' Danny put his knife and fork down, and was suddenly serious. 'There's something I haven't told you.'

'What is it?' Angel dropped her fork onto her plate with a clatter. 'What's happened?'

'I didn't know how you'd feel about it, but the bit of land I mentioned is part of the Grantley estate and Pa and I intend to make an offer.'

Angel stared at him in amazement and then she laughed. 'You're joking, of course.'

'Not at all. Pa is friendly with Curzon, Sir Eugene's land agent. Apparently Grantley's creditors were asking more than your brother wanted to pay. Pa used his life savings and mine to put in an offer for the orchard and the ten-acre field to the east of the deer park. It's been lying fallow for years.'

Angel sipped her tea, staring at him over the rim of the thick white cup. 'I know where you mean, but what would you do with the land?'

'We plan to go into fruit growing as well as expanding the market garden. We've been adding to our produce gradually and now is the time to expand.'

'Why Grantley?'

'Because it's close enough to manage, and I wanted to do it for you, Angel. Your brother has put in a bid for the house, which includes the gardens and the deer park, as well as the common land, and we added our offer. We're just waiting to find out if it's been accepted.'

She withdrew her hand, frowning. 'I don't want to take the house and land away from Hector and the boys.' She pulled a face. 'Susannah would have something to say about this.'

'If you were a vindictive woman you could treat her as she treated you and throw her out.'

Angel met his amused gaze with a smile. 'I could, but that would be too harsh. In a way I can't blame her because I was the interloper.'

'Not any more. You are Angel Montgomerie and your brother is a wealthy man.'

'I hope it works out for you and your father, Danny, and I'm glad that you're doing well. If I truly owned the land I would have given it to you for nothing. Your parents are wonderful, and you are a true friend.'

'You know I want to be more than that, Angel.

I've loved you since you were a skinny little girl, and now you're a beautiful young woman. I'd give my life for you.'

Angel dropped her gaze. Danny's eyes mirrored his feelings to such a degree that it hurt to look at him. 'I'm sorry, but...'

'But you're still in love with Hector. You might find that your knight in shining armour isn't the perfect being you've imagined him to be, Angel. For God's sake, we're just men and we're human, but I love you truly and always will.' Danny pushed back his chair and stood up. 'It's time I saw you home.'

They parted outside the house in Naked Boy Court. 'We can still be friends, can't we?' Angel said shyly.

'I'll always be there for you, if that's what you mean, but perhaps it's better if we don't see too much of each other for a while.'

'I'm truly sorry if I've hurt you, or if I've given you the wrong impression...'

He shook his head. 'It's not your fault. You can't help the way you feel any more than I can.' He put his hand in his pocket and took out a bag of coins. 'You've earned this today.'

'But we did it together. Half of the takings are yours.'

'I've enjoyed today, don't spoil it. Merry Christmas, Angel.' He opened the gate and was gone before she had a chance to respond.

She remained standing in the snowy courtyard, oblivious to the cold and the sleety rain that had started to fall. The day that had begun so well had ended badly and the feeling of loss was an actual pain, stabbing her in the heart. She was tempted to run after Danny and call him back, but that would be cruel if she could not give him what he desired above all things, and yet... Was it possible to be in love with two men? Both of whom she had known since childhood, and complete opposites to each other. Hector, the gallant soldier; handsome, charming and well-bred. Danny, a man of the soil; honest, hard-working and loyal.

She knocked on the door and waited.

'Good grief, what's wrong with you?' Lil demanded. 'Come inside before you catch your death of cold.'

Chapter Twenty-Five

The first that Angel knew of Percy and Blanche's return from honeymoon was when Percy arrived at the front door with an armful of presents. He had not forgotten anyone, even Baines. Angel showed him into the kitchen, which was the only warm room in the house as they were being forced to economise on coal. The money she had earned selling mistletoe was being used frugally, but at least they had candles and enough fuel to last until Christmas, which was now only two days away.

Percy laid the gifts on the kitchen table. 'They're just small things,' he said happily. 'Mementoes of our travels, which were wonderful. No doubt Blanche will tell you all about it when you see her, Angel.'

'Are you going to Westwood for Christmas, Percy?'

He shook his head. 'I doubt if we would be welcome.'

'Blanche is Sir Eugene's only daughter. I'm sure he'll come round in time,' Angel said earnestly. 'So do you intend to stay in London?'

'I thought that as you are the new owner of Grantley you would like to spend Christmas in your old home.'

Angel's hand flew to her mouth. 'Your offer has been accepted?'

'Indeed it has. I went to see my solicitor yesterday and signed all the necessary documents. It was quite straightforward.'

'You'll have a battle on your hands,' Lil said darkly. 'Miss Susannah isn't going to give up without a fight. She thinks she owns Grantley and a signature on a bit of paper won't make her change her mind.'

'Lil's right.' Angel sank down on the nearest chair. 'And to be honest Susannah has more right to be there than I do.'

'Nonsense,' Percy said firmly. 'You are the owner of Grantley now, my dear. I made certain your name is the one on the deeds and no one can take it from you.'

Stunned by his generosity, Angel took a moment to digest the full meaning of his words. 'But it was your money, Percy. I can't allow you to put it in my name only.'

'I can afford it, Angel. Our father left us a considerable fortune and a proportion of it should have come to you. Besides which, I wanted to put some of my inheritance to good use and to right the wrong that caused you so much suffering.' He put his hand in his pocket and drew out a folded sheet of paper. 'I sent for a copy of your birth certificate before I went to Italy.' He handed it to her, smiling. 'You'll see that you were christened Jane Elizabeth after your mother, but I think Angel suits you better.'

She stared at the neat copperplate writing with tears in her eyes. 'Jane Elizabeth Montgomerie. That really is me?'

He nodded. 'Yes, it proves beyond doubt that you are the legitimate child of Silas and Jane Montgomerie. My stepmother must have registered your birth, because Galloway wouldn't have done so. By the way, I gather he has been given a considerable prison sentence, so that's the last you'll see of him.'

'That's the best news I've heard so far.' Lil tore the paper off her parcel and unfolded a lace shawl. She stroke the soft material, shaking her head. 'It's the most beautiful thing I've ever seen, but it's much too good for the likes of me.' She folded it again and laid it reverently on the paper. 'I can't accept it, sir.'

'Of course you can,' Percy said sharply. 'I chose it myself. It's French lace, purchased in Paris. My wife and I will be very hurt if you don't wear it on Christmas Day at Grantley.'

'You want all of us to spend Christmas there?' Lil stared at him open-mouthed. 'Of course, they'll need extra help in the kitchen.'

'I think it's time we recognised you for what you are, Lil,' Percy said gently. 'You've been Angel's nursemaid, friend and companion all her life, and you should be treated as such.'

Angel clapped her hands. 'I agree. We've been through so much together, and I'm afraid I've taken you for granted, Lil.'

A dull flush stained Lil's cheeks. 'I don't know what to say.'

'Never mind that,' Baines said testily. 'What about me, sir? Have I got to shift my bones to Grantley?'

'You've been invited to spend Christmas with your friend Russell and his wife.' Percy slid a smaller parcel across the table. 'This is for you, Baines. It's a new pipe.'

'I dunno what to say, sir.' Baines unwrapped the package and took out the pipe. 'It's very fine, and you gave me some baccy, too.'

'I'm glad you like it, Baines.'

'Much obliged, I'm sure.' Baines tested the pipe, clenching it between his teeth and nodding. 'Very fine, sir. Very fine.'

'How do you know about these arrangements, Percy?' Angel demanded. 'Did you go to Grantley before you came here?'

'I must confess that we arrived home two days ago. I would have called here sooner, but I had a lot to do, including a brief visit to Westwood.'

'You saw Sir Eugene?'

'I did.' Percy pulled up a chair and sat down. 'I can't say he welcomed me with open arms, but we came to an agreement. He wasn't prepared to invite us to stay at Westwood, but he invited us to attend the annual Christmas Eve ball. It's a start, Angel.'

'Did he mention Dolly? I haven't seen her since Belinda took her in hand.'

'He included her in the invitation, but you'd hardly recognise her. Belle has worked wonders in such a short time, and Dolly has a natural grace and a sweet nature. I don't see how she can fail to win Sir Eugene's favour, especially now she's been given the opportunity to shine.'

'I hope he will let her stay with Rupert.'

'One step at a time,' Percy said, laughing. 'Let's hope the spirit of Christmas will bless us all, and make Sir Eugene a little less stiff-necked and more forgiving.'

'You've made me quite breathless, Percy. I can't believe that you've achieved all this in one visit.'

'You began the changes, Angel. But for you Grantley might have been lost to the Devanes forever, and whether they admit it or not, you are part of their family.' Percy nodded in the direction of a small package. 'You still haven't opened your gift.'

With trembling fingers, Angel tore off the paper and opened the shagreen-covered box. 'Oh, Percy, it's beautiful.' She took the gold pendant set with a ruby from its bed of black velvet and dangled it from the fine gold chain. 'I'm lost for words.'

'It goes well with your mother's ring,' Percy said, smiling. 'Blanche has exquisite taste.'

'She has indeed.' Angel replaced the pendant in its case. 'I'll wear it on Christmas Day.'

'Eudora won't be able to cope on her own, and the larder is probably empty,' Lil said thoughtfully. 'Miss Susannah doesn't know how to run Grantley. She was always a lazy young madam.'

Percy stood up and reached for his hat and cane. 'In that case, I suggest we leave for Grantley first thing in the morning.' He leaned over to drop a kiss on Angel's forehead. 'Don't get up. I'll see myself out.'

Ignoring his instructions, Angel went to see him off. 'I can't thank you enough for everything you've done, let alone the magnificent gift.'

'I'm just making up for the lost years. It's small recompense for the suffering that Galloway inflicted on you. I can't begin to imagine what it must have been like in the workhouse.' Percy opened the front door and gazed into the snowy courtyard. 'I can picture you out there when Sir Adolphus first saw you – a child in rags, barefoot, trying to sell mistletoe in order to keep yourself from starving. It doesn't bear thinking about.'

'I found myself short of money so I reverted to my old self, selling mistletoe on the street just days ago. Danny had stripped the trees in the Grantley orchard and we did a roaring trade.'

He gave her a steady look. 'I am so sorry. I've grown up with money and sometimes that makes me forget that others are not so fortunate.' He took a pouch from his pocket and dropped it into her hand. 'I apologise for being thoughtless, and I'll try to do better. From now on I'll give you an allowance so that you don't have to keep asking me for money.'

'Thank you, Percy, but if Grantley really is mine,

I intend to make it pay. The land will produce crops and I'll keep pigs and chickens, and cows.'

'I don't doubt that you'll make a success of whatever you do, my little mistletoe seller.' He tipped his hat and strolled out into the icy darkness.

The chaise was packed with hampers of food and crates of wine. Lil and Angel had been to market first thing and Baines had been sent to Smithfield to purchase the largest turkey he could find, and he had not disappointed. The prize bird was so enormous that it needed a seat to itself, but somehow they managed to squeeze everything into the chaise. Lil was about to climb up next to Baines when Angel caught her by the sleeve.

'I have a call to make on my way to Grantley,' Angel said in a low voice. 'I'll go with Baines, so I'd like you to wait here for the barouche and you can travel in style.'

Lil gave her a searching look. 'What are you up to?'

'Nothing, I promise. I just wanted to stop off to wish the Wicks family the compliments of the season.'

'You wouldn't be pining for that young man, would you?'

'Danny and I are friends, and no doubt he and his father will help me when it comes to managing the land at Grantley.'

'You're not telling me everything,' Lil said suspiciously. 'I know that look, Angel Winter. You were like this as a child when you'd done something naughty and you didn't want Mrs Wilding to

441

find out.'

'You're imagining things.' Angel climbed onto the driver's seat, next to Baines. 'I'll see you at Grantley.'

'Where to, miss?' Baines gave her a sideways look as he guided the horse through the busy traffic on Ludgate Hill.

'Pratt Lane, Hackney, Baines. I have some Christmas cheer for Joe and Sally. I want to tell them of my good fortune.'

'I should take something for Russell and his missis, but I haven't been paid for months.'

'Things will be better from now on,' Angel said hastily. 'I'm sorry, Baines. You're so much a part of the family that I forget about money.' She took a half-sovereign from her purse and slipped it in his pocket.

'Best wrap up, miss,' he said gruffly. 'It's going to get colder when we leave the city and that damp marsh air ain't no good for man nor beast.'

Angel pulled the coarse woollen rug up to her chin. She was looking forward to Christmas at her old home, but there was one huge hurdle to get over before she could feel relaxed and happy – Susannah. Toby and Humphrey would be surprised, shocked even, to discover that Grantley no longer belonged to them, but she had no intention of turning them out. The house was large enough to accommodate them all. But Hector was another matter. He might be far away, but she had spent half the night wondering what to do, and it was daybreak before she reached a solution. Hector was the rightful heir – the most practical solution would be for them to work together for the good of the estate and its tenants. Once such a thought would have excited her, but somehow it had lost much of its appeal. It might be fair, but would it work?

'Are you all right, miss?' Baines's gruff voice broke into her reverie and made her jump.

'Yes, just thinking, Baines. Just thinking.'

Sally's face split into a wide smile when she opened the door and saw Angel standing on the threshold. 'My dear, how lovely. Come inside out of the cold.' She held the door wide and Angel entered the front room, clutching the bottles. The warmth and friendly atmosphere of the cottage wrapped round her like a comforting blanket, and she felt instantly at home, although it must be a short visit.

'I can't stay, Sally. Baines is waiting for me. We're on our way to Grantley.'

'Jack told me last evening that your brother's offer has been accepted, and ours too. It's hard to believe that the Wicks family are landowners.'

Angel put the bottles down carefully. 'This isn't much considering all that you've done for me in the past, but I'm sure we'll see a lot more of each other from now on. I'm going to take an active part in running the estate, at least while Hector is away.'

A shadow passed over Sally's face, dimming her smile. 'Danny said that you were sweet on Captain Devane. Is it true that you have an understanding?'

'No, Sally. I might have had romantic dreams when I was younger, but I'm a grown woman, and I realise now that's just what they were. It's time to stop dreaming and get on with my life. Unfortunately I have to go now, but I'll see you very soon.' Angel glanced into the kitchen but the only occupant was Stumpy, who wagged his tail and went back to sleep. 'I was hoping to see Jack and Danny to wish them a merry Christmas.'

'They went to Grantley earlier to examine the land we bought. They're so excited, like two big children, chattering about their plans all day and late into the night.'

Angel laughed and gave her a hug. 'Merry Christmas, Sally.' She left the cottage with its inviting aromas and stepped outside into the cold damp morning. A grey mist covered the marsh, but they took the main road, and the horse seemed to know that a comfortable stable and a meal were getting nearer and he broke into a trot.

'I suppose you've come to gloat over our loss,' Susannah said bitterly. 'You'll probably throw us all out, but we won't go without a fight.' She stood in the entrance hall, shivering beneath the cloak she had wrapped around her slender body, as if to underline the hardships they had endured at Grantley. The great fireplace was empty, and a cold draught whistled through the ground floor, banging doors and rustling wall hangings like an angry spirit out for revenge. She turned on her heel and stomped off in the direction of the drawing room, where Dolly, Belinda and Percy were huddled around the fire. Damp logs hissed and spat and smoke billowed into the room.

'Why are you living like this, Sukey?' Angel

demanded angrily. 'There should be plenty of logs in the barn. We were never short of firewood.'

Susannah shrugged. 'I don't know. Maybe no one thought to chop down trees, or something. It's the servants who are to blame.'

'We haven't had a cup of tea yet. I offered to go and help in the kitchen but I wasn't allowed to.' Dolly's teeth were chattering so loudly that it was hard to understand what she was saying.

Susannah tugged the bell pull. 'Sit down, you silly girl. If we wait long enough someone will come.'

'You said that half an hour ago,' Belinda said crossly. 'You don't seem to know how to manage your servants. You need a housekeeper.'

'Or someone who knows what they're doing.' Lil jumped to her feet and made for the door. 'I'll stir them up in the kitchen. You'll get your tea, ladies.'

'Where are Toby and Humpty?' Angel met Susannah's hostile expression with an attempt at a smile. 'They should be helping you.'

'I don't know where they are,' Susannah said peevishly. 'Toby took his gun and went out first thing this morning and Humpty Dumpty is probably in his room reading a book, or acting out a part in front of the mirror. Although no one in their right mind would pay to see him perform.'

'I haven't seen him act, but he's a handsome young man.' Blanche moved a little closer to Percy as they sat side by side on the sofa. 'We saw some wonderful plays and several operas in France and Italy. Humphrey should go abroad and study, if that's where his heart truly lies.'

Susannah shot her a withering look. 'Who asked for your opinion? Just because your husband bought Grantley doesn't give you the right to tell us what to do.'

'That was rude, even for you, Susannah,' Percy said angrily. 'I think you should apologise to Blanche.'

Susannah shrugged. 'Perhaps I went too far. I'm sorry, Blanche, but all this is very upsetting. I don't want to lose my home to Angel or anyone.'

A feeling of sympathy overcame Angel's angry reaction to Susannah's verbal attack on Blanche. 'Grantley will always be your home, Sukey. Nothing will change.'

'I don't want to be beholden to you for anything.' Susannah's lips trembled and her eyes reddened. 'Anyway, I might well find myself engaged to a titled gentleman by the New Year. I can see that it's the only way out, unless I want to end up an old maid.'

Belinda leaned forward, holding her hands out to the feeble flames in the hearth. 'Really? That sounds exciting. Who is the lucky man?'

'We're all invited to the Westwood Christmas Eve ball,' Susannah said sulkily. 'That includes you, Percy, even though you aren't Sir Eugene's favourite son-in-law, and Blanche, of course, because it's her home. We're all to go, and I've got news for you, Angel.'

Shivering, Angel edged nearer to the fireplace. 'Really? That sounds interesting.'

'Yes, and it will put you firmly in your place. Hector is on his way home. I received a telegram

446

this morning. He expects to arrive later this afternoon.'

'That's excellent news.' Dolly glanced anxiously at Angel. 'I know that Rupert will be pleased to see him.'

'As will Angel,' Susannah said slyly. 'But Hector has a surprise for us.'

'It's obvious you're going to keep us in suspense.' Angel was curious, but she was not going to let Susannah draw her into an argument. 'I'm going to see about some logs for the fire.'

'He's married.' Susannah's voice held a note of triumph that echoed in the ensuing silence.

Angel had reached the door, but she hesitated, turning slowly to face Susannah. 'Married?'

'I thought that would bring you up short.' Susannah faced them all with a defiant toss of her head. 'What's the matter? Why are you staring at me like that?'

'If that was a joke it was in poor taste,' Angel said angrily. 'I was told that Hector had been called back to the army for some urgent reason.'

'You'll just have to wait until he arrives this afternoon to find out.' Clearly enjoying herself, Susannah sat down by the fire, holding her hands out to the feeble flames that licked around the mossy logs. 'Do hurry up, Angel. Send someone to chop some wood or we'll all freeze.'

She shot a malicious glance in Angel's direction. 'By the way, her name is Rosalind Cholmondeley-Charlton and her father is a brigadier. I'm sure we'll learn more when Hector brings her to Westwood.'

'But he wouldn't have had time to get to South

Africa and back,' Angel said dazedly.

'It was a lie.' Susannah looked round, smiling triumphantly at their shocked expressions. 'He only went as far as Malta where he met his fiancée and her father, who were returning from Durban. He's a dark horse, I must say. I didn't think Hector had it in him to be so romantic or so devious.'

Angel left the room, too stunned to retaliate. She knew that Susannah was enjoying her brief moment of triumph, but although the news was a shock, it was not devastating, and this surprised Angel even more than the fact that Hector had kept his romance a secret. He must have known the young lady in question for some time, and it seemed odd that he had never mentioned her, or even hinted that he was engaged. She should have been shocked, mortified, broken-hearted, but she was none of these. It was strange, but the only emotion she felt was relief. The dreams she had harboured as a young girl had held her captive and now she was free. She wrapped her mantle around her and made her way to Humphrey's room. Her first priority must be to get fires burning in all the main rooms, especially the bedchambers. She knocked on the door.

'Who's there?'

'Humphrey, it's me, Angel. I need your help.' She waited and was about to knock again when the door opened.

Tousled-haired and bespectacled, Humphrey blinked like a sleepy owl. 'Angel, when did you arrive?'

'About half an hour ago, but the house is like an

448

ice cave. Will you help me fetch logs and coal, if there is any?'

'I've had a cold,' he said miserably. 'I've spent most of the time in bed. Susannah's always in a foul mood and Toby takes off to the village at every possible opportunity. I think he has a love interest, although he pretends he's going shooting. He never seems to bag any game and I'm heartily sick of vegetable stew and potato pie.'

'Never mind him. Put your trousers on,' Angel said, averting her gaze. 'I'll wait for you downstairs.'

'Give me a minute and I'll be with you. I can't tell you how glad I am that you're home, and I'm glad that Grantley is yours. At least you'll look after it, which is more than Susannah has done. She's let everything go to blazes.' He closed the door and Angel retraced her steps, stopping at the foot of the stairs to wait for him.

It was mid-afternoon, but dusk was creeping over the flat marshland, blanketing everything in a grey haze. The sky and the land seemed to merge at the horizon as Angel and Humphrey set off towards the barn where the logs were stored.

'Dammit,' Humphrey said crossly. 'Only yesterday I chopped up a whole tree, or so it seemed.'

Angel shook her head. 'This won't last long, and there's barely enough coal in the cellar to keep the range going. Susannah obviously doesn't take much interest in housekeeping.'

'Mrs Kerslake used to do all that, but Mama kept an eye on what went on.' Humphrey ran his hand through his mop of tawny hair. 'Maybe Danny will help me saw some logs.'

449

'Danny? Is he still here?'

'I fetched some logs this morning and I saw him and his dad walking the field they've bought. It's on the far side of the orchard. We had a chat and he showed me where a tree had come down. Said it would make good firewood, but it's a two-man job with the log saw.' He quickened his pace and Angel had to run in order to keep up with him.

'We can't carry logs back from the orchard, Humpty. We need a barrow.'

'They had the donkey cart with them. If they're still around I know he'll give us a hand.'

The wind was biting and laced with sleet by the time they reached the orchard and Angel wished she had thought to bring her muffler, and she had left her gloves on the carved oak chest in the entrance hall. Humphrey let out a loud halloo and a figure emerged from behind a thicket of brambles.

Danny came striding towards them. 'What on earth are you doing out on a day like this?' he demanded, taking in every detail of Angel's unsuitable clothing with a swift glance. 'You should be at home, sitting by the fire, sipping tea like a proper lady, not roaming round in the twilight.'

Suddenly everything became clear and she felt like a bird released from a cage. She threw back her head and laughed. 'Danny Wicks, you sound just like your mother.'

A slow smile spread across his tanned features. 'I should know better than to tell you what to do. You'd think I'd have learned after all the years we've known each other.'

'We're in desperate need of firewood, Danny. Where is the tree that you were talking about?'

He gave her a speculative look. 'You're not thinking of sawing logs, I hope?'

'If you're offering I'd be a fool to turn you down.'

'Like you did when I poured my heart out to you.'

Humphrey cleared his throat. 'Ahem, I'm sorry to interrupt, but this isn't helping and it will be dark soon.'

'As a matter of fact Pa and I sawed the tree up. I knew you'd want the logs and we've taken a few for ourselves, but there are plenty left. If you'll give me a hand we can pile them in the cart and I'll bring them up to the house.'

'Thank you, Danny,' Angel said wholeheartedly. 'You can't imagine how cold it is in the house, and we have to get ready for the ball at Westwood.'

He smiled. 'Thanks for reminding me. We'd best get moving.'

Angel fell into step beside him while Humphrey hurried on ahead. 'You know about the ball?'

'Don't look so surprised. The Wicks family are landowners now and as such we have an invitation.'

'And you've accepted?'

'Are you afraid I'll show you up by behaving like a yokel?'

'No, of course not. I just can't imagine you in such a setting.'

He chuckled. 'You might be in for a surprise, my girl. I'm not one to give up easily.'

Chapter Twenty-Six

Thanks to Jack and Danny, and a little help from Humphrey, the fires were lit and the temperature inside the house began to rise.

Angel had intended to wear one of her old gowns to the ball, which was hardly worn and quite pretty, but perhaps a little old-fashioned. Aunt Eloise had made certain that Susannah had the best of everything, and Angel had always had to be content with hand-me-downs. She was about to step into her gown when Belinda barged into the room.

She dropped the bundle she was carrying onto the bed. 'I knew you wouldn't have anything suitable for tonight,' she said, smiling. 'This was made for me, but to be honest it's a bit too tight and this shade of crimson takes all the colour from my cheeks, but it would look lovely on you. Do try it on.'

Angel fingered the shimmering silk. 'I can't take this, Belle. It must have cost a small fortune.'

'I don't know about that, but I'll never wear it and the colour and style are just right for you. Put it on and see how you feel.' Belinda helped Angel into the gown and fastened the tiny, fabric-covered buttons.

'It's wonderful.' Angel fingered the delicate material. 'It's a pity I can only see bits of me in the small mirror.'

452

Belinda stood back, surveying her work with a satisfied smile. 'You look beautiful. It just needs the ruby pendant and your ring to complete the outfit. Oh, yes, and I almost forgot.' She opened her reticule and took out a small velvet-covered box. 'This is your Christmas present from me. It would be a pity to keep them until tomorrow.'

Angel opened the case and her breath hitched in her throat at the sight of the ruby earrings set in gold filigree. 'They're wonderful. I love them. Thank you so much, but I've only got a very small present for you, Belle.' She hugged her sister, blinking away tears.

'You're the best gift I've ever had.' Belinda mopped her eyes. 'Just look at us pair of sillies. We'd best hurry up or we'll be late for the ball. I'll put your hair up for you and then everyone will be able to admire your earrings.'

'But what about you, Belle? You need to change into your ball gown?'

'Walker has it ready for me and she'll do the necessary. But tonight is your night, Angel. I want you to outshine every woman there. You're my sister and you're the mistress of Grantley. This has been a long time coming and I want you to enjoy every minute of it.'

Minutes later, the young woman who looked out from the mirror was a stranger in Angel's eyes. She had never thought of herself as beautiful, but Belinda had put her hair up in the most becoming style and Angel had to take a second look to be certain that her eyes were not deceiving her. Belinda had hurried away to her own room to place herself in Walker's capable hands

453

and Angel decided to visit the kitchen to show Lil her new gown.

She found what appeared to be a party going on in the servants' domain. The rich smell of roasting meat mingled with the tempting aroma of freshly baked mince pies, and there was a hint of port and brandy in the air as well as the more earthy scents of ale and cider. Baines was helping to unpack a large hamper while Cook and Lil exclaimed over the contents, but they all stopped short when they spotted Angel standing in the doorway.

'My baby girl,' Lil cried, covering her face with her hands. 'Who would have thought you'd grow up to be such a lovely lady?'

Angel crossed the floor, taking care not to snag her gown on anything and she wrapped her arms around Lil. 'But for you I might not have survived infancy. You are my real mother and I love you.'

This time Lil's tears were real and she buried her face in her apron. 'Who would have thought it?'

Cook bobbed a curtsey. 'Congratulations, Miss Angel. I know I can speak for us all, but we're very pleased you're the new owner.'

'Thank you. I hope I can bring Grantley back from the brink, but we'll do it together.' She glanced at the hamper, frowning. 'Where did that come from?'

'Delivered from Fortnum and Mason an hour ago,' Cook said proudly. 'And there's another two in the scullery. We'll eat like kings this Christmas.'

Angel nodded. 'I hope you enjoy your evening. I'll say Merry Christmas now, because it will be Christmas Day when we return from the ball.'

The entrance hall at Westwood was dominated by a huge Christmas tree, blazing with tiny candles. Coloured glass baubles reflected their flickering light, and tinsel shone like frost against the dark-green pine needles. The reception rooms were crowded with county families and friends of the Westwoods, and hundreds of expensive wax candles shed their golden light on the revellers. An orchestra played in the ballroom and strains of a Viennese waltz greeted the guests. The spicy scent of chrysanthemums vied with the expensive perfumes of the ladies and the gentlemen's colognes, Macassar oil and bay rum. To Angel's surprise and Dolly's obvious delight, Rupert looked pale but handsome in evening dress as he sat in a Bath chair, although it was clear from his expression that he longed to be on his feet and whirling his wife around the floor. Dolly sat beside him, refusing all offers to dance with polite smiles, and Angel held her breath when she saw Sir Eugene approach the couple. She was too far away to hear what passed between them, but all three were smiling when Sir Eugene bowed to Dolly and walked away. He joined his wife and Susannah, who was talking animatedly to a distinguished-looking gentleman. He looked to be a good twenty years her senior, and was obviously charmed by her company.

'That's Lord Loughton,' Belinda whispered. 'He's as rich as Croesus and owns half of London, if the rumours are to be believed. He's been on the lookout for a suitable bride for years, so let's hope Susannah can convince him that she's the one.'

Angel unfurled her fan, holding it at an angle in front of her face. 'It looks as though she's doing very nicely. She's always wanted a rich husband and a title would be an added bonus. I wish her well.' Angel realised that she had lost Belinda's attention. 'Who are you looking at now?'

'Over there – talking to Humphrey and Toby.'

Angel turned her head and froze. 'It's Hector – and that must be Rosalind.'

'He's seen you, Angel. He's coming this way. Are you all right?'

Angel was calmer than she would have thought possible. The sight of Hector, resplendent in his uniform with his medals gleaming in the candlelight, would once have made her knees turn to jelly and cause her heart to hammer against her stays, but not now. She moved forward, holding out her hand as if greeting an old friend.

'Hector, what a wonderful surprise.' She came to a halt, looking the pale girl on his arm up and down, and liking what she saw. Rosalind Devane was tiny, like a beautiful child, with dark hair smoothed back from a high brow and large, pansy-soft brown eyes. 'And this must be your bride. How do you do? I'm Hector's adopted sister, Angel Montgomerie.'

Hector kissed her cheek. 'It's good to see you again. You look wonderful, Angel. And you're right, this is my lovely bride, Rosalind.'

'How do you do, Miss Montgomerie?' Rosalind

456

whispered shyly.

'I'm just Angel Montgomerie,' Angel said, smiling. 'This is Miss Montgomerie.' Angel urged Belinda to the fore. 'May I introduce my elder sister, Belinda, and I have a brother somewhere...' Angel peered into the crowd. 'He's no doubt showing off his lovely wife, Blanche.'

Belinda and Rosalind were talking animatedly and Hector drew Angel aside. 'I want to thank you for saving Grantley. I should have stayed at home and fought for my inheritance, but there are some things that are more important.'

'Affairs of the heart?' Angel met his gaze with a smile. 'She's lovely, Hector. I don't blame you for putting her first.'

'I didn't want to leave her when I returned on the *Orontes,* but I had a duty to Rupert and my men. I wasn't called back, that was just an excuse, although I apologise for not telling you the truth, my dear sister. You mean so much to me, Angel, but I knew I couldn't live without the woman I love at my side – nothing else matters.'

'I understand, Hector. I think I sensed that there was something you weren't telling me, but it doesn't make any difference – we'll share Grantley,' Angel said urgently. 'I don't want to take anything from you and your family. I owe you so much.'

His smile embraced her. 'I couldn't wish for anyone better to have Grantley,' he said softly. 'I know you'll look after my brothers and Susannah, but now my life has taken a different turn. Rosalind is an heiress in her own right and we'll be moving to Yorkshire where her family own a large

457

estate. It's her dearest wish, and that makes it mine, too.'

'Well, in that case I'm happy for you, but Toby and Humphrey will always be part of Grantley – it's still their home.'

'They're men now, at least Toby is, although I doubt if Humphrey will ever grow up entirely. They can choose their own destinies.' He glanced over her shoulder and smiled. 'And I see that Susannah has got her hooks into an earl at last. She'll be happy, but what about you?'

He had already lost Angel's attention. She was gazing at the new arrivals. Jack and Sally looked slightly embarrassed in their new clothes, and Jack was fingering his starched collar as if it were too tight, but it was Danny who caught her attention. He came striding through the crowd, seemingly oblivious to everyone in the room but her. Angel's heart began to thud and her pulse raced. Hector stepped aside to talk to his bride, but Angel was aware of nothing and no one other than the handsome, broad-shouldered young man who approached her, holding out his hand.

'You challenged me,' Danny said softly. 'You didn't think I could dance.' He took her by the hand and she did not protest. It seemed as though they were the only people in the ballroom as he led her onto the floor, and she felt herself melting as he took her in his arms. Danny moved with the grace of a panther and the gentleness of a dove, and Angel was transported to another world where love was all. How blind she had been, but now she could see and her heart was lost for ever.

'You are an amazing dancer, Danny Wicks.'

'With you in my arms I could do almost anything.'

'I've been a fool, Danny. I've been chasing rainbows.'

'Have you found your pot of gold?'

She looked into his eyes and saw her future. 'Maybe,' she said, smiling.

'That's not an answer.' He brought her hand to his lips and brushed it with a kiss.

'I was wrong to turn you down, Danny. I didn't know my own heart.'

'You know that I love you, Angel.'

'I love you, too.'

He swept her into a twirl, whirling her round the floor until the last note of the waltz echoed off the crystal chandeliers.

'Will you marry me, Angel?'

She smiled up at him. 'Yes, Danny, I will.'

The clock in the entrance hall struck midnight and Danny led her outside into the orangery where he took in his arms and kissed her. Angel slid her arms around his neck and she knew that she had come home at last. When they parted to draw breath he produced a small box from his breast pocket and flicked it open. 'I've been carrying this around for months – living in hope.'

The solitaire ruby gleamed with fire as he slipped the ring onto her finger. 'Merry Christmas, my beautiful Angel.'

In the distance Angel could hear the peal of church bells. 'Christmas will always be extra special for me now, Danny. I really do love you.'

He kissed her again. 'This is for ever – my own Christmas Angel.'

The publishers hope that this book has given you enjoyable reading. Large Print Books are especially designed to be as easy to see and hold as possible. If you wish a complete list of our books please ask at your local library or write directly to:

Magna Large Print Books
Magna House, Long Preston,
Skipton, North Yorkshire.
BD23 4ND

This Large Print Book for the partially sighted, who cannot read normal print, is published under the auspices of

THE ULVERSCROFT FOUNDATION